Praise for Barry Schechter's *The Blindfold Test*

"Barry Schechter regards the dirty tricks
with which life undoes his protagonist with a kind of glee.
We are reminded that Kafka was supposed to have
held his sides laughing while he read friends his stories."
—Lore Segal, author of *Half the Kingdom*

"*The Blindfold Test* is a beautiful and
terrifying pleasure, a metaphysically witty novel rich
with melancholy joie de vivre."
—Matthew Sharpe, author of *The Sleeping Father*

"Schechter . . . skews the horrible world to just the
right kind of acceptable lunacy."
—Han Ong, author of *The Disinherited*

"The kind of novel Woody Allen and
Hunter S. Thompson would've written together if they
could've gotten along . . . That Schechter can
combine HST's gonzo morality and pacing with Allen's
deadpan is almost too much. But still, we
couldn't get enough."
—Jonathan Messinger, *TimeOut Chicago*

"Part-comedy, part-thriller . . . *The Blindfold
Test* is blanketed with paranoia, quite Kafkaesque . . ."
—*New City Lit*

USELESS MIRACLE

ALSO BY BARRY SCHECHTER

The Blindfold Test

USELESS MIRACLE

a novel

BARRY SCHECHTER

MELVILLE HOUSE
BROOKLYN • LONDON

USELESS MIRACLE

First Melville House Printing: June 2020

Melville House Publishing
46 John Street
Brooklyn, NY 11201
and
Melville House UK
Suite 2000
16/18 Woodford Road
London E7 0HA

mhpbooks.com
@melvillehouse

ISBN: 978-1-61219-791-3
ISBN: 978-1-61219-817-0 (eBook)

Library of Congress Control Number: 2020931404

Designed by Betty Lew

Printed in the United States of America

1 3 5 7 9 10 8 6 4 2

A catalog record for this book is available from the
Library of Congress

For Lore Segal

USELESS MIRACLE

ONE

My ex-friend and -guru Harvey Bell called dreams "the gibberish of profundity." Sometimes it was "the profundity of gibberish"; Harvey was all about the music, not the words. I still smile when I think of him, grifter that he was, a short blobby Jew whose eyes grew more protuberant as he fasted down to bantam holy man trim. You've got to smile when you think of a professional Eastern Mystic in a turban who continued to call himself Harvey Bell.

He believed that if you hear the funniest joke in the world in a dream, and you wake up remembering "Dog walks into a bar then it rains"; and if the Dalai Lama confides the meaning of life in a dream, and what you've written in the notebook by your bed is "Folks needs Skittles," you have in fact heard the funniest joke in the world and known the meaning of life. The gibberish comes from what Harvey Bell calls the "Semipermeable Membrane." It's the barrier between sleep and waking where the gold coins of dreams are exchanged for the slugs of idiocy. This daily gyp is necessary just to go on living. Because . . . and here Harvey, who imparted his wisdom with a certain amount of weary rote, quoted Eliot . . . because "Human kind cannot bear very much reality."

I'm thinking of Harvey and his theories because I performed the first unassisted human flight as I was coming out of a dream. I wasn't sleeping well at the time. Rebecca was on some panels at a film conference at Ann Arbor—the Otto Preminger wars had broken out again among film scholars—and she'd taken Max to see his grandparents who lived nearby. I had to stay on to teach my classes at Northwestern, meet an article deadline, and serve on a dissertation committee, but I spent much of my time pacing the house. They'd never been gone this long. I have two Sylvia Herschel Awards for Outstanding Contributions to Criticism and Hermeneutics; just wanted you to know it wasn't typical of me to spend an afternoon playing with Max's soft trucks—VROOM!—or arranging Rebecca's bras and panties on the bed in invisible-woman poses.

The fourth day I got into bed at two in the afternoon, mashing her pillow over my face to try to catch a whiff of her herbal shampoo. The next thing I remember I was sitting on the beanbag chair in the living room, facing Rebecca and Max on the couch, my friend Toby in the armchair to the left of the coffee table, a vague blur in the armchair to the right (dream specialists always perked up at the mention of the vague blur. But it neither spoke nor stirred in its chair and played no further part in the dream). "Sorry, I'm not convinced," I said. "I think I've mentioned I have a little test to see if I'm dreaming." I struggled up from the beanbag chair, took my shoes off, and stepped up on the coffee table.

Max pointed and laughed. "Get dow!" he yelled.

"Good luck keeping him off the table now," Rebecca said, "but never mind. Let's see the famous test."

"Okay, move aside, please." Before I stepped off I looked around for something dreamlike. Apparently the blur in the armchair didn't qualify as dreamlike to my dreaming self. The daylight in the room was seething, but that was just leaves in the windows behind me. "The actual test is almost redundant. I never perform it unless I'm already dreaming."

I heard my old friend Toby say, "Why do you get to do the test? If anybody's dreaming here it's me."

"Sounds like the real Toby," I said and stepped off. I have parsed the distinction between flying and hovering many times since that afternoon, but this was hovering. I was standing still three feet above the carpet, positioned like the cartoon character who hasn't yet looked down. I looked down—Max's Ernie doll gaped up from the carpet—and remained in position. It was no big deal; I'd performed the test thousands of times. I started performing the test in puberty, I might as well add, just to give those of you who haven't given up studying me something to think about.

"This is creeping me out," Rebecca said. She and Toby were kneeling in front of me, chopping at the air between my feet and the carpet. "What happens now?"

"I wake up."

"Just a minute. Max wants to tell you a secret." She lifted him up; his breath was warm on my ear, apple juice and cookies. He whispered "bzz bzz bzz."

"That's just pretend whispering, buddy," I said. "You have to whisper the secret."

"A child whispers the secret," Toby said. "Come on, George, what kind of treacly Romanticism are you dreaming?"

The dream hadn't quite evaporated; my figments and I avoided eye contact while we waited for it to end. While we waited, Rebecca kneeled and rubbed a Kleenex at the corner of Max's mouth. He winced and tried to squirm away. Dream Rebecca was identical to my wife down to her dark, shiny new bob and her habit of crinkling her chin when scared or on the verge of tears. She glanced up, forced a brave closed-lipped smile, shrugged. Toby tapped his foot on the carpet and checked his watch.

That's all I could reconstruct over the years with the aid of a therapist, a federally indicted guru, and four hypnotists. I don't know how much extraneous material was added by the process. I'm not absolutely certain there's even a connection between the dream and what came next.

I awoke on my side of the bed, ensnared in the blanket and sheets, my head and chest dangling over the edge. I was half-asleep—sleepy enough to wonder what might happen if I performed the test. But first I had to extricate myself. I recall thinking that I'd like to surprise Rebecca and Max with a Houdini act; one minute straightjacketed in bedding and the next . . . my writhing landed me on the carpet, still entangled. I decided to lie there for a while. My polyester pajamas itched. These were supposed to be the new polyester. The room was cool but I was covered in sweat. All I had to do to get free, I reminded myself, was sit up. Instead I flailed at my confinement, still sleepy enough to imagine I could burrow deeper and come out the other side.

At this point of my account the therapist, hypnotist, or guru would pause and say, "Ah. The other side."

Static cling. It just occurred to me. Harvey thought my fight with the bedding was really the struggle to haul secret dream knowledge into the light of day. But I did laundry that morning and might have forgot to put in the dryer sheets.

I told myself to relax. I was like the man thrashing in quicksand, turning against the direction of the skid, flipped by my own judo. I breathed in, out. I was starting to fall asleep again. No problem, I thought, I'll just—I punched, rolled, kicked, scratched, tore. I don't know where this rage came from, but I was like those cartoon show antagonists I'd been watching all week, brawlers merged into a cyclone of arms, heads, stars, and exclamation points.

In the midst of these exertions I closed my eyes against a seasick feeling. I stopped thrashing, and my body—horizontal and facedown, unsupported by hands or feet or limbs—slowly touched down on the floor. I was awake enough now to wonder where it had just been.

. . .

I first performed the miracle in public—for people other than my wife and son—on April 10, 20__, some time between midnight and 1:30 a.m. It didn't seem worth the bother of checking our watches. As far as I recall, I didn't even win the talent show.

The evening was billed as a nonbirthday party. I'd missed out on my fortieth celebration because I'd kept warning my wife and friends—sometimes grabbing them by the lapels—that I dreaded and forbade a surprise party. "Just because a heart attack is a surprise," I'd say, "that doesn't make it fun. But at least *it's* a surprise." So when I came home from teaching on the big night and nothing stirred among the furniture; and when Rebecca took me to my favorite restaurant and the faces flickering at the other tables never looked my way, I began to realize the worst had happened: my wishes had been respected.

My lifelong friend Toby had his fortieth two weeks before mine and had expressed *his* wishes unambiguously: he'd left the country. But a few weeks later he too was missing his night of the little hats. It seemed pathetic to throw ourselves a consolation birthday, so our nonversion banned presents—again my wishes were respected!—and all mention of birthdays. The guests would be mainly our colleagues at Northwestern.

A half hour before the party my two-year-old Max and I were in the bathroom, Max standing on his bench making faces at our reflections while I tried to wet down and comb our identical cowlicks. By the time I managed to plaster down one, the other would come unstuck, and I couldn't find the glop. In addition to my cowlick he has my pug nose, Rebecca's hazel eyes, her pale skin, our dark hair, and my habit of compressing my lips while thinking.

I caught that look in the mirror. At two and a half Max seemed like a happy kid—liked jokes, games, music, the guy who read the morning stock quotes on channel 23, stories, hugs, rhymes, babbling, being chased, making motor sounds. But this pensiveness always startled me. I wondered what he was figuring out about the world, and how he could possibly get it right. It's on the basis of our misreadings, I suppose, that we become what we are.

"Iris is coming," I was saying.

"And?"

"And Toby."

"And?"

"And Jeff."

"And?"

"And and and and. Is that all you can say? . . . Marge Fredersen? The eco-feminist? She's coming."

"Uh-huh."

He was experimenting with his mouth, scrunching it up and trying to move it all the way to the right side of his face. I thought of my mother warning "careful it doesn't freeze that way" and wondered if that was my first real worry.

"You look a little sad." Rebecca had come up behind me; she took the comb out of my hand and began attacking my cowlick. "What's up?"

"Maybe a little. I've been looking at my friends. They don't look *old* yet—they just look like they've been woke up in the middle of the night."

She gave the comb a painful tug. "Thank you for that image! Come on, you're adorable." She put her face next to mine. Her smile is so spacious and employs so much facial machinery, it forces her eyes into glittering slits. She smiled at me in the mirror until I conceded with a shrug that okay, I'm adorable. "And hip," she added tapping the nosepiece of my frames. "Your little round glasses are back in style. You're youthful, popular, your lectures are packed, girls have crushes on you. Somebody gave me the address of a blog where your lecture hall baritone's compared to the voice of God. She marvels that that sound can come out of your—"

"Small?"

She winced. "Compact frame."

"It's the only useful thing Walter taught me. 'The diaphragm, George. Up from the diaphragm!'"

Max was singing "and and and and . . ."

"You don't have to worry for a while," I said. Rebecca was thirty-two. A month ago she'd had her waist-length dark hair trimmed to a springy bob. She wore a long black skirt and a black off-the-shoulders top that showed off her collarbones and the hemispheric outlines of her breasts. Being childishly adorable *does* have its compensations; you *can* trade it for sex and love, but you need to work harder than the ruggedly handsome or the lunkishly self-confident. You need, in pursuit of Rebecca, the perseverance of the legendary kid in my grammar school who saved up enough box tops for a dune buggy.

"I just got it," I said. "The hairdo: Greta Klimt. You *are* Greta Klimt."

Rebecca taught in the film department, and the pop quizzes in empathy that wives like to spring on their husbands—hints, codes, private jokes, telepathic transmissions—were in our case usually references to movies I'd forgotten or hadn't seen. This isn't the place to speculate on what that could mean, but I was doing my best to catch up.

"Greta Klimt," I went on. "Silent movie actress, did her best work with G. W. Pabst. Kansas girl, came to Berlin to join her friend Louise Brooks. Spent most of her time as a B-lister at UFA, but probably the most beautiful silent movie actress. Creamy pale skin, classic oval face. Cheekbones created to be lit by Germans."

She was working on Max now. "Thanks, but I've still got that image in my head."

I turned and kissed her shoulder. "Sorry."

If she was bummed by my first image, I wasn't about to share the other. When I looked at myself and my friends, I thought we hadn't *changed*, exactly: we looked *too much* like ourselves. Perhaps that's what Lincoln meant when he said that by forty you get the face you deserve: it's a self-caricature. Your face has cooled in the mold. Whatever you are, you're done.

She was watching me think in the mirror. "Regrets?"

"Didn't we have this conversation on my birthday? Okay. If I had it to do over I probably *still* wouldn't jump out of an airplane or raft down the Amazon or sleep with identical twins. Is that the same as no regrets?"

"You know it's not."

"The truth is, I'm pretty happy. I'm afraid that if I don't seem to have at least a tiny crisis, people will think less of me. If you teach hermeneutics and turn forty, you're required to say— maybe even to yourself—that you'd prefer to be in the jungle tagging monkeys for Greenpeace. In a few weeks people will let me enjoy my life without demanding my regrets."

She gave me a pat on the head. I half-raised an eyebrow at her in the mirror.

Let's get this out of the way. I am a small man. That day, before I'd been assigned my own press narrative, I still thought of myself as a *short* man (all right, sometimes small). I suppose I'd always been slightly bothered about my height. How could I not? I was the son of the astrophysicist and Distinguished Professor at the University of Chicago, Walter Entmen. Yes, *that* Walter Entmen, "the spaces between the stars." He was six five and bore the booming chest and cavernous cranium of the looming thirties movie star Raymond Massey. I'm hardly the first to apply Nietzsche's quotation—he looked like the abyss had been looking into *him*. Sometimes I'd walk into his study and break his nine-light-year gaze. He wouldn't get angry; he was just surprised, I think, that the same universe that contained 100-billion-square-mile walls of dark matter also contained that craning openmouthed blip by his shoe. Anyway, Walter did his best to prepare me for the world: boxing lessons, gloomy aphorisms. By the time I'd arrived at the morning of my nonbirthday party, I hadn't had much need for either—though I remained serene through squabbles at department meetings with the thought that I could beat up anyone at the conference table. That morning, as I smiled at my wife and son in the bathroom mirror, I was still a peaceful and happy man.

Later the press would assign me the role of small man. At first I was the plucky "small man who could." As the world grew more disappointed in me, the references to my smallness grew meaner. Later still . . . but far worse things happened to me than nicknames and bad press. So let me concede the point and move on. I am a small man.

Sorry, but I have to get this on the record: at five feet four and three quarters, I'm *not all that small*. I'm taller than most of mankind throughout history. Tall enough to gaze down on James Madison, for example, with my fists on my hips. Taller than average by the standard of many Asian countries. Taller than many of the people who on the slightest acquaintance feel entitled—despite my distinguished reputation in the field of hermeneutics, the theory of textual meaning and interpretation—to walk right up and muss my hair! So why bother? The sign has been taped to my back, so to speak, and to tear it off and stomp on it is to assist in my own diminution—there's nothing funnier than the pique of a small man.

I seem to be getting off point here so let's wrap this up. As I try to make sense of the phenomenon (the word the press settled on to skirt "miracle"), it all seems bound up with my presumed smallness. Toby, who despite everything he witnessed remained a skeptic, a cynic, and a smart-ass, quipped that it was all divine overcompensation—God's way of putting lifts in my shoes.

Of course my appearance of being small involves more than height. There is the matter of my cuteness. A man with tiny, symmetrical, boyish features—particularly if that man works in a profession of rigor and high seriousness—must constantly guard against the impression of childish adorability, must stand ready to impale it with the steel of his gaze! Don't know where *that* came from.

Granted: I get defensive. But to people who didn't know or care about my Auerbach Award, my gravitas was, I gather, cute; there's nothing funnier than a small man striving to maintain his dignity. A week before my fortieth birthday I went to get my driver's license renewed. It was one of those express facilities for people who aren't required to take the driving test: ten or eleven rows of folding chairs, nearly deserted that afternoon, an eye test machine resembling a submarine periscope on the counter, and behind the counter a blue curtain and a camera on a tripod. I passed the eye test and had sat down in front of the blue cloth when it happened. "Yooo Hoooooo! Eeeeeee!" This piercing noise, an exaggeration of the falsetto you might produce to make a baby smile, came from the photographer. He wore the standard white shirt, black necktie, and black pants, a skinny guy in his twenties with black horn-rims and patches of eczema. While he made the sounds, he crossed his eyes, wrinkled his nose, and bared his teeth. By the way, have I mentioned that earlier that month I'd gone to the Hague to address a conference on "Language and World Conflict," and Jacques Chirac praised my work? That's right. Jacques Chirac. In the license photograph my mouth begins to open in an anxious lopsided smile, my eyes bugging slightly behind my little round frames. In the days that followed I'd examine that photo, wondering if something about me had provoked the incident. But my cowlick was under control, the Windsor knot in my tie perfectly symmetrical, and, because I was headed directly for Professor Von Helberg's retirement dinner, I was wearing my Dunlap & Dunlap suit. I had to wait for the picture to develop, so I took a seat in the front row. Now the fun begins, I thought. I could watch other people react to the photographer's unconventional methods. But he was all business now: "Look up, sir," "little to the left, ma'am." When my license was ready I tried to strike up a conversation, waiting for the beast to burst loose again. "You're very fast here," I said. "Quite an efficient operation."

"Thank you, sir," he replied with impervious blandness.

But it's the accusation of another kind of smallness that I refuse to bear, and you might call the following pages my brief. As the subject of the world's only verified miracle, I was blamed for its measliness. This all changed, of course, but I cringe to remember it. The world had been waiting for thousands of years, and it felt entitled to something grander. Surely, the accusation went, the *intended* miracle couldn't have been such a gyp; it had to have been the meagerness of the vessel, my own paltry spirit, that brought forth such dinky wonders.

. . .

The talent contest was Toby's idea; no one had the energy to argue—no one had found the energy yet to get up and head for the coats—so he seized the role of dictator and MC. "A few rules," he said over groans too feeble to resist an actual intention. "Double-jointedness is a condition, not a talent. Kudos for your ability to recite *Paradise Lost* from memory, Edward, but no. Lip-synchers will be beaten. The ability to eat, drink, or swallow huge quantities of anything will have to be its own reward. As for air guitar, Jeff, you might as well put the 'guitar' aside and take credit for the air."

Toby has a big head, its massiveness enhanced that night by the tiny plastic derby secured by a rubber band beneath his chin. That head is set on a big body—not fat, exactly; his softness is dispersed, laundered, you might say, throughout a tall big-boned Clintonesque physique. He'd let his still solid-black hair grow out that year. Toby had small, surprisingly delicate features for a man his size, though the nose was oft-busted. He looked like . . . what? . . . a leg-breaker for the violinists' union. An apostate monk who'd been in some bar fights. That spring he'd been affecting a Rat Pack look: black sport coats with narrow lapels, white shirts, skinny black ties worn loose and askew. He brought off the Rat Pack/party hat combo with imperious deadpan, as if they were the vestments of some forgotten order.

I assumed that his Goth-looking black-clad Russian date was his motive for the talent show, but he was holding her in reserve. To begin he drafted Iris.

"Oh sweetie, I don't have a talent." These and other protests were shouted down and she stepped into the middle of the living room. Iris was an attractive woman, even if the only color I'd seen on her face was its own literary pallor, even if she carried her lanky body like something that exceeded union rules.

She was the funniest person I knew. And yet I have a little room for exposition here because I seldom remembered her jokes. I suppose it's because they made me worry about her. What

I recall of her improvised standup that night is the raw material: that she'd broken up with her boyfriend; that her mother was blowing her savings on some "voodoo cure"; that Iris dreaded turning thirty-eight, the age at which her father died of a heart attack and five years past the age when her grandfather died of a "heart condition." Oh, and she imagined that the strangers who took her body away would make cracks about the decor. And she mentioned a dream in which a man with the head of a bull stood over her bed and said, "That's it: I'm outta here." The dream was three months ago, and she hadn't been able to write a word of her latest novel since. Her twang was dialed all the way up, not a good sign.

As usual she reacted to our laughs with the pose of a lost, baffled, but resolute traveler. I know that's a lot to read from a disappointed gaze, but we'd shared an office for three years and she'd milked many jokes with it. She must not have sufficiently mastered the language, her pose implied, because the locals were laughing at her pleas for help. But if she persisted in explaining the problem, surely they'd grasp that none of this was funny.

Iris. I think we all wish we'd paid closer attention. But what should we have paid attention *to*? The gloomy jokes? There's nothing that pleased her more than telling them. The way she could tear up while smiling? It's a trick she and Rebecca practiced while watching Renee Zellweger on the DVD of *Jerry McGuire*.

Anyway, the talent show. My teaching assistant Jeff Bingham did something I prefer to forget involving objects up his nose. Marge Fredrersen, the eco-feminist, did a spot-on imitation of Britney Spears, I think. Our neighbor Mrs. Housbender juggled three tennis balls and a golf ball, explaining all the while how the size and weight difference made it harder until Toby disqualified her for special pleading. Rebecca did a lovely "My Funny Valentine," legs crossed on the piano, with jazz accompaniment from Paul Catlow, the science-as-narrative guy. Milly Steinman and her husband Warren Gustafson (Romance languages, Scandinavian literature) had taken up ballroom dancing in their fifties after her inoperable cancer was diagnosed; their tango ended with a full dip, Milly's shorn head nearly touching the carpet, a rose from our window box in her teeth. Nora Bales, the young linguist with slash-cut red hair, did an angry/perky cover from the Flaming Lips. Her sister Betty did something balletic with jumps and splits and stopped before it got ridiculous. The Beowulf scholar Thomas Willaston sang a cappella in Old English and stalked off to the kitchen when Toby razzed, "Aren't you ever off-duty?" Nobody razzed Professor Emeritus Maura O'Day, whose cracking voice and baffled pauses made her Gaelic song even more poignant.

Toby and Iris—who despite rumors had never been a couple—did their couples therapy skit, something they'd come up with on a department retreat. They gave a demonstration of the "trust exercise" where one partner, Toby, falls back, trusting that his partner will catch him. Iris was also the one giving the lecture. She'd stop to make one last point to the audience while Toby came crashing down. He was a graceful and fearless big man; his landings, even on the carpet, made the glasses jump. He demonstrated his trust again and again, while at the last second Iris would get distracted or check something in the "Trust Manual" or turn to the audience to take a question. It was just a variation of Charlie Brown and the football, but it brought down the house.

And then Toby's date Ludmilla disdainfully clacked through

our CDs. She needed music for her act: "otherwise only grunting and Toby making remarks." She nearly settled on the "Disco Inferno" compilation I ordered from cable at three in the morning the week Rebecca and Max were away, but finally she performed unaccompanied. I had assumed women in Goth-white pancake and bruise-colored lipstick, wobbly racoonish mascara round their eyes, tended not to be athletes. But Ludmilla did deep knee bends, touching her elbows on the floor, all while balancing various large, unwieldy, and asymmetrical objects on her head. I recall a wok, a table lamp, and our black-and-white short-hair cat Claude (I would have introduced him earlier but he'd been hiding that night) perched warily on three economy-size boxes of Calgon. Ludmilla wore, in case you worry about such things, a loose cheerleader skirt, black of course, and panties. For the finale she assembled what Toby introduced as "the Astounding Pile of Everything" on her head and smoothly squatted it up and down. He nudged me to point out her sculpted thighs and noted that she was circus folk. She overheard and snapped, "Not circus folk, performance artist!"

Except for Toby, the men in the room sustained a professorial deadpan. Iris, perhaps speaking for most of the women in the room, bounced cashews off the side of Toby's head. He knew where they were coming from and didn't look. She had a surprisingly strong and accurate pitching arm, good follow-through.

"That's a high point to go out on," I said when Ludmilla set down the atlas, the bird cage, and the anxious Claude. "I never thought I'd make it through another two and half hours, but I'm glad you thought of it," I said to Toby. "And by the way, happy nonbirthday, pal. Please don't start picking up things, Becca. I'll deal with it in the morning. Thanks for coming, everybody. It was the greatest nonbirthday ever. Sorry to rush this, I have to get up early."

No one had budged. Rebecca was next to me on the couch, Max sleeping on her lap. He'd insisted that his tiny rubber band top hat stay on. She took away the empty gin glass that had remained in my hand through Ludmilla's performance and set it on the coffee table. "I think you're going to have to perform, George."

Toby was on my other side. "Hermeneutics is not a talent," he warned, snapping the rubber band of the tiny hat I'd forgotten I was wearing.

"I dunno," I said. "Would anybody like to hear 'Rhapsody in Blue'?"

"I'm invoking the 'Fucking Boring' rule,'" he said.

Rebecca leaned close and whispered, "Why don't you do your trick?" That's what we'd been calling it while we tried to decide whether it was a trivial freakish ability like triple-jointedness, or the most important thing ever. Sometimes Rebecca believed it *was* a trick, and she'd used an old Hula-Hoop to check for wires. At first she thought I was gliding on "some sort of skateboard thing." For weeks I'd amuse her and Max with a performance every evening. Max was the first to get bored. Then it was once a week, then longer. My talent, in the form I'd been given it, seemed to have no use whatever except maybe tabloid notoriety. I'd already had myself scanned and blood-tested: nothing. When we realized that at least for now my ability would make no difference in our lives, we shrugged and moved on.

Her whisper had been overheard. "Yeah," people were saying, "let's see your trick, George." Ludmilla leaned across the coffee table and snatched off my little hat.

"Really," I said, and sometimes I believed it: "it's nothing."

. . .

I walked to the end of the hall, turned around, and lay face down on the carpet. The guests began to follow, and I ordered them back. They craned and squirmed in the living room entrance.

Rebecca sidled past them. Gathering the hem of her long skirt, she crouched down in a catcher's stance. She was holding the stereo's remote. "Ready, champ?"

I raised my head and exhaled. "Ready."

She pressed the remote and from the living room hyperventilating strings and imperial horns blared John Williams's overture for *Superman*. It was just dawning on me how embarrassing this would be. Max was beside her, holding out his arms. "Daddy, here!"

"Come on, George." She patted the carpet in front of her; a round of hoots and dog whistles began and abruptly broke off.

In the months to come everyone asked, "What do you think of when you do it?" You might as well ask what I think of when I lift my arm. By a similar though more strenuous act of will, my body rose horizontally three or four inches off the carpet (I'd never been able to get any higher) and flew (I couldn't just hover) very slowly (I'd never managed to go any faster) toward my wife and son. Partly for balance and partly for show, I extended my arms forward like Superman, my torso moving parallel to the floor. I didn't need to think about any particular thing to get airborne, but I had my cherished images. That night I pictured the Himalayas just below me, the searchlight ferocity of the snowcaps at noon, the delirium-blue of stark altitude.

You can't expect a bunch of drunken, supercilious academics to remain awestruck for long, and here came the flak. "Dustball

at six o'clock" . . . "Look! Down on the floor! It's a dog! It's a cat!"
and so forth. And I did look ridiculous in flight. As if my speed
and altitude weren't laughable enough, my exertions were often
accompanied by involuntary squinting or mumbling. Sometimes
my tongue protruded between my lips.

A few of the guests ventured into the hallway. Their looming
faces—the vastly jutting noses, the black depths of the nostrils—
looked grotesque from my baby's-eye view. Hands probed the
margin between me and the carpet. Ludmilla gave me a quick
but thorough frisk that set me veering (very slowly, fortunately)
toward the wall. Other women were saying, "Look at his little
mouth moving!" "And the way he kicks his little legs!" (I forgot to mention the kicking—I don't think it contributed to my
airworthiness; just another tic.) "Like he's swimming across the
pool to his mommy!"

A word about my dignity: no, I think we've covered that.

A shoe on my back pressed me into the carpet. "Just checking
your wind shear resistance, buddy," said Toby. He allowed me to
rise back up and fly on. The old twinkle-dust grin looked a bit
carnivorous from that angle. Despite his just-drunk-just-goofing-
around-old-buddy facade, I knew he was jealous; he thought if
anyone should be flying it was he, and he wouldn't look like a
moron doing it.

Flight is exhausting. I can't describe how I did it—it involved
no bodily movement except the useless kicking of my legs—but
like swimming it strained every muscle. Staying airborne caused
an agonizing muscular rigidity that made me dread paralysis or
stroke. The length of our hall was my limit, and by midflight
I'd be trembling, grunting, sweating, my shirt transparent. It
reminded Rebecca of Jimmy Stewart, I forget the film, flying

across the Atlantic with the engine sputtering, ice on the wings, bolts popping. I had reached that point. I fought not to expend the last of my energies thrashing and flailing. Three inches below me, our good, gray Stainmaster carpet beguiled like an exile's dream of home.

The guests backed off to the living room entrance; there were no more jokes. The only voice was Rebecca's, calm, almost a whisper, guiding me home. "Keep your arms straight. Do your breathing—slowly, slowly. Stop kicking, it's a waste of energy." Max was trying to run to me, but she held him back in the crook of her arm.

. . .

The stragglers and I ended up in the kitchen. Iris, Ludmilla, and Toby were there, and Rebecca when she'd negotiated the hat and put Max to bed.

Also at the table were Charles Blaustein, the other hermeneutist in the department, and his wife Karen, who worked as a loan officer at a bank. I didn't know why they were there, let alone *still* there. Charles and I weren't unfriendly, but he'd never invited me to his house, and this was the first pro forma invitation he'd accepted. Karen, tall, slim, tense, with long gray-streaked brown hair, mostly kept her eyes down where one thumb was rubbing the other on her lap. Charles was also tall and slim, with thinning silver hair, aviator glasses, and a way of sitting—he didn't seem drunk or stoned—that made me think he was battening himself in place. He sat there in his fully buttoned overcoat even though it was a warm spring night. My small talk had bounced right off. Perhaps he wasn't staring at me; maybe I only thought so because they'd barely spoken to anyone that night, hadn't eaten or drunk, just sat as if enduring a procedure. Maybe, I thought, he's just shy or watchful. After all our years together in the department, I barely knew him.

I thought maybe it's not as creepy as it seems. The pioneering Russian director and film theorist Dziga Vertov did an experiment. He took the same shot of an actor and inserted it into various kinds of footage. Then he showed it to test subjects. Depending on the context they thought the man humorous, menacing, happy, sad, angry, pensive. But I couldn't imagine footage that would make this not creepy. The best I could come up with was the Blausteins staring at each other at their own kitchen table, a pendulum wall clock slowly chopping up the minute.

The Blaustein Effect was seeping into everyone. The prospect of filling their silence was dreadful—like tossing cats down a well. I looked to Iris. When Rebecca forbade her to bring in dishes from the living room, she'd gone to some mental place where there were no Blausteins. She was fiddling with the Mary Tyler Moore curl of her muted blonde hair. I couldn't explain why we didn't all stand up and say goodnight.

Another possibility occurred to me. Maybe I was the only one who was spooked by Charles. Maybe everyone else was spooked by me. Or at least by the possibility they'd witnessed a miracle. Was that why Charles was stock-still in his overcoat?

Toby, leaning over the back of Ludmilla's chair, was smirking into the middle distance; I thought he was waiting for his blind-side moment to debunk me, but Ludmilla filled the vacuum. "You are filmmaker," she said to Rebecca.

"Not for a while—I'm teaching full-time. I used to make documentaries."

"You are political?"

"Yes and no. I don't like to know in advance what I'll think about my subject. Were you an acrobat in Russia?"

"Not acrobat, performance artist. This I do here. I was engineer in Russia."

"You know," I said to Iris, "I flew tonight and nobody's said a thing about it."

"I know, baby." She patted my hand.

Ludmilla turned to me. "You and Toby," she said, "are long friends."

"We grew up in Hyde Park, sons of emotionally distant U of C fathers. I used to dare him to call my father Walter. Or to ask him, 'Aren't the spaces between the stars just empty?' And he did! I think Walter respected him, in a ferocious scowling kind of way."

"Toby is charming but I do not think he is serious man."

I came to my friend's defense. "He's one of the foremost authorities on the seventeenth-century essayist and eschatologist Sir Thomas Browne. You can't be frivolous . . . and . . . you're not buying this. He can seem like he's just goofing around in his life, but he has great physical and moral courage. He was kind of a shrimp before his growth spurt, but when he saw bullies going after someone . . ."

"Those were Hyde Park bullies," he said. "Come on."

"He was the first one to make a stink on principle when the university wanted to kick some pariah off the faculty. You might think there are no consequences for a guy with tenure, but he taught all comp for a year just for that."

She mentioned that her uncle her been in the Gulag, and Toby said, "Got me there."

She turned back to me. "You and Charles. You are hermeneutists."

Charles spoke! "George invented the New Hermeneutics. You might say I'm his acolyte or disciple." He talked through the side of his mouth in a sneering voice reminiscent of Edward G. Robinson or the Penguin. I'd been told it was a medical condition, which was also responsible for the limited mobility of his features.

· It crossed my mind, not that I believed it, that Charles might have a gun under his coat. It seemed like a plausible modern religious narrative: man performs miracle, assassinated by his disciple. As I said, just a passing thought, though not, it turned out, entirely off-track. The knife rack on the counter was out of reach. Above the counter were hooks with shiny pots and pans, the wok, the egg whisker, and several gleaming pleasing things I'd never been able to identify. Sorry. I miss that life.

"Thank you, Charles, but you're my colleague, not my disciple. He's made many important contributions to the New Hermeneutics."

"Toby says you are number two hermeneutist," Ludmilla said to Charles.

"There are two hermeneutists in the department," he said curtly from the side of his mouth. Karen was looking down the hall to the door as if strenuous wishing might get her there.

I looked at Rebecca. She shrugged.

Putting a point on it, Ludmilla said, "Ah. You are number two hermeneutist in *department*." (After they broke up, Toby paraphrased George Sanders: "She's a graduate of the squat-thrust school of etiquette.")

Karen," Rebecca said brightly, "would you like something? We still have cake."

Karen was still yearning for the door. "No."

"Something to drink?"

"No."

"Charles?"

He shook his head.

The silence was making even Toby squirmy. "I was there with George when lightning struck. He invented the New Hermeneutics at the pancake house on Howard. He was eating the Big Boy Breakfast. Actually made notations on the tablecloth."

"You are hermeneutist, George," Ludmilla said. "You study what."

"My field is the theory of meaning."

"My father was killed by bus. What is the meaning?"

"I'm sorry about your father. I study the meaning of *texts*. Though actually contemporary hermeneutics is mostly the *theory* of meaning."

"Never meaning. Only theory of meaning. Like squirrel on wheel."

Toby kissed the top of her bright red bob. "Oh please, say 'Keel moose and squorrel.' I beg and she'll never say it."

"I will never say this. I am adorable for no man."

Cracking up, Rebecca and Iris high-fived her. With her accent, her smokey voice, and her ill-conceived mime/Goth look beneath her perfectly coifed bob, she was adorable. As an adorable man, I sympathized.

Ludmilla turned her wobbly-circled gaze on Iris, who couldn't hold back an anxious "Uh-oh!"

"You write funny novels. And yet you are sad woman."

"I'm with you so far."

"In Russia I read Twain, Lenny Bruce, Mencken. But American people are not like this. I want to understand real American humor." She unzipped her purse and turned it upside down. Along with a lipstick, a compact and so forth, dozens of paper squares flapped onto the table. I picked up a few. They were the sappy one-panel comics from the funny page: Family Circus, Dennis the Menace, Love Is, Marmaduke.

"Why is funny. I don't understand."

"Okay," Iris said, throwing herself on the grenade. "Let's go in the living room."

When they'd left, Toby seized the moment. "I guess nobody else can deal with it, George, so it's up to me. How about it? Laser mirrors, or the old magnets-in-the-pants?"

"You have no idea what you're talking about, do you? It's not a trick and I'm too tired to talk about it."

"Do you believe it, Rebecca?"

She shrugged. "He passed the Hula-Hoop test."

"Blausteins?"

They said they didn't know.

"Then let me give you some advice, my friend. Choose your narrative. Otherwise the press will hand you one. Do you want to be a paranormal guy, a saint, a superhero—"

"I can fly a few yards very slowly a few inches above the ground. Is that worth the tights?"

"How about wily fake, which perhaps has the virtue of being true? You'd better figure it out because what are the chances nobody got you on cell phone video tonight?"

"Do you really think I'm a wily fake?"

"No. I just don't want to process the alternatives right now . . . Or maybe you'd like to be God?"

"What?"

"They can't say you're God, but they can do a three-part series, Is He God? Ever hear the Lenny Bruce bit about missionaries? Your first lesson in PR, George. If the natives think you're God, they're cooperative, won't kill you and so forth. So you're a little vague about it. 'Well I'm not *God*, but . . .' And work on the flying. It's not that people won't believe in a pathetic God. But it'll piss them off. Right, Blausteins?"

I stood up. "We'll talk about it tomorrow." Toby and Rebecca also stood, and I had a bad moment when I feared the Blausteins might stay in their chairs. But they stood and thanked Rebecca and me for a lovely time. In the living room Iris was saying, "The cat and the mouse are in love, sweetie. What could be funnier than that? Oh, we have to go already?"

At the door Rebecca straightened Iris's collar. Iris had won two National Book Awards, been voted teacher of the year, was perhaps the highest paid professor in the English department. But Rebecca was always fussing with her, straightening her collar, brushing off a hair. Once she'd licked her thumb and rubbed away a smudge. "Say, would you like to come to dinner next week? We're thinking of inviting somebody else. I don't know if it's too soon after Lucas."

"Am I ready to get back on the horse again? Sure I am. If you fall off the horse and break your leg, they have to shoot you, right?"

Okay: I remember the jokes. Every damn one.

The Blausteins were the last to walk out; Rebecca closed the door, pressed her back against it, and slowly slid down to the welcome mat.

"Ancient fuckin' Mariner!"

TWO

The first time I saw Nelson Baim he was sweating into his beard saying, "Titanium, kids, it's the strongest metal on earth." He held up two interlocked hoops and asked the crowd of children, "Do you think I, a mere man, can pull them apart?" His birthday-party-magician voice had the booming stilted baritone of old-time radio, and the kids up front looked scared. "What do you think, boys and girls?" The kids shrugged, squirmed, threw covert punches and elbows.

Rebecca and Max and I had just settled in our lawn chairs, and already a trickle of sympathetic flop-sweat chilled my back. But Nelson had at least one fan; Max was tugging my pants leg.

I was succumbing to an outdoor nap—the tidal noise of the maple above my head, the confetti sprays of brightness through the leaves, the infantilizing smell of burgers. Sometimes I believe—mistakenly, I'm sure—that I might still have my old life if I'd stayed in that lawn chair and taken that nap.

I stood up and set Max on my shoulders. "Let's go see the magic. Rebecca?" Shielding her eyes, she frowned up from her recliner; freckles bunch around her nose when she wrinkles it. "Just don't let him touch the guy or his stuff."

The rows of chairs were full; holding Max by the ankles, I joined the grownups milling near the side fence. Nelson Baim (I didn't know his name yet) was about fifty, bald, sweat blinking in the copper filaments of his beard. His double-breasted powder-blue tux, too tight to button, looked like a seventies prom rental.

My first impressions of my future enemy ought to be vivid, but I don't recall much else; he was just a bad magician then. Surely I must have noticed the badge of his dejected vanity—the scant red hair tugged like catgut across his scalp. I soon learned that his stoic, defiant bearing in front of the audience was his usual posture. His barrel chest was always thrust out at some firing squad.

"Titanium—it's the metal they use in outer space." He gave the nonreaction a few seconds to die down. "That's right. Outer space." The oohs and ahhs of well-intentioned adults only made him wince.

Soldiering on, he called for a volunteer from the audience. "Somebody strong."

Ken Dreynen, the birthday boy's father and the chair of my department, stepped up, acknowledging the applause and whistles with a tilt of his Cubs cap and a magnesium-torch grin that flared against his five o'clock shadow. He held the Cubs cap over Nelson's head, bequeathing him his ovation, and the applause went dead.

As I said, Nelson was nothing more to me that afternoon than an inept birthday party entertainer, and he occupied only half my attention. It dawned on me that people were giving me looks and meaningful little nods. Others pretended, when I looked back, to be enthralled with the space to my left or right. This was two weeks after my performance for my drunken guests, but I didn't make the connection. I hadn't sworn the witnesses to secrecy—just mentioned that I found my talent slightly embarrassing and would appreciate their discretion. I thought that would be enough.

Chuck di Giorgio sidled up, raised his sunglasses, and winked. He hadn't been present two weeks ago, so my first thought was that I'd won the Twine. The award, named for the late poststructuralist Lyman Twine, was given out by the department every five years to a major contributor to the field of interpretive studies. I was rumored to be the front-runner.

Chuck nodded solemnly at Max—always shy and serious in crowds—then nudged me. This is it, I thought, a heads-up for the Twine! He held his arms straight out in front of him in what looked like the pose of a zombie or a sleepwalker. There was something heraldic about the sharp-nosed sunken profile, the sunglasses, the white long-sleeved shirt puffing around his rigid arms. Perhaps it was a ceremony; I wondered if this was how the winners were informed. "'Faster than a speeding bullet,'" he whispered from the side of his mouth. "'Look! Up in the sky!'—Lower! Lower!" He gave a tiny salute and walked off.

Rather than fume about who'd sold me out, I focused on Nelson and his volunteer. Ken was performing for the adults, feigning a precardiac struggle with the hoops. He made his neck veins bulge. "No good . . . can't . . . separate . . . hoops," he gasped, ignoring the magician's glare. "Titanium . . . too . . . strong. Uhmf! Just . . . a man."

Nelson placed a hand on his shoulder. "Thank you, Ken. Now, what if . . . Ken, thanks for your help. Now—what if someone was strong enough to pull the hoops apart? Could he do it without breaking one?"

A woman near the back fence called out, "What about the physicist who proved it's theoretically possible to turn a beachball inside out without making a hole in it?" The spirit of insurrection was at large.

If he'd laughed, Nelson might have reclaimed the audience. "I suppose you"—his stage baritone cracked on the word—"could separate the hoops without breaking one?"

"Of course I can. Anyone over ten knows how it's done. Shall I say?"

"Oh anybody can say, but, kids, there's been too much saying already. Let's do it! On the count of three. One!"

"There's a slit!" yelled Kyle the birthday boy, a shrill, fat eleven-year-old with a buzz cut. "That's the baby way to do it! It's so lame!"

"Two three." Nelson pulled the hoops apart and held them aloft to tremendous sarcastic applause.

In the futile hope that the birthday boy might shut up, Nelson recruited him to be sawn in half. I missed the preliminaries fretting about my secret. Would I be forced to clown around on TV now?

Nelson had closed the cabinet on all but Kyle's head and a pair of feet in his socks and sneakers. "It's not my feet!" Kyle yelled. "It's trick feet! Trick feet!"

Nelson held up his saw and aimed a sunburst at the audience. "What do you think, kids? Does it look sharp enough to saw a boy in half?"

Rebecca, who hated magic acts, had abandoned her recliner and joined us. "Train wreck," she whispered, "couldn't resist."

From my shoulders Max said, "He make him half, Mommy."

"Well I just might make you half," she said, "so I can have two. Look, there's Iris."

"Hi, sweeties." In sunlight Iris always looked like a Poe character, even in her jaunty red sundress. She glanced at Kyle and whispered, "That boy better celebrate now. This is the last year they'll call him husky." She touched Rebecca's hair. "Did I tell you how much I love the bob? Does it always stay that neat? Shake it, girl."

Rebecca did the Swim—holding her nose, gyrating down to deep knee bends and back up, her hair flying in place. She was teaching the films of the sixties that quarter. What can I say?: she was wearing her pink tube top, and Nelson might as well have made himself disappear. Iris joined in, dishwater hair whipping across her eyes. I set down Max and once again demolished the myth that hermeneutists can't dance. But wouldn't it be lovely to be Max, I thought, as he pumped his arms and shimmied, wriggling from the grasp of shame and gravity.

None of this seemed a big deal then. But at my most self-pitying I look back on our frolic as one of the last happy moments of my life. I know that can't be true. The good half of my life persisted a few more months. There are happy moments still, snowed under the rest. Perhaps it's just the absence of music that makes our little dance seem unreachable—sealed away in its bubble.

Iris froze in mid-Swim; she dropped the arm reaching for the sky and folded both arms across her chest. Rebecca, then I followed her gaze. His saw poised midair, Nelson stared at us with a loathing I assured myself had to be the sunlight in his eyes.

Max looked up at us and stopped dancing. The entire crowd was staring.

Things appeared to click back to normal, and people turned their attention elsewhere—everyone but Chuck di Giorgio across the yard, who fixed me in his sunglasses and resumed his spectral pose.

.   .   .

After the show we went up to apologize. There was an apology line; Rebecca, Iris, Max, and I queued up behind Ken Dreynen and the beachball woman. While his father placated the magician, Kyle walked barefoot to the end of the cabinet to retrieve his shoes and socks. They were still on the fake feet, which had been left protruding from their holes. He pulled away a sneaker and a sock, exposing a slim, bone-white, plastic female foot. Inevitably Kyle tugged the foot; he gasped at the erotic surprise—he was holding the complete device to the top of its well-toned calf.

I'll never get through my story without overusing phrases like "Nelson stared" or "Nelson glared" or "Nelson glowered" or "Nelson narrowed his eyes." The stare could be intimidating the first or second time; he was a powerfully built if flabby man, and his eyes were the silvery gray that "glint" in some prose. But the more he'd employed his stare on the audience, the more he'd resembled one of those slow-burning bullies in a Three Stooges short. By the time he turned the look on Kyle, repetition had diminished force to farce. He managed to intimidate an eleven-year-old boy, though: Kyle looked frantic to rid himself of the shapely half limb in his arms. I think he contemplated dropping it, as if surrounded by the police. Instead he walked up and formally presented it to Nelson, who didn't know what to do with it either. Cradling it like a baby, Nelson tried to will all eyes to his face.

The beachball woman turned around. "George?"

It took me a moment to realize that this short, fat old woman with her monkish white hairdo contained my friend Sylvia Nagle. "Sylvia? What—?"

She still had her gritty, raucous dirty laugh. "What *happened*, George? I got *old*."

"No, I didn't mean . . ."

Sympathizing with my distress, she patted me on the head. Did I mention that when I was given the Auerbach Award, one of the most prestigious honors in the field of hermeneutics, the presenter, by all accounts a heterosexual man, put his palm above my head and only restrained himself at the last instant?

But Sylvia. I'd known her at Princeton when I was a graduate student and she was on the faculty. People used to tell her dirty jokes just to behold that laugh discharge from her small trim body and bow mouth. She'd finally grown into it.

"Don't worry," she added tenderly. Her speaking voice retained its scoured sexiness. "It won't happen to you."

I thought she was about to pat my head again, so I asked how she knew the Dreynens (she'd known Ken at Sarah Lawrence), exchanged news, and made introductions. When I got to Max, she said, "A thinker, just like your dad!" She tousled both our heads. Lowering her voice she said, "What's the deal with this magician? How could he be so bad? There are books. I know a certified imbecile who can do the ring trick properly. You don't saw a boy in half and leave the fake feet dangling when you're done. You don't even *use* fake feet; you have an assistant in the rear of the cabinet. So the toes can wiggle. My point is, there's a level beyond which incompetence verges on the eerie. That's what it was—eerie."

"Maybe he's just lazy. Have you thought of that?"

"Come on, George. There *must* be a better explanation. And if you say 'performance art,' I'll tweak your nose."

"All right. He used to be a great magician. But his hubris, his will to perform not tricks but something verging on real magic, led to tragedy. It happened during the sawing the woman in half act. Something went wrong, and—let's not dwell on grisliness. Suffice it to say that Kathryn, his beloved wife and assistant, had a closed-casket funeral. Afterward he set out to atone for his reckless pride, enduring at countless children's birthday parties the ritual humiliation we just witnessed."

"That's *so* much better than the truth." Rebecca kneeled down to get at Max with a kiddy wipe. "He's Ken's brother-in-law. His ex-brother-in-law, really." She straightened up. "Ken's ex's brother. You'd be amazed what you can pick up if you sit in your recliner and listen." Her look italicized the remark, and I assumed there'd been talk about me, too.

"There you have it, Sylvia. Brothers-in-law: the reason Latin American regimes go bankrupt and children fidget through birthday party entertainment."

"Nepotism doesn't explain anything," Sylvia insisted. "Any imbecile—"

When Iris lost patience she spoke in her sweetest voice. "Maybe where you come from they just have better imbeciles.

You're on." She pointed over Sylvia's shoulder where Nelson Baim was waiting.

"Sylvia Nagle." She extended her hand.

"Just a minute. Oh Wendy! Oh Wendy, dear." He handed the amputation to a pleasant-looking redhead in a Columbia sweatshirt. "Nelson Baim," he said shaking Sylvia's hand, "and this is my wife Wendy."

At the mention of a wife, Sylvia's free elbow came back and poked me in the stomach.

"Sorry about the heckling," she said. "You were a good sport."

"No problem," he said tersely. "Makes me stronger. Thanks for watching the show."

"I've never seen a magic act like yours. Are you a professional?"

"Yes I am."

Giddy with amazement, she turned her back on Nelson and said, "He says he's a professional magician!" People seldom did this in real life—only in dramatic soliloquies or in cable reruns of Burns and Allen, when George Burns would address the audience while the other characters marked time and pretended not to notice.

I glanced at Nelson's reddening face; I was having second thoughts about his stare, his glare, whatever you want to call it. It wasn't just anger. I've seen it since on my own mass-reproduced face: it's the way you might look at a witness to your most private shame.

When our turn came and we'd introduced ourselves, I said, "Forgive me, I just turned forty."

He had a sequestered smile, a spare part for some other face.

Rebecca said, "Maybe you can explain my favorite trick. How do they make the elephant disappear?" It was her way of helping shy or uptight men relax—a chance to strut their expertise for the pretty girl. If she thought it through, she might have put an easier question to a man who didn't know the proper way to separate the rings or saw a boy in half.

His face reddening to Sunday-comics brightness, he mumbled most of his evasion. ". . . mirrors . . . cabinet . . . second elephant . . . the old switcheroo . . ."

"Pardon?"

". . . can't reveal . . . not at liberty . . . the magician's code." He looked away.

"I enjoyed your act," she said desperately. "Our son thinks you're terrific. Don't you, Max?"

It was true. Max was looking up at him with unconditional love, attempting to slurp the man through wide-open eyes. Nelson kneeled down and pulled a silver dollar out of Max's ear. Closing his hand on it, Max kept his eyes on Nelson. He was too young for the trick, of course; it hadn't occurred to him yet that coins *shouldn't* come out of his ears.

When I'd persuaded Max to give it back, Nelson straightened up and said, "You're the flyer?"

After all the thinking I'd done about being exposed, I didn't have an answer. I was ready to flash Rebecca the get-us-out-of-here signal, but she'd gone off to the beer cooler with Iris, Sylvia, and Wendy Baim.

You might be wondering by now: why did I dread publicity? I don't blame you for your suspicions. Check-kiting in the Dakotas? Second wife in Akron? Ice-pick job in Cedar Rapids?

No, no, and no. Then why not do my time on the talk shows and move on? Was it really because I didn't want to debase flying? Yes. That above all. There was also the matter of dignity: not just my own but the dignity of hermeneutics, a tiny academic field constantly anticipating the flash of the budgeter's scythe. We are unknown to the general public; one grainy portrait in the *Inquirer* can become the face of hermeneutics. I'm not speaking theoretically. Ten years ago Gunter Fjornow of Denmark was the most venerable practitioner of our discipline. I attended the party that ruined his life. That afternoon Fjornow had given the keynote speech at the "Theory of Meaning in the Digital Age" conference at Northwestern, and the party was in his honor. He got into the spirit by quickly disposing of an entire bottle whose label seemed all consonants. The question of cultural differences in humor came up, and Fjornow narrowed his eyes at a perceived slight. "Gloomy. That's what you Americans think when you see a Dane coming. Let's stand up straight and be serious. Smiles must be expunged. The arrival of a Dane is the end of clowning." Determined to smash the stereotype, he calmly unscrewed a lampshade and placed it on his head. "There," he said. He kept it on for the rest of the evening while discussing fine points of hermeneutics, his voice slightly muffled. I'd like to describe him, but all I can picture today is the lampshade. Somehow he slipped past us, and Fjornow was arrested a block from the party. For years afterward hermeneutics was associated in the popular mind with police video of Fjornow behind the wheel of his car screaming at the arresting officer, his voice deadened by the extant lampshade: "You Americans are so proud of your modernity! Why don't you light your fucking streets!" Cable news and the tabloids speculated about how he'd managed to find his car. Had he taken off the shade? If so, why had he put it back on? Did he think it was a hat? Fjornow himself had no comment for the remainder of his public life.

Nelson was saying, "I've heard you're not happy about having this publicized. I think I can help."

"You're an agent? A publicist?" I nearly added, "You're certainly too late if you're a blackmailer."

"No. Magic is just the way I earn my living. I'm a debunker of psychic and paranormal claims. You've heard of The Amazing Randi?"

"Yes, of course! You're the magician who debunked Uri Geller! proved that he bent the spoons by, uh—how *did* he bend the spoons? That's all right, you're probably sick of the question. So your little fiasco this afternoon was just a spoof. You had us completely taken in. We couldn't fathom how you could possibly be that bad!"

Nelson attempted to square his already squared shoulders. "I'm not the Amazing Randi."

"Oh well. Sorry."

"I was about to say that I'm in the same field. You might have seen some of my work on the internet—for instance in the miracle forum on *Ideas.com*."

"Oh, the . . . not really."

"Perhaps you're familiar with some of the skeptic newsgroups. *Alt.skeptic*?"

"I'm sorry. They still have newsgroups?"

"I haven't been on for a while. I'm a regular on *alt.frommissouri*. Was."

"I'm sure it's—" I couldn't think of any way to complete the sentence that wouldn't sound patronizing.

"You might have seen my letter on the Virgin-in-the-Oatmeal flap in this week's *Brighton Park Star*." Glasses had left indentations on the bridge of his nose. "Anyway, my interest in debunking psychics grew out of my dissertation."

I nearly said, *"Dissertation?!"*

"You can download it on *publishyou.com*," he was saying.

"I have a lot of catching up to do. Well, Max has been out in the sun all this time; we're going to get some juice."

"I'll get to the point. If I debunk your flying, I think the media will leave you alone." A Day-Glo-green beachball bounced off the side of his head. He kept talking, ignoring the sheepish kids who retrieved it. "You'll have egg on your face for a few days, then they'll chase after somebody else. Which is worse? Being proved a fraud? Or getting beaten up with folding chairs on *Maury*?"

I knew nothing about how celebrity worked; for all I knew, those were my options. "Wait a minute. If I'm a fraud, as you say, then I'm only *pretending* to avoid the press and I must really *want* the publicity. So you wouldn't be doing me any favor by 'exposing' me. And If I'm for real, you'd be one more hound in the pack. Am I missing something?"

"Stop, professor! Your twisty reasoning is too much for a simple illusionist like me." In sarcasm his voice rose to a pugnacious whine. "Oh you're good! Let the games begin."

The thought occurred to me: why am I standing here? "We have to go."

"Hold on. There's another possibility. You invented a trick to entertain your family and your professor buddies and things got out of hand. By now you're probably embarrassed to admit it's a trick. That's where I can help. If you and I put the truth out as soon as possible, I think I can get you out of this."

"So you're the magistrate of Salem, and all I have to do is recant."

Max took the red Matchbox car out of his shorts pocket and offered it to Nelson. Rebecca had made certain that at two years eight months he was past the world-in-mouth stage, and I'd bought him a set.

"Oh, it's a beauty," Nelson said holding it in his palm. "The '57 Chevy, my favorite. Do you have a collection—a lot of these?"

"Yeah. Lot."

"Well thank you for letting me see it." He handed it back. "Vroom! aye? Vroom! Vroom!"

"Vroom!" Max agreed. "Vroom! Vroom!"

"My wife thinks boys start making motor sounds before they ever hear a motor," I said. "She thinks that's why we have motors."

"Nobody's asking you to recant. You're a scholar, right? In your profession the truth gets tested. That's all this is. With all the people who know about you, it's a matter of days before the camera crews turn up. Let me run a few tests. I promise I'll treat you respectfully. If I prove you're a fake, you'll get your privacy back. And if you're real, I'll announce my findings without sensationalism."

That much I believed: I doubted he'd generate much sensation on *alt.frommissouri*. I said, "Didn't you already call me a fraud?"

"I don't want to judge your motives. I think some so-called paranormals believe in their alleged talents."

"So it's what. Hysterical flying?"

"I'd be more interested to know what *you* call it."

"I don't know what a miracle *is*. A miracle is just the interim before science—"

"Good." He narrowed his eyes in what he must have intended as a steely, searching gaze. "You don't believe in miracles yourself. Disarm the skeptics, good! You'd be formidable in a battle of wits. I'm looking forward to it. Why don't you join us for dinner next weekend? You'll do what you do, and I'll see if it holds up." As he got his own pun, his disconnected smile flickered on and died.

The smell of grilling burgers was making me lightheaded. "I'm sorry. I'd rather not be authenticated *or* debunked. When the camera crews turn up, I'll refuse to put on a show. They'll go away eventually." I nearly added, "Won't they?"

I took Max's free hand—he was drilling for another dollar with the finger of the other—and said, "I think we'll have to pass on the invitation, but thank you. Take your finger out of your ear, Max. There's no more money in there. All gone!"

Rebecca walked up with Wendy Baim. "You're fading, babe," she said holding her beer can against my forehead. "Guess who Wendy's great-grandfather was?" Max used the distraction to approach Nelson and gawk up like a tourist.

"I don't know. Let's see." I looked at Wendy. She was notable only for an elaborate perm and an expression of amusement verging on mockery.

"I don't know. Why don't you—"

"Hugo Freiles!" Rebecca whooped.

"Get out!" I whooped back. Freiles was the overlooked genius of silent films, one of the German expressionists. Rebecca had done a piece on him for *Film Comment*; she'd been thinking of a biography.

She hugged me and stroked the back of my neck with the can. "And guess what turned up a few months ago in her grandmother's attic?"

"No!"

"Yes! His letters, his diaries, his production notes, and some unscreened footage from *Tainted Moon*. I'm invited to go through everything starting Monday. And we're invited to dinner the following Saturday."

"That's tremendous!" I said hugging her. *Of course* it sounded like a suspicious coincidence. But what could I do? "Wendy, Nelson. I'll see you next week. I'm looking forward to it."

Nelson shrugged sympathetically, I thought, at my entrapment. "Me too. We live at Nora House in Lake Forest. Do you need a map?"

"The haunted house?"

Nelson winced. "Yeah."

"I know where it is. It's in our book on North Shore mansions. Magic is your hobby, then?"

"Yeah. Something like that."

I started for the grill then turned back. "Why should there be camera crews? Everyone will think it's a trick, right? Why would it attract any more attention than a magician levitating his assistant?"

"It's the smallness," he said.

My irritation with him gathered to a hot, bright point. "I am a small man. So what?"

I realized my mistake long before Wendy broke the uncomfortable silence. "He meant the smallness of the trick—whatever you call it." She raised an eyebrow. She didn't come into focus until then. She was, a moment ago, just the woman who lugged around Nelson's cases, the transparent worker behind the act's pallid wonders. Her red hair was in ringlets, an out-of-fashion style that always reminded me of Grimm Brothers children in the woods. I thought the eyebrow and her little smirk conveyed tremendous and misplaced confidence in her allure. At best, I kept telling myself, she was average or marginally pretty. A bit pear shaped. Small oval face and small nose. Small brown eyes in which, not for the last time, I seemed to be growing smaller even though neither of us had moved. Not that I was intimidated by an eyebrow: as an Entmen, I can lift mine with the best. But I had the oddly thrilling sense of being evaluated from a long list of criteria with checkboxes and failing.

"If you flew above the rooftops," she said, "people would always be looking for your jet pack. But three or four inches? Why would anybody fake a miracle so—I'm sorry—so *worthless?* It might be small enough to believe."

THREE

Our footsteps in the hallway seemed to follow just behind us, reverberating off the marble floors and high ceilings of Nora House. Wendy was saying, "The original house was built in the style of Van Doren Shaw and the Arts and Crafts movement. After the fire in 1946, my grandfather worked with the architect to design something that looked like a house out of Gothic novels or movies. The family's boilerplate version always throws in the phrase 'insane with grief' about now, and I suppose he was. He wanted a place his dead daughter might plausibly *haunt*."

The wallpaper's dense convolutions of blue and white hyacinths and Wendy's come-on perfume were making my teeth buzz. She was walking so close on my left her swaying hip bumped against me. I didn't want to say anything or start a pileup to my right. None of this registered with the spouses—Rebecca mentally lighting the scene, Nelson to her right snorting occasionally at the ghost stuff. Wendy *was* more attractive than I'd been willing to admit last time—not at all pear shaped in her black scoop-neck top and floor-length black skirt, her red ringlets less silly than I recalled. I suppose the eyebrow was the source of her power, with its taunt, "I've figured *you* out," or was it "I find you marginally attractive but so what?" or "You mean you're still *there*?" Not that I had any intention of flirting back. I wasn't even sure this was flirting. She'd been amused last time by the slightly disconcerting effect she had on me. She seemed like the sort who might follow up out of sheer mischievous empirical inquiry. Or did that fall under "flirting"? Anyway, I loved my wife.

"You're talking about Hugo Freiles?" I said to say something.

"Freiles was my great-grandfather on my mother's side. He died broke in Germany. I meant Jeffrey Wickander, my grandfather on my father's side. He designed the thingy on bombsights that helps us bomb better."

As we passed an open door, Rebecca nudged me; sheets draped over vague bulks of furniture rippled in a sourceless draft.

"Ducts," Nelson said with the weariness of someone who too often had to haul out the word.

"Lake Forest isn't zoned for ghosts," Wendy continued, "and for years the neighbors tried to buy the place and tear it down, even though you can't see it except on the private grounds. I think they were afraid his descendants might turn it into a paid attraction, one of those showily haunted mansions like the Winchester House."

"Have you ever seen one?" Rebecca asked.

"Ghosts?" Wendy laughed. "No. We thought there was something going on for a while. There's a legend that echoes sometimes come back with different words. And a few years ago it seemed to be happening. 'You say goodbye and I say hello?' You'd shout hello, say, and you might hear hello hello and just as it's about to fade, goodbye. So Nelson set up his equipment—the cameras and the voice print readers and the oscilloscopes and the rest. No readings. One day—"

"It was teenagers," Nelson said. "No point shining flashlights under our chins."

Wendy stepped in front of me. Her face was at most four inches from mine. Her perfume at that distance smelled like hyacinths and the chloroform the kidnap victim smells on the rag before blacking out. Something else . . . apples? That's it, apples. I decided to adopt the majority view that this was all normal and smiled pleasantly at the sharp white glint in her iris. "Now that I've mentioned the echo," she was saying, "it would be bad manners not to let you try it out. You probably wanted to but you were worried about misbehaving, hmmm? How about it, George?"

I backed up. "Help!"

Behind the echo the walls roared like a subway tunnel, then the noise faded and the echo died with an "elp."

The dining room was mostly in shadow beyond the long table and the dim reach of its candelabra. "This is where Nelson used to debunk mediums," Wendy said as we took our places in the middle, Rebecca and I facing them across the table.

The subject made Nelson grit his teeth. "Exposing gypsy mediums—the police and the reporters and the internet sites said, 'So?' Even the Gypsy mediums said, 'So?' But it was practice." He was wearing his powder-blue seventies magician's tux again, which I thought expressed some sort of vestigial countercultural disdain for dressing up. Rebecca was wearing her black off-the-shoulders, ankle-length dress. I was wearing my charcoal Armani jacket over a black turtleneck jersey selected not to drag on the floor when I gave my flying demonstration. Nelson's pastel tux gave him the only visible torso among our flickering, hovering heads.

"Igor!" Wendy called, and Rebecca and I cracked up as the

first course trundled out of the shadows. "His name is John, actually, he teaches at Kendall College," Wendy said of the shadowy nonhunchback in a white jacket who was now serving our soup. "We don't have servants; we use John for special occasions. He makes the greatest truffle soup. We don't actually live in this part of the house, you realize. We just like to give the guests goosebumps. Okay, just me." She gave Nelson a peck on the cheek. "Nelson doesn't approve of goosebumps. He's writing a book about it."

"It takes debunking beyond the paranormal," he said. "It's called *Against Wonder*—a reworking of my dissertation."

I'd already heard a bit about it from Rebecca; even as I resolved to bite my tongue I heard myself asking, "So everything that makes children wide-eyed? You'd—"

"Wide-eyed kids—that's where it all starts."

Rebecca placed a hand over her heart. "I love this soup. Where do you get your produce?"

"There's a market on Green Bay Road. We'll go next week. Nel, tell them why you became a debunker."

"I was seven," he said, candlelight glowing in the copper coils of his beard. "My parents took my sister and me to the circus. The act I was looking forward to was the human cannonball. I'd already seen him once the year before, and for weeks I'd been walking around at home with helmet, goggles, and a cape, imagining I was that guy. I insisted on being called . . . the great something-or-other. So now the human projectile steps into the center ring. Spotlight, drumroll. Tosses aside his cape and climbs into the cannon. His name was Orlando Toff—researched it for my book. I remember wondering, was it cold in there? Was it dark? Was there an echo? What does it feel like to explode into the air? As we wait for the big moment, my parents are watching me, hoping it'll bring back something they used to feel. The pretty assistant picks up the torch and lights the fuse. And while it's burning down, Orlando Toff silently flies out the barrel. He's already in the net by the time the cannon goes boom. It's done with a catapult, by the way. There was no sound from the crowd—I think they were confused at first, maybe embarrassed for the guy—except a few coughs and this braying laugh that stopped dead. My parents avoid looking at me. I avoid looking at my sister but I can picture her spiteful grin. But Toff's a pro. Swings down smartly, holds up his arms, and just as people are starting to laugh and applaud, the calliope strikes up and here come the elephants."

Like most people's stories about "the moment everything changed," this one struck me as glib, overrehearsed, and emotionally dishonest. I found out later that Nelson's parents had divorced that same year. I suppose it's reductive to blame even that as the source of his lifelong disappointment.

Throughout the story Wendy looked at Nelson with an expression I couldn't at first name. As she leaned toward him, wide-eyed, lips parted, I thought it was a joke, and Wendy did seem to have her antic side. But no, it was plain old worship.

Rebecca, who'd been there during the week going over the Hugo Freiles papers, had said, "There's this look she gives him— like he'd assembled her out of glitter dust in his magic cabinet. I'd like to say, 'Hooray for love,' but it creeps me out a little."

. . .

Rebecca had already given me an outline of Nelson's career as a scholar and debunker. Some of the details below come from my later research, when knowing everything about the Baims became a matter of self-defense. But that night I already knew he wasn't the surly idiot he'd seemed at the kid's birthday party. Well—maybe.

By the time he was a freshman at Columbia University, Nelson already had his weary skeptic act down pat. That's when he wrote a play about the man who sees through all life's snares and delusions. This protagonist, Niles Beam, throws a party for all his many friends. At first things proceed like one of those thirties mysteries Rebecca and I enjoyed, including the line "I suppose you're wondering why I've called you all together." Niles informs his assembled guests that tonight he will strip away their illusions, expose all the lies they've told others and themselves—"the very lies you people require to go on living!" A sample revelation: "Talent!? Jan, you have no talent!" Yes, I got hold of a copy. When he's debunked them all, the few guests with the energy left to fight try to turn it all back on "Niles." What about *his* delusions? How can *anyone* have "the strength and courage and moral clarity" to see through the world's "gauzy deceptions" to the truth! Doesn't he realize that such a seeker must go through life alone? Who would dare accompany such a hero on his life's journey! "Yes," he replies grimly, "I must take that journey alone. Goodbye." "Wait!" they call. "How do we go on! Tell us what to do!" But he walks out, and the lights dim as they stare at the door in glum tableau. My hermeneutic analysis: dumped by girlfriend. Or simply: no friends. Just a guess.

Shortly after the single on-campus performance of the play—a witness recalls that afterward the audience and the players "scattered like cockroaches when the light comes on"—Nelson changed his major to philosophy. And he "did brilliantly," which isn't the same, perhaps, as "was brilliant." I gather he was one of those stunt obscuritans who speak and write in such dizzying, torch-juggling jargon, nobody wanted to say it was bullshit. Nobody wants to be the guy who puts *The Tractatus* in the reject pile. His mentor, perhaps the most influential professor in the department, declared him a wunderkind and dragged half the department along. The other half included the professor who would listen patiently to Nelson's dazzlingly opaque questions, then continue the lecture at the point where he'd been interrupted.

Nelson stayed on at Columbia for graduate school, and with the lobbying of his mentor, he was allowed to do a dissertation under panel members from both the English and the philosophy departments. It was to be a modern reworking of *Thus Spoke Zarathustra*. My doctorate is in English, and I wouldn't presume to give a definitive summary of a turgid, complex philosophy dissertation, but basically it's this: Nelson's killjoy hero goes around dashing everybody's hopes.

At first the division of the panel kept various anxieties at bay. The philosophy people didn't like the writing but figured the English people would take care of it. The English people suspected the arguments were crap but left that to the philosophers. The philosophy people wondered whether Nelson's Zarathustra was even a philosopher—going around discouraging people wasn't enough to qualify. But Nelson was too intelligent, they thought, to propound simple hopelessness; it was all allegory, obviously, so let the literati sort it out. Besides, more than half the work consisted of Nelson's commentaries on his prophet's monologues—these gave the work a welcome density and complexity, though admittedly also a complete loss of clarity.

One day three of the panel members met off-campus for lunch in a corner booth at the West End. They wanted to share their concerns outside the baleful gaze of Tom Grand, Nelson's mentor and defender. There was much twitchy utensil tapping and deep gazing into mugs before an English department panelist observed that Nelson seemed not to be saying more than "Suck it up. Life is horrible." But this was only weeks before Nelson's defense of his dissertation, and there's always the feeling that to raise strong, previously unvoiced objections at the last minute is unethical. How do you answer the charge that you've been stringing the candidate along?

Nelson might have got through if not for a handout that appeared in the mailboxes of graduate students and faculty a week before his defense. He was widely feared in the department and had made many enemies. He'd walk up to his graduate student rivals in public—usually at a bar or some party he'd crashed—and before the victim had time to grasp what was happening, Nelson had slashed an artery with a stunning and possibly meaningless refutation. (Wendy insisted that he was never an intellectual bully, just someone who took ideas with the absolute seriousness they deserved.) And so the handout was passed around and served up raw: It was, of course, his undergraduate play, *Approaching the Abyss*. Whoever was behind it must have realized that its juvenile histrionics seemed to convey the same ideas—"Suck it up! Life stinks!"—as his dissertation.

Nelson's defense went well for the first half hour, until Ben Cardaman—a last-minute replacement from the English department who resented being there—said, "I have some concerns about your sentences. They seem to fall into two categories. The ones that make sense—mostly in Zarathustra's monologues—

but seem trite and simpleminded; and the ones in the commentaries, which strike me as something a very smart guy might say if he were drunk and mistakenly thought he could speak Albanian. Now it's possible that I'm not up to speed on my jargon, but is there anyone on the philosophy side who can unpack—this, for instance." He proceeded to read three passages and no one, not even Tom Grand, offered to translate. Nelson began to explain the first passage but Ben interrupted.

"Nothing you're saying makes any sense to me. Now maybe it was a mistake to have English professors on a philosophy panel. But I don't see the philosophers rushing to your defense."

"Now just a minute, Ben." Tom Grand unknotted his bow tie and removed his jacket. He was making it clear that no one was going to attack Nelson without taking *him* out in the bargain. In his early seventies then, Tom Grand was a legend at Columbia: a hubcap-stealing juvenile delinquent who discovered Rimbaud in high school and came to Columbia on full scholarship. Short, gravel-voiced, ruddy, brilliant, charming, and ramrod spined, his curly brown hair so dark and intact he challenged nervous graduate students to give it a tug, Tom sometimes encouraged the rumor that he carried his old brass knuckles in the pocket of his tweed suit. "You say when Nelson isn't being opaque he's being simpleminded. Let's start with simpleminded. That kind of reductionism is cute, but you can do it with anything. *Macbeth*: Murder will out! Bishop Berkeley: It's all in your head! That's why you guys in the English department can perform the act of interpretation. Because big, complex units of meaning can be reduced to simple bite-size ones. And if that weren't true of Nelson's work, you'd say, 'See? It *is* all a bunch of pseudo Albanian.'"

He was pacing the room now and had turned the color of papier-mâché. Marta Kuberlin begged him to sit down and catch his breath, but he kept on. "He can't win, because when he's not being simple, he's being complex. Or is it that his complex ideas are just simplistic ones in masquerade? So what if Nelson dresses up his ideas—ideas that could be summarized in a sentence or two—in the finery of jargon and literary tropes and dense argument? King Lear's daughters ask him why he needs an entourage. Why not just one or two flunkies? 'O reason not the need!' he roars. If utility were the point we'd walk around in burlap and win Nobels for Post-it notes." Breathing loudly he dropped into a chair, and someone on the panel began reading Nelson's next paragraph. Finally Marta Kuberlin, convinced that the recitation of one more sentence would propel her out the window, asked a question. "So Nelson: *does* life suck, and if so why?"

Realizing he'd soon walk out of the room with nothing to show for his graduate career, Nelson had never been so convinced it indeed sucked. And so he made the case for sucking, bringing in Schopenhauer, Nietzsche, Céline, and the second law of thermodynamics. He brought in the Sophists, who are refuted in every generation and come back to be refuted in the next because "we know the nihilists are right." He brought in the Holocaust. He cited Freud. He referred to dementia and bowel cancer. He paraphrased the scientist who proved there's a portion of the brain whose only function is to concoct a rationalization when a random misfire makes us do something for no reason. He quoted a passage from Baudrillard, who wrote that life was a one-time accident on this planet alone, and in a few billion years we'd be one more cold rock in the void. He realized he wasn't expounding a philosophical thesis anymore, just a gut feeling he'd been hauling around most of his life, but he continued uninterrupted for the next fifteen minutes.

Finally Marta Kuberlin said, "That was eloquent, Nelson. But tell me. Are you a *sad* man? Because it seems to me what you're doing here isn't philosophy. It's not even poetry. You want us to give you a Ph.D. so that some university will *pay* you to be *sad*."

Having quieted his breathing and run a handkerchief over his face, Tom Grand rose from his chair. "Come on. Let's get back to business." Through a series of questions and answers he guided Nelson through the dissertation, attempting to demonstrate how the candidate had taken ideas from eighteenth- and nineteenth-century German philosophy and combined them with contemporary brain studies. How he'd ingeniously reworked Kant's categories of pure reason to prove that the brain is a denial machine, placing a barrier, a sort of pillow, between our understanding and the world's incomprehensible awfulness. The world's true darkness was beyond our capacity to process or feel. The amount of truth even Nietzsche could drag past the barrier amounted to covering one's ears and singing loudly.

Nelson thought he did well on Tom Grand's Q and A, but it was too late. What had stuck in everyone's mind, even more than the play, was, "You want someone to *pay* you to be *sad*."

Afterward Nelson sat in the hallway while the committee deliberated. The only remark loud enough to hear out there was Marta Kuberlein's. "Sure he's qualified—if you count *being sad!*" Later he heard about Tom Grand's last-ditch defense. Tom pointed out that only five or six people in the world fully understood the new neo-Kantianism, and that George Garratos, the philosophy panel member charged with fully aquatinting himself with the subject, had done a half-ass job. "So here's your problem, folks. All this talk about Nelson being a fake or a mountebank. What it amounts to is *your* insecurity. You figure either Nelson is stupid or you are." Too late, Tom realized that that last remark was probably the final nail, indeed the first shovel of dirt. A few minutes later he was given the duty to inform the candidate that his oral defense had been rejected.

When six months of cooling his heels outside administrators' offices didn't pan out, and when his lawyer told him that he might as well find something to do because a legal remedy could take years, Nelson became "The Box Man." He showed up outside the main gate at Broadway and 116th one morning with a box strapped around his neck. It contained xeroxes of his dissertation, which Nelson offered free to passersby. He thought that once it was in circulation *someone* influential would recognize its value. Surely it was just a matter of time before the Zola to his Dreyfus came along. Meanwhile his constant presence as The Box Man would, he hoped, shame the university. At first he attracted sympathizers; he might not have been well-liked at Columbia, but he was respected in his department, and some people took him seriously when he said the committee had ambushed him. Nothing came of all this glancing sympathy—which had to contend, for example, with sympathy for the one-armed guy who sold paperbacks off a blanket a few yards away—and Nelson was gradually reduced to one more colorful campus attraction, sometimes forced to shout over the you're-all-goin-to-hell guy. But it seemed important not to give in. With Tom Grand's lobbying, he got a part-time job teaching Intro to Philosophy at Hunter College, returning every evening to the Columbia gates with his box. That winter he attended Tom Grand's funeral wearing the box. Some faculty tried to block his way, but Tom's widow Irene told an usher to look after the box and escorted Nelson to a chair in the front row.

Ten years later, Nelson had cut his box time to two evenings a week. He still enjoyed his bull sessions with passersby, the camaraderie of his "regulars," the friendly philosophical jousting with people who told him to get a life ("and by a life you mean what?"). Above all, he didn't want to let the bastards win.

When Wendy was a freshman at Columbia she told a group of friends she'd never seen the Box Man, so they took her to the gates to see the show. Nelson was reading an excerpt from his dissertation to the small crowd: the part where Zarathustra shows up at a child's birthday party and makes the kids cry. He'd become a polished reader by then, and Wendy thought he looked masterful putting down his hecklers. In his proletarian jean jacket, pushing back a flop of red hair, he looked like he was about to lead them all in a march. Wendy was ready to follow. She astounded her friends by asking him out. When they asked what she saw in him, she said it was his seriousness, his certainty. For her friends, ideas were something you picked out like clothes, depending on who was giving the grade. Nelson didn't share their cool irony, but to Wendy her old crowd was beginning to seem like a buzzing swarm of quotation marks.

They moved in together a few months later. I think Wendy saw Nelson as a fixer-upper. When Rebecca and I were looking at houses in Evanston, we were shown a horrible example of that genre: leaky roof, missing shingles, peeling wallpaper, rotting stairs, huge water stains, a fist-size hole in a wall of the master bedroom, a broken furnace and an omnipresent smell like mold and navel lint. The real estate agent told us that a fixer-upper required a strong imagination and a mighty will: we'd have to look *through* the squalor before our eyes to its distant transformation. I thought Wendy's adoring gazes at her husband were directed at some yet-to-be-realized sweat-equity incarnation.

When they were married ten years later, she told him she didn't mind supporting him—she was a VP at Harris Bank—while he worked on his book. It was to be a popularized version of his dissertation. He'd vowed to never use another word of jargon, which explained why he talked more like a birthday party magician than a near-Ph.D. His book would be the unified field theory of philosophy but in the language of rocks and baseball and shoes and TV—accessible to anyone who made the effort. When years passed and Nelson wasn't ready to show her any pages, Wendy began to grow anxious. She never heard typing when she passed his study, and she often thought of Jack Nicholson in *The Shining* (but at least *he* was *typing*).

Wendy had inherited Nora House and the family billions by then. She was gone during the day—she'd kept her job—and she pictured him pacing the huge house, its one true haunting. The birthday magician work was her idea—he could get some real-life experience of sleight of hand for his debunking, he could get out of the house and make friends. She saw to it that he got plenty of magic gigs: she had enough clout in Lake Forest to ensure that he'd never be at a loss for fidgety, disappointed kids. He must have felt like a teenager on summer vacation, taking some stupid job because his parents didn't want him to "just hang around."

But after his failure as an academic Nelson had no second act. He didn't bother practicing the magic tricks because that would mean he'd accepted being a birthday magician. He consoled himself for the failure of his psychic debunking by reminding himself that he was "really" the author of a book in progress that would reveal all previous philosophy as mere screwing around. And he wasn't writing the book.

"The book? It's going fine," he'd say when she asked. "I'm writing it longhand," he'd say to account for the lack of typing. "Where's the pad?" she finally asked. It was one of the rare occasions when he found the energy to raise his voice: *"Where's the pad?* What am I, some kid who hasn't done his homework?" It was such a close approximation of what he was, they never had the discussion again.

. . .

At dinner, when she wasn't talking up Nelson, Wendy wanted us to know that she wasn't just some rich bitch. She had an MA in English from Columbia—winner of the Sarah Seaton Award for best master's thesis—and an MBA from Northwestern. Long before the inheritance, she'd became the youngest vice president in the history of Harris Bank, and she was now second vice president and in charge of community outreach. The inheritance came as a surprise, not an entirely pleasant one when she learned that the heir had to live in Nora House ("I think he wanted Nora to have company," she said. "Not a joke," she added when we laughed.) She accepted in order to become president of the Nora Foundation, the charitable organization her grandfather had set up. Except for the allowance for the house and its upkeep, she'd returned all her legacy and her Nora Foundation salary to the foundation, and they lived on her income from the bank. She'd used her positions as head of the foundation and the head of community outreach at Harris to persuade Chicago's top hundred corporations to increase their giving.

She spent much of dinner discussing her favorite authors. That's when I started noticing her tics and affectations. All her enthusiasms—literature, food, painting, dance, sculpture— seemed weirdly sexualized. For example, she smoothed back her ringleted hair as she told us that "there's something *sensual* about Hopkins's sprung rhythms." Even more to the point: "Chaucer—oo!" Rebecca had to put a napkin over her mouth and feign a cough. Wendy seemed to find it amusing to occasionally adopt a British accent, as in "*ec*tually." She used expressions that made sense to nobody else, for instance the infinitely flexible "pod," as in "A. E. Houseman—what a pod." Or "George, podling, would you like some more ice cream?"

I begged off on the ice cream.

"Then let's take a look at your little miracle."

.   .   .

"Tell me, George." Wendy crouched down with the videocam. I was lying on my stomach on the ballroom floor, ready to give my demonstration. "When you fly do the people look like ants?"

I beat her to the punch line, from a famous *New Yorker* cartoon. "Those *are* ants."

Klieg lights gleamed clinically off the expanse of white and gold tiles. My suit jacket, watch, glasses, and the contents of my pockets had been placed in a bin near the ornate entrance doors, where Wendy had scanned me with a metal detector and told me there'd never been a ball in the sad history of Nora House.

Nelson flicked a switch; cameras and monitors along the walls caught me looking a bit anxious. Nelson had promised that he wouldn't give the recording to the media without my permission. But I imagined myself cringing across campus past snickering colleagues, their arms extended in that damn Superman pose. It was worth it; Rebecca thought the Hugo Freiles papers were substantial enough for a biography.

Wi-Fi sensors taped to my forehead and chest fed blips and squiggly green lines to a nearby computer. What appeared to be a red Hula-Hoop leaned against the same desk. Six yards away Rebecca, my guide and coach and cheerleader, assumed a catcher's crouch.

"Let's get our definitions straight," Wendy said. "If you're 'down there,' are you flying? It would be levitating, assuming you were actually doing it."

"It would be levitating if I hung motionless in the air or moved only vertically. But I move horizontally with my torso parallel to the ground. Like Superman but not as high. That's flying."

She raised her face from the camera and wielded the eyebrow, implying, I thought, that she saw me as an intelligent and perhaps attractive man and that she'd be disappointed in me if I didn't see things her way. The solid mass of her perfume leaned up against me.

"I think of levitating as a floating, weightless condition. What I'm doing is more like the effort of powerlifting myself by the bootstraps. Completely exhausting. Maybe that's the difference—flying is work. Or look at it this way. If while I was 'levitating' over to Rebecca, a fly traveled along just beneath my nose, wouldn't you say the fly was *flying*? And therefore *I'm* flying. Altitude has nothing to do with it."

"George George George." She pushed the camera an inch from my face, as if a good blinkless stare would make me drop all this nonsense. "If a levitation train levitated three or four inches above the tracks, wouldn't you say the levitation train was *levitating*? Doesn't flying have to take place in oh, I don't know, *the sky*?"

"Actually the sky starts here." I placed my hand a sliver above the floor. I lifted my head and raising my own eyebrow added, "Or if that's too hard to get your mind around, the air."

"Really? So Icarus flew into the sun for nothing? He could have just flapped around in his yard?"

"Are we ready?" Nelson called from across the room. "I'll cue the music. Your usual?"

"We have your Superman theme." Wendy lowered the camera. "Or just in case you're in the mood for something different, George, I found 'Stairway to Heaven.' Hmmm?" The eyebrow again, augmented by a flaring of the nostrils. For the first time it occurred to me that she might be a little off.

I lifted my head and looked at Rebecca, wondering how she felt about her new friend flirting with me—or whatever the hell this was. Rebecca seemed to find it a riot; we exchanged shrugs.

Wendy poked me in the side with her pointy-toe shoe. "All right, George. Slip the surly bonds of earth." The music cued late, and for a few seconds there was no sound but my breathing until it was lost in the mighty orchestral swoon.

Arms extended forward, legs kicking uselessly, I rose to a height of four inches and began to fly to Rebecca. For the record, I am not a clumsy man. When I wasn't flying, people admired my quick sure movements dancing, lighting a woman's cigarette, swimming at the health club, changing a diaper, eating prawns with chopsticks. I'd been practicing at home, hoping to bring that same grace to flight. But so far I couldn't fly any higher or farther or faster, nor avoid grunting, drooling, extending my tongue over my upper lip. Panting like a drowning man among the feet of observers, I sometimes wondered if this horrific awkwardness was a hazing into my new element. Perhaps evolution required the flop-sweat of its forebears. How many fish had to twitch and gasp on the beach before the first successful amphibian? Perhaps each new move in the human repertoire—walking, running, dancing—must first pass through its Jerry Lewis phase.

Wendy placed her heel on my back and pushed me down to the floor. "Buoyancy test," she said. I recalled Toby doing the same thing. Was the first humanoid to walk upright similarly mocked? I made swimming motions on the floor until she released me and I flew on.

Months later, an ear, nose, and throat doctor told me that my clumsiness in flight might have stemmed from a disturbance of the inner ear. It couldn't process unsupported flying, even inches from the ground. To the inner ear it was all baggage pouring out of the overheads, The High and the Mighty, bells clanging, oxygen masks dropping.

Perhaps that explains my startled yelp when Nelson lowered the red Hula-Hoop. It was merely the magician's device to detect wires or other supports. I drew a breath, stopped kicking, and emerged from the portal having performed the world's first authenticated miracle.

.   .   .

I was lying on my back on the tiles, getting my breath, Rebecca and the Baims on the floor beside me. The klieg lights had been shut off and we all looked a bit golden beneath the chandeliers.

"Did I pass?" I asked Nelson.

His grudging "yes" steamed through his teeth. "You passed the hoop test."

"What about the squiggly line test? What did that measure?"

"The hoop was it. All right? I went to the magic store on Lincoln Avenue and asked the counter guy how he'd prove whether or not someone was flying. I didn't like the look he was giving me—they don't like me there—so I said it was for a story. He said if it was him he'd use a hoop." Wendy was rubbing his shoulders; she unknotted his bow tie and unbuttoned the collar.

"So the equipment—it was just to intimidate me?"

"Did it work?" Wendy asked brazenly. "The Nora Foundation donates medical equipment to the Third World. They'll come back tomorrow and box it up." She hugged Nelson from behind and put her chin on his shoulder.

"Why are you guys so sad?" asked Rebecca. "Instead of debunking George, why can't you *bunk* him?" She glanced wryly at Wendy: "I mean *antidebunk* him. What's wrong with affirming something if it's true?"

"The magic store clerk said if you pass the hoop test you're flying," Nelson conceded.

"Well?" I said.

"David Copperfield can make an elephant quote-unquote fly above the Mirage Hotel, and nobody believes it. Should I believe *you're* flying because your claims are more modest? . . . But I promised that if you passed I'd concede." He extended his hand; I sat up and shook it. We all stood up and exchanged hugs.

"We're invited to a party tonight," Wendy said. "Come along. Romulus Goins, the debunker? He's in town this week and they're giving him a party. Magicians and skeptics and professors.

Paisley, patchouli, pipes and, um, elbow patches. David Copperfield's in town, so he might be there. Probably some people you
know from Northwestern. Come on, I'll bet you've never seen a
thousand-dollar mullet up close. There will be several.".

"Sounds like fun," Rebecca said.

"I'd have to phone the babysitter."

"Wait a minute." Rebecca took my elbow. "Toby and Iris,
remember? They're coming over." They were on one of their
hopeless dates, which they'd backstopped by arranging ten
o'clock drinks at our house. To skip yards of exposition, Toby was
in love with Iris and believed he was too rotten for her (possibly
so). He believed, Iris said, that she was some tiny brittle Glass
Menagerie figurine whose warranty could be voided with a hard
look. Afterward they'd hide from each other for a few days and
go on being friends. As for his Russian acrobat—performance
artist!—I hadn't kept track.

"I remember Iris from that snotty kid's birthday party,"
Wendy said. "I like her. Why don't you have them meet us? It's
at 2944 Pratt."

Rebecca didn't flash me her get-me-out-of-this look—a wistful gaze into some happier distance—so it looked like we were
going.

I said we'd have to call the babysitter and our friends; Wendy
mentioned bad cell reception and directed us to the phone in one
of the guest rooms ("we keep the extensions connected in case we
get lost").

More ghost furniture beneath sheets; in a black-and-white
photo on the wall a frail girl in dark bangs gaped. It had to be
Nora. The points of her lips tweaked up in a secret smile, which I

probably wouldn't have studied if not for the horrible glamour of her death. The casement was open but there was no sound from the garden; the wind seemed massed in the lightless trees.

"Creepy enough for you?" I said.

Rebecca nodded. She gave her bob a vigorous shake and it settled back in place. It had become her reset button.

"Speaking of creepy," I said, "if you're weirded out by what Wendy was doing—whatever it was—we don't have to go."

She laughed and whispered, "The eyebrow? She's been giving me the eyebrow for days."

"Wow. So either she's coming on to both of us or it's some kind of neurological tic?"

"If she's flirting with us her agenda isn't sex," she said. "It's like smiling at the traffic cop. You're not planning to have sex with him."

"Somehow that never works for me. You're saying . . . What are you saying?"

"Come on, George. You've seen how she looks at Nelson."

"Oh. She wants me to let Nelson debunk me. Or failing that she wants *you* to persuade *me* to let Nelson debunk me."

"There ya go!" She extended her hand— "oh, go on," I said, "do it"—and mussed my hair.

"I don't think he had any real hope that the tests would work," she continued. "He put about as much effort into it as he does into his magic. So I guess it's up to Wendy.

"You don't have to hang out with these people," she added smoothing my hair down. "I don't even have to do the Freiles book. I've got other projects I'd enjoy just as much. I haven't put much work into it yet, so let me know soon."

"Nonsense. They're so damn odd, it'll be fun figuring them out. She doesn't lack for self-confidence, I'll say that."

"Wendy believes she can make anybody do anything."

"A billion dollars must help," I said.

"She gave the money to the foundation, remember? Besides, she thinks she can do it through sheer will. She thinks most people are weak."

"Okay, then. Let's party with the Hitlers. I guess they just kept going after Nietzsche."

Rebecca laughed and gave me a shove. "No! I sort of *like* them. They're kind of sympathetic, aren't they? She's so in love with this guy who's beneath her, and he's so sad."

"Okay, we like them. As for Wendy's plans, she can *will* till the cows come home, but we can out-brow her."

"I saw something weird the other day. It was when she was showing me the library. She showed me the shelves with her childhood books, and one of them was *Controlling Yourself and Others: The Science of Power*, by Edwin Flesner. I thought it was misshelved, but there was her signature on the endpaper in perfect, serious ten-year-old child's penmanship."

"While the other girls were reading *Little Women*—"

"She read *Little Women*, too," Rebecca said. "If you think about it, she does a lot of the stuff all the talk show guests who write books on power recommend. She doesn't exactly whisper but she speaks softly enough that you have to lean in and concentrate."

"Oh—right."

"Or sometimes if there's a lull in the conversation?" Rebecca lowered her voice. "She'll sit and watch you, not staring, just . . . watching, until you start talking just to make noise."

She put her hand on the phone. "What if she were offering money—a million dollars, say—instead of come-ons and eye-brows?"

"I'd talk to you first, of course."

"It's completely up to you," she said. "We have tenure, we're comfortable, we can afford any college for Max."

"Then I'd say no."

She asked me to explain.

"I'm not usually at a loss for words, but it'll sound stupid."

"I doubt it's stupid if you feel so strongly."

"Because it would *defile flying.*"

"That *does* sound a little stupid," she allowed.

"I'll work on it."

. . .

Wendy said she wished she knew more about her great-grand-father, and Rebecca charged into the breach. We were riding to the party in Nelson's SUV; Toby and Iris would drive up from Lincoln Park.

Rebecca was saying, "Freils had all sorts of ways to show you a character is going mad." She's usually poised and calm, but her gestures get bigger when she's excited (in conversation together the women in her family gesture like shaken puppets), and Wendy leaned back to avoid getting clipped. "For instance he kept experimenting with the image of a man falling into his own eye. I'll shut up in a minute."

"No, please. He *was* my great-grandfather. The only one I've seen is *Tainted Moon.* I keep promising myself to get out to the UCLA archive. But please."

"Anyway, the first time he tries it—in *Infernal Melody*—the falling man stays the same size and the eye below grows bigger. That looked too much like an oncoming collision. Directors are still inventing film grammar, and they aren't always sure what will make sense to the audience. So in *The Crooked Tower* he tries it with the eyeball filling the screen and the falling man shrinking as he plummets into it."

Nelson glanced at her in the rearview mirror. "This is how many years after an audience ran from a train on the screen?"

"That didn't really happen . . . His cinematographer Walter Casmiri comes up with a variation for *Mesmer.* You see a woman, the hypnotized subject who's about to become Mesmer's slave, falling into his eye, getting smaller and smaller. Then the eyelid blinks and she's gone."

When I realized we'd stopped moving, I faced front. Pratt had dead-ended against a park filled with gumdrop-colored abstract sculptures. There was something suspenseful about the empty, overlighted paths; I think we were waiting for someone to make an entrance. Wendy stepped up and rubbed Nelson's shoulders.

"The park's not backing down, Nel. You'll have to turn around." If either of the Baims suspected that Nelson's brother skeptics had fake-addressed him, it never came up.

Nelson cruised the side streets, mostly upscale ranch houses. I squinted to catch a number, the streetlights twitching through dense leaves. And then we were back at the dead end. Crickets revved up to underline the point.

"Remind me how you heard about the party," Wendy asked Nelson.

"Raymond at the magic store was talking about it on the phone. You remember Raymond. He's sort of a friend, my only friend at the magic store, and I asked him for the details. I'll call him."

Nelson tilted his chin at the park. "2944—would that be *in* the park?" He pulled out his cell and dialed. "'Raymond? It's Nelson. That address you gave us? I said it's Nelson. How about now? He'll call us back from a landline."

He began driving out of antsiness. He turned north on Lincoln. "I think Pratt picks up again somewhere near here."

"On the other side of the park," Wendy said.

"There's a shopping center," I said. "It's west of the shopping center. Or maybe just south."

While Nelson had been talking to his "friend," Rebecca had phoned Toby. She said, "Toby thinks Evelyn Janks will be there. She wrote that book about credulity and the right brain. He'll try to get the address and directions from her. You know, there's a hotel around here, used to be a Hyatt, I think it's a Radisson now. They have this philanthropist bartender—the man who puts the gin in gin and tonic, remember, George? And those scrumptious golf ball–shaped eggrolls. There's a jukebox and a dance floor, guys. Let's go there if the party doesn't work out—oh, stop here!"

We were passing a gas station with a minimart. "I'll ask directions," Rebecca said, "and who wants an ice cream cone? My treat!" That year the convenience markets were experimenting with wrapped, preassembled, triple-scoop ice cream cones, the scoops snugly fused through some mystery process.

Wendy raised her hand. "Me me me! As long as you're up, Nelson."

"I'm not up."

"*As long as you're up*," she said pointedly, "get some drain cleaner, toilet cleaner, Special K, Kotex, and paper towels. Should I write it down?"

"I'm not stupid," he muttered before stepping out and slamming the door. Rebecca was waiting in the lot; they stepped up onto the raised sidewalk and into the store.

Wendy clambered over the gearshift and onto the driver's seat. She extended her legs over the console onto my lap—she was still wearing her black floor-length skirt. I decided that telling her to put them down would be playing whatever game it was.

"I bought this skirt at my neighbor's yard sale. It's from the late seventies or early eighties—these snaps up the middle? Usually this style came in midcalf length. And yes, at this length you have to think about wind velocity. Do you like it, George?"

"It looks nice, but when I see pictures of women with the snaps open, I imagine them struggling to hold themselves together."

"Do you imagine that I'd ever struggle to hold myself together?"

"No," I admitted.

"Are you sad that the snaps are all closed?"

"You're acting ridiculous."

"And yet you haven't asked me to put my legs down."

"Put your legs down."

She kept them where they were. "Do you know why they call them snaps? It's because each time you undo one it makes a satisfying snap!" She rubbed her thumb on the top one.

"You were an English major, so you must know that the connection between words and sounds is completely culture-bound. If we were in Japan—"

She shook her head and laughed.

"Do you like me, George?"

"Of course I like you," I said innocuously.

"Here's an exercise in deductive reasoning. It's not quite in syllogism form, but you'll pick it up. A: The Nora Foundation is the sole private sponsor of the Chicago Folk Dance Festival. Did you know that, George? B: Because of my immersion in world dance, I've mastered the steps of all nations. What do you deduce?" Eyebrow up.

"That you're saying random stupid things to see how I'll react."

"The correct answer is, my legs are unimaginably great. If I were to undo all these snaps right now, I honestly believe it would destroy you. Was that a snort? Did you *snort* at me, George? Let's try a little test. I'll keep my legs here and undo the bottom snap. I'll bet you'll be glad to see me, if you know what I mean, even though I've always thought my ankles are a little thick."

You must be wondering: how do I remember every damn thing everybody says? I've always had a good memory but not a photographic one. When the flying started, I thought my experience might be a tiny asterisk to history. And I thought that if I looked closely at my daily life, it might give me some insight into the flying. And so I started jotting keywords in a pocket notebook; at night I'd expand these fragments into full recountings in my journal. During many of the events you've read about here, there'd be a moment when I pulled out the notebook and made a brief entry. I left all that out of *this* book because the last thing you want to do is read about my writing down the phrase you're reading.

I have to admit that Wendy's test, ludicrous as it was, was near to having its intended effect. So I retrieved the notebook from my inside suit coat pocket and jotted a few keywords from that evening: cannon, squiggly, power, unimaginably. I held it on the palm of my left hand and wrote with the right. I'm adept at writing in the dark in tiny orderly script.

"George, what are you doing?"

"George . . . what," I muttered as I wrote, "are . . . you . . . doing."

"Is this your version of 'thinking about baseball?'"

". . . thinking . . . about . . . baseball."

"George, don't be a pod. This is so immature."

"*Immature?*" I laughed. "What are you, Wendy, twelve?" Granted: I wasn't operating at my highest order of wit. I turned the notebook over to the right-hand page. "Immature," I muttered as I wrote. "What . . . are . . . you . . . Wendy . . . twelve.

"Look," I said, "Rebecca's asking directions. When she's as fired-up as she is tonight, her gestures are a caffeinated hula. Watch. The meaning, as they say, is in the hands."

The skinny kid behind the counter—so pale he seemed to have the fluorescent light version of a tan—was floored by Rebecca's onslaught of giddy gesticulation.

While Rebecca spoke, she traced a series of verticals and right angles in the air. "Ah, here we go." I interpreted for Wendy. "We're lost. California, Lincoln, Pratt, the park. McCormick, Touhy, California, side streets, back to Pratt, back to the park—" Rebecca spread her arms, turned her palms up, cocked her head and froze. "Crickets."

Wendy and I applauded. When our laughter subsided, she clapped me on the shoulder. "That was glorious! I really like her."

As he rang up the ice cream cones, the kid spoke slowly and gravely. "*He* doesn't know directions," Wendy said. "He just wants to keep looking at her tits. 'Hmm. A park. Let me see. Now, wait a minute. Ah. Yes. Hmm. You know, I seem to recollect . . .'"

"He's not a bad fake thinker. He's like some of my C students—they go for that Montgomery Clift agonized earnestness."

"Speaking of faking."

"What?"

"George. Come on."

"I thought the hoop test resolved everything to everyone's satisfaction."

"Magicians kept saying 'if he passes the hoop test he's flying.'"

"And yet!"

"Seriously, George. They only said it because they were sure you wouldn't pass."

It had occurred to me that I could give the Baims a new life just by recanting. I suppose I took Rebecca's view: Odd as they were, I sort of liked them. All I had to do was be famous for a week—a dreadful prospect, but it looked like the press would find out soon in any case—get debunked, and go back to my old life.

Then why *not* give Nelson his second act and let poor Wendy stop whoring—or whatever this was. I don't like to lie, but it wasn't as simple as that. I couldn't recant because . . . all right, because it was *flying*. Do I have to explain? *You* know what I mean, you who've buzzed the housetops in your ghostly pajamas. It's not that I'd found something celestial at the altitude of four inches. But I'd been given a gift. I wasn't about to drag it in the dirt.

And there was one other problem. "To debunk me you'd have to figure out how I faked it."

"So? You'll tell me."

"I can't tell you because I didn't fake it."

"You're a smart man, George. I'm sure you'll figure out how you 'would have' faked it."

Checking out at the counter, Nelson glared in our direction. I recall saying that Nelson's glares and grimaces and glowerings had begun to seem comical. This wasn't funny. I thought of swiping her legs off my lap.

"He can't see us, George. It's dark in here and the windshield's tinted," she said, making me feel complicit. But she stood up, climbed back over the console, and returned to her seat. "He's a good man. No. Somewhere in there there's a *great* man. A lot of people are afraid of him, but he's just unhappy. Can't you help him?"

I opened the door for Rebecca, holding a cone in each hand. "Ice cream!" she sang, handing one to Wendy and peeling the wrapper off her own.

"Drain cleaner!" Nelson sang, setting the bag on the mat.

We began to circle the neighborhood while we waited for Toby's call. On Lincoln, Rebecca pointed her cone at the window. "There's a 7/11! I'll ask there." Nelson pulled into the lot and was about to get out when Wendy said, "Stay here. I have to show you something."

We watched Rebecca speak to the round-shouldered man behind the counter, her gestures with the ice cream cone big enough to land an F-16.

Stooping behind the cup holder with her ice cream, Wendy narrated: "California, Pratt . . . the park. . . ."

I don't know which part of the story led to Rebecca's sudden operatic sweep of the arm; the three scoops, still welded together, continued their arc outside the cone. The clerk gazed fatalistically at the pantyhose display they'd sailed behind.

Rebecca looked in our direction—for a moment I thought she could hear our laughter, shrill and startled as horror movie screams—and pathetically held up the empty cone. "Awww," we sighed in chorus.

Toby phoned as she was getting back in the van, still holding the empty cone. The party was at 750 Belden; Nelson did a U-turn and we drove back south. "Wait!" Rebecca shouted. "There's the gas station. I'll ask for new scoops." She held up the empty cone that I thought she'd been grasping from shock.

The last thing we wanted to do was talk her out of it: we were fans of this new form of theater. Wendy gripped Nelson's arm as Rebecca walked into the minimart. The clerk and two mechanics from the garage broke off their conversation. All three leaned forward while she recounted our adventure from the beginning, including, it appeared, reenactments of her *previous* reenactments. When she got to the ice cream mishap, wielding the empty cone and launching the bygone scoops, the pale boy and the jumpsuited men craned their necks in unison.

We applauded and whistled when Rebecca came back with a new triple scoop. As she got in, Nelson leaned over the seat and gave her a pat on the arm. "You were magnificent! I'm so glad we met you guys."

I couldn't fit the sappy sentiment or the catch in his voice with the look he'd flashed through the store window earlier. For now I decided to take Rebecca's view of Nelson. "He's a teddy bear," she'd said that morning. "The faces? I dunno, stomach acid."

FOUR

Seven-fifty Belden was a remodeled court building in Lincoln Park. As we walked into the party, the music and talk snapped back from us as if on a high-tech fishing line.

All sound hung suspended with the pot smoke. We smiled and nodded at frozen stares. Then a crumpled beer can bounced off the side of Nelson's head and the party resumed.

"What a bunch of assholes. Should we leave?" Rebecca gave the stink-eye to the crowd, who'd turned back to each other. I'd expected a lot of paisley, ruffled shirts, and mustaches—I'd always associated magic with that era—but aside from some well-fed, silky mustaches and the occasional sculpted mullet, it could have been a university party. I recognized a face or two from Northwestern.

Nelson straightened his cuffs and bow tie. "It's all right. There are people in the community who don't like me. I won't give them the satisfaction . . . Okay. Someone told me how a certain magician did a certain trick and I posted it on the internet. There are people in this room who've threatened to beat me up on sight. I guess they meant in their dreams or their blogs. And don't tell me about the damn magician's code. The man I exposed doesn't even call himself a magician. He's one of those magical-mystical guys. You know: goes right up to the line to imply *he's not just doing tricks*. How is he less of a fraud than some psychic? Wouldn't the world be a better place if everyone was a little less amazing?"

The host came over, his thin lips and bright panicky eyes straining toward congeniality. "Sorry about that," he said not to Nelson but to our group in general. "Please don't let it spoil the rest of the evening. Food's on the dining room table, alcohol's in the kitchen." He exchanged greetings and handshakes with the women and me and walked off.

Wendy caught up with him and whispered something in his ear; he tried to disguise his flinch as a whacky double take. He rolled his eyes at the room, but his intended audience were talking in clumps or dancing. He walked back to Nelson, shook hands, and speed-walked away while Nelson rubbed his hand on his pants. "See you in a minute," Wendy said, "we're going to look for Nelson's friend."

"That could take more than a minute," I said to Rebecca as they set off.

"I'm going to start drinking," she said, "and not stop till I imagine this party is fun. First let's find Toby and Iris."

A cloud of pot smoke materialized around me so suddenly I expected a magician to step out of it. It was Toby, standing to my side, smoke streaming out of his giant head, his sweep of the arm indicating something witty about the state of things in general. When he was stoned he sometimes skipped the aphorisms and just posed for the book jacket.

I could tell he wasn't happy. "Try it," he said handing me the joint. "It produces a Chandleresque black curtain of oblivion. A beaded black curtain of Chandleresque semioblivion, to be precise. Hi, Becca. One look at those creamy shoulders and I'm blivious again."

"Back at ya, Tobe. Where's Iris?"

"Sobbing in the kitchen, I think. Don't worry, it's the funny sobbing."

We knew about the funny sobbing, which is the reason I felt free to examine the joint. The smoke was making my eyes slit. "Will this be pleasant? Remember the last stuff? Like bad unlicensed acupuncture, tiny, tiny needles everywhere."

"You have to *smoke* it. Close hermeneutic analysis won't get the job done."

I shrugged and took a hit. A vibrating electrical hum came up from the floor and fizzed along my spine. It wasn't pleasant, but it seemed like a good distraction from things less pleasant still.

"One hit's enough," he said. "You're good."

I handed it Rebecca, who paused to ask Toby, "How was your date?"

He started a shrug—couldn't find the heart to complete it. "I don't know. Go ask her how she is."

Iris was sitting with five or six other people at the big kitchen table, reading aloud from a book titled *My Long Sad Road to Magic.* As advertised, she was sobbing, her voice cracking, wiping at her cheek with her wrist, pushing back a side curl that had stuck to her face.

The book's covers shared the same black-and-white photo of the magician Ricardo Dean. The man himself was leaning against the kitchen sink. Dark, wiry, spiky haired and black turtlenecked, he performed the most ordinary gestures with the quick, lithe movements of his act. "And now," I imagined him announcing, "I will drink a glass of water." He was the most gelled man I'd ever seen. In photographs his hair had a moonlit-forest effect, but up close you could almost hear it squish. He greeted us with his trademarked (seriously: there'd been lawsuits) "haunted stare." It seemed to be saying, "You understand nothing of my long sad road to magic. And yet, I forgive you."

Between sobs, Iris read, "And so I looked at my parents for the last time. I loved them, but they would never see the magic. Below us only rocks and dead things, above us the blackness of space, and beyond that, at best, a heaven without wonder."

She looked up and gave us a brave moist smile. "Oh, hi."

"This is the *funny* sobbing, right?" I asked.

"Oh, sweetie. There *is* no funny sobbing. But isn't it pretty to think so?"

"The funny sobbing" was Toby's coinage. Once a year he taught a graduate seminar in pop culture, and when his students got too snide and condescending, he invited Iris in to view some piece of kitsch from his collection—the *Hawaii Five-O* episode where Mickey Rooney dies, that Joan Crawford movie where she makes friends with Bigfoot, maybe the "very special episode" of *The Facts of Life*. But always something tear-jerking and risible. And predictably, amid his students' snickering, Iris would break down and weep. "This," he admonished the class, "is how someone with feelings watches 'the very special episode' of *The Facts of Life*. It isn't that she's incapable of 'irony,' to use your favorite misused word. This is, after all, Iris Ransler, winner of the PEN/Faulkner and two National Book Awards, possibly the funniest writer in contemporary fiction. She can put more irony in a character's 'hello' than the sum total of all you think you're hoarding behind your twitchy smirks. Sure," he summed up, "be analytical, be merciless in calling crap crap, but if you don't let yourself feel, you're cowards."

This rant, of course, was largely a joke. He didn't really believe that hers was the appropriate response to crap. But the annual "Iris Day" served two purposes. It gave him a chance to remind his graduate students that criticism wasn't just squinty analytical watch repair, reassembling Lear's howl out of tiny doodads. If you can't howl with Lear, you're better off assembling jigsaws. And it gave him a chance to explore the mysteries of Iris. How could anybody so funny and sharp—who was capable of being tough, sarcastic, and resilient—be so defenseless? He was in love with her (not that he'd admit it), and the incongruous tears frightened him—reminded him that she'd had two nervous breakdowns. He was terrified of her breakability. How could an asshole like himself *possibly* blah blah blah; even if he could reform, he'd feel like a blindfolded oaf at Pottery Barn. Could the crying be a put-on? Impossible. And so he took refuge in the idea of "funny sobbing": Even if the sobbing was absolutely genuine, she was somehow, simultaneously, making a joke. He actually researched it. He called me once at two in the morning and said, "Maybe it's not possible to be funny and sad at the same instant, but George Steiner thinks we can do quick change-ups that are close to instantaneity." I think the concept of "funny sobbing" had become the bulwark for all his frail hopes that they could be together.

Iris was smiling through tears once more, an expression so poignant I had to remind myself that she and Rebecca used to practice it while freeze-framing Renee Zellweger on DVD.

I said, "Toby thinks—"

"God didn't wire us to laugh at our own crying while we're crying. That's what our friends are for."

"Sorry."

"That's okay. It's funny. 'Iris is crying at some piece of shit again.'"

We glanced at Ricardo Dean, but he remained imperviously haunted. He took the book out of her hands. "Don't hide your pale beauty behind a book."

I wrote that one in my notebook. When I was finished Iris held out her hand. She read it and handed it back. "Hearing check. Lovely but pasty, that's me."

"I surrender." He raised his hands. "I can't compete with your wit. Just as *you* can't fight what's happening between us. Let's get out of here."

"Know what I'm thinking?" she asked.

He folded his arms. "Yes, I do."

"Jell-O surprise. It's the gel. You could suspend marshmallows in there."

"Yes. Delicious—and surprising."

She looked helplessly at me and Rebecca. "I'm *doin'* my best to *insult* him." It hadn't escaped me that her twang was turned all the way up. Never a good sign.

"It's tough when the guy's shameless *and* humorless," Rebecca said. "Mind if I take a shot? Fuck off, gel-slick."

"It would have been coarse of me to use that word," Ricardo Dean said to Iris, "but there it is. We'll see, you and I, where the night takes us."

"Thanks for trying," Iris said to Rebecca. "It's like winning an argument with some idiot who just comes back and says, 'Oh yeah?'"

. . .

I found Toby speaking to Wendy and a short gray man with round, steel-frame glasses.

I took him aside. "I think Iris is about to leave the party with Ricardo Dean. I don't know what happened on your date, but do something. Go!"

"Leaving a party with some douchebag is a small price to pay for our freedoms. What do you think I can do? Anyway, she'd never—"

"He meets her mother's three criteria. Has a job. Not in prison. Uh . . . what's the third?"

"Has his own car," he said. "Forget it. I'd just mess her up." His big frame deflated like a parade float. "I think she and I—"

"Look, *you're not that much of* a bastard."

"Thank you, George. Decent of you to say that. That's Romulus Goins, the debunker," he gestured at the man in the steel-frame glasses who was standing next to Wendy.

I refused to be distracted. "Don't you know what all the sobbing is about? It's guys like Ricardo Dean. And the funny sobbing? It's a way to get in *even more sobbing.* Go!" I clapped him on the back. "Be her ninja!"

"She and I came to an understanding tonight. She wants no part of my 'saint/whore dichotomy.' I'm going to have to practice a tougher discipline than ninja: her old friend Toby."

"I'm sorry, Toby."

He put an arm around my shoulder and guided me over to his previous conversation. Goins and I shook hands.

Toby wasn't quite so devastated that he couldn't tweak me a bit. "Tell me, Romulus, suppose I claim to be able to fly. Suppose that as far as anybody can tell, I *can* fly. How would you debunk me?"

"A pass of the hoop would probably do the job. Otherwise I'd figure out your weak points and work on those. Your basic *Crime and Punishment*. You big guys go down fast.

"Wendy and I were discussing the so-called Flesner Magic Show," he added.

"Edwin Flesner," she explained breathily, "was a Harvard psychologist who worked with the CIA after Korea. They were worried about the Russians or the Chinese programming brainwashed Manchurian Candidate assassins. Flesner did astounding things with his test subjects. He said, 'You have to tear the subject down to nothing before you can build him back up.' Experts are still arguing about whether the infamous magic show took place at all. I believe it did. This is the one where through mass hypnosis Flesner convinced an audience of five hundred people that he was performing miracles. Levitated a herd of flaming hippopotami thirty feet in the air, turned an eighteen-wheeler into a baby. In reality it was just Flesner on an empty stage, gesturing."

"I was one of the last cops on the Chicago Police Carny Squad," Goins rasped in his razor-gargle. I noticed that his right blue eye was glass. "The Flesner story is all so much elephant crap. The so-called magic show never happened. I don't care how many degrees the guy had—I have a Ph.D. in psychology myself—I know when I'm walking behind elephants."

"Regardless," she exulted, "no one understood more about power. He thought his work should be kept from the public, but after his death, his students came out with a popularized version, *Controlling Yourself and Others: The Science of Power*. I found it on my father's bookshelves on a rainy Saturday when

I was a kid, and it changed my life. Not the sort of thing you'll ever find on the bestseller list. And it was all based on that old brainwashing premise: tear the subject down to the ground and build up something new. Beside it all the other books on power are worthless—and I include Machiavelli."

"More elephant crap," Goins growled. "And that cuckoo bird ideology. Flesner's just Ayn Rand with a dungeon."

"As you know, Romulus, a skilled interrogator doesn't need a dungeon. The best way to tear the subject down is with small, seemingly glancing blows to his self-esteem. For example: George, genealogy is a hobby of mine, and I discovered that your grandparents changed the family name—to Entmen from Antman."

"Yes," I said warily.

"Do you know why?"

There was no point letting her draw this out. "It was the plurals. People kept saying 'Antmen.' And the correct version, 'Antmans,' had always sounded faintly ridiculous."

"Did it occur to your grandparents that Entmen has an equally incongruous plural?"

"Their English wasn't so hot. What's your point?"

"Doesn't it ever seem to you, George, that you dodged a bullet on Antman, your small man problems being what they are? Remember my joke about the people down there looking like ants? Did you think, 'That's me?' All right, enough. I don't want to do any real damage."

"You're kidding. *That's* the science of brainwashing?"

"Flesner used to say, 'Once you've got a thread standing up, you can go back later and pull it.'"

"Say, Wendy," Romulus Goins leered, "do you still do that dance? What is it, the I-don't-care dance? We missed you at the parties. It's almost worth having your husband around. That dance, though," he said to me, "it scares me a little, and I worked homicide for twenty years."

"It's called the I-don't-care-that-I'm-dancing-with-you dance," she said. "*Ec*tually, it's based on Flesnerian principles. Care to take me for a spin, Rom? I promise I'll be gentle."

He backed off, making push-back motions with his hands.

"The I-don't-care-that-I'm-dancing-with-you dance is exactly what it sounds like," she said to Toby and me. "Men have burst out crying." She smiled, flared her nostrils, raised her eyebrow. "They whimper things like, 'I don't understand. Don't you *like* me?' It's a display of absolute power but all in fun. How about you, Toby? You look like a tough guy."

Toby stepped back to Goins's side of the imaginary line.

She turned to me. "George? I don't know, podling. I'm afraid I'd destroy you."

Rebecca was standing behind her now, mocking her with raised eyebrow and flaring nostrils, fists on her hips.

I said, "Wendy has challenged me to the I-don't-care-that-I'm-dancing-with-you dance."

Wendy turned to take Rebecca, who said, "George is strong enough to face any stupid mind game you can dream up. He'll dance your dance *if he feels like it*, and he's also strong enough to turn you down without feeling like some twelve-year-old boy who's walked away from a dare." I don't think Rebecca had thought that through.

"Let's go," I said backing toward the dancers, "do your worst." How bad could it be? The stereo was blasting Thelma Houston's

"Don't Leave Me This Way." Romulus Goins gave me the gladiator salute.

She was a better-than-average dancer, but her movements, though in time with the music, were in no way synched with mine. Nor did they seem deliberately not in synch. I tried following *her* lead. She didn't react by changing her step; she did everything she would have done alone for exactly as long. Sometimes she hugged herself or leered at some dirty joke in her head. She was an attractive woman, but not so much that her dance was a sexual torment. Whatever power it had, it wasn't the power of longing. Then what was making me so sad?

No matter where or how close I positioned myself, she looked through me. None of this seemed like a show-stopping performance, but the other dancers had formed a circle and ceded us the floor. I snapped my fingers in front of her eyes—she didn't blink for ten seconds, exactly when she would have blinked, I thought, if I hadn't snapped my fingers. A more suggestible man might have begun to doubt his own existence. I suppose I looked foolish, like a guy who tries to cut in while the dancers remain oblivious to his hapless grindings. Finally I let Wendy dance with the invisible while I concentrated on moving without reference to her. It took me a moment to notice that she was watching me. It was, after all, not the I'm-not-dancing-with-you dance but the I-don't-care-that-I'm-dancing-with-you dance. I don't know how to describe that look. Until then I'd thought there was caring and not caring. It had never occurred to me that there were higher orders of not caring. It wasn't dislike or hatred or contempt or indifference, and I wouldn't have been bothered if she didn't like me. It wasn't quite the way you'd look at an ant. It wasn't the cat who'd eaten the canary, leaving some of it behind just to watch it slowly comprehend what happened—that, come to think of it, was her default expression.

"Yeah, she gave you the famous look," Romulus Goins chortled as the song ended and I stumbled away to faint applause. "It's been compared to the expression on God's face when he decided to never answer our prayers. Oh, come on. Pour yourself a Jameson's and forget it."

I decided to spend some quiet time in the room with the coats. "Don't follow me," I said to Rebecca, Toby, and Wendy (whose hand on my arm I shook off when she tried to apologize).

It was late spring, so there weren't many coats on the bed. Mostly light jackets, a few dry raincoats and umbrellas (rain had been forecast), and a magic wand. I shook it, twisted it. Nothing. Then I squeezed it just below one of the bulbs and a bouquet of paper flowers erupted from the other end. I tried without success to shove them back in and hid the thing under the bed.

"Knock knock," Iris said in the doorway. "What is it, sweetie? Don't tell me you're upset about that stupid dance." She sat next to me on the bed. "What was it like?"

"Imagine that moment in the future when your name is spoken for the last time. That's what it's like."

She gave me a squeeze of the shoulders and sang, "It takes fewer muscles to smile than frown. Turn your existential crisis upside down!"

I managed a feeble laugh—more of an air laugh. "I don't know. Maybe it's the flying. I had all those hopes. When I fly I'm starting to feel like the person 'down there' who looks like an ant. I practice every day and I can't do any better than I did at the talent show. Maybe that's all it will ever be. I spoke to Annabel Reardon . . . theology? I described my talent, said it was an idea for a novel. I asked her why God might want to create a useless a miracle. I thought she'd say something inspirational—no miracle too small. You know what she said? 'Neither God nor I have any interest in bar-trick miracles.' I don't know why we're all talking about God tonight. I'm still an atheist. That'll show 'em."

"If God did the kind of bar-trick miracles they do in the Budweiser commercials," she said, "he could triple his audience. Water into beer? Come on. Anyway, as Dr. Johnson would say, it isn't that you do it well, it's that you do it at all."

Ricardo Dean had walked past the doorway twice. "Really, Iris? Ricardo Dean? I always thought you and Toby—"

"His famous 'saint/whore dichotomy' doesn't bother me so much—as long as I get to be both. But I don't."

"But Dean!"

"What I need now is an obtuse man. I'm tired of all these sensitive guys who want to explain me to myself. I prefer a guy who checks his watch while I'm sobbing. You're sitting on my coat."

While she buttoned it, I pulled the wand bouquet out from under the bed. She mussed my hair. "Just when I'm saying sensitivity is overrated you go all Jimmy Stewart on me. Thanks, sweetie. Last guy who gave me flowers wanted to borrow a thousand dollars."

"Better hide it under your coat till you get outside. Anyway, be careful with that guy. I guess it's too late to tell you not to do something immensely stupid."

"I won't be any more immensely stupid than I have to be. Promise."

When I was alone I pushed aside the jackets and lay down.

. . .

Yelling from the living room woke me up. Rebecca and I were lying across the bedspread, her head on my chest, the jackets piled up at the foot of the bed, the light still on. Like a hospital visitor, Wendy had pulled up a chair to the bed and been thumbing through a copy of *Architectural Digest*. She impatiently turned each glossy page with a whip-crack snap.

"George? I wanted to let you know how truly sorry I am."

Rebecca opened her eyes: "Noted. Why don't you twirl away or whatever it is you do."

Toby appeared in the doorway as Rebecca and I were sitting up. "Job and his comforters! If you ladies don't mind waiting outside, Dr. Toby will administer years of intensive psychotherapy in a one-minute lightning round."

The women left—Wendy getting in a last "sorry" on the way out—and Toby sat down on the chair.

"Wendy's kind of hot," he whispered out the side of his mouth. "If I were a thirteen-year-old boy—and I am!—I'd think it's pretty neat, an attractive woman who talks like a Bond villain. She radiates power. She's the complete Yalta Conference, George—Roosevelt, Churchill, *and* Stalin."

"Looks like you're the patient here," I said combing my hair with my hand.

"Right. I'll get to the point. This dark night of the soul you're experiencing? It's not Wendy and the brainwashing. It's not the flying. It's not midlife crisis. It's the dope."

"The dope? I forgot all about it."

"And *that's* the dope! I didn't see how I was going to get through the night. And then I realized: it's not me, it's the dope!"

"Stay with us tonight. Who drove?"

"Iris. She was more likely to leave comparatively sober. She's gone, huh?"

"Yeah. We left our car at the damn Baims' house. We can try to get a ride from one of the horrible guests, we can take the El, we can get a cab, or we can ride back with the Baims . . . Damn. We'll have to pick it up tonight. The Camry's in the shop."

"It's the least they can do. The Pottery Barn rule, George. She broke you, she owns you."

"No she didn't. It's the dope!" I stood up; whatever it was seemed to have worn off.

There'd been no music for a while, and I could make out some of the yelling: "Dickhead!" . . . "Nelson!"

. . .

In the living room the party had encircled four men. There was a tall skinny old man in a traditional magician's black tux, his spray-tan contrasting vividly with his platinum pompadour toupee. Odd bulges formed around his gritted smile. Nelson Baim struggled to break loose from the two men holding him back. His shirttail was sticking out the bottom of his powder-blue tux, which had lost its buttons. The magician nodded to the minders; they let go of Nelson and stepped back.

"We're just having a little fun, Nelson. Just a few magic tricks, that's all. I realize you have very little idea of what magic *is*"—raucous laughter from the audience—"so maybe it's time you learn. Let me reassure you: There's no real *magic* involved in magic. *Or is there?*" He winked at the audience. "Don't be scared. It's just a discipline involving sleight of hand and misdirection, much like what a pickpocket does. Speaking of pickpockets! How's that for a transition? Remember the famous wallet-ectomy your doctor performs?" He placed his hands on Nelson's scantly occupied crown. "I'm willing your wallet up through your body, through the top of your head and into my hands. Come on, wallet." His concentration gave even more definition to the eerie bulges. "Here it is!" He flourished a wallet and handed it to Nelson. "Is this yours? Better make sure your wife's money is all there." Applause.

Wendy and Rebecca were standing at the back of the crowd. I observed to Wendy that she looked remarkably unperturbed.

"When do I ever look perturbed? That's Oscar Birfman. Stage name: Mysterio. He used to do those Magic Card commercials on TV. Oscar wants to refurbish a community theater in Lake Forest and teach magic workshops to kids. He applied for a grant from the Preservation Council, and guess who's on the board? It'll work out fine. Oscar groveling, new gigs for Nelson."

"The money's here," Nelson said going through the wallet, "but all the credit cards are gone."

Oscar patted himself down and pulled out a handkerchief. He loudly blew his nose and handed the handkerchief to Nelson, who took it by reflex, then held it with disgust. Oscar took it back and placed it in his inside tux pocket. "Nelson Baim! Good to see you! What brings you here! Did we have an appointment? Can't remember!" He winked at the audience. "My senile dementia's acting up again. Well, it couldn't be that important. It's getting late. See you!"

"Come on, Oscar. Just give me the cards. Please."

"Please! That's what we magicians call a magic word." He pulled the handkerchief out of his pocket. "What's this!" It was tied to a cascading assembly line of handkerchiefs, red, pink, orange, brown, black, purple, striped, polka dotted. Oscar kept pulling. Tied by a ribbon to the final handkerchief was a long accordion holder of IDs and credit cards. Nelson held his hand out but Oscar was reading the IDs. "Impotence Club for Men! Just kidding, folks!"

"He picked Nelson's pocket earlier in the evening and then arranged the stuff in his own pockets," Wendy said. "Oscar hasn't had a new trick in fifty years."

One of the plastic windows contained a folded sheet of paper. Oscar pulled it out and began unfolding it.

"Leave that alone!" Nelson lunged for it, but Oscar held it behind his back. Nelson shoved him to the carpet.

The crowd gasped; someone yelled, "You gutless fucking parasite!"

"I'm sorry, Oscar," said Nelson, extending a hand.

Ignoring it, Oscar gathered his various parts off the carpet. "It's okay, folks, I'm okay. Let's see what the big deal is about this piece of paper." It was a yellow sheet from a legal pad: Oscar read, "The secret insight philosophy has missed for 150 years: the deep connection between Kant and Nietzsche. Neither philosophy truly complete without the other. If I can make people see this truth, maybe I won't be a failure after all. My life isn't over!"

"I know where I've seen him!" someone yelled. "It's The Box Man!"

Nelson wasn't a man who took humiliation stoically. It showed on his face as rage and physical pain. But now he'd gone blank. I couldn't predict whether he'd go on standing there or walk away or put a face through a wall.

Oscar neatly folded the paper, replaced it in its plastic, detached the plastic windows from the train of handkerchiefs, folded the plastic windows into one compact rectangle, placed it in Nelson's jacket pocket, and gave it a little pat. Nelson put his hand in to see if it was really there.

"Don't worry, it's there," Oscar said. He held out his hand, and after a brief hesitation, Nelson shook it. "Just one more. I know you folks have been razzin' me about the old tricks—how about something I didn't perform for Bess Truman? And you're not so impressed when I name-drop Bess Truman, are you?" Laughter. "So for tonight I have a brand-new trick. Mr. Baim, if I could have your assistance just once more.

"It's a good trick, so I'll keep the patter to a minimum. I once met a man in the Orient, blah blah blah." It got a laugh. "Let's get right to the trick. I'm going to reach *through* Nelson's pants and remove his underpants. All without opening his pants or loosening his belt. And *no one else* meddled with his pants either. But I'm a magician, not a lawyer, let's just do the trick.

"Nelson? If you wouldn't mind removing your jacket? Very fashion conscious, by the way, you never know when it'll be 1977." Nelson's shirt was torn; he tucked it in. "Now Nelson, I have to warn you. I'm going to have to touch your balls. Just through your pants. There are many women who could testify that I don't touch men's balls for pleasure, but regrettably they're all dead. I'll speak with *them* when I get a gig that *pays*." Big laugh.

"Take a good look at Nelson's pants." Oscar extended his arm in that direction. "Belted, zipped, not breakaway pants— they don't make pants like his anymore, thank God. Now, let's be frank. Nelson doesn't like me. Is there anyone who thinks he'd shill for me, because we all know how the trick could be done that way. But if I don't come up with Nelson's actual underpants, he'll gleefully tell you so. Right, Nelson? Okay, don't be ticklish." He placed both hands across Nelson's crotch. Nelson clenched his jaw. "Okay, here come the underpants. One two three!"

He held up a pair of paisley bikini briefs to floor-shaking laughter and applause. "Nelson Baim, are these your underpants?"

"Yes."

Nelson's expression shifted from blank to serene. "Are we finished, Oscar, because there's a little trick I'd like all of *you* to see."

"It will be our pleasure. I'm glad to see you're finally taking your craft seriously. But first, Dr. Irving Fleischman is here with us. I'm sure you all know him as the dean of psychic investigators but Irving is also an MD. He's been my friend for over sixty years—I'm sure you'll all agree he's above reproach. Retired, yes, but never retired from medical and personal ethics. What are you waiting for, Irving? A plaque? Dr. Fleischman, if he ever *gets* here, will look inside Nelson's pants and verify what's what down there."

My back and neck ached from tension; I'd been waiting for Nelson to go berserk, and this sudden serenity was the shriek of air raid sirens.

The crowd stepped back, and Dr. Fleischman, a fat guy with a combover and crumbs on his shirt, walked up and shook Nelson's hand. He undid Nelson's belt, unbuttoned the button, pulled out the waist, and peered down. "Naked as Adam. But he should clean up a little better down there."

When the new eruption of stomping, hooting, laughing, and

wall pounding ended, Nelson said, "And now I'd like to show all of you *what's what*. You call what you do *magic*? Could any of you perform a miracle? Sure you could. If you could arrange the lighting, the videotaping, the editing, the camera angles, and the holy roller shills you pay to scream and faint. Pathetic. I know a man who can fly, and he's here tonight."

"That bastard," Rebecca said. "Let's go."

"George? Show them. Show them how pathetic they are."

We headed for the door.

"George?" The derisive laughter was building.

I heard glass break and turned around. Nelson was being restrained again, the circle tightening around him. "Nelson, you fucking suckbag." "Do you know how many birthday party magicians can't find work because the parents think we might be *you*?" "Why don't you learn to do the ring trick before you worry about miracles, asshole." "Why are we even talking to him? Let's fuck him up."

"Hold my jacket," I said to Rebecca.

"What are you going to do?"

I wanted to hear myself say it. "I'm going to fly to the rescue."

I got down on my stomach, rose up, and collided with the back of some guy's boot. I repositioned myself on my stomach, rose up, and called, "Coming through!" The backs of a woman's stilettos were in my way; she turned, looking for my voice, and I collided with her instep.

"*Crawling?* I hope you're enjoying the view."

"Flying! Gotta go!"

Why didn't I walk up front and give a demonstration? Because I didn't want it to be a performance. If I stepped up there I'd be one more act. Maybe the whole point was in the inches. I wanted to show them that right here, above the carpet, among your shoes, next to the cat, something impossible could happen.

I rose up and bumped into the cat; it hissed at me. Still airborne, I yelled, "Coming through!"

People were beginning to notice. "What's he gliding on? Some kind of skateboard?"

"Nothing there."

"Hey! You heard 'im! Clear the way!" It was Romulus Goins, crawling backward in front of me. "So what you got there, kiddo, the old magnets in the pants?"

I dropped to the carpet, got my breath, and rose up. "Nope. No magnets in the pants."

People were clearing a path now, and soon I was up front with Nelson and his antagonists. "What's the gag?" "Some combo of crawling and gliding." "Couldn't book him as an opening act with his tongue sticking out like that and his legs kicking like some spaz at the Y."

Panting, I flopped onto the carpet and rolled on my back, watching the ceiling throb. The bullies stood over me. The leader of the pack—Mr. Let's-Fuck-Him-Up—said, "How do you do that? And why're you doin' it down there? Gotta buy a ticket to see the full airborne gag, right? Come on, what's the secret?"

"There's no secret."

"Great. Okay guys, let's fuck up Nelson."

"Wait," I said, "Let me get my breath . . . All right, uh, *what's* your name?"

"Rod." He looked like he was in his forties, but his goateed face had the same sorts of bulges Oscar's did—years of smiling at unenthused audiences through sheer will.

"Rod, you look like a good guy. Can you keep a secret? Come

down here. Closer." Rod put his ear in front of my mouth. "Turn your face a little bit. I need to look you in the eye. Just wanna be sure I can trust you. Good, just a *little bit* closer." When we were kids in Hyde Park, Toby and I used to imagine scenarios of how you might get a guy to lower his guard so you could knock him out. I'd always claimed that Toby's old "I have a secret, lean closer" plan would never work. But I punched Rod in the face and he went down, nearly on top of me. As I stood up Nelson took out one of the guys who'd held him back, a gut shot that set the man whooshing.

"Nelson! George!" It was Toby. "Leave these magicians alone! They're just fighting for the honor of magic." He brought his elbow back into a magician's nose. All his scenarios worked!

We ran down the hall; a man lunged and Nelson shoulder-checked him into the wall. "Go!" I yelled to the women. "Run!"

Outside on the empty sidewalk I massaged my knuckles while we watched the door; the blaze of chandeliers made the lobby even emptier. It was a cool drizzly night, the smell of the lake coming in on a breeze. Rebecca handed me my jacket and I put it around her bare shoulders.

"Nobody chasing," she said.

Nelson undid his bow tie. "You'll probably hear from Romulus and the other debunkers tomorrow. But the magicians? They know what a magic trick looks like. Maybe they're scared."

. . .

Toby dealt with emotional crises through the principle of exchange. If you can't face the problem, trade it for one you can. Broken heart? No, it's the dope! Solutions were equally fungible.

Terrified of looking within? Then order a really big stack of pancakes.

And so Nelson, Wendy, Rebecca, and I were drinking decaf at 2:00 a.m. in the pounding brightness of a pancake house while Toby sliced away like the lumberjack of pancakes. When the waitress had set them down he'd started to untie his skinny black Rat Pack tie, then changed his mind and tossed it jauntily over his shoulder. "Better already," he was saying now. "See, George? It was the dope." He was the happiest man in the International House of Pancakes.

"Keep your voice down."

"Dope lowers the blood sugar. By the way, I've solved the underwear trick." He started to get up and I grabbed his wrist.

"Don't," I begged, "pace around while you tell us how you solved the case. Please." He stayed in his chair.

Wendy looked bored. She pulled out a compact mirror, gave herself a "hey there!" glance, tossed it back in her purse. I was sure she'd figured out the trick—I had it mostly figured out myself—but unlike Toby she didn't need to impress us. It was evident at the party that *she'd* learned quite a bit about magic, just in case Nelson ever wanted to be helped.

"Let's get to the heart of the matter," Toby said. "How did the underwear get from inside Nelson's pants to the hand of Oscar Birfman? It's very simple, really." He poured more maple syrup on the remnant of the pancakes and let the moment accrete.

"The underwear," he declaimed, "was never *on* Nelson!"

Nelson was trying to be a good sport. The resulting queasy smile looked like he'd picked up a pizza slice from the floor and finally decided to eat it.

"But why," Toby asked us, "would he assist in this deception when he so clearly despises Oscar? It's a matter of—philosophy! As Nelson told me during our conversation at the party, he is . . . *a Nietzschean*. For Nietzsche, society is the herd. And the Superman of Nietzschean doctrine stands *outside* the herd and its 'cattle'—or 'slave'—morality. Nelson might not come out and say so, but in his . . . in his dreams? his interior life? . . . *he* is the Superman. As for underwear? Here's a riddle: does the Superman wear boxers or briefs? Trick question: the Superman will not be trammeled or confined. When the Superman hears the word 'underpants,' he reaches for his gun."

Rebecca placed her head on my shoulder, closed her eyes, and made snoring noises.

"Almost there. I believe that tonight, as he was about to leave for the party, Nelson decided to *brave the winds*! But I sense that he's a little . . . reticent? shy? He'd want to keep it to himself. I think you'd all agree that he still hasn't mastered the Nietzschean imperviousness to shame. Now: a man without underpants isn't so hard to detect, and Oscar—let's just say Oscar would have noticed. Before the performance he borrowed the ghastly briefs from the host or a guest. They *could* have been Oscar's own, but I don't want to think about that. Conclusion: Oscar knew that Nelson would *not* want to discuss the preexisting nonexistence of his (Nelson's) underpants. Better to own up to somebody else's horrible paisley thong. And so the Adam-nakedness testified to by Dr. Fleischman was the very state of underpantsless nature in which Nelson arrived at the party."

"Just as I suspected," I said. "It's the worst magic trick ever. So Nelson—I guess you've decided that I'm not faking?"

He looked at Wendy, who apparently had become his spokesman in matters of flying and debunking.

"Nelson said the magicians might have been scared by your performance," Wendy said. "All that means is that nobody has figured out yet how you do it. But all that's beside the point now. You're a private man, and the press is going to be camping on your lawn. Just let Nelson debunk you, and pretty soon they'll go away."

Toby balled up his napkin and spiked it on the table, catching it on the bounce. "Sounds like a good plan, aside from the 'laughingstock' and the 'complete disgrace' parts."

"Not at all. George is no con artist. Nobody will be *exposing* George. He never claimed to be performing a real miracle. In fact he's an amateur magician. That's why, when Nelson figured out how the trick is done, he followed the magician's code and discussed it with no one but George. The trick will remain secret. All you have to do, George, is give Nelson a public tip of the hat for figuring out how you did it."

"I'm sorry. I can't," I said.

"And why is that?" she said calmly, almost cheerfully.

"I'm not going to dishonor flying by telling lies about it."

"*Dishonor flying?*" Wendy laughed. "And who'd be the victim? Flying?"

"Honor," I said.

"We'll discuss this further in a few days," she said.

"There's nothing to discuss."

"I don't understand why you're afraid of me, podling. What frightens you about a discussion?"

"He's made up his mind," Rebecca said. "Why don't you drop it? You know, we have a babysitter at home."

"She lives in Evanston? We'll pick her up and drop her on the way." Wendy had kept her eyes on me. "But you *are* afraid of me."

"No I'm not!"

"I'm five four, I weigh 115 pounds. Rebecca says you're trained in boxing. You've certainly got the edge intellectually. I truly don't understand: what do you imagine I could *do*?" She was enjoying herself. "Beat you up? Leg wrestling—I'm pretty good but you'd win. *Debunk you*? But nobody can figure out how to do it. Isn't this fear of yours just a little bit *funny*? Come on, George, admit it." She laughed, not the echo-chamber cackle of some villainess but a girlish, coltish laugh. She was laughing, I thought, at the obvious lie of her helplessness. I'm not sure why, but the rest of us were laughing along. Faces leaned out of the booths, just wanting to quietly eat their pancakes at 2:10 in the morning.

When the rest of us stopped, Nelson kept going, clutching his gut, narrowing his eyes, his deep laugh booming off the ceiling tiles, rising in pitch to a keening noise, then slowly sputtering out in a series of coughs, squeaks, groans, and *hee . . . hee . . . hees.*

FIVE

On waking I like to lie in bed with eyes closed and assemble the who-what-where. That morning it wasn't coming together. I was lying on my stomach, my ribs aching, my face pressed against something scratchy, my eyes squeezed tight against dizziness. "Rebecca?" No answer.

I didn't recall opening the window, but the room was a riot of wind, birdcalls, and rustling leaves. I squinted out one eye, and the mesh of eyelashes in my vision seemed to continue in the world. I closed my eye, counted to five, and tried again. I'll skip the next rounds of looking, failing to process what I saw, and closing my eyes. Suffice it to say I was lying on an upper bough of an oak tree, my arms wrapped tight around the limb, which was, I estimated, twenty feet off the ground. It was the tree on our parkway. The street was empty, the old Tallmadge street lamps still on. Past the glinting housetops the sun bobbered up from the lake. The back of my hand was bleeding. I was wearing my navy-blue pajamas with the white piping.

"Good morning!" A man with a collie on a leash smiled up. He wore a black Syracuse sweatshirt and a Cubs cap that he sometimes pressed down against the wind. Tall, seventyish, pinch nosed, he regarded me as if pajamaed men bloomed commonly in our local trees. "I envy you. Sometimes I'll wake up at two in the morning and think, 'Damnit, why don't I get up right now and climb a tree?'" He spoke in a stagey baritone, and I assumed he taught at the university. "Of course there's always a good reason not to. You've got the right idea. Don't put it off—run outside in your pj's and romp among the leaves! Otherwise some unremarked day when you were thirteen will prove to be the last time you climbed a tree. I'm James, by the way, and this is Daisy."

"Uhhh George."

"I think we can forgo a handshake in the circumstances. Say hello to George, Daisy." He gave her leash a tug and she barked. "Daisy doesn't actually bark, by the way. Or rather, she barks sarcastically. She *says* 'arf,' like Orphan Annie's dog."

It had sounded like a bark to me, but I was more concerned with how I'd got here and how I was going to get down. I'd already experimented, using an eight-foot stepladder, with whether my flying ability could break a fall at three or four inches. It could not. And yet I'd possibly just performed the greatest flight in history in my sleep.

I was a sleepwalker when I was a kid, and I once somnambulated two blocks in pajamas and slippers to a locked-up Dairy Queen. I'd also been an avid tree climber. So what was this—sleep climbing or sleep flying?

After James and Daisy left I sat up on my tree limb and relaxed, sighing in a choir of leaves, confident now of my ability to climb down.

Could this possibly be a new improved flying? Would it ever come to me again? Be grateful it happened once, I thought. If it happened. "Thanks," I whispered to whomever. "What next?"

Charles Blaustein—my fellow hermeneutist, the angry over-coated starer who spoiled my party—was out for a dawn run. He wore a black tracksuit with white stripes up the sides, and his orange glasses turned deeper orange as he stopped just short of my tree and looked up. I think he was glad to see me there, brought to bay at last, treed. He seemed to be attempting a triumphal sneer but the limited malleability of his face cut it down to a smirk.

"All right then," I said. "Have we concluded our business?" He checked the fitness gizmo on his wrist and ran on.

.   .   .

"There's a man in a turban downstairs to see you." Rebecca leaned against the doorway of my study, arms folded, enjoying my efforts to surface from my work and accommodate the fact of the turbaned man.

"Is it one of those huge magician's turbans? It's not . . ."

"No." She sculpted a small oblong above her bob. "It's a mini. Very chic."

"Take a message and his number. Please?"

"He says he's an old friend."

"I don't—"

"From college, he says."

"You're having a grand time, aren't you? I suppose you already have his name. Do I have to wrestle it out of you? C'mere. Wait a minute. That would be Harvey Bell. I never mentioned him? Guru to the stars? He's marginally famous now, goes by the name Swami Harvey. No, wait, that's just what his old friends call him. Not to his face, which I haven't seen for eighteen years. Actually his swami or guru name is . . . hold on, I know this . . .

Harvey Bell. When I knew him at the University of Chicago he liked to smoke pot in a dirty bathrobe he called a smoking jacket. In between he was a respected minor poet. Well. Let's see what's left of *him*."

"Maybe you'd better get down there," she said. "I didn't invite him in. He seems nice but a trifle eerie."

The Harvey Bell I knew in college would stand in your doorway glancing anxiously left and right, as if friends on either side of him had knocked and run away. This new (that is, older) Harvey in my doorway had shed all shyness, baby fat, wistfulness, and the fretful aerobics of his nervous tics. He'd grown distressingly thin but somehow there was no less of him, as if he'd passed through a car compacter or a black hole. His newly gaunt, tanned face had the bulges I'd seen on the magicians. No, they were more like the facial muscles weight lifters get from grimacing or that gurus get, apparently, from grinning prodigiously into the infinite. He was doing it now.

He wore a white Ralph Lauren suit, an open collar, and a small white turban—not cocked at an angle like the fedora he'd worn at his poetry readings—and the look he gave me blazed right through on its way to someplace light-years further.

A visit from the swami should have been a hoot. Why did it make me nervous? He was one of the group of poets I'd hung out with at the University of Chicago; I was going to be the critic who'd canonize the Fifty-Fifth Street Tap movement. As you can imagine, poets tend to be less psychically constant than the average U of C grind. Over the years I was unnerved to watch people I thought I knew metamorphose into Buddhists, Republicans, drug addicts, lawyers, slackers, hackers, speakers in tongues, brokers, herbal healers, and eco-terrorists. At least one had seemed to be working his way alphabetically down a list; some eventually orbited back to something like their default selves. But I was the rock, renowned for being George. It made turning forty both easy (still George) and bittersweet (still George!). One of the good things about forty was that aside from getting old, you don't have to *become* anything. Whatever you are, you're done.

"Harvey?"

"George." His handshake was cool and dry.

"Why are we standing here? Come on in. Rebecca? Rebecca! She'll be down. Can I get you anything?"

"I'm fine." Of course. How else could a guru be?

I sat on the couch and he sank into the beanbag chair.

"Sorry," I said. "It was a present from my wife's dad. It was a gag gift, but not so much that he wouldn't be sad if it wasn't here when he visited. And now he's dead and she'll never get rid of it. Why don't you sit in the armchair?"

Harvey waved off the suggestion. He looked comfortable, legs extended, hands folded over his scant stomach.

It's not that I didn't want to see him. But after the Blaustein incident at my birthday party, I was a little wary of people who materialized without explanation. I tried to think of a polite way to ask why he was here.

He rose from the beanbag without stumbling when Rebecca and Max came in; he shook their hands, let Max touch the turban.

Max, just up from his nap, was wearing his cowboys with lassos pajamas. "Daddy, am I dreaming?"

I turned to the expert on consciousness, who said, "No, Max, you're the most awake person in this room."

Max bugged his eyes to convey super awakeness.

"I wish we knew you were coming," Rebecca said. "Why don't you stay for dinner?"

It was the phrase I'd been searching for: I wish we knew you were coming.

"I wish I could. I'm on a panel at the university in an hour. My second, actually. I'd heard you're at the university, so I looked you up, I walked over, rang the bell, and then there's now."

Rebecca and Max sat next to me on the couch while the beanbag redigested Harvey.

"This is the conference at Tech Auditorium?" she asked.

"Oh, please, don't be polite—you're officially excused. These things are always dull. They choose the topics from the same old pile of words in the same old hat. This time they pulled out 'society,' 'digital,' and 'inner.'" He sighed. "I'm inner, as always."

We exchanged news: he was divorced; had a five-year-old daughter; had indeed been a guru to the stars; was a consultant to hospices, helping them set up meditation programs. He took down Toby's number and email and mentioned that they'd run into each other years ago at the St. Mark's poetry reading series in New York. "Completely freaked out by the turban. Tilted his head sideways at a 180 degree angle to take it in. I think he was drunk. He said I could make a bundle sponsoring 'meditation slams.'"

All the while I was trying to recall if there'd been some foreshadowing of the new Harvey in college. Of course there had. The first time I visited his apartment he'd led me to a closet at the end of the hall. It was lit by a bare bulb dangling from a cord and filled with stacks of old *TV Guides*—there must have been hundreds. He'd seemed to be waiting for a reaction; I couldn't think of anything except "nice *TV Guides*."

"The light isn't very good here," he'd said, "look closer. Go on, pick one up." I was looking at a cover from the late sixties; it took me a moment to realize why Ed McMahon from *The Tonight Show* was so unnerving. Ed's irises had been erased, the eyes reduced to bulging zombie-white eyeballs. Maybe they changed the cover stock since then, but Harvey told me he did it with a pencil eraser. If he told me why, I've forgotten. I picked up more, and on each cover saw the lunar stare and capped teeth of the TV undead.

He was at it again, gazing out at The Invisible. I tried to think of some reminiscence to get him off it—anything but the *TV Guides*, which I thought might embarrass him and creep out Rebecca.

"Back in college," I said to Rebecca, "I was seeing a dermatologist for my psoriasis. The medications he prescribed were just making everything worse, and I could never talk to him during visits—he was always rushing out of the office. So one day I phoned him. 'My ankle's itching like hell, nothing you give me helps,' and so forth.

"As you can imagine he wasn't the most compassionate, attentive doctor, but that afternoon he seemed concerned. 'This shouldn't be happening,' he said. 'I hate suffering.' That's what he said: 'I hate suffering.' You probably think this was sarcasm. At best a rusty bedside manner. Or that he meant he hated listening to patients *talk* about their suffering. But the tone of human kindness was unmistakable. The conversation went on for a while—he just seemed easy to talk to. And then I stopped. 'Wait a minute,' I said. 'Is this Harvey Bell?'"

Rebecca yelped and Harvey released a surprisingly boisterous laugh. "I don't remember this."

"I'd confused your number with the dermatologist's. Of course you were messing with me, but I've always thought the empathy was real."

"Back then? I was probably just messing with you."

It would have been impolite not to ask him about his philosophy. To his credit, he kept it under five minutes. Like many hot spiritual properties of the time, Bellism (he didn't call it that) was syncretic, combining ideas from physics and several religions. It involved taking energy from various mental and bodily regions, turning it into other kinds of energy, and moving it around. I tried to follow, but it was all too squishy for me. I'd soon gone to the place I go during departmental meetings—where everyone in the room goes eventually, except the two people arguing for the bone china or the blue. The trick—and without it there'd be no departmental committees and thus no university—is to leave behind an attentive-looking simulation.

You might be thinking that I owed my old friend a better effort. Really?—then why don't I share some thoughts on hermeneutics? I'll start with a few observations about Dilthey's concept of the Hermeneutic Circle and conclude with some brief remarks on typology. Ah. You're still there—the reader who came for the hermeneutics. Thank you, my friend, but everyone else has gone on to the next paragraph. Shall we join them?

Harvey's lips had stopped moving and he looked hurt, attempting to blink it away. He hadn't changed as much as I'd thought.

I gathered he'd stopped speaking some while ago. I opened my mouth to fabricate a vague reply to a range of things he might have said—instead I apologized.

He waved off the offense. "That's all right. Some people are allergic." Maybe this was still the old Harvey—stick a turban on him and all that wistfulness looks meditative. I hoped he was happier than he'd been in college. Back then he wrote pining love poems in the troubadour style. They had a defensive glaze of New York School humor, but you knew he slid them under some door and slunk away.

Rebecca stepped out and I was pouring myself a gin and tonic when Harvey sidled up and muttered, "Can we speak in private?" His eyes had snapped back from their thousand-light-year guru gaze; they glittered with rabbity unease. He was about to whisper something in my ear, but Max chose that moment to grill Harvey about his "hat."

Max was wearing his rubber band top hat and would have worn it twenty-four hours a day straight through old age and death if we'd allowed it. Harvey waited patiently until the fire hose of questions subsided. No, Harvey replied, his mommy didn't let him wear the hat to bed, and no, it didn't have a rubber band to go under his chin but no, it didn't fall off, and as for wearing it at the table—Harvey glanced at Rebecca, back on the couch, who shrugged—maybe once in a while if Harvey had been very very good. Perhaps it was more than the turban that made Max think Harvey was an oversize kid, and Harvey seemed to enjoy playing along.

Rebecca had pasted on her deflecting cheerleader smile; Harvey was making *her* nervous, too. "George, why don't you take Harvey outside and show him the miracle of dirt-level flight?"

.   .   .

There was just time for a short demonstration in the backyard. I'd quickly learned that my practice sessions out there wouldn't create a sensation on the block. Unless you were up close, you'd think you saw a man sliding or crawling or writhing or spazzing out or just searching for a tiny object in the grass. The only neighbor who even took an interest was Mrs. Housebender next door, who far from seeing me as the modern Prometheus, initially asked whether she should dial 911.

"Just flying," I'd said, "low altitude."

She thought this was droll, and whenever she came out to trim her rose bushes and saw me practicing, she always asked how my "altitude" was doing, figuring, I'm sure, that it was plenty high.

Harvey and I were alone in the yard. Rebecca had stopped watching my practices; "I'd rather watch the grass grow," she'd said. "Oh, wait, you mow it three times a week now, so there goes the comparative excitement." (I kept it close-cropped to keep my flight gap visible and because I believed that unmown grass or any uneven surface slowed me down, even if I didn't brush against it.) My practicing had become a sore point between us, ever since I confessed that sometimes instead of taking Max to the park I let him squirm with boredom watching me fly on the lawn.

It sounds pretentious to say so, but I thought it was my solemn duty to fly better. Once I'd perfected my talent I planned to share it with the world. Every day I worked out at the gym for ninety minutes and practiced for two hours in the yard. I was in the best shape of my life, but my flying—height, speed, distance—remained unchanged. Rebecca said I was auditioning for sainthood— "first Jew!"—and that the exhaustion and soul-withering boredom of flight were a form of self-flagellation.

Did I think it was a miracle? Yes, but I remained an atheist. I'm perfectly aware that my beliefs were muddled and contradictory. My belief that flying was a gift I'd been *given* stopped short of *by whom*. My belief in sharing my talent with the world existed alongside my belief that publicity would defile it. Even my belief that I was performing a miracle was based on the empirical observations of campus scientists, who'd cautiously, privately, and nearly inaudibly spoken the word. I'd set all these clashing beliefs together on a mental shelf where they couldn't coexist for long; eventually I'd come back and see what was left.

Harvey walked in front of me, backward, crouched, as I flew from the back fence to the bushes behind the house. I was hoping to show off, but, maybe because he made me nervous, all my tics were on display, the kicking, the flailing, the protruding tongue, tremors, a slick of drool working down my chin.

At the end I lay on the grass and squinted at the pulsing blob of late afternoon sun. "Okay, it didn't look pretty," I panted. "I'm in the old flyboy tradition, spit and bailing wire." I could hear clippers in the next yard. Mrs. Housebender was probably more curious about my turbaned friend than anything I was doing.

Harvey was sitting next to me in a lotus position (I'd offered him a cushion from the recliner; "I don't care about the damn Ralph Lauren suit," he'd said, raising an obvious question I didn't bother to ask). "No need to apologize for the modesty of the miracle. If you turned water into wine I wouldn't complain about the vintage."

I laughed. "That's very rabbinical, Harvey. So you're really a holy man now?"

"I was about to offer my services. I know, you're still an atheist. Think of me as your coach. Just a wiseman with a gym whistle. A few months of training and I'll have you zooming the skies."

"Don't you live in California? Anyway, we don't have the big Mia Farrow bucks for our own guru."

"Don't worry about that. I need the gig."

"Oh . . ." I sat up. "If you need money, of course we'll help out."

"No no no, I'm not hitting you up for money. I wouldn't *charge* you." He was fidgeting with the turban, making tiny adjustments that set it slightly askew then straightening it out again. "Look. Frankly I'm having some trouble with the IRS. It'll all be cleared up, it's just accounting errors, but it's the first thing you see when you google me. And when vindication comes, it never gets the bandwidth of the lies. But if I trained the world's first flying human? I think that would be good for both of us. I know you think anything spiritual's a joke, but I honestly think I help people. I don't want to lose my following, I *like* being a guru."

"I don't know. I couldn't bear it if what I just did was televised. I like my privacy—all right, I don't like looking like an idiot. People already come up to me on campus with their arms extended forward in that damn Superman pose. Sometimes they make the whooshing noise."

"Of course they wouldn't be mocking you if you were flying *up there*. I think your sense of privacy is at least part of the problem. Flying isn't for the secretive, the wallflower-ish, the hermeneutical. A true flyboy doesn't hide. No wonder you're practically crawling in the mud. A man who flies *up there* needs a largeness of spirit. He needs *magnanimity,* George . . . Oh, uh, madame? Do you know what your neighbor George has been doing all these months in his yard?"

Mrs. Housebender had peeked over the fence and her deeply

tanned face somehow blushed when Harvey addressed her. She was around seventy, eyes the shade of blue I associated with bolts from the blue (though she was a mild-tempered woman), white hair churning in the shadow of her garden hat. She stood stock still for a moment and I thought she was about to back away from the fence.

"Is it the turban?" Harvey said. "Really?"

"Hello, I'm Ruth."

"I'm Harvey." He extended his hand over the fence; she set down her shears and shook it. "Please join us, Ruth. George would like to give you a little demonstration. As silly as what he's doing might look from that side of the fence, it's truly miraculous. Come on over, take a look."

When Mrs. Housebender came through the gate, I was about to demur. Harvey cut me off. "Magnanimity, George!"

"I've known George ten years," Mrs. Housebender said to Harvey, "and he still calls me Mrs. Housebender. I know he thinks it's a sign of respect, but to me it's a sign that I'm very very old."

I said I was sorry; "Ruth it shall be."

Harvey sighed. "Can we get to the *miracle*, please? I have to leave for my lecture in a few minutes."

And so I flew toward the back fence, Ruth and Harvey walking stooped on my left and right.

"When does the miracle happen?" she asked. She touched the corner of her mouth to indicate I was drooling.

"It's happening now," I said. "If you look beneath me, you'll see a small space between my chest and the lawn. I call that the flight gap. It doesn't look like much, but it's the first verifiable evidence of unassisted human flight."

"Oh, uh, that? You're levitating?"

I tried to keep the exasperation out of my voice. "Not levitating, flying."

When I'd reached the fence we all sat down on the lawn. "You can be honest," I said to Ruth. "What do you think?"

Harvey and I recognized her look—it was the pitying avoidance you get in writing workshops when your work is a dud.

"It's such a little gap," she said. "And why is it a miracle?"

"I've been doing what I just did for scientists at Northwestern. A psychologist who used to study psychic phenomena at Duke in the Rhine Center's heyday, a biologist, a physicist. I asked them to keep it quiet for now, but they agree that what I do violates some bedrock assumptions of science. In other words it's the first scientifically verified *miracle*."

"I don't want to hurt your feelings, George, but if small things count, I can perform a miracle too. When I go bowling? I know before I release the ball which pins I'm going to knock down. I can see them sort of light up. I think a lot of people have some trick like that, but most of us don't go running to the Rhine Center. Oh, I *have* hurt your feelings. Maybe they're *both* miracles."

"Thanks for stopping by, Ruth. I have to get back to my manuscript, and Harvey has his lecture. And by the way, has it occurred to you that maybe you're just a good bowler?"

When she'd gone back into her house, Harvey said, "I think I can help you, but I have to be honest. The glory you're dreaming of—come on, George, don't pretend you're not—maybe that'll never happen. Maybe the look she gave you will be part of an endless line of pity and condescension."

"You're not one of those *groovy* gurus, obviously. Okay, let's give it a try, see if it works out."

Harvey refused to be distracted. "Maybe you were *picked out* to fly three inches above the ground, very slowly, and not very far—no more, no less—for the rest of your life. If that turns out to be the case, it still means *something*, and you and I will figure out what that is."

SIX

Flying! flying! flying! By now you must think it was the only theme of my life; that I spoke of nothing else with family, friends, students, colleagues, indeed with the heating duct guy or Max's pediatrician. This was hardly the case. That spring I realized one of the dreams of my professional life: my essay on J. L. Austin's "performative utterances" and their application to the theory of meaning won the Twine Award for Outstanding Achievement in Interpretive Studies. As I worked on my acceptance speech I spent much of my time blindly and absentmindedly pacing the house; after days of this Rebecca nudged me out the door one morning and pointed me toward the nearby indoor mall.

The mall unlocked its doors two hours before the stores opened to allow early risers, mostly seniors, to take heart-healthy walks in a hushed, air-conditioned, Muzak-glazed, *Dawn of the Dead*–alluding environment. Wafted on Muzak, I would glide past the oxygen tank woman, past the Day-Glo-green-sweat-suit guy with the pumping arms, while I drafted sentences about my debt to Gadamer or an opening joke about a structuralist, a deconstructionist, a new historicist, and only two parachutes. I paced the mall every morning for a week.

On the day before the Twine Award ceremony, my last morning in the mall, I was walking toward a Carson's at the end of the deserted hallway, and I made out what appeared to be my mirror image in the dimness behind the window. Nothing odd about that; the store was filled with shiny surfaces. But the closer I got the clearer it became that although the doppelgänger imitated my every move—sometimes a few seconds late—it was not my image . . . it was a woman . . . it was Wendy Baim, in dark sweats like me, her red hair tucked beneath a black beret. Separated from her by only the plate glass now, I ran my comb through my hair, while Wendy, no comb handy, pantomimed hair combing. We'd seen the same Marx Brothers movie.

"George!" she said stepping out of Carson's. "What a coincidence!" She spoke the last word in quotation marks palpable enough to poke your eye out. Smirking, she looked down at her iPhone.

"How—" The competing questions had formed a traffic bottleneck. How did you know I'd be here? Are you following me? What the hell do you want? How do you get into closed stores? Are you still trying to resuscitate Nelson's paranormal skeptic career by getting me to conspire in my own debunking?

"How? How did I know you'd be walking toward Carson's when you're walking laps around the mall? Hmm." She radiated her usual perfume (I can never remember the name—Whore In Fog?) and to inhale too deeply was like being worked over by thugs with fur mittens.

Wobbly, I put a hand against the wall. "I thought the stores were closed at this time."

"Yes, but I wanted to go in," she said, as if that covered it.

"So Rebecca told you I walk here in the morning?" The

oxygen tank woman clattered past us, sneering at me triumphantly.

"Are you all right, George?" Wendy unzipped her purse. "Why don't I throw cold water in your face and slap you till your teeth hum?" Who else could say that like a dinner hostess offering more salad? "You'd enjoy that, hmm?"

"Let me have a sip of that."

She handed me her bottled water. I took a swig—everything smelled like her perfume—and I can't remember where the bottle went from there.

"I just wanted to tell you in person," she said, "that we need to move forward with your debunking." She returned her attention to her iPhone, pressed a button, and studied the screen.

"Yeah," I sighed, "but, not a trick, remember? The honor of flying, remember? The reputation of hermeneutics? Children's sense of wonder? Dreamers buzzing the housetops in their pajamas? Nothing's changed."

"Oh, but a good deal has changed." She looked up from the phone. "Remember Ricardo Dean from the magicians' party? The magician who was sitting in the kitchen with your friend Iris? The one she left with? Well he got very interested in your flying performance that night, and he's reverse-engineered the trick. In a few weeks he'll be a guest on *The Tommy Thorne Show*, providing commentary on cell phone videos of your pathetic so-called flying. Which incidentally he dismisses as levitating. And then he's going to demonstrate how a real man flies—zooming supersonically among the spotlights, high above the bald spots of Tommy and the other panelists. Some unimpeachable guest will frisk him—*I* wouldn't mind frisking him!—he'll find nothing but Ricardo and his fashionable clothes. You can't compete. Ricardo and his team get the latest black-budget tech from sources at NASA and DARPA. So forget your dignity and honor. What you have to think about now is how ridiculous you want to be. Ricardo will make you out to be a pathetic charlatan; Nelson will respect you as a fellow magician. Whose trick only another great magician (Nelson) could figure out."

"Nope."

After studying her phone a while longer she said, "Tell you what. You can fuck me. One-time-only offer. Fire sale at the mall. We'll do it on the train."

"The Northwestern? People I know ride that train. Thanks for your generous offer but I must decline the fucking."

"I had a different train in mind. You're not going to pretend you don't want to fuck me, are you? Then how do you explain this?" She handed me her iPhone. "Look at that. You're besotted with me."

"I was dizzy."

And so it went as we scrolled through the photos she'd taken while pretending to be checking messages or something.

"That one. You're staring at my body."

"Trying to decide if you're pear shaped."

"There. I'd call that expression longing."

"Just confused."

"You have an erection." "How can you deduce that from snapshots of my face?"

"I mean," she replied, "you have an erection *now*." She snapped a photo and showed me the screen. "Here's a reminder if you've already forgotten *the present moment*."

I quickly reached into my sweatshirt pocket, produced the notepad I used to jot notes for my journal, and began writing—muttering as I wrote, "you . . . have . . . an erection . . . now."

She snatched the notepad out of my hand. "You can't look at me, can you? And now you're just transcribing dialogue—she says, he says. You're not going to acknowledge, even to the one-man readership of your private notebook, that I'm looking at your erection as we speak."

I took back the notebook.

" . . . erection . . . as . . . we . . . speak."

"Let's continue this on the train."

I replaced the pen and notepad and faced her smirk, flared nostrils, and raised eyebrow, once again growing smaller in her canny brown eyes even though neither of us had moved. "You know what? I think you're all bluff. Serious people don't say 'let's fuck.' And speaking of looking, I've seen the way you gaze at Nelson. Like he created you in an empty top hat. You're not going to cheat on him. So I call. What train do you have in mind for this unlikely fuck? The Orient Express?"

She glanced over my shoulder; I turned. At the opposite end of the corridor, in front of Kohl's, a uniformed "engineer" sat in the "engine" of the toddler train.

"He's here because the mall office was told to expect VIPs early this morning," she said. "He's been instructed to look straight ahead until we say the ride, so to speak, is over."

"I thought there'd be more room," she said when we crammed in. "Good thing you're so tiny, podling."

"We're exactly the same height."

"True," she said, "but by rights I'm five nine."

We rode hunched under the ceiling, trying not to slide off our narrow plank seat (at first we sat on opposite planks but our heads collided when the train braked). We were smooshed together in a way that didn't bring back the romance of train travel. Sex was out, along with most unconstrained movement. All right, sex was theoretically possible, at least a hand job, maybe oral, but allow me to spoil the nonsuspense—we just sat there. Her face that close was reduced almost to comic book dots: pores, hairs, blackheads, clots of makeup. Her perfume seemed more solid than my own woozy body. I turned my head to the unpaned window in the door and inhaled. In the window of Spencer's a serene female mannequin sported skinny jeans and a T-shirt whose legend, DOPE, spoke directly to me.

"Know any good jokes?" she said to break the ice.

I told her my Twine acceptance speech joke about the structuralist, the deconstructionist, the new historicist, and only two parachutes.

"You forgot one of the conventions of the genre," she said. "The pilot. The pilot always bails out first. You need *three* parachutes. You look crestfallen. You didn't spend the past week in the mall writing that joke, did you?"

"Uh."

"Just add a sentence. Oh, I see." She pried her arm out from between us and tousled my hair. "Poor George. You built a perfect crystal palace of a joke and now it's all smashed. Never mind that. I wanted us on the train because I'm about to make a threat. Sometimes people try to short-circuit a threat by walking or running away before I can get it all out."

"Well they're just rude." You wouldn't have to be a stuntman to jump out. I pushed the door handle. Locked.

"Child safety, George. What I wanted to say is that if you

don't help Nelson with his debunking I'm going to take away your Twine."

"What's the plan? Mug me as I step off the podium? Maybe borrow it and never give it back?"

"The committee is reassessing."

I laughed. "They've already announced it. They can't 'take it away' without being sued. Not to mention looking like jackasses."

"I think you'll admire my strategy. It was classic Flesner. It's all laid out in his book, *The Reaches of Power.* Really, George, you ought to read it. I used a tiered threat system. What Flesner calls the Pyramid of Fear. The English department gives the award. So I threaten the School of Arts and Sciences. Arts and Sciences threatens the English department. And all to threaten you, George—the man *under* the pyramid." There was a breathiness in her voice. For her this was all daisies by the riverbank.

I stopped laughing to catch my breath. "The Pyramid of Fear!" I said in my best Lugosi imitation, driving myself into another laughing jag. "Excuse me. Whew. I don't know where to begin. All right. What did the arts and sciences dean threaten the chair of the English department with?"

"The dissolution of the English department. Poof. Gone."

"Well I'd like to see the press release on that one. Ridiculous. Are you going for so-unbelievable-it-could-be-true? Well that's not even a category. And what did you threaten the School of Arts and Sciences with?"

"The Nora Foundation contributes about seventy percent of nontuition funding to Northwestern's humanities and liberal arts curricula. You're not laughing *now*, George. Oh, please do. You have a lovely, musical laugh." An Asian man with jogging shorts and varicose veins was walking alongside, staring into her window. I couldn't see the look she gave him but he stopped cold and thought about it.

"That's a lot of money," I said, "but it wouldn't be worth the public outrage. How could they spin shutting down the English department?"

"I don't know. Call the dean. Hold on, I have him on speed dial." She pressed the button and handed me the phone.

Dean Samuel Weinberg used to teach in the English department; we'd been friendly acquaintances. He picked up on the sixth ring, croaking a sleep-cracked hello.

"Sam, this is George Entmen. I—"

"George. What time is it?"

"Sorry about the time." I rolled up my sweatshirt sleeve. "7:30. It's about my Twine Award."

"Yes. Congratulations."

"So there's no problem with the award?"

"Just do whatever that damn woman wants. You're not recording me, are you? . . . Forget the award for a second." He raised his voice. "How could you be selfish enough to sacrifice hundreds of people in the English department—not to mention severe cutbacks in all liberal arts and humanities departments. And you'd wreck all those lives just to keep doing that creepy masturbatory thing you do in the dirt?"

"That reminds me." My voice had acquired a jaunty, this-is-too-absurd-to-go-berserk tone. "How will you justify shutting down the English department?"

"Well, you know. Blah blah the internet. Kids these days. The job market. Elitism. You can't tweet a seventeenth-century periodic sentence. What do they call the ratio of tuition to lifetime earnings—you know, the something/something ratio. Gotta have that. We don't need more baristas who can quote from 'The Dunciad.' What else. Probably more about Twitter—the heights of the English language just make the kids feel bad. Obviously, George, I don't *know* how I'd justify it. I was only threatened yesterday, and I'm assuming you'll behave like a sane man. And right back at you, George: how will *you* justify shutting down the English department?"

"Wait a minute. That won't happen either way. If I agree to Wendy's terms, the English department and the School of Arts and Sciences stay just as they are. If I refuse, the English department takes back my Twine and remains intact (the bastards) along with the School of Arts and Sciences."

"You fucking idiot!" I held the phone away for the next minute of shouted abuse. Wendy flashed her what-a-jerk look (eyebrow, smirk, slow shake of the head) but I wasn't about to ally with her even on that.

"Regardless of what I do," I said when the shouting stopped, "nobody's going to shut down the English department. It's inconceivable."

"Ha!" After popping this mighty bubble of bile, Sam continued in a tone of self-enforced calm. "Apparently the English department doesn't believe it either. They're not going to take back the award— 'the ceremonial banquet will proceed as scheduled.' Enjoy your rubber chicken, assholes, while the missiles fall. You're familiar with Cold War terminology? Here's one you oughta be thinking about right now. Mutual assured destruction. The principle of deterrence. If one side doesn't believe the other's threats, that whole structure of fear and prudence—well it *fucking blows up*, doesn't it? Of course in this case Wendy is the only party with nukes. The rest of us can only kill each other before she kills us worse. So here's how it plays out. You get your fruity award. The School of Arts and Sciences faces devastating cuts. Arts and Sciences closes down the English department, and not just for revenge. We've done the numbers, and it will do even more damage to the university if we try to save English by letting Arts and Sciences take massive across-the-board cuts. The only way we could take that hit would be to eliminate a department. And as bogus as those justifications for killing English sounded to you and me, an awful lot of people believe them. Of course we should never have allowed ourselves to become so dependent on one donor. I suppose that alone will be grounds to shit-can me. We can restore our budget in a year or two—raise tuition, hit up the remaining donors, find new ones—but that just means we can start clearing the rubble. I just remembered something. You know what? During the Cold War one scenario for Armageddon was that a low-flying bat—don't ask me why it can't be a bird—it crashes into a radar dish and the early warning system goes haywire. You are that low-flying bat."

"Hi Sam!" Wendy said girlishly.

"She's *there*? Just kidding about 'that damn woman.' What kind of game are you playing, Entmen? Am I being recorded? Listen. I heard that you speak about 'the honor of flying,' and honor of any sort ought to be treasured in these times. But what kind of asshole would sell out hundreds of colleagues to protect his right to self-importantly writhe in the dirt? Come to think of it, you could go on doing that anyway. Sure, think about your honor and your ethics. But what kind of ethics sacrifices real people for something symbolic? Satanism? Frankly, there are rumors."

He hung up.

I handed back the phone, regarding Wendy with hatred and grudging respect.

"What are you thinking about, George? Strangling me? If I had a million dollars for everyone who'd like to strangle me— well, I do. Too bad, I enjoyed our friendship." She gave her door two loud slaps. "Mr. Engineer? The ride is over."

The dyspeptic engineer came over with his keyring, tipped back his cap, and took a long look at these VIPs who, he must have imagined, had despoiled the innocent whimsy of his train. He unlocked the door and walked off swearing, I thought, under his breath.

I had my hand on the handle. "One thing I'm confused about. This fuck you were offering. It *was* transactional, right? Because you didn't say it would be in exchange for helping Nelson. Did you just forget? You only wanted to get me on the train to make your threat, nothing else?"

She'd always lifted her right eyebrow, but for the first time here was the left. "Focus on hating me. You'll be much less confused."

.   .   .

"There he is, the Twine man! Mister Twine!" My department head Ken Dreynen raised a high-five, wiggled his fingers to indicate it wasn't being reciprocated, and returned the hand to his armrest. He studied me a moment, then flicked the hand toward the chair in front of the desk. The window was open on a brilliant spring morning, the branches behind Ken's head exhaling a riot of lights.

I'd come straight from the mall; I sat down while Ken mur-

mured, "No high-fives from the Twine Man. Mister Twine, keepin' it low."

"I appreciate the department's courage in taking a stand for me," I said. "But you've got to take back the award."

"The presentation's tomorrow. Tell me what you'd like us to say, George. Trouble is, anything that would justify taking back an award this prestigious would justify, practically make mandatory, terminating your contract."

He shrugged and grinned at the insanity of this; I usually found his immensely toothy smile cheering, but today it was making me squint. He folded his hands behind his razor-shaved head. Friday office hours were his casual Friday, which in warm weather involved Hawaiian shirts—today's had toucans. The old button-down Ken was barely discernible beneath the toucans and the stubble. He believed that meditation, stoicism, a sense of humor, a titanium will, the love of his family, and an intense love of the world had helped him beat stage 4 lymphoma (in remission four years now). He was one of my heroes, and his resemblance to a rejected Jimmy Buffett album cover didn't diminish that one bit.

"You do know," he said, "that Wendy's my ex-sister-in-law? Nelson's my ex's brother. That's why he was the magician at Kyle's birthday party. That and the millions Wendy gives to Northwestern. Plus the sheer enchantment of his act, of course. She phoned about fifteen minutes ago to give me her final terms. Charming woman, always asks about Jennifer and Kyle even when she calls to make threats. Of course we can't back down."

"You can't possibly believe it's worth putting the entire English department on the sidewalk. Or do you think she's bluffing? Is there a deadline?"

"Yeah, the deadline's just after you finish your acceptance speech. I could walk up to the podium, announce that your award has been revoked and take it back even then. I think she'd enjoy that most of all. You can renounce it yourself, but you can't get away with magnanimously giving it to somebody else. She dictated the required language—it's hair-raisingly humiliating, my balls shriveled just writing it down."

"She does all that charity work. Doesn't she worry about being seen as a monster?"

"She pointed out, and she's right, that she does more measurable good in the world in one day than the whole English faculty will do in a lifetime. She said she could stab you in the eye, George, and her aggregate goodness would barely change by a decimal."

Following a protracted silence, I said what I thought was the most reasonable thing anyone had said that morning. "Even if she's not bluffing, I've never heard of a major university closing its English department. Department closings are rare enough, but they never close English, despite all that digital age crap about the death-of-whatever. It's hard to believe it could ever happen. It violates my sense of reality."

"Doesn't comport with your sense of reality. We've got *that* going for us."

"Okay, I'll say whatever she wants. I don't have to say anything that would dishonor flying, do I?"

"I'm not entirely certain what that means, but oh yes you will."

"I see." I saw that every escape route would be barricaded but I continued to go through the motions. "What if you took back the award and just didn't offer an explanation. Would she allow that?"

"Yes, but I'm not taking back the award." Shouts too distant to carry words dissolved above the pathways. "You're really worried about *dishonoring flying?*"

"I ought to be able to explain it by now. See if this makes sense. When I was an undergraduate at the U of C I worked as a copy editor on one of the campus poetry magazines. E. F. Singleton was our faculty advisor. I applied for a summer job with *Poetry Magazine*, and to pump up my resume, I asked E. F.—some of the staff called him 'effin Singleton,' but I liked him—I asked E. F. if in his letter he could burnish my role at the campus magazine. He shook his head in anger or disbelief or sadness or disappointment—all of it, probably, and it was a memorable sight. E. F. was extremely nearsighted, and he wore these thick magnifying lenses that gave him the eyes of a gentle sea monster. He asked me if I loved poetry. I said yes. He said how much. I said with all my heart. Then why, he demanded, would I use poetry in a lie? He said, 'Your finest instincts require fidelity—like a wife. Don't honor them, and they go bad on you, they curdle inside you.'

"And he told me this story about the early English poet Caedmon, the stable boy who gained the gift of song in a dream, but I haven't found it in any of the biographies. Anyway, Caedmon betrayed his art somehow. I don't remember what he did—somehow he sold out. And then Caedmon has another dream. A creature with the body of a man and the head of a bull appears to him and says, 'You're killing us' . . . And that's how I'd feel about dishonoring flying. Does it make any sense at all?"

"Honestly, George, no. It sounds like a lot of things I said to girls in bars to show I was sensitive. But if you feel that way, it's all the more reason for us not to back down."

"I can't blow up the English department just to feel good about myself. Do you have the renunciation she wrote?"

He reached into his top drawer and handed me, with two fingers, as if wishing for hazmat gloves, a folded sheet of paper.

Folding it smaller, I put it in my pocket. "I won't read it in advance. I heard an interview with a champion eater—he was going to eat a ground-up school bus during halftime at a Bears game. Well, some of it, the windshield and the seats, maybe. He was asked how he was getting ready for the big event. The most important preparation, he said, is *don't think about eating a school bus.*"

Ken laughed; I said, "I'm going to wing it for now. I'll go to the ceremony and give the speech I've written. Maybe we'll find out she *was* bluffing. Maybe I'll find an angle that I can't see yet. I'll keep looking for that angle till the moment I have to cave. And I'll have until the end of my speech to renounce the award I've worked for my entire career and will have just accepted. Oh God, my mother will be there."

Ken swiveled halfway to the window, and we watched the show in the branches. "What a gorgeous campus," he was saying. "When I was having my medical problems I'd look out that window and think, whatever happens to me, at least this will still be here. Life goes—"

"That doesn't do a thing for me. Really. Not a goddamn thing."

. . .

It struck me as I was walking down the steps of University Hall: What about Nelson? Did he know that for his sake Wendy had shrunk metropolitan Chicago to a shoebox diorama, rearranging

134

the shrieking populace at will? If he found out, would he try to stop her?

I stepped onto the pathway and into the guillotine breeze of a bicycle, whose rider tossed a laconic "beep" in his wake. This was the old neo-Gothic part of campus, clock towers, masonry, steeples, ivy, stained glass, chimes, monumental shade. You couldn't help noticing the contrast between that weightiness and the tanned screen-deep students. All that sparkling ease beneath the oaks attracted a few scolding preachers every spring. This morning's version was the campus-renowned you're-all-going-to-hell guy, a horn-rimmed suited young man shaking hands and giving out pamphlets, his hair battened down with some sort of ancient hair oil. He handed me a pamphlet titled, with perfect foresight as it turned out, "Hello, You're Going to Hell."

But what about Nelson? I thought on the walk home. He was like one of those literary characters who'd chosen his own hell; perhaps he'd literally picked out the curtains. Wendy had granted him an eternity in his study—it must have seemed like eternity—to produce the great milestone of philosophy he'd always sworn to write when he had time.

But I think his catastrophic dissertation defense was the end of his intellectual life. It pretty much tore out all the wiring. Anyone who's gone for a Ph.D. can break into a sweat imagining it—the committee turning on you. You have to calm yourself walking into that exam room. You tell yourself, I've spent years proving myself to these people, I wrote the dissertation, I picked the committee, I've had long conversations with all the members, my advisor can't think of a single further revision, I know my subject down to the molecule, what happens now will be pro forma, a few probing questions, then attaboys and slaps on the back, my Ph.D. all but handed to me on the way out. Nelson was handed his vital organs. Did he sit in his study reliving it, the committee's faces hovering in expressionist black and white, his faltering attempts to type a sentence bringing down their echo chamber sarcasm, their reverb guffaws? "Are you a *sad* man, Nelson, because I think you want us to give you a Ph.D. so that some university will *pay* you to be *sad*." ". . . like a very smart guy wrote it in Albanian."

When it became clear that he wasn't writing in there, Wendy set him up as a birthday party magician to give him a diversion "while he finished the book." And when she saw that his suffocatingly boring act would never be more than a cross between clinical depression and child abuse, she thought up the psychic debunker gig: it would help him research the varieties of fraud and self-delusion without which, he would have claimed in the book if he were writing it, the human race could not survive. Rebecca had spent much of the past month at their house cataloguing the Hugo Freiles papers, and she was certain Nelson didn't want to be a debunker either. Perhaps he just wanted to sit in his study and feel sad on Wendy's dime.

And yes, I suppose you could see Wendy as the true hero of my story, climbing down into the pit of hell to save the man she blah blah blah, but I don't. As James Joyce said, of an argument with his publisher "There are two sides to this story. But I cannot be on both sides at the same time."

But did Nelson know how much damage she was doing, Godzilla-footing everything in the way of his "career"? What would he do? Was he bitter and spiteful enough to stand back and let it go on?

Wendy would be at her office downtown; I decided to pick up my car and drive out to Lake Forest to see Nelson. But as I was stepping onto my front walk I saw him, striding up the block beneath the shade trees like some fairy tale character who could be conjured by his name. He was walking a little too fast, and something about his bearing made me put down the arm I was raising to greet him. The usual rod up his ass seemed charged with high voltage. Ten yards away he ran at me head down like a wide, flabby, middle-aged, but credibly terrifying semipro tackle. I ran up the steps, the door opening while I groped for my keys, and stepped in allowing Rebecca to slam it behind me an instant before Nelson hit it like a cannonball.

Rebecca smiled grimly. "A1 Home Protection—Extravagant? Yeah?" There'd been home invasions in the neighborhood last year, and one of A1's security measures—and the reason we nicknamed the house Chez Alcatraz—was reinforced doors that would do for a bank vault.

"So," she said, "Nelson showed up half an hour ago yelling something"—she lowered her voice— "about 'the fuck train.' Luckily I had the chain on the door. He started leaning against it and luckily you didn't listen to my nagging about the baseball bat." (I'd left it out after the recent hermeneutists versus new historicists softball game.) "It's still on the floor by the coatrack."

"Wait. You waved a baseball bat at him? Wow."

"He wasn't as impressed as you are. So I told him there was a sick two-year-old boy, no doubt just awakened from his nap and terrified by all the screaming, who'd be demanding to know what kind of train that is. And he looked ashamed and walked away. And speaking of luckily: good thing I was keeping an eye out the windows after that."

You could classify people by the way they behave in an emergency, and Rebecca was one of those who start tearing up clothing for tourniquets. She was like her bob: she could shake it and shake it and when she was done it all fell back in place.

I looked out the pane in the door, expecting that any moment Nelson's hate-crumpled features would mash against the other side. The porch looked empty. Had he knocked himself out? I stood on tiptoe and looked down but couldn't see the part nearest the door. "How's Max?" He'd had a low-grade fever when I left home that morning.

"Good. His temperature's back to normal. And he slept through all the racket. Still asleep."

"Do you have Nelson's cell number?" She called it sometimes to make sure there'd be someone at home when she wanted to see the Freiles papers.

I entered it in my iPhone's directory, and it occurred to me that I'd better discuss the fuck train with her first, before she heard about it from one nervous side of a phone call. "This needs a preface."

We dropped onto the couch like two sacks of laundry. In my fear of withholding anything I spared no detail: the low-flying bat, the parachute joke, the fuck train, the looming destruction of the English department, my upcoming acceptance-and-renunciation speech, the devouring generosity of the Nora Foundation, my erection.

I had anticipated any number of responses, but not her gleeful "hold on. There's something you have to see."

She returned with her iPad and scrolled through her mail. She was giggling softly: if it were anyone but Rebecca I'd wonder if she were hysterical.

"There." She handed it over. The photo, a selfie taken by Wendy, showed the two women sitting on Wendy's living room floor in neon yellow underwear. Newspaper was spread on the carpet beneath them. Rebecca was applying polish to Wendy's toenails while staring at her body, unaware at that instant of the camera. Wendy smirked exultantly, her eyebrow ready to take wing. It was an image out of my worst nightmares and perhaps my fantasies. "We'd gone underwear shopping at Nordstrom's, and at lunch we agreed that we missed being the age when girls braid each other's hair and paint each other's toenails. So we bought a couple of bottles of Revlon Chill Cherry"—she wiggled her nails— "and the rest is recorded history. Oh, and she held up her phone with that picture and said, 'See? You have a crush on me.' All part of her plan to get me to get you on board with the Nelson Baim reclamation project. I just laughed."

I said, "The way you're looking at her—what does *that* mean?"

"That she has a rockin' body, of course. But just so you don't think I'm evading the implied question, no. There's nothing between us. . . Are you all right, George? You look like you're being whacked with a sledgehammer while simultaneously grooving on IV morphine for the pain. Is this torture for you or a turn-on?"

I shrugged glumly. "Both? That's why there are tickle-fights in hell."

"You're not seriously jealous. She's a character and she looks good in underwear, maybe a little pasty in neon yellow, and that's it. Though I look better in underwear, so who needs her?" She stroked my cheek. "Right, George?"

"Damn right you do!" I glanced at the screen. "If that were a fashion shoot, she might as well be the grip or the lighting technician. She might as well be best boy!" Mandatory but true.

"That's a movie term," she said, "but thanks."

"So you never gave a thought—"

"With *Wendy*?" Rebecca took the iPad out of my hands and closed the cover. "She's borderline insane, as you know. I'd rather lick a hot stove. Anyway I prefer my lovers short, bespectacled, hermeneutical, male, and airworthy. Obviously I won't be returning to their house anytime soon. I have xeroxes of everything I need for the Freiles book, and I've already interviewed Wendy. My publisher has signed a contract with the estate, so she can't fuck with us on that." She smoothed down my cowlick, which had sprung up cartoonishly. "You know, George, we're not Catholics. We're allowed to *think* anything we please. . . What *are* you thinking?"

"Ah! You see?"

"She has some sort of fascination for you. What's *that* about? Midlife crisis? You just turned forty, you're successful, one of the most respected figures in hermeneutics, you love your family, we love you, it's all perfect. Is perfect boring? Scary? Not scary enough? Maybe it would be interesting to pull out a block in the bottom row? You look at that imperviously confident expression she has, the raised eyebrow, the slightly certifiable glint—insanity runs in her family, by the way—and maybe for an instant you wonder what it would be like to throw everything away for no damn reason. Is that it?" She cocked her head, as she did when she wanted a better view through my skull.

"I'm one of those people," I said, "who fears the edge of subway platforms. We think we feel the attraction of jumping. Turns out we're statistically the least likely to jump."

"I'm having trouble with your metaphors today. Are you fucking her?"

"No!"

We watched each other breathe for a while. I got up and went to the front door, put the chain on, cracked it open, and verified that Nelson Baim wasn't lying unconscious on our porch. Good for him. I dialed him and listened, on the line, to quavering underwater ringing. Even his ring made me sad.

I returned to the couch. "I'm forgetting how to speak plainly."

"I'm sorry. Usually when someone answers a straightforward question by the scenic route, I figure he's being evasive. But I forgot—you're George. So. Is Wendy the platform, the edge, the train, the tracks, or the attraction of jumping?"

"She's the woman," I said, feeling like I'd been cast in the role of George, "who pushes you off the platform then climbs down and administers first aid. Say. I wouldn't mind seeing you in the new underwear."

"Later," she said. "Here's what I think you should do. All your choices in this Twine business stink. You can get a much better deal if instead of worrying about her Twine Award threats and conditions, you satisfy her original request. The Twine stuff is just her revenge because you didn't give her what she really wants. So hold the press conference with Nelson and congratulate him for figuring out how you did the trick. She'll need to make you famous first, and she has the resources to do it. Don't worry about that. For a week strangers will say aren't you that guy. Then after the press conference strangers will say aren't you that guy that guy debunked, and then the caravan will move on. You've got to hand it to Wendy for thinking up a cute way around the nonexistence of a trick: you tell the press, 'I can't reveal the trick—magician's code—but kudos to Nelson Baim for debunking the hell out of it.' The irony is that the press won't report it. No trick, no story. Wendy would realize that if the whole business didn't have her so crazed. But after you make the announcement, you're out of it. There's nothing more you can do because there's no trick. Sooner or later she'll realize that. She'll have to leave us alone. Uh-oh. You're about to invoke the honor of flying."

. . .

At that moment the worst idea I've ever had came to me—at me, really—with the brilliance and proclamatory kettle-drumming of a subway train. "No, I can save the department *and* flying—maybe not my dignity but so what?" I said as I fished out the iPhone, went to the directory, and selected a number. "Don't worry, babe, I've got this."

"Don't you want to tell me your plan first? I thought we were going to strategize."

"Let's just get on with it," I said as the line began ringing. Perhaps the bad idea that possessed me knew its lifespan would be short.

An elderly male voice panted hello.

"Hello, Preston? It's George Entmen."

Rebecca put her mouth to my ear and whispered, "For godsake hang up now!" I slid away.

Preston was Preston Twine, founder and endower of the Twine Award. The Lyman Twine Award, to give it its full title, was named after his only child, a beloved young professor of

English at Northwestern and a rising star in the emerging field of poststructuralism who died of liver cancer in 1973.

Preston, a widower, the retired owner and CEO of North Shore Bank, liked to hang out with the English faculty. In the years since Lyman's death he'd been reading up on literary theory. He often stopped by the department offices at University Hall for shop talk. With his ramrod bearing, rosy cheeks, sparkling eyes, and magnesium-torch-white hair, Preston looked like a five-star general in a children's book. Always smelled like a barber shop, always a red carnation in his lapel. He'd slowed down a bit in recent years, and once when I came across him and his caregiver sitting on a bench on campus, the old man pretended to know me but clearly didn't. Usually, though, he seemed sharp as ever—we'd discussed the works of Gadamer less than a year ago—and I was counting on that. It was reassuring that he and not the helper had answered.

"George, congratulations again on the award! There's never been a choice that's pleased me more, and it couldn't happen to a nicer guy. What can I do for you?"

"About the award. Will you be presenting it yourself?"

"No, it'll be someone in your field. If you don't mind having the surprise spoiled, it's Ben, uh, Tomilson of Yale. Good man."

"This will sound very strange, Preston, maybe even offensive, but I need to beg a favor. I'm not at liberty to explain why I need it, I just hope we've known each other long enough that you'll have faith in me."

"You know I have faith in you, George. We've been friends, mygod, it must be ten years. I remember the—"

"I need you to take back the award." Rebecca lunged for the phone; I switched to the other ear. "The head of the English department won't do it. You're the only other person authorized to take it away."

"Legally? I'm not sure about that. I'd have to run it past my lawyer. Lester McGonnigal. Good man. Everybody calls him Knuckles. You know him?"

"Regardless of legality," I said, "nobody would dispute your right to do it. So. After the award is presented I beg you to go up to the podium and take it back. I truly wish I could tell you why, but I can't. Only that the future of the English department depends on your doing this."

"If you don't want it," he said peevishly, "don't accept it."

"As I said, the English department won't take it back." Wendy had told me that I couldn't rid myself of it just by personally giving the thing back or away. First I'd have to read her prepared remarks at the award ceremony (yes, I'd broken down and looked at them. They were mostly about my flying. You say you can't imagine what it means to debase flying? That's because you haven't read those ninety-three depraved words. Even now I can't bear to repeat them). I'd be deemed insane of course and could never teach again, but never mind *that*. What I couldn't abide is that the ancient dream of unassisted human flight would become nothing but a dirty joke—no more poetry than the one about the trucker, the big vagina, the flashlight, a second trucker, I think, and the eighteen-wheeler.

Preston wasn't done trying to reason with me. "Well then you should speak to the committee. They gave you the award, George. I thought it was a great choice, but I had nothing to do with it."

"Preston. Please."

"I get it. Your modesty speaks well of you. Of *course* you hate the egotism involved with awards. You believe the life of the mind is a team sport—shoulders of giants and all that."

"It's not that."

The warmth drained out of his voice. "Then what is it?"

"This isn't a joke, Preston. Please trust that I'd never disrespect you or the award." I didn't want to mention Wendy and her threats; what if he had one of his spells and blurted it out at the podium?

Rebecca was trying to whisper something. I plugged my ear. "Preston, has someone ever threatened everything you care about?"

"Sure," he said sarcastically. "Hitler, Tojo."

"Well imagine that one day you're practicing your acceptance speech for an award you've worked for your whole professional life, and suddenly Hitler . . . and Tojo, uh—" Rebecca grabbed the phone; I grabbed it back.

"I don't understand." Preston was saying. "What's going on, George?"

"All I can say is that something very bad will happen to me and the department if you don't help me with this. You're the only one I can ask. I'm not at liberty to explain why." I knew I was repeating myself as inanely as my two-year-old begging for a horse, but I was brainlocked with shame and panic. My shirt had turned transparent and was pasted to my chest.

After a long pause Preston said, "All right. I'll take it back."

I forced myself not to melt into gibbering gratitude. "Thank you."

"And when I'm up there holding your award what do I say?"

"Just say, 'I take back this award' and leave the podium."

"You know," he said, "I used to wonder if all that high-end lit-

erary theory was just a gag. Maybe the point isn't to *find* meaning—maybe it's to take away whatever meaning we already have. I
guess it was only a matter of time before the joke landed on *me*. But
I don't want to believe that. I want to believe you're the good man
I've known for ten years and I'm going to bet you are. And if the
point of all this is to make an old fool of me, I beat you to it ages ago.
When in the speech do you want me to step up to the podium?"

"Let's say five minutes in." I doubted that anyone would try
to stop him.

"When you're up there," I continued, "just say 'I take back
this award' and leave the podium with it. And I swear to you, I'm
not trying to make you look foolish. I hope that some day I can
explain why all this was necessary."

"And after I walk away with the award, what then? Do I
keep it? Do you want it back later?"

"No." I wished I could find some doggie door and scuttle out
of George Entmen. "Just give it to a better person."

"Whatever you say." He hung up.

Rebecca was looking at me pityingly, and by now I understood why, but I let her spell it out. "I don't know where to start.
How old is Preston? Late nineties? Didn't you think of how much
damage that call could do to him? He probably thinks you were
gaslighting him. As for the chances of your scheme working, did
you think that having Preston take back the award is some sort of
loophole? The only judge who'll rule on your loophole is Wendy.
She has all the power, she sets the rules, she's the referee. Wendy
wants you to help her husband, and she's not going to stop until
then." She cupped my face in her hands. "Please. If you fuck this
up dozens, maybe all of your colleagues—never mind *you*!—
will end up unemployed in the worst-ever job market for English

professors. And, yes, if you give her what she wants maybe flying will be 'dishonored.' Which I think we agree is preferable to something measurably awful happening to visible, palpable, nonabstract human beings. Flying has been dishonored before—think of all those grammar school productions of Peter Pan—and it seems to be doing okay."

My thumb hovered above redial. "You're right. First I'll call Preston back."

She put her hand on my arm. "Maybe you should wait. Taking back your first call a minute later might completely disorient him."

"I need to undo this now. Believe me, he'll be relieved."

A baritone cop voice answered on the first ring. Had to be the caregiver.

"Can I speak to Preston?"

"He's resting."

"Can you take a message? This is George again. Tell him—"

"Got it. Anything else?'

"I haven't finished."

"I'd say you're finished, Mr. George Again."

"That's pretty insolent. Does Preston know how you speak to callers?"

"Does your mom know you masturbate to Justin Bieber videos?"

I heard voices muffled by a hand on the phone.

"Hello, George." It was Preston.

"Your assistant was being incredibly abusive. Did you hear what he was saying?"

"I'm not feeling well, George. Why are you calling now?"

"Please forget everything I said about taking back the award. I'll accept it in the usual way. All I can say is that I was receiving threats about what would happen if I accepted it and—just under a lot of pressure today. Please pretend my last call never happened. I'm *so* sorry."

"So when you accept the award I should—"

"Just stay in your seat, enjoy your dinner, do me the honor of sitting through my acceptance speech—not that I deserve it!—and know that you have my eternal respect and gratitude and the love of all of us in the English department."

"And when I go up to the podium I say what?"

"*Don't* go up there. Please. As I said, just stay in your seat and absorb—not the right word, but you know what I mean. Accept— the love of the entire department for all your good works. Please forgive my mistake and pretend that call never happened."

"This call never happened? Then what *is* happening?"

Was *he* was gaslighting *me* now? "All right, Preston. I should let you get back to your rest. Once again, I'm abjectly sorry. Bye!

"That went well!" I said to Rebecca. "On to Wendy!"

She put her face in her hands.

.   .   .

"Hello!" Wendy pronounced the word, as she often did, with a breathy, bad and pointless British accent.

"This is George," I said.

"Of course. Ready to schedule your press conference?"

On the line I could hear the distant sound of objects breaking. "Is there—"

"Oh that's just Nelson letting off steam. Sometimes he requires a little wrangling, but not a problem. How does three weeks from today sound? I believe classes will be out. And I have you booked the week before on Tommy Thorne. Gotta get you famous, podling. Nobody's going to care that you were brought down unless you fall from a height. Only kidding. There's no disgrace involved. You won't be *debunked:* our spin is that you're an amateur magician and Nelson simply reverse-engineered the trick. Nobody did anything disreputable. But since you're a *magician*, the trick itself will naturally have to remain hush-hush."

"I've been meaning to ask. Do you ever sit in the shadows going mwa! ha! ha!"

"Why no, George, I don't. Today I was busy seeing to it that a tiny West African nation has the resources to fight malaria. There's something I must say for your own good: I think you're attracted to my dark side. Your fantasies about me aren't healthy, and frankly I find them a tad creepy. Work on it, it makes our friendship awkward. Why don't I send you an email to confirm the dates?"

"And there won't be any problem with the award ceremony?"

"Only that I can't wait to be there for your well-earned triumph."

"Thank you!" I said before I could stop myself.

"I think we're done here," she said, "don't you?"

She broke the ensuing silence to say, "Poor George, trying to think of some withering put-down to deliver before you hang up."

"Give me a minute."

She began humming. To give her her due, she had a lovely singing voice. At last she said, "We both know it won't come to you until you don't have to say it to me."

"Fuck you," I said and hung up.

SEVEN

Tonight, I resolved, I would allow myself to be happy. The honor of flying could fend for itself a while. I was driving my mother and Rebecca to the Twine presentation banquet. Mom had been jet-lagged since she flew in from Palm Springs that afternoon, her sentences trailing off in ellipses and mumbling.

When I glanced at her in the front passenger seat she seemed slightly out of focus; maybe it was just the borderless blur of her lipstick. But I imagined that all the versions of her I'd known or seen photographed were superimposed, including the pretty kindergarten teacher who'd written a letter introducing herself to Walter Entmen—my future father, late father now, the famous, glowering, towering, vaguely furious astrophysicist—and asking him to come speak about the stars and planets to her class. He taught at the University of Chicago, "just blocks from us," she'd emphasized with three exclamation points. The accompanying photo showed Mom and the kids imploring ("one, two, three pleeeeze!"). Her smile, practically an astronomical object in itself, was large and bright enough to draw Walter from his office on Fifty-Seventh Street through the unimaginable vastness and darkness in his own head to the Ida Tarbell Elementary School on Fifty-Fifth Street. Another photo shows him posing with the class, attempting not to loom, attempting to smile through brute force. Mom and the kids stand bunched together at the opposite side of the frame. Sometimes not even my own existence convinces me that things could have progressed from there.

Of course she must have been seeing me with the same simultaneity—distinguished soon-to-be-award-winning hermeneutist tugging at the model jet plane superglued to his hair.

The mob of her snapped back into the outlines of one slightly baggy still smiling seventy-year-old woman. I didn't recall the chin wattles from our visit six months ago. Her years of experimenting with her hair color had ended in a dim sorta-brownishness that could have been the sum of all colors or their absence.

"George," she enthused, street lights gliding across her glasses, "I nearly forgot! When your book came out I bought copies for all the relatives!"

Our Lexus had what the salesman called a ninja-quiet ride, so I restrained myself from sighing. I knew how the story of the relatives would end—this one had never varied since she handed out my first book— but I feigned eager anticipation. "And?"

"And they didn't understand it!"

I rolled my eyes in the mirror. Rebecca's teeth flashed in the back seat. She adored my mother, and the ritual story of the books and the baffled relatives—and my exasperation with it— always gave her a kick.

"Mom, I've never understood why you think it's a good thing that they don't get my work."

"Because it means you're *very very* smart!"

She reached out for my head and I held up a hand. "Wait, the cowlick! No hair-tousling till after my speech."

"Your cousin Joe said he started your book *three times* and then quit!"

"You know, writing isn't wrestling. The point isn't to force the reader to give up. And please, next time let me give you all those copies."

"I can't give them freebees. These are gifts!"

Rebecca and I laughed, and finally Mom joined in. "They're the new fruitcake," I said.

"Your Uncle Izzie said he wanted to *pound* and *pound* and *pound* his head until he lost the ability to read."

"We'll blurb it. Thanks."

I wondered if my father would have been proud tonight. Mom had told me that when my first book came out he'd leave it lying around in places where visitors would have to "come across it." And he'd say something along the lines of, "You want that copy? Really. Go ahead, we have more. His mother sees to that. Me, I've never seen the point to hermeneutics. What does it have to do with the price of potatoes in Idaho?" An odd criticism from a cutting-edge astrophysicist. "Frankly I wish George would do something useful. He was lauded in the *Sunday New York Times Book Review*, you know. Quite a distinction for an academic book. Also a fulsome review from Fitzgerald Weems in the *New York Review of Books*, who I understand is one of the top men in George's field. Whatever *that's* worth. Did I mention he won the Pegg Award for best first work of literary theory?" Perhaps there *was* some faint praise in all that damning.

It occurred to me: Now that I knew that one local corner of the supernatural was real, the odds for the existence of ghosts had gone up. Why couldn't Walter Entmen be attending tonight—invisibly, of course—still in one of his identical dark suits, scowling behind some corner table, holding up a commanding spectral finger in a fruitless attempt to order his one daily bourbon? I wondered how he likes death. After all those years specializing in "the spaces between the stars" maybe he dived right in.

. . .

"It's too dark. You're going to have to guide me, George." My mother tightened her grip on my arm.

Built in the early seventies, the Zaggernaut Hotel lobby was a knockoff of the Hyatts from that era: glass elevators gleaming like Xrays; dark corners seething with climbing vines; nearly every surface composed of mirrors or shiny black marble; the lighting all firefly glints and tiny nova-bright spotlights; the huge atrium overhung by balconies whose highest stories melted in expressionist shadows. In the days when this lobby was bustling it must have been exciting, like an optimistic version of Fritz Lang's *Metropolis*. But now, dark, empty, AC-ed to the chill of the grave, all they needed to achieve full dread was to turn off the Muzak and let our footsteps echo.

Rebecca, lit perfectly noir-licious in her bare-shouldered black dress, craned at the upper stories. "Among architects it's known as 'Where the future went to die.' The only reason this place still exists is its dubious landmark status. Come on, the Zebra Room's this way. Don't look up, Rose. You'll get dizzy."

"George." At first I thought that breathy syllable came from the AC or some crevice in my brain, but the perfume was louder.

I turned around. "Hello Wendy."

She too was wearing an off-the-shoulders dress—even tighter

than Rebecca's—and in the cinematic light her pasty shoulders were luminous. "Hello Rebecca. I don't think I've met—"

I introduced her to my mother.

"We're wearing practically the same dress," Wendy said to Rebecca, using the occasion to eye her up and down. "But mine's red."

I was having a hard time navigating between distance and politic courtesy, but Rebecca seemed to be enjoying herself. "Of course it is," she said. "In case there's someone who wouldn't get the point in black."

"Let's settle this like civilized women." Wendy raised the eyebrow. "Lobby wrestling. Three falls."

We didn't want to be charmed, but Rebecca and I couldn't help laughing. My mother looked baffled.

"Nelson's in the bar," Wendy said. "He has something he'd like to say to you both in private before the presentation starts."

"We'd love to hear it," I said, "but my mother's kind of disoriented by the lighting, and I'd like to get her to our table."

To be helpful, Mom said, "Rebecca could do that. Why don't you go talk to your friend?"

On the way to the bar Wendy said, "Don't worry, Nelson just wants to apologize. I think you're feeling a little guilty yourself, aren't you? About saying 'fuck you' to me this afternoon and hanging up?"

I opened my mouth and—realizing what I could say on the subject of what *I* owed *the Baims*—closed it. I was done placating her.

"That's all right," she said. "I'm sure you only meant it carnally."

I was about to ask what she'd told Nelson about the kiddy train; I wondered if she'd lied about it to drive him into a rage and further demonstrate the chaos she could make of my life. But before I could bring it up, she said, "Look who's joined us."

Toby and Iris were sitting with Nelson at the bar.

Iris was wearing the sparkly yellow formal dress her mom had made for her a few years ago (if you brought up the dress she'd say something like "I'm competing for Miss Florida 1962," but she accepted the National Book Award in it). Hoping she'd dumped her sleazy magician, I blurted, "Did you kids come here together?" Immediately I knew it was the wrong thing to say. Toby took a long clinking gulp of his drink. I was probably the last person who believed in a future where they'd be a couple, even if it seemed increasingly like an alternate future. I think Iris loved him about 20 percent of the time. It was different for Toby; his entire public self was the gleam on the carapace around his love for Iris.

He chewed an ice cube, the noise resounding through his large distinguished head. When he finished, he said, "Iris is waiting for magic boy. His hand is demonstrably quicker than the eye. Look at her eye."

The lighting in the bar was slightly better than the lobby's— just bright enough to see Iris's shiner beneath its dab of makeup. The blonde upturned Mary Tyler Moore curl over each of her ears drooped; she was drunk. "Door," she said straight-faced, meeting my stare.

"You couldn't come up with something better?" I asked.

"Of course I could," she said attempting a breezy tone. "Why would I use that one unless it were true? . . . Okay it *wasn't* an accident. The door meant it." As always when she was sad, she spoke at full twang.

"Not funny *at all*."

"Of course it wasn't funny. Oh sweetie, everybody thinks I set out to be funny. Being funny is just my nervous tic. If a punch in the eye is all it takes to get rid of it, then . . . then I don't even have to finish this joke."

"Drop that guy like a burning bag of stool," I said. "You don't hate yourself, do you?"

Wendy put a hand on her shoulder. "You need to break things off with this man. I'll bet he promised to never do it again, they always do. But abusers never stop. The Nora Foundation sponsors counseling for battered women, protective services including shelters, and workshops on toxic relationships. Look for our link to Flannagen House."

"Wait, *workshops*? Like, 'Tod, Leslie, your toxic relationship has some interesting ideas but it needs work?' Not funny. Good."

"All your self-deprecating humor." Wendy shook her head. "Like so many women you've turned all your power the wrong way. Read *The Reaches of Power* by Edwin Flesner. Every woman should know the work of Flesner."

"Sure. I'm writing that down," said Iris making writing motions in the air.

Once we'd all decided there was nothing else we could say to Iris, Wendy turned to Nelson. Since I'd come in he'd sat there looking down at his full shot glass on the bar.

"George," she said, eyes on her husband, "Nelson has something he'd like to say to you."

Nelson continued to study his shot on the bar.

Transferring all his anger to Nelson, Toby yelled, "Just drink it! This isn't cliff diving!"

Wendy tilted Nelson's chin up and waited.

"I'm sorry I want to kill you," he said to me. He looked even sadder than Iris.

"At least he's sorry," Toby said.

"Remember what we talked about, baby?" Wendy stood behind Nelson rubbing his shoulders. She kissed the lonesome red filaments brushed tight to his crown. "Remember what you were going to say? Can't you say it?"

"No," he said with genuine regret.

I patted my inside suit pocket to be sure I had my speech and stood up. "I'd better get over there, talk to the organizers, have a last look at the speech. Don't worry, they'll serve dinner first. I'm actually a little nervous."

Toby slapped me on the back, gave me a two-hand hand-shake. "If there's a sentence you think is weak, just attribute it to Marcus Aurelius. Never fails."

Wendy gave me a hug. "You'll be spectacular."

Iris, still sitting, put her head on my chest and hugged me. When she let go she wiped her eyes and said, "You'll knock 'em dead." She snorted at my discomfort with her choice of words. "Oh come on!"

·   ·   ·

Pointing to a woman in a dark corner of the lobby, Toby said, "I'll bet she's the loneliest whore in Evanston." I could just make out a woman in a black cocktail dress leaning against a wall next to a potted plant.

I'd asked him to walk over with me because I was worried about Iris. "Is it out of the question to stage an intervention? With Iris, I mean, not the woman by the plant."

"It would be easier to kill the guy," he said. "You know, God must like the sound of that because here he comes."

Iris's magician Ricardo Dean was walking toward the bar, his

157

inevitable black turtleneck showing beneath an Armani jacket, his spiky hair glistening. *"Entertainment Weekly* says he has the grace of a Pharaoh's cat," Toby scoffed. "They say he's mastered the arcane secrets of the ages. Oh, and his eyes, they say, *harbor an ancient sadness.* They will in a second."

"Please don't—"

"Door!" Toby shouted as Ricardo approached and, when he looked our way, jabbed him in the eye and kept walking.

. . .

It was called the Zebra Room because long after the fad of op art a famous op artist had painted the walls with eye-befuddling purple-and-white diagonal stripes. They were one of the features that had gained the Zaggernaut its landmark status. I'd been warned not to stare at the stripes because after a few seconds they could seem to move—bloating, squirming, flickering. The dangers of this effect were obvious, especially in a place that served food, but tweaking by designers, psychologists, lighting specialists, inner ear specialists, neurologists and post-op artists had never quite stilled the walls. Despite the occasional explosion of nausea, the stripes had proved to be a feature not a bug because, like hot sauce, diners took them as a challenge.

I stood at the podium and scanned the audience as I waited for the applause to stop. The most enthusiastic clapping came from the honoree's table, closest to the stage: my mother, Rebecca, Iris, Toby, my guru Harvey Bell, the department chair Ken Dreynen, and his wife Alice. At my request the seating committee had moved Ricardo Dean to a distant table, but Ricardo had worked his magic and was back next to Iris, bumping Preston Twine and his helper to Outer Siberia. His eye already purple, Ricardo performed a graceful mime of clapping—but clapped loudly and sarcastically whenever Iris was looking (he was two seats away from Toby but never turned his head in that direction). Wendy, one of the most avid applauders, had also got herself and Nelson upgraded to my table, no doubt through her usual nuclear diplomacy. Nelson stared at the tablecloth. In the least welcome seating switch of all, my hermeneutist colleague Charles Blaustein—who at my birthday party had sat silently glaring in his overcoat—was next to Nelson. What did I ever do to Charles? Maybe it was just his corpse-eye stare, but he seemed to have calculated the bare minimum of hand motion, sound, and enthusiasm that could constitute applause.

Except for this bunch at the speaker's table, I'd never had an enemy in my life. Why had they come here to see my triumph, needing to be up close? Was this a new spin on *schadenfreude*? It's not enough that I succeed, my enemy must succeed too?

In retrospect they seem like vultures in a western, circling the same empty spot or perched on the roof of the saloon, waiting. *How do they know?*

.   .   .

"Three critics," I began, "a deconstructionist, a new historicist, and a hermeneutist, are traveling by private plane to a conference, the only passengers." I focused on Rebecca, who was grinning already. "The pilot announces that all four engines are on fire, that he's about to bail out, and that there are only two remaining parachutes." I wasn't sure it was necessary, but I added, "He bails out."

I realized then that for a while I'd been hearing a tapping sound. As it grew louder it was more like a hammer pounding a spike against a bank vault door.

"The deconstructionist says, 'I deserve to live because—'" Croink! Croink! Croink! Croink!

Even Rebecca turned around to look for the source; Preston Twine's home health aide was guiding him by the arm up the center aisle between the tables toward the stage. Preston had changed since I'd seen him just a few months ago, stooped now and walking with a cane, one of those gleaming new "miracle alloy" models. He wore a Brooks Brothers summer suit with a red carnation. He looked like he'd lost fifty pounds.

Not knowing what else to do I kept talking. "Uh, so the deconstructionist. He's making the case that *he* deserves to *live*." Croink! Croink! Croink! Croink!

"And so he says, uh, this deconstructionist, to the other two literary theorists, each of whom wants very much to, uh, live, of course, so the deconstructionist says . . ."

Preston and his helper, a squat man with a razor crew cut, stopped in front of the stage.

I covered the mike and whispered, "Preston, you remember we canceled the plan, right?"

"I'll be right up."

I looked at the helper. "Please tell him—"

"The ramp's over there," the helper said to his boss. "Let's go." It was the guy who'd insulted me on the phone. He looked too happy not to know what was going on, twinkling at me like a mean steroid elf. But really, it was all my fault.

The Twine Award sat next to my speech on the podium. It

was a silver-coated statuette of a helmeted Minerva because there is no goddess of hermeneutics. I picked it up and clutched it protectively as they stepped onstage. "Preston," I whispered, "it's all taken care of. You don't need to do a thing."

"Beat it," said the helper. "And leave the paperweight." He eased Preston into the chair I'd sat in when I was introduced.

I resorted to what seemed the least fractious option. "Ladies and gentlemen, it's my honor and my pleasure to introduce the founder and endower of the Twine Award, Mr. Preston Twine."

Half applause, half befuddlement. The room was filled with the noise of literary theorists theorizing.

The helper stepped up next to me and whispered, "How do you want to leave, 'cause I can throw you back to the head table like a minnow. *She* stays," he added grabbing the award and setting it back next to the microphone.

As I stepped down he guided Preston to the podium and stood there with him propping him up. "Don't look at the walls, boss," he whispered. I decided to sit in the chair and wait. I felt obligated to finish the speech; my wife, my mother, my best friends, and my colleagues were all there. If Preston left with the award, fine. I decided to give back the five thousand dollars that went with it.

The helper adjusted the mike for his boss. Preston's first words were lost in a wheezy rush of breath. I'd never heard his voice so weak. He raised it. "George wanted me to take back the award. Oh, I almost forgot." He picked it up and half turned to me; the helper steadied him, took the mike off the stand, and held it to Preston's lips. Summoning his commanding voice, Preston said, 'I take back this award!' He gave me a thumbs-up. "Are those the words, George?" He looked like he'd already been drained by the embalmer. I smiled at my friend and gave him a thumbs-up.

As they walked toward the ramp Preston sagged out of his helper's grip to the floor. The helper rolled him over and began chest compressions. "Is anyone here a doctor?"

Three or four people ran onstage but Preston was already dead.

. . .

Afterward some of us sat with Sonia Twine-Mills, Preston's granddaughter, waiting for the body to be removed. She was gripping her husband's arm, a boney woman with a dazed blue stare. "He was ninety-eight, I thought I was prepared," she was saying, "but how could you prepare for *that*?" She was still in that moment after a car crash when the car has stopped and you haven't. For the past few minutes she'd been holding a handkerchief in the vicinity of her eyes which only now began streaming. "Should I wait up there with him? He looks so alone." We glanced at the stage, where Preston lay beneath a blanket someone found backstage.

Her plate of melting chocolate ice cream drew her horrified gaze until someone placed it on another table. She looked up. "George, what were you and my grandfather talking about?"

"Oh." I knew I'd have to answer that question, but not that I'd have to answer it now. "One of our big donors thought that I shouldn't get the award"—across the table Wendy's sad, shaken face barely flickered— "and the department refused to take it back. I thought it might spare us retaliation if Preston did it. I tried to cancel the plan but we got our wires crossed. It was all just stupid academic politics."

"Except it killed him," his helper said. He got nothing but

shocked and offended silence during which it occurred to me that I'd killed Preston.

Iris came over; she'd been sitting with my mother a few tables away. "You'd better take her home, sweetie. The air's all running out."

Rebecca and I stood up, said goodbyes around the table, numbly accepted congratulations, offered some last words to Sonia and her husband, and asked about the arrangements.

"Tonight as soon as we get through the rigamarole Arthur and I will just go to bed. But come over any time tomorrow."

The helper gloated, as if we were fleeing his accusation.

As Rebecca and I walked out with my mother holding on to us— "Just sleepy, dear, and upset for that poor man of course" —Blaustein stood at the doors. He was holding out the Twine Award. I'd set it on a food cart hoping to never see it again.

"You forgot this," he said with a grin stretched so torture-wide (I didn't know his condition allowed for such a grin and wondered if it had done damage), he might have been trying to block the doors with it.

"Keep it," I wanted to say. "You can pretend you won it." But there was my mother, beaming at the blunt instrument.

. . .

"George?" Rebecca's sleep-slurred voice.

I opened my eyes, listening in the dark for Max or a burglar.

She raised her head. "You were dreaming. You were yelling 'I killed Preston!'"

I could make out the shimmer of her face, the power light of the child monitor, the breathy smoke-wisps of the curtains. "No," I managed, "*you* didn't kill Preston, *I* killed Preston."

"I'll give you a second to catch up. Okay? You think you killed Preston because, according to your hair-shirt theory of causality, your call might theoretically have knocked *how* many seconds off his life? The chicken they served at the banquet was disappointing—how many seconds did he lose there? The misery of being named *Twine* in high school—I'll bet that cost him a full year. Can't you just be sad he's gone and leave it at that? I miss him too."

"He was a beautiful man," I said, "and I was too desperate and selfish to realize how upsetting my call would be."

"George, do you remember when he was convinced I was related to him through his cousins, the Highland Park Carltons? He must've misunderstood or misheard something, I can't imagine what. I couldn't talk him out of it, so whenever I ran into him on campus I played along. Until one afternoon last year he came here with a bagful of enormous fold-out charts of what he believed was our shared family tree. I never told you this, it was too sad. I put up with it for a couple of hours until finally I thought I'd flip out along with Preston and we'd end up in some *ward* together squinting at his charts. The branches . . . the sub-branches . . . the sub-sub-sub," she yawned, "twigs." She put her head on my chest. "So I gently told him there were no Carltons, let alone Highland Park Carltons, in my family. It was painful to see his face. He looked like a Philip K. Dick character who wakes up in some inconceivable alternate universe where I'm unrelated to all these Carltons. I thought he was about to have some sort of medical event, but he just thanked me for my time, very cordial, very chipper, made a little joke about his memory, a little joke about his confusion, and I begged him to sit and have more tea, but he walked out. I'll bet I shaved at least as much time off his life as you did."

"Who do you think will be the first one at the funeral to accuse me of killing Preston? Blaustein, Nelson, or Preston's helper?"

"Preston's helper already tried that and people were appalled. Nelson? I don't think it's his style. A *violent* man, but not the passive-aggressive sort who spreads gossip."

"There's *his* eulogy."

"As for Blaustein," she said, "who knows? He says he admires your work. At your birthday party he said he was your 'acolyte or disciple.' Maybe that was sarcasm, but could we call him a deranged fan? Does hermeneutics *have* those? ... I hope you didn't throw out your Twine Award again because I'll bet he's been through our garbage tonight."

EIGHT

Even a man with his nose scraping the ground can find vastness. A lawn at the altitude of four inches is unexplored country; down here the uniform green you see up there is yellow, brown, russet, sometimes newborn proto-colors that have their moment on the lawn and vanish forever. And yes, it's mostly green but every imaginable shade, from the delirious green of the jungle to the queasy face of a beer-bonged frat boy. Even my severely cropped (for flying) lawn was no mere Soviet collectivity of grass; each shivering vibrating blade was its own self—subtly spotted, muddied, flattened, fatter, faded.

You think your lawn is just dirt and grass? Get down and look. I found a Bazooka Joe comic strip, still smelling of bubblegum, fluttering on a grass blade. A red plastic fingernail. Three condoms. A scrap of paper with the word fragment "arve" in lovely cursive. A total of eighty-seven cents in change over five days. A doll's brown eye. A one-inch businessman figurine toting a molecule, perhaps, in his briefcase (none of the toys were Max's). A blue plastic whistle that my guru Harvey Bell appropriated (was somebody throwing this stuff over the fence? I had well-mannered elderly neighbors on either side).

With Harvey's encouragement, I filled my head with such inspirational horse shit and bogus wonder—and don't quote me on the colors. I needed to motivate myself for flaying, I mean flying, but that's how boring it had become. A flailing man with his nose in the dirt can still find the stars, he insisted. He was teaching me to see, "truly see," my lawn.

I'd asked him to cut out spiritual jargon like "chakra" and perhaps this was all he had left. It was only our second session, and already I suspected he wasn't a very good guru.

He wore the whistle I'd found over his University of Chicago sweatshirt (he still wore the turban). It was a joke between us, based on an Octavio Paz poem we'd loved as students in which a guru teaches his disciple self-mastery through track hurtles and a gym whistle.

I was lying on the grass panting from a round of flying and "seeing." "I'm sorry, Harvey, but perceiving each individual grass blade isn't enlightening. It's numbing and exhausting. Thank God for collective nouns."

He was twirling a blade of grass between his fingers. "But I'll bet you were too tired," he said slyly, "to obsess over whether you killed Preston Twine. See? It worked."

"It worked perfectly until you just mentioned it."

"Oh." Harvey looked off into the far distance and I thought he was about to paper it over with some mystical epigram. "Sorry about that."

"And why are we concentrating on making four-inch flying palatable? Have you already given up?"

"No. There's one impedance to flying that I'd like to work on now." He was back to business. "Are you a good swimmer?"

"Not at all," I said. His intuitions were better than I thought.

"And how did swimming lessons go?"

"Catastrophically," I said. "Did I tell you this before?"

"No. It's just that there's a lot of drowning in your flying."

"I certainly know what it's like to drown. And with my parents watching, *sitting in lounge chairs*. Mom smiling like I was about to be handed my degree and graduate to the next life."

"That's it," Harvey said. "Get the narrative hook in, then *dramatic pause*."

"The camp was run by fundamentalist Christians . . ." I continued.

"Why would they send you there?"

"Another one of my dad's schemes to toughen me up. Like the boxing lessons. I think he believed that Jews would be too nice. Plus it was probably cheap. He was always getting 'deals.' Like the particle board 'universal storage organizer' that cracked down the middle when he tried to insert the first shelf. Once a complete stranger saw him getting out of our old Buick with the long scratch in the paint. The scratcher, as I think of him, promised to fix it for seventy-five dollars. It came back with some sort of glop over the crack. The glop broke off a week later and the crack was even bigger. My dad never researched any of his 'deals.' He was too busy and too distracted with the universe. How could anything or anyone except my mom compete with the universe? It's not that he didn't toss me a baseball once in while but he'd be thinking of the universe.

"So. Visitor's day at Camp 4-Fun. Have I mentioned that I was eight? My mom smiling rhapsodically as I braid my lanyard, dad thinking about the universe. And in the afternoon we get to my swimming lesson. The swim coach wasn't just that; he was also a hellfire preacher. Those sermons were something; if I ever get to hell I might not like it, but there won't be any surprises. And his approach to swim teaching was religious too: throw 'em in the pool and let God sort 'em out. He looked like the actor James Woods; you could calibrate a carpenter's level on his flat-top. That day—in fact starting with the first lesson—he was screaming at me because I couldn't swim or float on my back. The day's lesson was floating on my back. As usual the reverend was apoplectic, screaming stuff like 'Why can't you relax!' and I'd start taking on water. Not sinking like a rock—call it sinking in a slow stately manner. That is until he screamed 'You're sinking like a rock!' and focused all that hellfire rage in a punch to the stomach that emptied my lungs and pushed me underwater.

"So I'm thrashing to stay afloat and he gets out of the pool. Giving me his high-decibel manhood lecture from the sidelines while I drown." I'll have to write this next part outside the quotation marks because I can't distinguish between how I phrased it for Harvey and what I wrote in journals, confided to Rebecca and Toby, or relived years before in therapy. There are a couple of other beginners holding on to the side of the pool looking terrified, trying not to look at me; no one has the guts to extend a hand. So it's thrash, burst above the waterline; gasp, grab at the water; try and fail to thrash to the side of the pool; watch the water line rise above my eyes; inhale water through my nose and mouth; make climbing motions as I sink; attempt to mime swimming; attempt to punch my way out or fly into the shaky blue; burst into air; try and fail to shout; croak 'help' inaudibly, sink beneath the water line; gag on a tremendous burning snoot-ful of water; rise and fail to draw a breath.

"And there are my parents *still in their lounge chairs.* Mom is smiling. Why is she smiling? It beat the hell out me then but now I know. She's smiling because, one, she believes people should smile, two, people will *like* you if you smile, three, there's an authority figure standing nearby and Mom trusts authority figures, which leads to four: Dad is just sitting there, therefore Mom will just sit there. As for Dad, he's thinking life is dark and dangerous and awful—he'd be diagnosed with depression now—and better get used to it and if you don't save yourself this time who'll save you next time and the coach will dive in when it gets truly bad and okay, back to the universe. Finally some kid gripped the side with one hand and held out the other to me. I wish I could remember his face; I'm certain he saved my life. All I can remember is the coach's face verging toward purple and Mom and Dad *still in their lounge chairs*."

"Wow. Have you been in therapy?"

"Of course. My mother took part in a session, and she tut-tutted all the drowning talk. 'Your swim coach was *right there*. Your father was on the swim team in high school, and he was *right there*.'" And I started yelling at the poor woman. 'You were both right there right *in your lounge chairs!*'"

"I like your mom," Harvey said.

"Everyone likes her. I love her. She's a great mom. But if she's the only one there, don't bother to drown."

"I'd like to try an experiment. Do you think you've got any flying left in you this afternoon?"

I sat up, rubbed my face, positioned myself on my stomach, and launched.

"Attaboy, George. Head for the back fence. Okay, everything you're doing, the flailing, the kicking, the drooling, the protruding tongue, the grunting—is that new?—they have nothing to do with flying. They're about not drowning. The result is you're drowning. You're grabbing at sinking bits of wreckage that you think will keep you afloat. You have to trust that The Invisible won't drop you. So let's start with the tongue. Back in the mouth, behind the teeth, that's it. See? That tongue wasn't doing anything but crampin' your style." I laughed.

"The arms extended forward like Superman's? They might have some slight aerodynamic property but not if you keep slapping at the air. Arms at your sides. There ya go, sleek as a missile. Except the kicking. Not helping, George, and what will Tommy Thorne think?" Harvey had been on the show twice, and he'd been coaching me for my upcoming appearance. "He never outright mocks, but lately when a guest disappoints he'll look very tired, and that boyishness we all love falls away, and you see him thinking *maybe it's time I stepped back.* I mean that literally. The backdrop behind Tommy and the guests is solid darkness—not really, but it appears to be—and all he has to do to disappear is take one step back. Not really, but it's a nice image. You want to be responsible for that? I like him. He's a nice man, as far as anyone can tell."

He released a long shrill burst on his whistle. "George. You're wasting energy. *Stop kicking.*" He employed both arms as a vice around my shins, and next thing I knew I was reenacting the Patty Duke mad scene from *The Miracle Worker* on my lawn—a frightened frustrated Helen Keller flinging dishes, writhing out of her tutor's grip, throwing punches and mashed potatoes. Only the punches in that description were non-metaphorical, and one caught Harvey on the jaw.

"I'm sorry. Are you okay? I'll get the first aid kit from the house."

He was probing the jaw with his fingers, making yawning

motions with his mouth. "Never mind that." He tilted his turban back Stetson style and assessed me coldly. "Is this all you want to be? You've been handed a miracle, George, and it requires a towering heart."

"I'm working on it."

"I think we'll have to deal with a second fear. You take pride in your rationality, and—I think you're afraid of your miracle. What if Moses was afraid to part the Red Sea? What if he deployed his sea-parting talent George Entmen style—in his bubble bath, for instance, watching dinky waves push around a rubber duck? . . . Let's try one more experiment. Could you find that Hula-Hoop Rebecca used to test your flying?"

I was glad to get away from him for a minute. The hoop was leaning against the washing machine in the basement, where our cat Claude liked to keep an eye on it. I think he was a little afraid of it but he held his ground: *If you think you can take me, Hoop, let's do this thing.*

"Sorry," I said to Claude as I picked up his archenemy. It occurs to me that except for a passing reference in the first chapter I haven't mentioned our cat. He was old—though his fur, black with white paws, stomach, and snout, remained glossy— and I was taking away one of the few things he still did for fun. He didn't enjoy chasing Max or being chased anymore, and as soon as he hid in his grocery box in the living room he wanted to be hiding in his other grocery box in the kitchen. He gave me a sad suffering look that I took to mean *You think it's easy being a cat? Wait till your turn comes.* "Really sorry, buddy. Hasn't been an easy day for me either. Camp 4-Fun, you know? Did anyone ever tell you that you have a calming presence? You do. Sad but calm. Stoic dignity. I know you're mad at me, buddy, but if I was

drowning *you'd* save me. You'd alert the authorities, like Lassie."
He gave me a look that I took to mean *Just get the fuck out.*

I brought the hoop outside to Harvey. "Sorry about before,"
he said, setting the bottom edge on the lawn. "It's not like anyone
else is flying *better.*"

"Or at all," I corrected. "Look. I've taught most of my life, and
I understand how frustrating this assignment must be for you.
Just bear in mind that I hold the altitude, speed, distance, and
gracefulness records for unassisted human flight. The dignity
record, too, regardless of what you and Tommy Thorne might
think."

"Sorry I was such an asshole. I thought the drill sergeant
approach might work. What I'd like you to do now, champ, is fly
through this hoop without touching it. You can't do it if you're
squirming around. All right? Olé!"

I positioned myself on my stomach and launched, arms at my
sides, legs still, tongue behind my teeth. Not a single grass blade
registered my passing. I floated out the portal, effortless as a blos-
som on a slow current.

"Lookin' good! Keep going! Think you could fly a little
higher? That's okay, you're doing fine. Can you speed it up? Don't
worry about it, not a problem. Oh. Race that fly to the back fence.
Never mind, he's already there. What could be more serene—a
guy out flying on his lawn on a sunny Sunday morning. What
could be more American? Uh-oh. You're kicking a little bit. Regular breathing, feel the sun on your neck. Good. I suppose flying
without the tics is scary—like working without a net. I know
you want to start fidgeting, making those twitchy 'course correc-
tions' that correct nothing." He repositioned the hoop. "Let's try
another pass. That's it," he said as I flew out. "Stay just like that.

You make this new flying look easy. Maybe you'll at least be able to fly farther now. You're tightening up. Relax."

I suppose it was "relax" that did it. The old fear spread through me like a vibration, the lawn and sky spinning (though Harvey told me afterward that I myself wasn't spinning). I clawed at the air, batted the hoop away, and dropped to the lawn panting. "It was worth trying, anyway," I said.

"I wouldn't call our experiment a failure. For one thing we proved that you're not flying. Can you describe what you were feeling when you floated out of the hoop?"

"I was . . . no. I can't. Wait a minute, what do you mean I'm not flying?"

"Have you considered the possibility that your will has nothing to do with it? That you're not flying, *you're being flown*?" He checked his watch. "Let's explore this next time."

NINE

The enormous head of Tommy Thorne loomed out of the darkness. People assure me the head is proportionate to the body, perhaps even a bit on the small side, but it loomed like a hovering lead balloon. Like many heads of aging celebrities—caricatured, analyzed, photographed, and intently observed for a lifetime—it had become hyperbolized, its droopy features magnified as if by the sculptors of Easter Island or a close-up that never drew back.

Black curtains surrounding the table generated darkness and swaddling quietude; black camera lenses peeped through the folds. Not one for chit-chat, Tommy asked me to pronounce my name then focused, in the seconds before airtime, on a patch of nothing just to my left. I imagined the space inside that head as a cavernous blackness, its silence broken only by the whispers (which I couldn't hear) of his flesh-colored earpiece.

"Okay," he said, "let's roll tape." The segment began when after three or four run-throughs of the introduction he delivered it with the required polish. "George Entmen is a professor of English at Northwestern University. He is one of the most esteemed practitioners of hermeneutics, the study of how a *text* generates *meaning*. But Professor Entmen has an even rarer dis-

175

tinction. If a growing host of distinguished physicists, engineers, debunkers, and magicians is to be believed, George Entmen . . ." He paused out of a sense of drama and perhaps embarrassment. ". . . can fly." Appending, deadpan, "At a height of several inches." I thought I saw a series of microexpressions fight for possession of that facial acreage—solemnity at a possible milestone in human evolution; resentment of a guest who probably should have been on some chair-busting tabloid show; a flick of a shamefaced smile from a man who knew Nobel laureates not only by their first names but their nicknames.

The famous boyish enthusiasm revved up, and I flinched as he leaned across the table. "Professor Entmen. George. We've been in touch with the experts you cite. And this morning you flew, as you call it, for our own experts. If you're doing a trick nobody knows how you do it. *And yet.* Scientists always tell me that extraordinary claims—especially of the paranormal— demand extraordinary evidence. But your problem is more than that. Even among paranormal claims there's one category that people—well, grown-ups—resist with all their might, and even if we were somehow convinced we'd never admit it. We deny these things with the same intensity we believed in them as kids. When they were torn away from us they left a residue of hardness and cynicism that the most cynical among us call 'being an adult.'" I fought an impulse to flee as the megalithic head leaned even closer. "I mean, suppose I said I was Santa Claus. I can produce the magic sleigh and the magic reindeer. I'm timed climbing down all the chimneys in the world in five hours. The documentation is all there. And yet, *could you ever bring yourself to say Tommy Thorne is Santa Claus?*"

I'd been up most of the night anticipating questions, but I'd never thought of that one. The next day an assistant producer would phone to thank me for my appearance and to apologize profusely for the events I'm about to describe. She let slip that a head cold and a powerful antihistamine had Tommy "a bit off his game."

I could feel my sweat-soaked underwear constrict as I tried to frame an answer. Sometimes there's nothing to do but open your mouth and see what comes out. "I'll bet at least one hedge fund crook came into being when Santa's beard peeled off in his hand . . . But if people don't want to believe I can fly, I don't blame them. If it were someone else who claimed to fly, and not me, and I were home watching him on *Tommy Thorne*, I'm sure I'd be snorting and shaking my head and asking my wife to change the channel. I'm not trying to win converts. Well . . . I suppose I am. At first I just wanted to entertain my wife and son, and when they got bored with it I would have been content to stop. But cell phone videos have been making the rounds; and besides, I don't think I have the right to keep this to myself. A physicist said unassisted human flight changes everything we thought we knew about the universe. That's just as true with my limited capability as it would be if I flew a mile high."

"That's another thing. Your limited capability. What is it—three inches?"

"Very often four," I said defensively.

"Our next guest, he'll join us in a few minutes, calls it 'the micromiraculous.' He thinks you're hoping people will be more easily convinced if it's not that much of a miracle—if it's practically, but not *quite*, just a man crawling on the floor. Nothing to differentiate it but a sliver of light between the man and the floor. Are you hoping that when you demonstrate your ability in a few minutes, people will believe it because why would anyone go to the trouble of faking *that?*"

"Again, Tommy, if I were someone else and not the man who has this talent, and I were home watching that guy on *Tommy Thorne*, I'd ask that very question. But actually I'm doing everything I can to fly better. I work out two hours at the gym every day and practice on my lawn for two hours. I work with a"—I nearly said guru— "trainer. Anyway, reality as we know it is just as screwed at three inches."

"Let me ask an even more basic question. Is this a trick?"

"It's not a trick. It's flying." My press conference with Nelson—when I'd be forced to recant—would be in two weeks. In the meantime I hoped to convince people of the miracle. Why would I work to convince people of one thing now and of the opposite in two weeks? Wouldn't I be a laughingstock when it all played out, my professional reputation totaled? My hope, I guess, is that once people saw the miracle, not even the press conference could convince them they hadn't. Or that even if nearly everyone were finally disabused, believers would remain. Perhaps the ability to keep believing would itself require a superpower— accessible only to some corps of the credulous, a super league of saps. But I wanted to believe they'd be out there.

. . .

The next segment—the demonstration and especially the counterdemonstration—required more space than the Tommy Thorne Studio afforded. Tommy and I rode the elevator to another floor of his building where the Berman Business Network was lending us one of its studios. I don't know why we didn't tape the whole thing there. Perhaps he'd needed the intimacy of the Tommy Thorne Studio to look me in the eye and know if I was lying, the darkness playing bad cop. I wanted to ask, but he was watching the floor numbers, lost in thought. I imagined the earpiece whispering, *"You're a man on an elevator, lost in thought."*

We were accompanied by hypergelled magician and abusive boyfriend, Ricardo Dean. Ricardo's participation was distasteful but it wasn't an ambush. I'd been told when my appearance was arranged that he would watch my interview from the green room, then demonstrate some Vegasy "reverse-engineered" version. I wasn't worried about being upstaged, confident that the size, smarm, and spectacle of his performance would brand it for what it was—a miracle with a drumroll.

He too was watching the numbers. Up close his mustache seemed to have bubbled out of an oil slick. "You look very relaxed," I observed. "I guess punching Iris in the face will do that."

He smirked, eyes still on the numbers. "Killed anyone else lately?"

Tommy reluctantly intervened. "The elevators in this building are being converted to the new MULTI system. Ropeless." We'd arrived.

.   .   .

That morning, before the interview, I'd been frisked, stripped, politely and apologetically cavity searched, bleeped and blipped at by enigmatic devices, and scanned with a portable ultrasound. I'd been closely observed since then, but I submitted to a patdown before the demonstration. The scrutiny to which Ricardo Dean and his team would submit had been the subject of grueling negotiations—limits were placed on searches, on the distance of cameras and observers, on how much of their preparations could be observed at all. The Tommy Thorne people pointed out for the final time that with so little transparency Ricardo would hardly be able to make the case for a reverse-engineered miracle. He gave a whatever-ish shrug. "I have to protect my work," he insisted. "The time, the expense, the trade secrets, and don't forget the kids—their sense of wonder. If anyone thinks they see a trick, let's see them reverse-engineer it. I don't want to get into the weeds of theology here, but the only part of a miracle that matters is the wow. I can promise you that. Wow in caps."

While Ricardo and his team went off to manufacture the wow, I lay on my stomach on the studio floor. They'd put me in a black unitard to contrast with the white floor. The desks and other furniture had been taken out and additional lighting wheeled in. Supplementing the usual cameras, a man with a hand-held squatted in front of me. He did a couple of deep knee-bends and practiced squat-walking backwards.

Tommy had decided against giving an introduction. "I don't want to be a ringmaster," he said before the tape rolled. "Let's give this as much dignity as we can."

The man with the handheld gave me a nod; I rose up two, three, four inches and set out for the exit sign fifteen feet away. Don't kick, I reminded myself. Arms at your sides. Sleek as a rocket. Tongue securely behind the teeth. No mumbling. Drool contained. Dignity. No thrashing—nobody's drowning today.

The cameramen looked up from their lenses; no one had ever had a clearer view of the miracle. The handheld guy—a short round man with a crew cut and morning-after stubble—peeked over the top of his camera, bug-eyed. It was my proudest moment of flying.

Soon I was short of breath. Something was off—something about the air, as if I'd flown into a low-pressure front. It felt like only kicking and thrashing could restore my equilibrium, but I clenched my teeth and tried to concentrate all the tension there. I was nearly at the halfway point when something exploded near the back of my head and an elephantine downdraft smacked my face into the floor. I shook it off and kept going. I looked up: Two feet above, a supersonic blur in gold lamé buzzed me with another Jehovah sonic boom. I dropped to the floor and tried to get my breath. The handheld guy was on his back trying to aim the lens, turning his head spasmodically left and right. On the next pass Ricardo dived from the ceiling—twenty feet up!— braked at two feet, grabbed me by the hair, and pulled my face along the polished floor. "You looked tired, George. Thought you might need a tow."

.   .   .

"I want this on the record," Tommy said when tape was rolling again and the three of us were seated on stools. "I want you to know, George, that I and every member of the crew will testify to the assault we just witnessed."

Ricardo looked as smug as ever. If invulnerability to shame qualified, the man was a superhero.

"Nothing's been injured but my dignity," I said to Tommy. "And I still think I won on dignity compared to—" I tilted my chin at Ricardo, who'd donned a red superhero cape to go with the gold lamé tights.

Ricardo smiled liked God's gold-plated baby. "The first dog-fight in the history of unassisted human flight, and you lost. But you're handling it well. The great air aces of World War I couldn't have taken it more stoically, especially the floor polishing. You're a real sport." I wasn't going to let him provoke me. Just sit back and let his dickishness shine.

"Speaking of unassisted," Tommy said. "Ricardo, your demonstration was amazing, but it's widely known that much of your act is accomplished with black budget gear from DARPA, the pentagon's cutting-edge research agency. Your detractors say you're little more than their test monkey, but no doubt a magician helps them find novel applications for the stuff. I think most of our audience realize that if you were truly flying at the speed of sound, you'd have burned to a cinder. The crew thinks you've got woofers on you for the boom."

I said, "Tell me, Ricardo: how was your demonstration a reverse-engineering of something I can do without tech? You might as well say that anyone who flies in an airplane is debunking me."

"Can you reverse engineer what *I* did?" Ricardo said irritably. "Then shut up. Tommy, admit it. Even if what he's doing is a miracle, who would you rather watch for an hour?"

Tommy thought about it. "Okay, you have a point. I believe that what George does is a miracle. And yet, you said you'd deliver wow in caps and you did. It was spectacular! And it reminded me of something Arthur C. Clarke said: 'Any sufficiently advanced technology is indistinguishable from magic.' Sorry, George. It's just that you're not the first one to come to us with a negligible miracle. These people don't get on the show because who'd watch? Who wants to watch a bowler who knows before she releases the ball which pins she'll knock down? Verified by Stephen Hawking himself."

"Wait. You're talking about my neighbor Mrs. Housebender? She says she—"

"Actually we've turned down dozens of people who work that particular miracle. I suppose we could put them all together for a panel, but why? Your neighbor might reduce all physics to smithereens, but who'd be watching? Did you know there's a magician who can pull a rabbit out of a hat for real? What's his name, Ricardo?"

"Clarence Fonderbine."

"Clarence has just as much claim to a miracle as you do, George. The problem is, it looks exactly like a magician pulling a rabbit out of a hat. No difference except metaphysical. Neil deGrasse Tyson vouches for him. Nobody cares. Clarence suffers for his miracle—covered with bites, some infected, rabbit droppings all over the house. He can't make the rabbits *dis*appear. And meanwhile, as far as most of us can tell, reality as we know it goes rolling on. Luckily most of these people don't have a patron with as much clout at PBS as Wendy Baim." I guess that had been rankling him the whole time.

TEN

My appearance on *Tommy Thorne* generated exactly one piece of fan mail. It read:

Dear George,

Are you some kind of Jew? My husband Judd thinks probably not because you don't have a Jew first name. He says the Jew names are Myron, Shlomo, Jacob, Saul, Bernie, Izzy, Isaac, Irving, Moses, Stan, Norm, and Lenny. I said but what about his last name? He said Entmen sounds like the people who make the little cakes. I said George reminds me of a cute little flying Jew cupcake, and I think Judd got jealous. Married forty-five years, and still jealous.

My point is this, we love people of all religions. Christians, Buddhists, Catholics, Muslims, Hari Krishnas, Zorros, all the Jews, Greek Orthodox, and the people who built the Baha'i Temple, namely the Baha'is.

On Fox News they showed you flying on Tommy Thorne, and I said to Judd, "I bet you could do that."

He said that if he flew at all he'd fly *better*. Please don't take that the wrong way. Being an intellectual and a Jew and so forth, you have your own way of doing things. Judd is a big man, and it just seems logical that he'd fly *bigger*.

And that brings me to why I'm writing this letter. Judd worked hard his whole life, but he don't have enough money to retire. We used to have a small farm but we had to sell it. We still live in the house because we want to leave it for the kids. Somebody said we could get a reverse mortgage, but Judd heard you have to let Ed McMahon live in your house. And I said you ninny, he's dead. And you want to hear the sad part? Now that the paint store closed, he don't have nothing to retire *from*.

What I'm trying to say is this. Could you please teach Judd to fly? He looks like a big lunkhead but when he needs to learn something he learns it. If he needed to learn Herman Nutics to fly, he'd be your best student. Instead of sitting around the house feeling sad, he could save people. He could fly people out the window of a burning house, he's very brave! Maybe some nice woman in the Ukraine wishes she could visit the grandkids here in Blane, Missouri (our neighbors!), but she can't afford it? Judd could whisk her here at the speed of sound. Plus, he could make millions putting on a network show for the kids. Plus endorsements! And he'd give you half!

I hope this letter finds you well, and please say hi to your wife and little son for us. Even if you can't see your way to helping Judd, please stop by and visit any time. There's a slice of pecan pie waiting for each of you. And even if you only fly four inches now, you'll bounce off the ceiling when you taste my pecan pie!

God Bless You,

Cathy Toms

PS

Judd says hi.

The day it arrived, Toby and my teaching assistant Jeff had dropped over in the hope of watching me flop around on the lawn. Harvey Bell, sitting in a lotus position beside me on the grass, handed the letter to Toby. "Note the penmanship," Harvey said pushing back his turban with a thumb. "A perfect copy of the Kittle Method chart on the classroom wall. Death threats and Kittle perfection—that's the mail you flag first." We took this seriously—he'd been a "guru to the stars."

Jeff sat down on the lawn. For the sake of his narrow-lapeled Rat Pack suit, Toby pulled up a lawn chair. "She loves the Zorros," he said when he'd finished, handing the letter to Jeff. "She's good people."

"That can't possibly be the only response," Harvey said. "Have you checked your social media?"

Jeff muttered, "Uh oh." He was my best student and he never came to class drunk. But his beer patina had become as permanent as his blonde hair and the slightly damp blue eyes women thought sensitive.

I tried to force eye contact. "Jeff? What are you hiding?" A year ago I'd told him that I thought social media were a waste of time, that I'd been stampeded into thinking they were as necessary as breathing, that the only reason I didn't quit them was that getting out was much more of a bother than keeping the accounts and never using them. He'd looked at me with such horror that I turned it all over to him—Facebook, Twitter, LinkedIn, Instagram. "If something important turns up," I'd conceded, "let me know."

I took out my smartphone and went to Facebook. Jeff had written me a new bio, which I read out loud. "'Professor of English and James Lydecker Chair of Hermeneutics at Northwestern University, Twine Award winner for best work of theory-based criticism, and *lord of the fuckin' sky!* Bow down to me, nudniks, for I am the reincarnation of Quetzalcoatl, the winged Aztec god. Married, one child.'"

I laughed. "Is that what your ominous 'uh-oh!' was about? I'm honored to be lord of the fuckin' sky. I'll have cards printed."

He drew a breath, opened his mouth, closed it, drew another breath.

"Jeff?"

"Okay . . . no? Rebecca made us promise not to tell you what's happening on Twitter."

Toby snatched the phone out of my hand. "You know what? Let the social media do its thing in its universe and you do your thing in yours. There's never been a better example of what you don't know can't hurt you. Think of all the teenage suicides who'd still be with us if they could stop checking Twitter to see what the bullies are posting now."

"Think of all the bullied teenagers who don't get around to committing suicide," I said, "because they have to keep checking Twitter to see what the bullies are posting now. Sorry. Just trying to see the bright side."

"Should I continue?" Toby asked irritably. He hated to be interrupted in mid-holding-forth.

"Please."

"The experience of a true Twitter-swarm must be close to that horror story we loved when we were kids. There's this organization, remember, that recruits millions of people to wish the latest person of its choosing dead. Just wish. Your enemies can engage their services. Their representative—a very polite man in a Brooks Brothers suit—shows up at your door one day and tells you that those millions of people are wishing you dead as he speaks. And knowing, you die. Supposedly that's the basis for voodoo. So be careful what you know."

"Millions of people wish me dead?"

"Mostly no, as of now. I'd say 300,000 wish you dead, two or three million hate you, and another eight million haven't yet put a name to that roiling in their gut every time they see your face. Look. I think your fear of publicity is at least partly the dread of something like this. You pretend to be your own man, impervious to the opinions of the crowd, but *come on.*"

"Why do they hate me?"

Toby looked for guidance to Jeff, who shrugged.

"All sorts of reasons," Toby said. "There are the religious zealots, of course. They think you're blaspheming the very idea of miracles. There are the people who think God had intended a powerful zooming-through-the-stratosphere miracle but you were too much of an impotent little putz to carry it off. There are people who might be part of that last group, it's hard to be sure, I don't get their point, but they think you're 'cock-blocking God.' There's a small but growing faction, no doubt the work of our colleague Blaustein, who think you killed Preston. There's a bunch—mostly thirteen-year-old boys, I think—who will never regain their sense of wonder because they think they saw your wires. There are the people who intuitively know you're vulnerable on the small man theme: Lots of obscenities with the formula 'little this, micro that,' and of course the inescapable 'ass pimple.' I haven't seen you turn that shade of red since grammar school. Should I stop? No? Most of the people who don't quite hate you yet find you creepy or pathetic. Plus a bunch of marriage proposals if that's a consolation. Oh, remember the magician Tommy Thorne mentioned who can pull a rabbit out of a hat for real? He wants to know if you have an agent."

"And you're saying that none of this can hurt me if I ignore it? That it's all off in its own parallel universe?"

"Let's put it this way. For now at least your Twitter is roiling but it hasn't reached critical mass. Twitter *seems* to be its own world—Digitalia, with its own strange catastrophic weather and weird excitements. And it's true that mobs of trolls haven't turned up on your doorstep to beat you up. But imagine your Twitter is a giant laundry bag filled with angry cats. If you find the sack convulsing on the sidewalk do you open it to see what's going on? No. A smart guy would call animal control and keep walking. The cats are in a *sack*, after all, no interaction with the world outside. But what if it's a sack of a *half billion* angry cats? It's not going to just lie there. Its bounces and writhings and rolls can destroy neighborhoods and entire medium-size towns. It can reach the point where the ticked-off cats, albeit sealed in a bag, are reshaping the extrabag world. Keep your head down."

. . .

Soon afterward I was the most famous man in the world. I'd dreaded fame as an invasion force landing on our lawn: microphones and TV cameras flailing like clubs, sobbing moms holding babies aloft, church groups singing "Michael Row the Boat Ashore," television lights blazing through our shades as if the caves of sleep had been converted to all-night discos.

But my fame arrived not as a torrent but the unending plink! of droplets. So quietly I can't quite say when it began. I learned that by the time I appeared on *Tommy Thorne* everyone had already heard of me, they just didn't want to talk about it. Strangers passed me with that curt nod that says yeah, you. Reporters showed up at our door not by the hundreds but by grudging ones. They said, "All right, let's see it," as if I were the sad uncle at Thanksgiving dinner who must be allowed to show you his rash. They nodded after my flying demonstrations, said they'd be in touch, and waited, at least the "serious outlets" did, to see what their competitors would do. And so I was vaguely familiar to readers of *The New York Times* but on inescapable first-name terms with readers of *The Holiday Shopper* and center stage in the hallucinations of readers of the *Weekly World News*. The actual news that the laws of physics were smithereens and that the next stage of human evolution was being prophesied three inches above my carpet—this was consigned to the "lighter side" segment at the end of newscasts. If it was the local news, they'd joke about it with the weather forecaster.

By now even the experts who'd confirmed my ability didn't want to talk about it. The seminal works they'd planned—"This will change the course of . . .!"—were abandoned. It's not that they'd changed their minds, not even that anyone challenged their findings. It's that my squalid little miracle was beneath their dignity, and they were sick of being mocked by colleagues with their arms extended forward in that damn Superman pose, the wits leaning from side to side to indicate the buffeting of wind.

ELEVEN

"I don't think you're flying," Harvey Bell had said at a recent lesson, "I think you're being flown." And with that remark he'd checked his watch and left.

At subsequent lessons I pressed him on what he'd meant. Was it one of those deep guru aphorisms I'd learned to disregard, or did he believe that some trans-dimensional toddler was picking me up and putting me down like a Tonka Toy? And why did I only happen to fly when I thought I was engaged in the exhausting physical activity of flying?

He reminded me that the exhausting part of flying was the tics—kicking, drooling, flailing, and so forth, all manifestations of my fear of drowning. We'd established that none of these contributed to getting me off the ground or keeping me there. And I couldn't spell out what I *did* to fly—what muscles, rules, skills, instincts, thoughts, or feelings I employed.

Harvey seemed reluctant to tell me who or what he thought the pilot was. "For now," he said one afternoon in my living room, "let's concentrate on that dream you had just before you flew for the first time. I'm interested in the vague blur that was sitting in that armchair." We both looked at the empty chair.

"We don't want to draw any conclusions just yet, but consider the blur a suspect. For now let's see if you can get to know it a little better." Standing over me while I sat on the couch, he took off his watch and used the inside face to beam sunlight from the bay windows at me. "You know what else I've been wondering, George? Suppose you were driving a long featureless highway. You see an intense bright point on the horizon. You can't look away, you want to go on gazing at it, you want to go on looking no matter how tired . . . how sleepy . . . and you drive right inside it. Imagine being inside that bright . . . bright . . . point, and now you're back in your dream."

"This is very entertaining, but I'm not suggestible enough for hypnotism. And I can't be compelled by shiny things. I'm not a cat, Harvey. Harvey?"

I was still in the living room but no longer on the couch; I found myself in the beanbag chair. Harvey was gone, replaced by the Rebecca, Max, and Toby of my old dream. They looked like the real thing, but they just had that aura. It was unsettling to see them through a hypnosis-induced fabrication of a dream. Hypnosis is not, as you might believe, a "waking dream." This hybrid state was making me queasy.

Rebecca looked around, as if she too had been transported from somewhere else. She gave her bob a shake and let it set-tle back in place, but I was still there. She smiled at me and shrugged. Next to her on the couch Max was lazily swooping his blue Lego jetliner through the air. Toby was in one of the two armchairs next to the coffee table, tapping his shoe on the carpet, waiting for something to happen. He was wearing his perennial narrow-lapeled Rat Pack suit minus the last several months of heavy wear.

"Do you see it?" asked the voice of Harvey Bell. "Take a minute to study it."

I forced myself to look. It occupied the second armchair. Its outlines were blurry, naturally, but it was about five-feet long and two-feet wide. Inside the outlines it was filled with floating shimmers and glints and vague stillborn proto-shapes. Was it a living thing or some sort of portal?

"Do you see that thing in the armchair?" I asked Rebecca.

"What a cruel thing to say about Toby. Though I do wish he'd change his suit once in a while."

"Very funny. You do see that dingus there?"

"I'd rather not discuss it just now," she whispered.

"Are you afraid of it?"

"Can we discuss this *later*," she said out the side of her mouth.

"Toby, the distinguished whatchamacallit is two feet away from you."

He folded his arms. "And your point is what?"

"Any opinion?"

"The most tedious thing about being a professor in the humanities is that people are always expecting you to have an opinion. Things will tootle along perfectly well without our opinions attached."

"So you're afraid, too. Come on. What do you think it is?"

"It's *your* dream, George. Why are you asking me? To paraphrase what they used to say about Sinatra, it's George's dream and the rest of us just live in it. But all right, here's a theory. You're not looking at the thing itself—no one could bear it. I think it's some sort of Vaseline shot. Rebecca knows what I'm talking about. As Doris Day got older, the cameramen wanted to hide her wrinkles. So for close-ups they rubbed Vaseline on the lens. With each succeeding film a bigger schmear. By With Six You Get Eggroll things got really gloppy. Waterlogged blobs of rotting light deliquesce in the air around her face. Now our friend here"— his eyes darted to the left— "has been around, they say, since before time began. That's a lot of glop."

Maybe the vaunted wisdom of children worked in dreams. "Max, buddy, what do you think of that thing there?"

"Vroom!" he said concentrating on his plane.

"Harvey?" I called out. "I'm going to see if there's any change in these pockets. I wonder if I could toss a quarter into the blur."

"Never mind that, it could be dangerous. I want you to make contact. Talk to it."

"Hi," I said to it. "We're being terrible hosts. Can I get you anything?"

The blur shivered as if rippled by a breeze.

It felt like the most miserable party ever was being held in the vacuum of space. I looked imploringly to Rebecca. *Help*, I mouthed.

She turned her palms up in a rare display of helplessness.

I put my hand behind my neck: code to Rebecca to use her charm.

She turned to the thing and flashed a smile so vast and bright she squinted. "I like your lights. Are they alive?"

TWELVE

Not writing this next part can't make it not happen. Typing slowly, I keep reminding myself, won't slow it down—*it's already happened*. Okay. Here we go.

Iris phoned, speaking with the amped-up twangy cheeriness that was always bad news. "You guys gonna come see me disappear Friday night at Club Blasé?" She sometimes filled in for Ricardo's assistant.

After the usual it's-your-life boilerplate, I said, "Why are you still *with* that guy? Make *him* disappear."

"Funny you should say that. My mom passed along a vanishing spell she got from her 'advisor.' It just made Ricardo even more *there*."

"Maybe if you weren't living with him he'd—"

"Think of him as the wallpaper in the sentence 'Either that wallpaper goes or I do.'"

"If you're implying you're about to leave him, I'll be glad to go with you when you pick up your things."

"Did you know, George, that contrary to popular lore, the line about wallpaper was *not* Oscar Wilde's last words?"

"Yes I did. Are you leaving Ricardo?"

"And the actual remark about wallpaper, which he made weeks before his death, was—"

"I know all that. Why are you being so evasive about Ricardo? Tell me something. Anything."

"All right. I won't let him slide this time—not on all the hair gunk in the world, and believe me, it's on his head."

. . .

Who cares that Ricardo was chained up and tied in a bag and seconds later strolled in through the fire door? Or that the pigeon in the box was now a pit bull, that the card in the woman's cleavage was now the pigeon, that the cat was where the dog was, and the dog was where the cat was? Of course I despised Ricardo (stink-eying him from the closest table and chewing the ice in my drink as loudly as I could until Rebecca elbowed me), but that's not what had wrecked magic for me. "Eroded" is more accurate. I'd seen too many magic acts, that's all. Eventually you still don't know how they do it, just that when the dog and the cat and the card and the pigeon and Ricardo disappear, they're smuggled someplace else for a bit and then they're smuggled back. Who cares?

A word on someplace else. I believe it was Yogi Berra who said, "Everything in the world is either someplace or someplace else." There's nothing magical about this someplace else; I suspect that in Ricardo's act it was often a tight space reeking of animal shit. I looked the pigeon in the eye. It gave no sign of having been reassembled from the void. *(Obviously, I'm trying not to arrive where I'm heading, practically grabbing at trees and lamp posts.)* In those last calm moments at Club Blasé I was woolgathering: why, in an age when rabbits are conjured from hats for real, and your neighbor might be flying in his backyard, and the laws of physics are suggestions at best, should the sense of wonder shrivel to a mote? I wished there were no someplace else; I wanted things to disappear for real. My worst wish ever, and it would be granted.

Iris was a capable assistant, except for the flailing. When Ricardo addressed the audience she illustrated with a lot of arm-sweeping "indicating." Her gestures grew broader as the act went on. This was her passive-aggressive revenge, I supposed, and it was beginning to get laughs. Ricardo's annoyance was clamped in his smile, which only provoked her to giddier heights of spokesmodeling. She went beyond the operatic and the semaphoric, to what I can only describe as Vanna White in flames.

At the end of the trick where a man and a woman from the audience disappear then reappear a second later in each other's clothes, Ricardo grabbed Iris's arm just short of "indicating" his nose. She winced as he tightened his grip and whispered something in her ear.

He turned to the audience. "How about it, folks? Would you like to see my lovely assistant disappear? I would!" The exertions of his eyebrows and mustache couldn't force a single laugh or clap.

"I can't wait," Iris said. "Vanish me outta here and send along my stuff!" The audience laughed and applauded. She spread her arms wide, bent her knee in a tiny curtsy, and—a true rarity— smiled. She gave him a peck on the cheek. Their fight, I was thinking, was fake. No wonder I couldn't get a straight answer on her plans for leaving him.

"Plucky, isn't she? She'll give nonexistence the fight of its life." Ricardo tilted a black box toward the audience and called for a volunteer to inspect it. A nervous man in a corduroy jacket—why do I remember he sold dental supplies?— climbed in and verified there was no sliding panel in the box. After helping him out Ricardo moved the box aside; the nervous dental salesman, on all fours, confirmed there was no trapdoor beneath it. "You're sure?" Ricardo asked him. "Feel around." "No," the salesman reported. "I mean, yes, I'm sure." On his own initiative he began knocking on the floor. "The staid music of the respectably solid," Ricardo orated. "Not really. Of *course* it's hollow—we're on a stage, remember? But no trapdoors, right?" "Right!"

Ricardo slid the box back in place, shook the salesman's hand, and let him return to the friends flashing thumbs-up near the back.

Ricardo took Iris's hand to help her into the box. She let go of him for a moment, still smiling, and waved to the audience.

I wish I'd had my smartphone out to record my final look at Iris Ransler, master of the Southern Gothic-comic-tragic-tragi-comic novel, beloved daughter, sister, professor, friend. She looked good, a long-legged girl in gold-spangled tights, net stockings, and long white gloves. It was easy to forget she was pretty, which was how she wanted it. She never wore makeup, not even for the act, her dishwater hair had been left for dead long ago, and at times she seemed to be sinking behind her water-gray eyes. Ricardo once told her that he'd chosen her for her pallor, "the perfect Poe-like glamour for the theater of the uncanny."

But I don't need a smartphone to recall that smile. It crinkled her eyes and, lacking the full set of muscles of a practiced smile, strained to keep tugging itself over a bright expanse of teeth. It seemed a bit self-conscious, like any creature that lives mostly in the dark. I wondered, not for the first time, how sad she was. The smile was just as ambiguous as her usual deadpan. You could never be sure whether she was telling a joke, or pouring her heart out in the format of a joke, or ripping out every one of her vital organs in the pretense a joke—just to see if you were cruel enough to laugh. In every case you laughed.

Once at a barbecue in my yard Max fell down and started crying. I hugged him: "Everything's okay, I'm here." "I wish," Iris said, "somebody would say that to *me*."

.   .   .

Technically it wasn't my last look. Every time Ricardo was about to close the lid she got laughs by raising herself for instantaneous Whac-A-Mole peeks over the top. Then just from the forehead up. Then the quietly blonde top of her head. When none of her was showing, Ricardo looked down in the box. "We don't have to do the trick," he sulked. "Is that what you'd like?" ("Is this part of the act?" Rebecca whispered. I turned my palms up.) Her hand came up in a final wave, energetically scouring the air—there. My last glimpse—and as soon as it went down he slammed the lid. It made a booming chunk! as it shut.

Once an audience volunteer had verified that the lid was locked, Ricardo gave us a crash course in the physics of vanishing. "Here's what's going to happen. My spell will deagulate all the molecules—indeed the atoms—of Iris's body. Mind and soul will disperse as well. She'll escape as a subatomic mist moving through and between the box's atoms, spreading in all directions throughout the universe. So don't feel sad when I open the box and you don't see Iris. In a sense she'll still be there. Why, you might get the feeling she's sitting next to you. She will be. But she'll also be at the Skylark Bar at Halsted and Cermak. She'll be everyplace simultaneously. Skokie, Tinley Park, Bangkok, Alpha Centauri—you get the idea. Bratislava? Yes, among everyplace. Oh, and that blinking red dot you half-saw in the night sky for an instant and can't find again and you wonder if was just a defect in your eye? She'll be there. No one could be less gone. And minutes later, after I cast the counter-spell, she'll be back in the box. And now, the spell."

While he chanted syllables in a made-up language—"Woonga-bazoonga!" recurred among more Latinate sounds—Rebecca whispered, "This trick stinks." It was true. He'd been slick and masterful in the earlier illusions, but now, for the finale, he might as well have been Nelson Baim blundering through the ring trick. The whole thing seemed lazy, and Ricardo seemed to have lost interest. Maybe they'd been fighting after all and it was getting to him. His tuxedo jacket was missing a button, tortured filaments coiled out of his mustache, and his eyes, gazing into an infinity that would soon be filled with Iris, were bloodshot. It was strange to be feeling sympathy, if not empathy, for Ricardo Dean. I hoped that when he got to hell he'd be handed one ice cube.

"Are there any questions about the deagulation process?" Why was he killing time?

I asked about the various escape routes he'd seemed to leave open for Iris. "Great question, George. One I anticipated." He gave a loud clap and a stagehand came out with an electric drill. Ricardo looked at the box: "Hunker down, baby." The stagehand drilled a hole in the lid and screwed a hook into the hole. Ricardo clapped again and a second hook descended at the end of a cable. The stagehand connected it to the hook on the box and the box was winched four feet off the ground. "Escape routes closed."

She'd already had plenty of time to escape but I decided to let the sorrowful asshole get through his trick. I thought the lack of further questions meant everyone else had made the same decision. But then the inevitable whiz kid raised his hand: "How could she reach Alpha Centauri so fast? It would take the mist, traveling at the speed of light, like, four years."

"I dunno. Space warp," Ricardo mumbled rubbing his face. "Have you vanished from this mortal plane and dispersed throughout the universe yet?" he asked toward the box.

"I'm workin' on it, sweetie. Gimme a minute." It was the last thing she'd ever say.

"Exactly one minute," he said looking down at his watch. "Don't worry, folks. People who've deagulated say there's no pain involved."

I won't milk the countdown. At the end he ordered the box set down, unlocked it, raised the lid. He was too miserable, I thought, to convincingly fake surprise: he made the kind of face I make when reading Max a story. "What are *you* doing here?"

The dental supplies man sat up in the box, looking windblown and disoriented. He rose to his feet and Ricardo helped him step out; the man made pat-down motions over his own torso then staggered out of Club Blasé, his friends running to assist him. Laughs and applause.

Ricardo tilted the empty box toward the audience, shut the lid, had it winched again. "All right, folks, she's uniformly disseminated throughout the universe. That's the easy part. Now let's bring her back." He chanted the B-side of woonga-bazo-onga, "the reagulation spell," and concluded with the "reentry countdown."

"Let's see if she's found her way back to the material plane

yet." He knocked. "Anybody home?" Not even crickets. "In rehearsal she popped open the lid open herself, but maybe she's tuckered out." He unlocked the box, cracked it open, then grimly closed and locked it. "Not yet. She must be on her way. Don't worry folks, the universe is, after all, um . . . " His pleas to the suspended box— "come on, babe. Iris? Come back, baby. Iris, please?"—reverberated through the theater unrequited. Then yet another countdown, followed by his mightiest "shave-and-a-haircut!" knock that sent the box gently swinging on its cable. During the wait that followed, the box might have disappeared sound itself. Making the best of things, he had it lowered, unlocked the lid, showed us it was empty, and announced, "There you have it, ladies and gentlemen. The miracle of subatomic deagulation. The second show is canceled. And remember: life itself is magical. Goodnight!"

Rebecca thought that over for a moment. "Fuck you. Where's Iris?" No one had gotten up to leave.

"On rare occasions," Ricardo sighed, "the subject fails or refuses to reenter our mortal—"

"Fuck you."

"Sometimes the allure of the world beyond is too powerful to—"

"Where is she, asshole?"

He turned and walked briskly backstage to scattered applause and broke into a run, Rebecca then I charging up the steps in pursuit. She outran the elderly stagehand who lunged at my feint left; we pursued Ricardo down another flight of steps and a narrow corridor. He slammed his dressing room door and locked it behind him. Iris's was unlocked. Her clothes—the brown suit she wore to her classes, her underwear tucked in a pair of brown

flats—and her purse with her wallet and cell phone inside were on the dressing table. In the hallway Rebecca was pounding on Ricardo's door. ". . . *you* in a box, you bastard."

The hallway was crowded now, mostly with Iris's students. The widest man with the flattest haircut kicked in the door on his second try. Ricardo was working on the window bars' padlock with a nail file. On the wall next to the dressing mirror, a framed poster for the Bellagio Hotel showed Doug Henning and a mulleted Ricardo, both in tuxes, making spell-hands at an elephant.

When the crowd had frog-marched Ricardo back onstage, two jocks sat him on a stool and held fast to an arm apiece. We returned to our tables.

Having regained his composure, Ricardo said, "Let's settle down for a vigil. She might materialize yet. Sometimes there's a bottleneck between the mystical plane and our own."

Rebecca threw a ball of napkins that landed in his glistening hair. "Cut the mysterioso crap."

Stoically he removed the crown of napkins. "Aren't you people overreacting a tad? You do know the difference between making someone disappear and making them disappear in a magic act?"

"The difference," Rebecca said, "is you're supposed to put them back."

"Oh come on! You think she's ceased to exist? She'll turn up. Why all this panic? Say. Wasn't there a *Banacek* episode in the seventies where a magician killed his girlfriend while disappearing her?"

"You're baiting us now? You think that's funny? You're an abusive boyfriend, and it's apparent to all her friends that the fighting's been escalating. Dozens of us saw her black eye."

"Did she ever say I her hit her? It was a door." *Was* he trying to provoke us? I was glad Toby was out of town at a conference.

"Maybe it'll hit you on the way out!" Rebecca said. "We've all been wondering why your act was so crapulous tonight and I think I understand. One of the final derangements of abusive boyfriendhood is the 'now look what you made me do' stage. The boyfriend blames her for all his fuckups. It can go further. He starts sabotaging *himself* just to have an excuse to punish her."

"You people are the rageaholics. I'm just sitting here on this old historic stage enjoying our vigil and trying to reason with you. Why *don't* you call the police? I'm the one who's been roughed up. I'm the one who expects to be attacked. So tell me. Most of you are well-behaved scholars from Northwestern. Have you even noticed that you've become a mob? You've fallen prey to the kind of bumpkinated terrors that should have been left behind in the Middle Ages. Are you proud?"

There were murmurs in the audience; some people were shame-faced; a man at a nearby table cringed.

"I do understand why you've resorted to torches and pitchforks. It's been in the air at Northwestern lately, hasn't it? And you know who's the locus of it all? George Entmen."

A startled laugh escaped me.

"That's right. The man evil-eyeing me right there at the head table. *He* thinks it's a laugh riot. You probably know about the vicious prank he played on Preston Twine—the beloved philanthropist who did nothing more to George than endow his fucking Twine Award—and George made that ninety-eight-year-old man drop dead at the ceremony. And perhaps you've heard that Wendy Baim and her Nora Foundation might withdraw their endowment from the English department, wrecking dozens, maybe hundreds of careers. Do any of you students have a scholarship or a fellowship? *Will* you have it? Guess who's mired in that one up to his little round glasses? George. And guess who Iris's cell phone lists as the last person she called before she disappeared? Bingo."

That last one was a slur too far and it elicited some hoots and laughs; he regrouped. "But I understand why you're reaching for your pitchforks. A Gallup poll shows that belief in Satan has risen by twelve points this decade, with a similar bump for the Antichrist. I'm not saying George is either. It's just that, as he himself *brags*, his little talent negates the laws of physics. If we can't rely on science anymore why *not* revert to savagery? You think we live in a world now where magicians' assistants can disappear for real. And yet some of you still think George is a good man. Most people will think well of the Antichrist, too. Have you ever watched George 'fly,' as he calls it? It's this creepy mix of writhing, twitching, drooling, arm waving, and Exorcist–type mumbling—all with this eerie sliver of light between George and the ground. I don't know about you but it makes me shudder. Imagine walking a dark deserted street at night and having *that* bump against your ankle."

Some of my students were in the audience. I turned to share a smirk with them but most avoided eye contact. The rest looked back at me as if I'd just scuttled down the wall from the ceiling. It was my first clear look at my fame.

"Why is he such a *small* man?" Ricardo was freestyling now. "Small? Hitler? Remember how Hitler—" There was a thunk! and he fell through the floor, stool and all, nearly pulling his two minders after him.

. . .

Some of us ran onstage. A trapdoor hung open; Ricardo lay on a mattress below, lucky he'd fallen clear of his metal stool. The room was the length and width of the stage, its floor all mattresses. A downward flight of steps connected it to an even larger mattress space—perhaps for trapdoors on the floor of the club.

"Don't worry, I'm okay," he said, overestimating what was at most our curiosity.

A short sixtyish man with steel-gray hair, round steel-frame glasses, and a military bearing emerged from backstage. "I couldn't listen to that windbag one more second. Wherever Ricardo is, there should be an eject lever."

I recognized the razor-gargle voice of Romulus Goins, ex–Chicago police detective, Ph.D. in psychology, and the dean of Chicago debunkers. I'd met him at the magicians' party. He looked down the rectangular hole at Ricardo. "How ya doin'?"

"No thanks to you but—"

"Alive is *more* than enough, thanks. Don't bother with the door down there. I took the liberty of locking it."

I said to Ricardo, "Why don't you tell us where Iris is and we'll call it a night? Ordinarily you wouldn't have much to fear from us but we are, as you say, a mob." Granted: not as intimidating as it might have been.

"I guess you haven't heard of a little point of honor called the magician's code."

"I just noticed," I said, "that punch in the eye Toby gave you has healed. It's time for your tune-up punch."

Romulus put a hand on my chest as I was about to jump down there. "That guy was born for a tune-up but it won't be necessary.

Iris went down the trapdoor before I locked the room. So she has to be—do you know the history of this place?"

"All I know is this floor used to be Harrison Sullivan's penthouse. He owned and I think designed this hotel."

"Sullivan was the last of the great Chicago robber barons—construction, real estate, and waste disposal. Architecture was his hobby. The Sullivan Hotel is the last of his projects still standing. He claimed to be a black sheep descendent of Louis Sullivan but in fact he was a black sheep Levine.

"This wasn't the family residence; it was his home away from home, if you catch my drift, but no one ever proved it in court. According to the lease it belonged to the mistress, Anna Mae Windsor (she was a Windsor like he was a Sullivan and I'm a mallard duck), and no one ever managed to catch the two of them alone together." I heard one or two groans as he inhaled and continued his lesson in forgotten Chicago history. "The wife was always sending over detectives, but he was a master of the getaway. He installed over two dozen trapdoors and a labyrinth of corridors and secret tunnels. Through the basement he could connect with the network of service tunnels and disused subway lines under the loop. He even had his own miniature train engine down there and he tootled around under Chicago blasting the whistle and wearing an engineer cap. In 1975, at the height of the Chicago magic revival, the penthouse, with all its secret passages and trapdoors, was converted to the Funny Bunny Magic Lounge (Sullivan had been dead for thirty-five years: cirrhosis, syphilis) and later they changed that unfortunate name to Club Blasé."

"This is all interesting, but we're worried about our friend."

"It's a snap. The room we're looking at contains a concealed

207

door that opens on a secret corridor—by the way this stage was here from the beginning. Harrison's infamous so-called midnight puppet shows—"

"Romulus. Please."

"Sorry. The corridor takes you to the stairwell—fifteen floors down to the basement. Those steps aren't on any blueprint. There are no access doors except the concealed one from the secret corridor. Because of all that unaccounted-for space, the building seems slightly asymmetrical. But Harrison was a drunk, a cokehead and a bad architect, so it didn't arouse suspicion. If somebody pressed the point, he said something about ducts. Sorry—there are fifteen flights of steps to the basement exit. At the bottom there's an exit door. But Iris wouldn't be able to open it; the owners of the club had it sealed after the underground floods of the nineties. There's no way out."

"So she has to be in the corridor or the stairwell?"

"Yep. There's nowhere else she could be. I'll just drop through the hole and unlock the door to the corridor and we can go say hello to her. Shove over, Ricardo."

"Just a minute." I looked down at Ricardo. "How about it, is that the secret of the trick?"

He sat up on the mattress. "As long as I'm about to be a has-been magician, people might as well know I was a smarter one than I seemed tonight. After she dropped down Iris was going to walk to a designated spot in this room. There's a concealed closet with a lever on the back wall and a box containing stage makeup, a wig, facial prosthetics (nose, wrinkle-pack, neck wattles, and so on), a pair of thick eyeglasses, and a pile of folded clothes. She puts on the makeup, glues on the prosthetics (these are the ones with the cutting-edge stick-em on the back, right out of DARPA), she's been practicing for weeks. She puts on the drab flower-print dress, the glasses, the wig, the orthopedic shoes, and so forth. She had the whole routine from nose to shoes down to six minutes— that's why I needed the time-wasting rigamarole. So now she's a dead ringer for my aunt Agnes, who's sitting directly above her at a table at the back of the club. Iris checks the all-clear light—which my aunt activates with a customized app—and if it's green Iris pulls the lever. Agnes, along with her chair and a circle of the floor underneath it, descends by hydraulic lift, and Iris takes her place on the chair. A few moments later Iris is sitting in the back of the club. Yeah, like in the Bond movie. So Iris is sitting there, waiting for my shave-and-a-haircut knock on the box. And *then*—," he closed his eyes, ecstatic, an eyeliner-fouled tear running down his face, "she stands, cries out my name, rips off her prosthetics, throws off her wig, tosses away the glasses, rips off the dress revealing her gold-spangled tights, and declares she is back from the other plane! . . . But instead she ditched me. I thought she loved me. We were making plans."

He was convulsively weeping now, and I was faced with that old dilemma in morals and manners: what do you say to a sobbing asshole?

"It might not seem like it now, but you'll get through this. Other fish, right?"

He opened his eyes and gaped as if it were a Zen koan. He wiped his face with his hand, spreading eyeliner. "By the way, when she went down the trapdoor the dental supplies man was already here. Should I explain how—"

"No!" we said in unison.

He removed a paisley handkerchief from his tux and loudly blew his nose. "You know, George," he gulped down tears, "I invented a noise-reduction system for hydraulic lifts just for that trick. I've applied for a patent."

"You're a smart guy, Ricardo. I never doubted it. If you'll shove over a bit so we can drop down—"

"And remember when Agnes's glass fell and shattered during the first trick and everyone turned around? That was so everyone would think she'd been there the whole time. Good detail work, huh?"

"You thought of everything, Ricardo, except, you know."

"Look!" the wide student with the flattop yelled. "She's there! I think that's Iris!" He ran to the back table. "There's this putty stuff on her face! I think I can . . ." He grabbed a cheek between his thumb and forefinger, pulled, and stretched . . . stretched.

"Ow! I'm not her, you idiot!"

"That's not Iris," Ricardo sobbed.

.   .   .

Rebecca then I jumped down the hole after Romulus and stooped-walked behind him under the low ceiling to the door. Ricardo sat against a wall with his knees drawn up, his face a bleeding wound of eyeliner. He mumbled something as I passed.

I turned, walking backward. "What?"

He said, "Tell her 'be happy.'"

Students were dropping down one by one behind us. Romulus unlocked the door; I was expecting something madcap, but it opened on a corridor of buzzing fluorescents, institutional green walls, and dirty tan linoleum.

The linoleum made a gritty hiss behind our footfalls. Two students ran past us and Rebecca took off behind them, inciting the rest of us to stampede—except Romulus, pressing his back to the wall, pleading "three-pack lungs."

The front-runners threw open the door to the stairs. The cement steps were snugly contained between two walls, offering no place to hide and no view beyond the nearest landing. "Iris!" Rebecca screamed; her cry seemed to hunch down among the close walls. Soon we were all screaming as we ran until Rebecca screamed "Stop!" We stopped screaming and running. "Hey, girl!" Rebecca called. "Iris! We scream and we scream for you and not even a hello?" Not even crickets. We sprinted the rest of the way, lucky no one was trampled in our mad screaming blur to the bottom.

I was in good shape from my flying workouts, but after running fifteen floors screaming while having an anxiety attack, the dim lights throbbed to my pulse. When I crossed the final landing I had to sit down at the top of the steps. Students near the bottom were doing stretches or taking out their phones or looking around baffled, nothing beyond them but the cement-sealed door. Rebecca stood in front of it talking on her phone, leaving messages for Iris and anyone she might have confided in.

Romulus, sweat soaked, came down last. He held onto the rail and lowered himself beside me. "Obviously we've been scammed. I can think of a few possibilities. One. Ricardo's trick is still playing out, but that doesn't mean Iris will turn up tonight or any time soon. After avalanches of notoriety, hundreds of tabloid theories of her disappearance, he'll announce his return to magic. HBO pay-per-view from Madison Square Garden, and for the finale he conjures Iris back to this mortal plane. If that's where this is headed, you have to face the depressing probability that they're in on this together. Or two. Maybe she learned enough magic to disappear from the disappearing act on her own. Not likely. But as you've seen, a lot of magicians hate Ricardo. Maybe *they* worked it out for her. Or three. Let's just say I want to take a good look at that *Banacek* episode. But stay positive for now."

"How could she disappear from the stairwell?"

"I haven't the slightest."

"What if the concealed corridor has its own concealed corridor, or the secret stairway has a hidden secret—"

"Settle down, George. Students of magic have literally gone insane pursuing that line of thought. Anyway I've seen the real blueprints for the Sullivan, and all the modern add-ons. There's nothing that mystifying. Sullivan was trying to hide from his wife, not visit Narnia."

"No," Rebecca was saying on the phone. "Listen to me. I said top to bottom. What do you mean *look again?* What—wait. Oh God." She looked stricken. Everyone else stopped talking. "Rebecca?" a mouse voice bleated from her phone. She pressed the end call button. "Around the twelfth floor. There's a window. It's the only way out. It's over the Chicago River."

Romulus said, "Sullivan would never—oh, wait. I saw it."

We'd all seen it and its only effect was to nudge us slowly toward recalling it.

"I suppose," I said to Rebecca, "you could make something of that if you want to take the darkest view possible."

"I'd be happy just to take *another* view. What've you got?"

We trudged back up, Rebecca calling the cops on the way. They usually waited twenty-four hours before classifying a person as missing but made an exception when that person might be in the river.

The window, as I'd dreaded and faintly recalled, was open. It faced west over the bridges. The river smell is a miscellany of fetid things, but this was one of those breezy summer nights when they catalyzed into something lyrical. The green water is black at night, the quaking reflections below somehow brighter than the city above. There was a ledge—not wide enough for Iris to edge along the building, as the urban legend has it, and climb through the first open window she saw, where Mr. Right was about to dine alone. It was just wide enough to allow her to step out, brace her back against the Sullivan Hotel, raise her arms in the posture of a diver, and aim for the brighter city.

. . .

The Chicago Police Department Marine and Helicopter Unit found nothing of Iris but her long white glove. The more hopeful among us (I wasn't one of them) thought the glove was a ruse, dropped from the window before she carried out a plan to disappear. Why else the striptease with the glove, they argued, except to perform the ultimate striptease of shedding her identity? Others thought the impact or the water might have dislodged it, tight as was. In the weeks to come we all became experts on the currents down there. We could intelligently discuss gravity currents, density currents, and bilevel flow, but it was just a busier way of grieving. When a month passed and nothing more of her had turned up (there was some excitement over a YouTube clip of a girl's charm bracelet bobbing past an outdoor cafe in River North, but the sane fan's reliquary never expanded beyond the glove), and when the drawer had closed on the last lead, the memorial services began.

Rebecca and I attended the three in Chicago: at Northwestern, at the Chicago Cultural Center, and the public one at Daley Plaza for her fans whose numbers were a shock to anyone who thought her a coterie writer. At the plaza a succession of Chicago celebrities and politicians read excerpts from her novels. Ricardo was there; nothing short of incarceration for felony battery could have prevented him from sobbing into a microphone. I'm sure Iris would have been entertained by the alderman who drew religious meaning from the break in the rainy weather. It was a bright sharp-edged day after weeks of rain, the plaza a shell-burst of color. Sunbathers lying on the benches at the back, security watching a toddler trying to climb the Picasso, a mime-faced unicyclist doing figure eights—it all had the ache of the hyperreal. I was one of the speakers, but I can't remember what I said—certainly not that her funniest lines seemed, now, like suicide notes awaiting a rimshot.

THIRTEEN

Nelson Baim was seated at the bar of the Dorring Hotel, poking a shrimp fork at ambiguous lumps beneath a gobbet of orange cheese. He was wearing his trademark powder-blue seventies magician's tux, and he'd never looked more like the loneliest boy on prom night.

"What's that?" I marveled, taking the next stool. I'd arrived early for our press conference, thinking I'd use the time to jot down some talking points. But after ten minutes in a folding chair in the empty conference room—distant footsteps reverberating, giant steel doors banging someplace—I needed to get my sobriety down to something bearable.

"It claims to be bar food," Nelson said. His expansive scalp, the filaments tugged across it, and the copper coils of his beard twinkled in the light of a blinking sign. He'd yet to stick the fork in. "Keep watching and it seems to move."

"You obviously got a head start on me," I said signaling the bartender. A half hour from the dreaded event, we seemed to have reached a foxhole detente.

"Rebecca couldn't make it," I said. I hadn't wanted her to see me humiliated.

"Wendy won't be joining us either," he said.

I nearly said, "I assume she'll be puppeteering us remotely?"

I steered us to a safer topic. We traded accounts of worst bar food, mostly at academic conferences: the buffalo wings that reduced a west Texas bar full of Analytical Leibnizians to a pit of quivering intestines, the shrimp cocktail that took down the Modern Language Association in '07, etc.

As my drink arrived, he handed me the shrimp fork. "It's all yours if you want it." It did seem to breathe when you looked a while. "It looks substantial enough to crush my butterflies, and maybe that's all I need." I tentatively started chewing and seconds later stared at that same glistening mouthful in my napkin.

"What was it like?" he wondered.

I gave a side-eye to the spot where I'd pushed the dish. "If God came down to us in the form of seafood and melted cheese, the sight of His or Her face couldn't be any more overpowering. I think it demands something of us—more, I think, than the ritual kneeling over porcelain. I don't know. Maybe they just kept the damn thing under heat lamps too long . . . Last time we spoke you were still working out how I do my trick. You haven't called again so I assume you found something you can use?"

He gave me a wised-up smirk. "Nope." It was the smirk of a banker turning down a loan to a man who had fucked his wife.

"Wendy constructed this farce for your sake. It was all so poor, poor Nelson could revive his career as a debunker. Aren't you worried about being a laughingstock?"

"Nope."

I felt like I was plummeting down an elevator shaft—the honor of flying, the colleagues in the English department who'd lose their jobs along with me, and the seafood-cheese-and-cement appetizer all chained to my ankle.

"And you know why?"

I hated to feed that smirk. "Why?"

"Because every time I bring up the trick, you tell me it's not a trick. You say ask other magicians and I keep telling you, they can't find the trick."

"What does *that* tell you?"

"You've got a little less than a half hour to tell me how you do it."

"Nelson, this will be worse than your dissertation defense. I'm cringing just imagining it."

"Twenty-six minutes."

"All right. Fake a bit of magician's tradecraft. Sometimes when a magician wants to give others in the field a hint at how a trick is done they'll allude to sources and methods. 'Blackstone and Carter—the bloody rabbit diversion.' That sort of thing. Get out your smartphone, go through some magic sites, and find something that sounds good. Just be vague. It's only a hint."

"Do you think they're all idiots, George? A room full of journalists and magicians?"

"Maybe I'll just go home," I said.

"You're bluffing," he said.

True. I planned to follow my agreement with Wendy to the letter in the preposterous hope she'd let me go.

"How about another round," he said, "while you think through your options?"

In all his threats he never brought up Wendy's to wreck the English department. Maybe he was ashamed. Maybe this sudden kamikaze obstinacy was aimed at her and her Nelson Baim Reclamation Project.

"So you'll shoot *yourself*," I said into his smirk, "in the hope the bullet catches me on the way out. Let's stick to Wendy's original plan. You announce that you've figured out how I do my trick, and I'll say yes you did. Unfortunately, we say, we can't divulge anything more. Magician's code. Then you can kill some time by thanking a list of people who inspired you during your long years in the wilderness." My hope was that the press wouldn't bother to report such a nonevent at all, giving me at least a respite from disgrace.

"Yeah," he said. "About that. She didn't really think they'd go along with us saying I've figured out the secret but we can't tell them what it is. She thought you'd be so humiliated by the reporters, you'd give up and tell us all the secret that I've figured out. She said, 'Nobody is more terrified of losing his dignity than George. Or as George calls it, the honor of flying.'"

"What?"

"Twenty-four minutes."

"If there was a secret why wouldn't I have told you by now?"

"Good point. Twenty-three and a half minutes."

. . .

We had agreed only that I'd speak first, praising Nelson's brilliant, tireless work in debunking me. But he took the spot behind the mic and silently glowered at the press with an expression that must have laid down the law at children's birthday parties but here elicited bafflement. He blocked my attempts to change places or lean toward the mic. He elbowed me when I cleared my throat to speak without amplification. Fine. It was *his* event.

Reporters asked when and if this thing was going to begin, and he answered with further silent glowering. Standing next to him, I saw tremors of rage or stage fright. I thought his plan was simply to face them down and that the final destination of his death ray stare was his old dissertation committee.

Romulus Goines was seated in the front row, polishing his glasses with his tie. "George, does your friend require medical attention?"

"Let's give him a minute," I said. As someone who'd had his share of public mortification, I thought I recognized the bravado that comes from thinking, "It can't get any worse so what the hell." But hell is like a steam cabinet in a James Bond movie: there's always a mysterious hairy hand ready to turn up the dial. That thought, or some variant, must have occurred to Nelson because his military bearing steadily froze to paralyzed deer.

Deciding they had no time for a staring contest with a catatonic birthday magician, the press put away their laptops and phones. A few were already in the aisle.

"Hold on, folks." Romulus said and they all stopped. "This is potentially a milestone in the history of debunking, so give the guy a minute to stifle his heebie-jeebies. Meanwhile, George, I think the TV folks will need a flying demonstration."

Predictably the press sighed. No one, least of all I, was eager for yet another display of low-altitude floundering. I came down off the stage, got down on my stomach on the carpet, rose four inches, and began to fly up the aisle. When did the lure of flying—that dream of falling upward, that throttled melody that makes you pause in your lecture on the phenomenology of emptiness and hum softly, eerily—when did flying become another bodily function? Panting, flailing, kicking, mumbling, drooling,

tongue protruding—by now it was all as miraculous as the crap-
per without magazines. In his pep talk that morning, Harvey
Bell had said, "How can you be bored with flying? When you
give your demonstration today I want you to see, truly see the
carpet. You'll be the first man to view it unsupported from four
inches in the air. Survey your realm, George! The tiny altitudes
belong to you alone."

There was probably some honest holy man doctrine among
the jokes. I surveyed my realm below. The carpet was royal blue;
Wendy had chosen a room with short carpet pile to show off my
flight gap. Fresh vacuum cleaner tracks. A woman's nylon-stock-
inged foot on the aisle, big toe tapping. The backward-moving
black-and-white track shoes of the cameraman in front of me.
The distant dull traffic hum of conversations, none of them, I
came to realize, having to do with me. Where was the empyrean
in all that?

I landed—the carpet was just a carpet from any distance—
and stood up. The press went on talking and texting. Did this
happen in the lives of the saints, too? Did someone have to take
them aside, thank them for their service, and explain that they
were washed up?

.   .   .

Nelson placed a hand over the mic and whispered, "Last chance,
George. Tell them how you fly or I'll do something."

"Ooh. Sounds scary. You picked the perfect time, we're all
bored. What are you waiting for?"

"I don't want to do this." More a plea than a threat.

"Oh what the hell, do it."

For the next minute all he did was sweat fat droplets that

skied down the sides of his nose and lit a sparkling constellation in his beard.

The soaked transparency of his tuxedo shirt revealed a silver metal rectangle beneath it with a large recessed black button in the center. I supposed that Wendy had bought him some DARPA tech and we were about to see another exercise in reverse-engineered flying.

"Where'd you get the gear?" I whispered, hoping a little conversation might calm him down.

"The guys at the magic store on Lincoln set it up. They have connections; magicians have done trials for DARPA before."

"Okay. I'm assuming this wasn't Wendy's idea?"

"Nope." He was holding back tears. "I just want to show her that I tried everything."

I remembered the guys at the magic store hated Nelson. "Have you at least tested it?"

"There wasn't time. They brought it here an hour ago. The energy charge is only enough for one flight. It was for backup, okay? I didn't think you'd be this stubborn."

"I have a bad feeling about this, Nelson. It'll probably be a dud, and that's the *best* we can hope for. Let's go back to the original plan: We bullshit them. Bullshitting never killed anyone. It's not worth god-knows-what because you're afraid of disappointing Wendy."

"Fuck you." He turned to the audience. "Good evening, members of the press. I'm here to prove, through reverse engineering, that George Entmen's flying does not require a supernatural explanation."

"More DARPA tech?" Someone asked. "Ricardo Dean did that on *Tommy Thorne*."

"This is the second-generation tech. You're comparing a Model T to a Bonneville Salt Flats test car. Believe me, you'll always remember where you were today. Those of you with sensitive hearing, cover your years—there may be a sonic boom."

I can't explain his reckless hyperbole. Maybe he hoped to deepen his disgrace to the point where he'd never have to leave the house again.

Another question summed up the skepticism and impatience in the room. "I don't really see the point of this so-called reverse engineering. George has undergone body searches, even cavity searches, and it's clear that he doesn't use tech. How will your demonstration debunk the way *he* flies? It's not even apples and oranges. It's apples and prairie dogs." Nelson ignored the question.

"If you flew at the speed of sound," someone observed, "you'd burst into flame."

Nelson thought about this, no doubt realizing it was true. "Fuck you."

He reached behind the podium and removed a blue football helmet, wincing at snickers from the audience as he strapped it under his chin. He stepped down from the podium, gazed upward, slapped the button, and raised his arms above his head.

"Uh-oh!" some wag said. "Aims at the stars, hits the ceiling."

The inevitable nothing followed, to laughs and applause. Ignoring them, arms still raised above his head, Nelson gazed wistfully at the ceiling. He got up on his toes, took a few small jumps and an unimpressive leap that brought more laughs.

"What's that?" someone called. Beneath the ruffles of Nelson's shirt the device was emitting a deep hum.

The sound swelled to a migrainous bone-juddering roar that

made people in the front rows flee up the aisle. I might have joined them but I was afraid to let go of the podium; tiny vibrating fizzy black dots crowded my vision, perhaps marshaling toward a complete blackout. All that remained of my shattered hearing were occasional kazoo sounds.

Nelson went rigid and hit the stage like a chopped tree. My vision and hearing were coming back; the hum had stopped. I stepped down from the podium, rolled him over—his nose was bleeding—and ripped open his shirt.

A convulsion passed through him and he stopped breathing. I tore off duct tape, pulled away the device, began alternating chest compressions with mouth-to-mouth resuscitation. "Call 911! Is anyone here a doctor!"

His breath came back in a loud rush, a nasty brew of Jim Beam, bar peanuts, and whatever sour horror he'd held down all his life.

FOURTEEN

"Let's skip the minutes." The visor of the chairman's Cubs cap nearly covered his eyes, meaning closed for business, let's get outta here soon. "Before we discuss graduate assistant compensation is there any old business?"

It was the last faculty meeting of spring quarter, classes over, our grades turned in, no one wearing a suit except the great classicist Winston Kendrick: "Because I am a professor," he explained as he sat down at the conference table and immediately fell asleep.

The end-of-quarter meeting was always pervaded with a drowsy satisfaction, as if we'd climbed a medium-size mountain. The nearly deserted campus at the windows sated us: the cathedral chiming, a bicycle bell tinkling, the massive oaks mumbling old business of their own, a distant girl's laugh flashing tipsily among leaf shadows on the wall. As Nabokov said, "You can always count on a murderer for a fancy prose style."

You must be wondering if you missed something! No, I'm not a murderer. But my enemy Blaustein, rising to his feet now, would soon beg to differ. Ever since my fortieth birthday party, when he'd sat silently glaring at me and my guests, I'd been meaning to ask him, "What's your beef?" By the time he stood blocking the exit at the Twine Award ceremony, handing back the cursed statuette after I'd thrown it out, angry pinpoints trembling in his aviator glasses, I'd decided he was simply unhinged.

This was my first close-up view of him since then. He calmly looked around the conference table, his smile as detached as a Mr. Potato Head piece—a tall, slim, poised man whom Toby had dismissed as "a smart-looking guy whose degree came from posture school." Blaustein was wearing a black shirt and black jeans, the gunfighter effect enhanced by his silver hair but marred somewhat by his orange-tinted aviator glasses.

The chairman raised his visor a millimeter. "You don't have to stand, Charles. This isn't *Witness for the Prosecution*. You're not going to give a speech, are you? Oh, please don't."

Blaustein, still standing, reached into his briefcase, and I don't think I was the only one who considered hitting the dirt.

His hand came out with the Twine Award, which I'd thrown out a second time the night before (having disabused myself of the paranoid notion that Blaustein was hiding somewhere waiting for me to throw it out again). He set it on the table, fastidiously removed a piece of arugula from the face of Minerva, and holding the leaf fragment between thumb and forefinger raised it aloft. "Garbage," he said. "George put his Twine Award in the garbage."

Someone stifled a laugh. As I mentioned elsewhere, Blaustein's sneering nyah! nyah! voice, delivered from the side of his mouth and recalling the voice of 1930s movie gangster Edward G. Robinson, was said to be a medical condition. So perhaps it was politically incorrect of me to hope he'd say "arugula."

Toby smiled at him. Toby had stopped crying about Iris weeks ago, and everything he looked at now provoked this moist-eyed smile—the smile you might give a frail child who shows you his effort trophy. "That's some fine surveillance work, Charles. Good binoculars would be essential; you strike me as a Bushnell PowerView sort of guy. How did you know when he'd dump the award? Did you use private investigators? Students? Where did you or your henchmen open the bags? When you were studying great literature and dreamed of being a professor did you imagine you'd have henchmen? Say, what kind of leaf is that?" He, too, was hoping to hear "arugula."

"Yes, Charles," the chairman said, "the Twine in a garbage can makes me sad, but have a little empathy. Because of the award's tragic associations George wanted no part of it, and let's just say it's not easy to give it back. At any rate, this committee isn't the venue for your complaint. You can contact the disciplinary committee but frankly you have no case. Now we *must* get to the graduate students. The teaching assistants' demands—"

"I'd like to begin my case against George with this quotation from Marcus Aurelius," Blaustein said.

"He's unstoppable," Toby marveled. "The Terminator in *Mr. Smith Goes to Washington*."

"Do you have the blue pamphlet Arts and Sciences distributed last month?" the chairman asked Blaustein. "It provides a list of, er, *social services* for faculty who are, ah—*stressed*. Your insurance provides for a, ah, rest at a stay . . . uhrm, a stay at a rest—"

"'The gesticulating fool is the saddest man of all.' —Marcus Aurelius."

"He never said that, you idiot." Winston Kendrick appeared to still be sleeping as he spoke, the esteemed profile pillowed on his folded arms. "Every professor in the humanities knows that when you have a weak line, attribute it to Marcus Aurelius."

"Charles," Linda Tummelty said, "you're the one who becomes increasingly absurd and pathetic the longer this goes on."

"Really? Has there been another faculty member at this university as ridiculous as George? Have you watched his Jerry Lewis version of flying? The flailing, the drooling? What does it do to children's dreams of soaring among the clouds when unassisted human flight becomes this shameful rite in the dirt? Does it make you *proud* to be on this faculty, Linda? . . . Do you know why so many people fear insects?"

"Huh?" she said.

"You're no Marcus Aurelius," I said to Blaustein. "I liked you better in the days when you quietly loomed."

"The insects," he said, "down there in the dirt, Linda. We fear them because we don't know what they're doing down there. You never know when out of nowhere one will start climbing up your leg. Can you be sure it's not happening now?"

Linda replied pleasantly, "Maybe you can work that out with your doctors at the—what are we calling it?"

The chairman spoke into his cell. "Security, please . . . Hi, I'm going to need someone removed from our meeting. Would you please send up some personnel? Uh, one would probably be plenty, but if our colleague is blessed with the strength of the mad—sorry, Charles—maybe two. There will be no shortage of volunteers to assist." He hung up. "Meanwhile, Charles, you have five minutes to make your case, and we'll look at you with our best Serious Faces. Go on. As I understand it you were arguing for George being somehow vaguely awful. Serious Faces, everyone."

"I hope you realize," Blaustein said, "that those Serious Faces you're making are the same ones you make when you listen to each other . . . I'll get to the point. George is responsible morally if not perhaps legally for the deaths of Preston Twine and our dear Iris—convinced her to break up with her boyfriend and it drove her to suicide—and the near-death of Nelson Baim. And speaking of the Baims, this department will be open to the blackmail and extortion of Wendy Baim as long as George remains with us."

"Preston Twine died of old age, everyone told Iris to break up with her boyfriend, and George didn't cause Nelson's accident," the chairman said, "he saved his life. Wendy is my sister-in-law, and I know she's very grateful to George. But never mind. Have you made your case?"

"Oh, she's grateful all right," Blaustein said.

"Is that it? Can we get back to teaching assistant compensation?"

What terrifying bolt of power coursed through Blaustein at that moment? "Grateful!" he boomed, his voice no longer that of Edward G. Robinson the misunderstood gangster; this was Robinson of *The Ten Commandments,* stomping on the rubble of the tablets, dancing in the mosh pit of the golden calf, jeering, "Where's your Messiah now?" (Actually Robinson never said that famous line, but I hoped it might come out the side of Blaustein's face.)

He was saying, "Wendy is grateful *to me.* Remember Monitor Press, George? When they gave George the Lydecker Chair of Hermeneutics, the editorship of Monitor came with it. When he got bored with it he fobbed it off on me."

"Dozens of faculty would have jumped at it," I said. "It was a recognition of your scholarship and taste."

"Sure it was. Nobody else wanted it, it doesn't pay. Guess who I'm publishing this fall? We're branching beyond critical theory with this one. It's a huge work of speculative philosophical synthesis. Your face is about to droop right off your skull, George. Do you see where I'm heading?"

"Yep."

The chairman raised his visor. It was dawning on him, too. Toby was a few seconds behind.

"A vast tome," Blaustein continued, "combining Nietzsche and Kant, brain research, contemporary nihilist studies, all in service of the thesis that the world—"

"You're publishing Nelson Baim's dissertation," I said in the hope of cutting him short.

"—the world is a pile of shit. Nelson's dissertation, plus every random thought he had while staring at the wainscoting in his study for the past twenty years. Needless to say, Wendy is extremely grateful. *To me!* Sure, she knows you're a good man, saved Nelson's life Blah! Blah! Blah! Blah! Blah! Blah! Blah! Blah!" We cringed at each Blah! as if at gunfire. "And she knows that anyone but you would simply move to some non-Wendy-funded university, except you fear she'd take vengeance on your colleagues at Northwestern for your escape. She told me she finds your ethical agonizing admirable. But Wendy is *very* grateful *to me!*"

Blaustein took a clipper out of his pocket and began cutting his nails. "I'll see to it that she never relents in her pressure on you and the department. Wendy—it's better than having the bomb."

I saw no point in asking Blaustein why. I didn't want to ask for his demands, because I dreaded there were none. I said, "This must be the most joyous event in Nelson's life, but when I saw him he didn't seem to be celebrating—anything."

Blaustein didn't mind making small talk with the enemy he'd so resoundingly Wendied. "I only offered him the book deal yesterday."

I jerked my head to avoid a nail fragment in the eye. "Is he finally happy?" My distant hope was that if Nelson were happy, someday Wendy would allow me to be happy.

"Of course he's been clinically depressed for years. Wendy hasn't given up. She thinks a little adulation—"

Two security guards were standing in the doorway. They looked us over, and we'd all seen that expression of relief on the faces of jocks. "I don't think your services are required," Blaustein told them. "You don't need security guards after all, do you?" he said to the chairman, who avoided looking at us as he sent them away with a melancholy swipe of the hand.

Blaustein continued. "And so, George, Wendy will expect you to devote most of what remains of your career to discussing Nelson's book. It's quite awful you know. It reads like something he mumbled while shaking a fortified wine at the moon. And you'll be out there every day shredding what remains of your reputation, praising Nelson's book on the tabloid shows, analyzing his place in the American nihilist canon while a woman with a meth hairdo accuses you of fathering her one-eared baby. Poor George, your father was a physical and intellectual giant, and you've spent your life as a *small* man haplessly squinting up at the heights of esteem. All that horseshit about the need to defend the honor of flying—it was just your recognition that if you lost any more dignity you'd be flying *under* the dirt. Outside of Ripley's Believe It or Not you'll be remembered, if you're remembered at all, as one of the truly silly men of academe."

We applauded sarcastically, a last act of rebellion, knowing he could make us fill our briefcases with rocks and swing them at each other gladiator style in a fight to the death.

"You're forgetting," the chairman said, "the department gave you the editorship and what the department gives, the department can take away."

"You're forgetting I have a contract with Monitor Press. I have three more years."

"Really? We don't ordinarily pay the editor. Say, I don't think we paid you the dollar that makes it a binding contract."

"You did, though. All on record. Nice try."

"A contract," Toby said, "because Charles is a man who demands to be taken seriously. It's all about respect, right, Chuck?" He flinched as Blaustein turned his way and glared.

"Charles, there are—" The chairman glanced at Winston Kendrick, sleeping quietly now, "four witnesses to your threats."

"You have witnesses, I have *Wendy*."

"I'm not a lawyer, but surely we've got something fireable."

"Weh—" Blaustein saw no need to waste further breath.

"I could fire your ass, take on Monitor Press myself, and publish Nelson—I'll take that hit for the team."

"Wendy and I agreed she wouldn't allow that sort of uprising."

"Why doesn't she burst our faces between her thighs and get it over with?" Toby wondered. "We've all dreamt of it, admit it. You too, Linda, don't give me that look!"

"That's enough new business for me," Blaustein said. "I'm taking the liberty of adjourning the meeting."

The chairman flicked a nail clipping off his shirt.

.   .   .

As I left the building the "you're all going to hell" guy stood on the deserted pathway with a full armload of leaflets. He gave me his usual cheery "Hello, you're going to hell!" Feeling sorry for him, I took one. "Not much traffic on the road to hell," I observed. "But good intentions, aye?"

He didn't laugh. With his black horn-rims, hiked-up black pants, black skinny tie, and white shirt buttoned tightly at the neck, he looked like Pee-wee Herman with decades of conversion therapy. "The people who do pass by are usually alone, taking a rare look at this beautiful world, not staring at their screens or trading eye rolls with their friends when I approach. People are more open to the message when they're away from the crowd."

"You know, you've been telling me for years that I'm going to hell. Good call! I really am going to hell!" I can't account for my cheerfulness; sheer horrified giddiness, I suppose. "More of a *living* hell but still—"

"Pray. Get down on your knees right now and—"

"Sorry, not my mode."

"You'll be praying to *Wendy* soon enough, George." I turned around. Blaustein was standing a few yards down the path; he must have been waiting for me. A shit-eating grin was trying to take hold on his face but his condition tugged it into a lopsided smirk.

"Renounce false gods," the you're-going-to-hell guy whis-

pered. "Renounce this so-called Wendy! And that man's voice—
I believe it's the voice of the devil himself."

"Actually," I whispered, "it's the voice of the late screen actor
Edward G. Robinson. And don't bash the voice, it's a medical
condition. Still, you might be onto something."

"You people always think evil is a medical condition," he said.
"I knew I'd seen you on television. You're the so-called flying
man."

He held up his forefingers in a cross and thrust them toward
my face. "What you're doing is a mockery of true miracles. It
stinks of the devil."

"All right," I shrugged. "Say hi to God. And by the way, *nice
hair tonic*. What is that, Vitalis?"

"Aw, it looked like the beginning of a beautiful friendship,"
Blaustein jeered as I approached. "Mr. You're All Going to Hell
and Mr. I'm Going to Hell. I forgot to give you your itinerary for
the Nelson Baim tour."

"Even if I were doing the damn thing, the book won't be out
for a year at the earliest."

"What we're envisioning won't be an ordinary author tour
that begins when the book is released and ends a month or two
later. How could you raise Nelson to immortality in the Western
canon—and Wendy will settle for nothing less—in a month or
two? Why not give immortality a push by hugely extending the
longevity of the tour? Your role, George, will be a combination of
seminar leader and carnival dunk-the-man. We'll be using your
waning academic reputation and your bizarre flying monkey
notoriety to keep people talking about Nelson's stupid brand of
nihilism. You'll be with Nelson every day but don't worry, the

motel rooms will be doubles. The tour starts on Thursday. That gives you two days to . . . what's the phrase? . . . to get your affairs in order. I just emailed a copy of your itinerary."

"I have a family, you realize."

"Yes. Regrettable."

"Good gag. Back at the meeting I totally bought it. You exploited my normal human terror of Wendy and the simple peasant awe she inspires about her capabilities."

"You know, George, I don't *have* to convince you. But I'll give you the courtesy of a reply: oh yeah?"

"Really, I'd love to but we had other plans this summer."

"You really think it's a gag? You think it couldn't possibly be true? You thought her threat to destroy the English department was impossible until you were willing to do anything to get her to call it off. For Wendy we have to rewrite the old adage: the impossible she does immediately; immortality takes a little time. But seriously, let's make an important distinction. A place in the canon for Nelson: that *is* impossible, despite her torrent of grant money to the leading opinion makers in his field. But her resources to force you to work for that goal until it 'happens': unlimited. Don't hate her, George. She loves her man."

He was right, I thought. There was no limit to her selfless love and can-do monstrousness. I assumed that the immortality scheme, with its gratuitous cruelty to me, came from Blaustein. Since it distilled all her dreams for Nelson, she probably didn't think it was crazy.

It was time to ask.

"What's *your* beef, Charles?"

He did a double take. "Your question disappoints me, George. Just a few minutes ago I was thinking, at least he never asks why.

He doesn't pretend not to know. So tell me—how would you describe our acquaintance? What do you think of me?"

. . .

The truth is, I didn't think of Blaustein. Let me amend that slightly: his behavior at my birthday party, where Raging Blaustein first appeared, upped my attention level. But I soon got used to his apoplectic stares, his attempts at menace (how frightened should you be of someone whose home number shows up on the caller ID for a breather call?), and his sarcastic best wishes (When he said, "Don't get run over by a car!" I replied, "Thanks, I'll look both ways." When he said, "Don't get bowel cancer!" I replied, "Thanks, I'll watch my diet." My collegial counterattacks made his eyelid twitch).

Until today he just hadn't been a very convincing threat. In our peaceable days I was used to thinking of him as a hole in the scenery, or as Toby put it, "the tap water of guys." A few nights after my birthday party as I was turning out the lights in the living room I saw him through the bay windows. He was out on the sidewalk avoiding the street lamps and weighing a brick in his hand. I don't think he saw me; we were both standing in the dark. I watched him hefting and pondering for ten minutes before he walked away as I knew he would. Did he refrain out of cowardice? A pang of conscience at terrifying the two-year-old sleeping nearby? But I guessed he'd decided to use it for a bookcase.

I don't want to give the impression that I'd been snubbing him in the pre-rage days. I'd always stop to chat when we ran into each other on campus. But even though my memory is better than average, our conversations, even seconds old, seldom found purchase there. Toward the end of Blaustein's tirade at the meeting, Toby and I had exchanged a look: if we'd known he could be that witty and eloquent, and if he could be that way when not drunk on his own bile, he might have become a pal.

All right, there's more to it. I tended to forget him because there was a lot I didn't wish to remember. I recruited Blaustein for Northwestern, you know. We met at a party, and when I learned he was unhappy at Cornell, I mentioned my high opinion of an essay he'd just published and urged him to apply. Not only that, I lobbied for him. I thought we sorely needed another hermeneutist in the department; in fact, my dream had always been a quasi-independent Department of Hermeneutics. When he arrived that fall I took him around the department offices making introductions. Rebecca and I had Charles and Karen over for dinner (he hadn't seemed crazy that evening; I might have mistaken his gloom for an admirable seriousness).

Near the end of that quarter he asked me to read and comment on the manuscript of his latest book, a study of Dilthey and Hirsch and the concept of the Hermeneutic Circle. It proved to be wrongheaded and inanely written; I had to read it a second time to be sure I hadn't fallen asleep and read it in some nightmare. How had the same man written the journal essay I'd admired? I recalled that the publication was known for an interventionist approach to editing, sometimes assisting their authors in reworking their arguments, editors sometimes rewriting whole pages.

I broke into a sweat when I remembered all the commitments I'd made to Blaustein, including my promise to introduce him for his Arthur Fretton Binghamton Lecture the following month. I ran to the library holding on to the desperate thought that criticism, like literature, can be a matter of inspiration. Sometimes you reach down deep and bring up *Seven Types of Ambiguity*, sometimes it's your small intestine. But the other works I could find at the library were equally dispiriting.

What could I do? I assured myself that a mediocre professor who'd had tenure at Cornell and had already been given tenure at Northwestern was probably in the ninety-eighth percentile or above of college teachers in general. His students could get what they needed; he wouldn't be an embarrassment to the university. Maybe not deserving of the highest superlatives, but I knew how to scrupulously traverse the labyrinths of praise. "It couldn't have been better," right?

One rule of the wise two-faced critic is to avoid "fine." It's a squirmy word with kaleidoscopic connotations. A "fine" wine: okay. A fine book: careful, you're negotiating a mountain road with no guardrail. "Your book is fine": duels, certainly fistfights, have been fought for less. I made it through my Binghamton introduction without legally fibbing, and even blurbed the awful book I'd read in manuscript: it couldn't have been better!

I suppose my sense of obligation was slightly deranged. I felt obligated to the man I'd brought to Northwestern where he and Karen had apparently made no friends. She was rumored to hate her job and to be suffering from depression. She blamed the recent death of her father on the need to place him in the care of her incompetent sister back home. And word was spreading among his colleagues that Blaustein was a hack: his reputation, like the fabled Hovering Orb, had required the mass belief of the Cornell English department to remain aloft. In those years I'd see him wandering the campus muttering to himself, and each run-in was as dread filled as trying to make small talk with the Ancient Mariner. Guiltily I continued slathering ambiguous praise on his work and inviting him to parties while all but mouthing no! I found it possible to look him in the eye only by looking *at* his eye. I suppose the advent of his insane rage came as a relief: no more reviews and introductions. If his fury had been a bit more proportional, I might have seen the connection to everything I'd done and hadn't done.

.   .   .

I decided I owed him that true account even if he used it against me. He listened silently, arms folded, expressionless except for the smirk of his condition. When I finished he opened his brief-case but my hit-the-dirt impulse passed quickly. Just a padded envelope; "hold this," he said, and when I took it, he reached into his pocket for his phone. "I have a video of you introducing me, George. You did me the 'kindness' of introducing me when I gave the Claudia Vapors Lecture in the Humanities." Not kind-ness but 'kindness.'

"'Thanks for those 'kind' words." I kept my fingers at my sides, reluctant to start an air-quote war.

I'd secretly lobbied for his Vapors lecture, hoping the honor of it might halt his disintegration. The lecture was the night before his hateful performance at my birthday party, and I'd always wondered if there could be a connection.

He pressed play, handed me the phone, and took back the envelope. My introduction was as I recalled it. I hadn't said "fine," I'd scrupulously avoided double meanings. I'd concentrated on the parts of his work I could praise, because, to quote the joke about the woman trying to compliment a rotten egg, "parts of it were very good."

When the video was over I said, "And what *exactly* is your beef?"

He took the phone back and removed some photographs from the envelope. "Do you know what microexpressions are?"

"I get it. I looked at you funny *microscopically?*"

"We have an old Leica that can take pictures in tiny fractions of a second. If you photograph a person's face at that speed you can capture microexpressions—I use 'microexpressions' in its original meaning, not the pop culture term for body English or face reading. I mean expressions too fleeting to detect with the unaided eye. Often our microexpressions contradict the truth of what we say or pretend to feel. Some people argue that with the advent of the high-speed shutter we discovered the secret self— the one that gives the raspberry while we recite our wedding vows."

"I've heard the theory. It has about as much validity as that old craze for scanning liquor ads to find hidden genitalia in the ice cubes. The microexpressions can look weird or menacing because our features are in flux from one expression to another."

"I started wondering about *your* secret self, George. You recruited me for Northwestern, you've praised my work, and it's led to nothing but my misery. I can't leave—can't get tenure anywhere else—and Karen might be in even worse shape than I am. And who's been spreading the slander about my work? Really, how many people in the department have even *read* my work? I thought I was having a nervous breakdown when I began to believe that your seeming kindnesses were your way of destroying me. Good thing I was crazy enough to put that hypothesis to the test. So I recruited Karen and her Leica. Didn't you think she was a bit too dedicated to *documenting* stuff, especially you?—zzt!zzt!zzt! So now we can see Bad George in the photos—or as I think of him, Real George—reacting honestly to what Good George is saying in the video.

"On the back of each photo," he continued, "I write the time on the video and what you were saying. For example. On the video Good George says 'Blaustein brings new life to the interpretive quest,' but here's Bad George"—he handed me a photo—"in a mean girl trifecta: eye rolling, nose wrinkling, and see how he seems to be in physical pain at the nice things Good George is saying about me?"

"The fluorescents were giving me a headache." I rewound the video. "Look. You can see the lights flickering."

"What about this? Good George praises my insights into Dilthey's work on the techniques of biography while Bad George nearly vomits."

"Just a bit of dyspepsia," I said. "And that's not even a microexpression. I'm sure I'm equally green around the gills in the video." I fast-forwarded and arrived at the part where Good George and Bad George pause to take a Maalox.

"Charles," I said, "I told you I don't agree with all of your hermeneutic theories and I've admitted I find some of your work disappointing. I've tried to help you through your bad times and I'm sorry if you've taken that as an evil plot. Now that we've aired things out I hope we can be friends. And can you *please* call Wendy off?"

But he was already on to the next photos, at one point comparing Bad George's smile to Hitler's when he crushed the Czech resistance. I walked away as he pulled put a dozen more, fanning them like a poker hand as he sought out Bad George. That's when I remembered my earliest conversations with Blaustein. He'd told me that my work had been one of his major influences, that it was the reason he chose Northwestern, that he considered himself an acolyte of my New Hermeneutics.

Now I got it: of course he believed I was his implacable enemy. It was preferable to believing I was meh about his work.

Microexpressions aside, what if my true opinions had leaked out of all those reviews and introductions? I had a fair amount of influence in the field—what if I'd sparked the widespread view that he was a hack? What if I *had* ruined his life?

The you're-all-going-to-hell guy had been standing a few yards up the path spying on us for God. He glumly held up his forefinger cross; I'd hurt him, too.

"Sorry about the hair oil remark," I said as I passed. "Your hair's fine."

FIFTEEN

On the walk home I imagined Blaustein's madness fused with Wendy's power. To keep that away from Rebecca and Max, I needed to flee, alone, to some map-blink off some decommissioned highway.

I walked in the house prepared for a grim discussion of my options. But Max wanted to play a video game, and I imagined a future where I sat alone in an eggshell motel room in the Badlands, peering through a gap in the blinds at acres of squat and regretting that I blew Max off today.

Even Wiffle Bat Hero can be poignant the last time. Max miraculously homered and Rebecca and I were whooping and giving him thumps on the back as the ball soared over frenzied dots in the stands; it ascended through the clouds and seemed ready to pinball among the stars. I froze it before it could drop: "Let's remember it this way." I was crying. Max gave me a pat on the arm and told me everything would be okay. It didn't work so he tried a thumbs-up and a trembly smile. That's when the headlong sobbing began: seismic, hippopotamine. Rebecca cupped my face in her hands. "George, what is it?" I shrugged, sobbed, shrugged.

"I have to work on something," I said crossing the hallway to my study. "Let's talk later."

I sat down at my desk and took a last look at the room. The professor's study, no description necessary—visualize every cliché attached to the phrase because that's how I chose and furnished it. Oak! Mahogany! Here was a serious man. A man of substance. The books not just books but mighty volumes that could crack your spine if you were foolish enough to read one in bed. If you stacked all these books they'd reach all the way to—my late father? A tall man, a giant of astrophysics. A serious man, a man with a study, a man of substance. What substance would that have been? Gloomothol? Bleakodine? I asked my mother what he thought about in there and she said "the spaces between the stars." He seemed to think about the same thing everywhere else. Was he my role model? Couldn't I have found a middle course between "black hole of gravitas" and "spasmodic miracle clown"?

I was having second thoughts about going into hiding. How was I going to hide when I was possibly the most recognizable man in the world? Not that people asked for autographs anymore but they nodded or grunted or shuddered or sneered their recognition. I didn't even know if Rebecca and Max would be safer at a distance or with me. My anxiety attack was receding; I inhaled the heady scent of slowly decaying paper. It seemed impossible that in the Wendy-Blaustein alliance *he'd* be in control, so I put aside my worries for our physical safety. I mimed a casual ease by putting my feet on the desk. Already my worries were seeping back out.

The new chair wasn't built for Whitmanesque loafing; I put my legs down.

My plan was simple. Go on with my life until Wendy and

Blaustein made it impossible, then sue them. Meanwhile here I was at my desk in the posture-fascist chair I bought when I turned forty. You couldn't nap or daydream in this baby: the whip and the chair were one. Why not start the memoir of flying I'd been planning?

I turned on my iMac, brought up a blank page, and blinked back at the cursor. Was I the hero of my own life? Was I even the protagonist? Was anybody the protagonist of their own life anymore?—Wendy did that for us.

In what sense had this been an adequate life? The story of my flying would be an epic of passivity—of being blown about like a leaf, but not nearly as fast or far or high. Had I upheld the honor of flying? No future Yeats would write a version of "The Irish Airman Foresees His Death" (the "lonely impulse of delight" among "the tumult of the clouds," etc.) to describe my one aerial battle—Ricardo Dean polishing a television studio floor with my face. Okay, I saved Nelson Baim's life, and, if you can remember that far back, I saved him from a beating. But really, was my life worth the breath? The case seemed weak. For the past few winters I'd used my snowblower to clear the sidewalks and parking spaces on our side of the block. I wrote letters for jailed writers and scholars. I demonstrated for causes and spent a night in the lockup trying, incidentally, to explain hermeneutics to a drunk who said he was with the CIA and could kill me with an inch of dental floss. I lobbied to help my students find work, I met with them whenever they wanted to discuss a problem, course related or otherwise. Once, in an epic conference with a student, I explained the entire quarter of Introduction to Hermeneutics including "What is hermeneutics?" Once a week I mowed the lawn for Mrs. Housebender, and cleaned her gutters in the fall. I'd worked with a volunteer organization teaching ESL to Russians. I spent an afternoon walking around our neighborhood with a woman who couldn't remember her name, though we never did find her house and I had to call the Department on Aging. I'd sat up with Iris in suicide prevention marathons. I was, as they say in the obits, a loving husband and father and son. I was honored and respected as a hermeneutist and had won most of the awards in my field. Jacques Chirac had praised my work. That's right, Jacques Chirac.

It occurred to me that my freshmen students could read from their college applications and make a better case that they were heroes of their own lives. One of them had modernized the agriculture of the Yucatán and had documented his claim. ("Fuck!" Toby said when I pointed to the line in the application. "Let's slit our throats and get out of their way.")

. . .

Rebecca knocked; would my memoir have to include my saying "come in"?

We left the door open. Max was watching cartoons across the hallway, and in the sometimes angry discussion to follow, we remembered, mostly, to keep our voices down.

She rolled the second chair over to my side, sat in it, put her hands on my shoulders, and eyeballed toward my brain. "So, you gonna tell me about it?"

"I'm sorry I upset you guys, but problem solved."

"I have ways to make you *talk*," she said in her spot-on Marlene Dietrich. "Something to do with flying?" She put her legs (white shorts, tan) on my lap. "Something go wrong with the *flying?*" Lately she spoke of flying in the sarcastic tone of a golf widow or a two-timed wife.

"No, not—okay, flying related."

She removed her legs.

"Hey! Put 'em back!"

They stayed over there. "They say men think of sex every six seconds," she said. "When was the last time you went that long without thinking of flying?"

"Only when I'm flying. Sometimes I'll zone out and think of nothing. I haven't told you—"

I was about to describe Blaustein and Wendy's plans for me when she broke in.

"When was the last time you took Max to the park? He ends up sitting in the yard watching you have your low-altitude epileptic fit. And don't give me that crap about flying and a child's sense of wonder."

"I fly him around on my back sometimes. How many dads in the park can do *that?* He has fun. He plays with his truck. Harvey lets him wear the turban—his whole head disappears in there and he shouts, 'Look! I'm a turban!'"

She made a face.

"True, we don't know where it's been," I said.

"He hates it, George. He told me. We can't imagine what it's like for a two-year-old to spend all those afternoons in unrelenting boredom. He can't distract himself with sex or hermeneutics or flying. You used to talk about how neglectful and emotionally absent your father was. You said you'd never let that happen to Max."

I thought I might start crying again. "Of course you're right.

I'll take him to the park from now on, I'll tell him I'm sorry. And I don't love flying as much as you think. When I gave my flying demonstration at the press conference, I looked down from the altitude of four inches—Harvey Bell says I should always survey my realm below—and spotted a cigarette butt on the carpet. And I thought, that's about as exciting as flying will ever get. Why not stop? But what if the next training session is the one that sets me zipping around the skies?"

"And so Max ends up squirming through another afternoon watching your display of avian rabies on the lawn."

"You're right," I said. "Can I just print up a sign to that effect and hold it up when necessary? I'll use my gym time for my flying practice. As a bonus, let me get my first page down and I'll take him to the park this afternoon."

"Sure you will."

"You'll see. Come with us."

She walked out.

I sat there trying to recall the first moment of flying: I'd felt disoriented, feverish, and for a moment felt the presence—

I nearly fell out of my desk chair as something exploded. It was volume one of the two-volume book club edition of the Oxford English Dictionary crashing down on the desk.

"It's the grandeur of the word, isn't it?" Rebecca demanded. "Suppose you called it 'floating'? Would you be sacrificing your family for 'floating'?"

Max hadn't turned around, focused on the explosions in his cartoon.

"It's not 'floating,'" I said. "Look it up. There's a dictionary."

"Look up 'fly,'" she said, "and while you're at it look up 'float' and 'levitate.'"

"You know, I *am* a professor of English."

"Don't pull rank on me. Your colleagues in the English department call it 'levitating' behind your back. What if you're no more important in the story of mankind than some bored assistant Nelson Baim might *levitate* above a birthday party?"

'Fly' and 'levitate' and 'float' were bookmarked. I turned to 'fly.' Like everyone else, we'd lost the little magnifying glass that came with the two-volume OED and I had to search my desk until I found a different one. I'd looked up flying in the OED before and recalled feeling a bit anxious when the definitions that could cover unassisted human flight seemed to mention the sky. "I'm too scattered to process dozens or hundreds of definitions right now."

"Giving up already?"

I tried my old defense. "Suppose a fly was flying at the same height I do. Wouldn't you say the fly was flying?"

"From a fly's perspective three or four inches is much higher than it is in ours," she observed.

"Then let's say it's flying at one inch. Or half an inch. You still wouldn't say the fly is levitating. Maybe you could also say it's floating but that would be in addition to flying."

"No, the fly's just flying. It's your geriatric pace along with the low altitude that suggests floating. George, you're not the only one who can perform some tiny miracle. Mrs. Housebender can see which bowling pins she'll knock over before she releases the ball; they seem to light up."

"As I constantly remind you, my darling, maybe she's just a good bowler."

Ignoring this she said, "Mrs. Housebender doesn't act like she came down from the mountaintop to give mankind the gift of

Precognitive Bowling. She doesn't strive in all things to maintain the honor of Precognitive Bowling."

I looked around. The tonnage of books, mahogany, first editions, galleys, awards, plaques, framed letters, and wainscoting could hold it back no longer—I was a short man and a fool, even my wife thought so.

.   .   .

I walked straight to the front door— "George?"—down the front steps and started up Ridge. Breathe, I told myself, let it go.

It was that ghostly hour in the early afternoon when the deserted sidewalks, the nearly empty streets, the Tallmadge street lamps (imitations of nineteenth-century London gas lamps), the seething shade, and the old wood frame houses seem about to revert to their late-night dream versions. Exactly the setting where your footsteps begin to echo, and the echo, like some impish doppelgänger in the mirror, proves to be not quite you.

I turned around. Five yards back a man in a magician's top hat and a dirty white tuxedo froze and turned to the empty sidewalk behind him. He faced forward again and stared back nervously and defiantly—a tall sickly skinny kid, nineteen or twenty. It was hard to observe anything about his face beyond the purplish wound on his left cheek.

Were the magicians we beat up months ago finally about to take their revenge? Were Wendy and Blaustein recruiting all my enemies? No sign of any more magicians. Were they waiting to make an entrance, columns of them marching out of the traditional puff of smoke?

The kid approached. He wasn't physically imposing, but up close his infected wound looked like a bite and I thought of rabies.

249

His voice broke as he said "George Entmen?" The George Entmen craze was about over, but occasional strangers still wanted something: a ride, God's plan, the secret of my trick, a selfie, a letter of recommendation, a blurb for their poetry chapbook, a miracle for their sick child, a chance to perform their act.

The day had been humiliating enough already without running away from some shy magician. "All right. Amaze me."

He took off the top hat. His poorly confederated brown hair stood up, lay down, or blew in his face. He pushed it back and said, "Please inspect the hat."

"You're kidding." I took the empty hat, looked inside, felt around for hidden spaces, handed it back. "Not a *rabbit*, surely?"

His entire musculoskeletal system sagged.

"Oh." I tried to put it more kindly. "It's just that people don't want—"

"Ya think?" He reached in and pulled out a rabbit by the ears. "Ta-da," he said bitterly. It was a good rabbit anyway, lustrous white coat, brown-eyed, placid. He cradled the rabbit and stroked it. It closed its eyes.

"You know, the rabbit's fine. I'm sure it lulls your audience, and just when they're thinking that that's all there is—"

He sagged even further, looking only at the rabbit.

"Sorry," I said. "I'm hardly one to talk about disappointing people."

"See I really pull a rabbit . . . this rabbit didn't exist before I pulled it out of the hat just now. Six Nobel physicists say that what I do demolishes our model of the universe. Why isn't that enough?"

"Oh. You're *that* guy. Tommy Thorne mentioned—"

"Clarence Fonderbine." Securing the rabbit in the crook of one arm, he extended a bite-marked hand.

I shook it. "So what now? We team up and fight crime?"

"Actually, I wanted to ask if you have an agent."

"No, but I get calls from agents—not interested. Say, this isn't an agent, but I got a call for a gig you might be perfect for. It's a commercial for a product called The Fishin' Magician. Could you pull a fish out of that hat?"

"No, rabbits only, and my power's limited to one per day. And it only works with this hat. And nobody else is able to pull rabbits out of it. And I can't make the rabbits disappear by stickin' 'em back in the hat."

"That could be a load of rabbits if you've been at it awhile. What do you do with them?"

"I don't want to talk about it."

"And what's with all the rules?" I asked, thinking of my own severe limitations.

"I dunno," he said, "but somebody on the other side of the hat must be laughin' his ass off."

.   .   .

"'But somebody on the other side of the hat must be laughin' his ass off!'" I concluded, dreading the awful silence if Rebecca didn't laugh.

She laughed, despite my vocabulary slip with Max in the room; Max fake-laughed to keep us company, and hostilities seemed at an end.

Rebecca and I returned to my study and I filled her in on the Wendy-Blaustein onslaught. "What's the or-else?" she asked when I'd finished. "Do it or—? Or what?"

"That idiot—he forgot the threat. I'll phone Wendy and ask."

"No!" She gripped my arm. "If she hasn't committed herself

there's always a chance she'll think twice about hurting the guy who saved Nelson's life."

"If we know what it is, maybe we can think of countermeasures."

"'Countermeasures?' What are you, a secret agent? You just want to hear her sexy voice on the phone."

I took out my phone. Why did I have Wendy as my number five contact? In case I wanted to be more quickly harmed? "The more information we have, the better we can defend ourselves."

"That's ridiculous."

"If it works with hurricanes it can work with Wendy." It was ringing.

Wendy picked up. "George? How are you? It's been a while."

"Fine. You?"

"We're completing a project to bring potable water to two million people in South Sudan. And what are *you* up to, podling?"

"Blaustein forgot the or-else."

There was no need to explain the expression to Wendy. "Just between us, the man is no joy to work with. Let me give you a protip, George. Never ask about the or-else. There's always the chance your extortionist might change her mind if you don't commit her to something. But you'll have to save that for next time. The or-else is awesome. First I destroy the English department—unfinished business from your never telling us your trick. Then I destroy hermeneutics."

"Really. How do you propose to do that?"

"We'd brand you as a scientology-like cult. We've got the psychologists, the pundits, a bipartisan group of politicians, some washed-up movie stars, and of course the hermeneutics survivors, including Blaustein."

"You're delusional."

"That could be. I've been reading a lot of hermeneutics, and all that cultish gibberish does subvert the rational mind."

"I don't know whether to laugh or—"

"Laugh, dear, by all means laugh while you can. Saving the best for last, I'll steal Rebecca from you."

"Really. And just how would you do that?" I asked, avoiding Rebecca's tilted stare.

"She's there, isn't she? Then I'd better whisper," Wendy breathed. "Remember the selfie of Rebecca and me in our underwear painting each other's toes? Just before we got started on our toenails we got started on each other. We're sitting on the carpet. I extend my foot into the crotch of her new panties. I'm pretty dexterous with my toes and—"

I was about to hang up but instead asked, "So you didn't really—"

"Second base," she said, "though emotionally it was an inside-the-park home run. Now. Do you want to hear how I'm going make her mine, as they say in country-western songs? Hang up if you don't want to hear this. Still there. Of course. It might happen like this. Some rainy afternoon—a Tuesday or a Thursday when you're at the gym and Max is taking his nap—I come over there in my wet clothes. I have on this tight white dress. You've seen it. Do you like it?"

"Yes."

Max was standing there; he handed me a truck with a wheel coming loose and shrugged. For the most part he was a happy kid but lately he'd acquired an old man's shrug, palms up, eyes enlarged, chin crinkled, lips compressed and turned down, shoulders bunched at the neck. It was the fatalistic shrug of my great-uncle Eddie, who'd died thirty years ago. We'd thought it was cute at first and damn funny, but it worried us a little. Was this the sadness of all those afternoons watching me claw at the air?

I placed the iPhone between my ear and shoulder while I worked. There was a specialized tool just for the wheels of that truck, the wheels were shoddily attached to make you buy the tool, and no mob leg-breaker could be more persuasive at making you fork over an outrageous sum than your child holding out his crippled truck. I had a tool in the top drawer of my desk (they're tiny; you'd better buy two) and I tightened the one-of-a-kind screw while I listened.

"I'll have a story," she was saying. "A charity reception at the Orrington. Car trouble. Bad cell coverage. But the last thing she'll be thinking about is the auto club and cell towers and the laws of coincidence. Just me in my little white, wet dress. And then me peeling myself out of it."

Max and Rebecca were eying me curiously. My shame and guilt should have squelched the eroticism of the call, but instead everything had mixed into one hot pie seething with live blackbirds. Our cat Claude came in; even he was giving me the stink-eye.

"Do you like the word 'peeling,' George? It doesn't make you think of potatoes, does it? No, I didn't think it would. Rebecca helping with the zipper—with all the summer colds going around we've got to get those wet clothes off fast!—and pretty soon I'm peeling her out of her university sweatshirt and yoga pants or whatever else she's wearing on a Tuesday or a Thursday afternoon in a hopeless attempt to look frumpy. This is even more fun with her sitting there, isn't it? There's a lot of nervous chatter when we start peeling. Her Hugo Freiles biography, something funny Max said, the South Sudanese and their potable water. But by the time we start on her it's just rain and breathing. I know it's implausible but I imagine her pussy has a taste, at least an aftertaste, of tapioca."

"That's more than enough," I said tersely. "Goodbye."

"A little late for the moral indignation, but, you know, honored in the breach. Say hello to Max and Rebecca. One more thing. Your wounded-butterfly shtick is no fun for either of us."

"By that definition of 'fun'—"

"Fight back! You need to power up, my friend. Read your Flesner! Start with Chapter 7 of *The Reaches of Power,* 'The Pyramid of Fear.'"

"I'm sorry I don't find wrecking my life as much fun as you do. Tell you what. Why don't I just write Nelson a blurb?"

She had a laugh for running through a meadow beside a brook flinging daisy petals. "Now that's just silly. Bye!"

. . .

Max was back in the living room playing with his truck. He was shouting "vroom!" at the top of his voice, so evidently the truck was in good repair.

"To sum up," I said to Rebecca, "she'll destroy the English department, destroy hermeneutics, and turn up here on a rainy day and make you her lover. And I can't just sit back and be destroyed—there's assigned reading. She suggests the contest would be more sporting if I read my Flesner. Always with the Flesner! Oh, and she says that the day you two took the underwear picture she got to second base with her toe in your crotch."

"She didn't make it to first. Thrown out. It occurs to me that if she lies about *that,* maybe her *threats* are bullshit. They've always sounded a little grand even for someone as powerful and relentless and evil-ish as she as is."

"I agree." I dialed Wendy.

This time Rebecca didn't grab my arm or lunge for the phone. She just looked sad. "You get impulsive when you're worked up," she said. "This can't possibly help."

"She's right," Wendy said.

"We think you're bluffing," I said to her.

"Poor George. You've forgotten my protip from ten minutes ago."

"Usually you're sort of charming, even when you're making threats. But what I just heard, that was bad Cruella de Vil—I won't dignify it with a more literary reference. Your original threat to take away my Twine Award and wreck the English department? Magnificent, bravo. But this—clearly your heart's not in it."

I was pleased that I'd at least made her stop and consider her next remark. It was during that pause that I first heard calliope music. It wasn't coming from the phone. "Do you hear that?" I whispered.

Rebecca nodded warily. The circus gave her strong feelings of "don't touch it, you don't know where it's been."

"Poor George," Wendy was saying, "you want mommy to say it's all over and everything will be fine. Sure, I might have overdone the threats. I thought I could get you to acquiesce here and now if I piled it on, and believe me, for your own good, we *must* settle this today. And since you fantasize about me as this omnipotent omnibitch, I thought a little sexy domestic turmoil might undermine your resistance."

"Sounds like you're out of threats."

"Oh George, there are as many threats as there are grains—"

"Are we done with the author tour?"

"Sadly, we are not."

The calliope music had reached attack volume. "Look. Nelson has his book contract. Christ, I can't *think*! Okay, I assume there's no provision in the contract to send me on the perpetual book tour? Then fuck Blaustein. Just have your megalawyers enforce the contract as written."

"Don't you think I thought of that? I told Blaustein we wouldn't be honoring anything outside the written contract." Even at full volume I couldn't make out everything she was saying beneath the quaking, shrieking whimsy of circus ditties. "[Something something something] it provides [something something something] and the provision that [something something something]. Blaustein said maybe he'd just kill you."

"What! Blaustein said he'd what?"

"Kill you! He said maybe! I know, George, I should have mentioned it. I thought that once I did, everything would escalate [something something something] off a cliff tit over ass. Nobody has to get hurt if you play along with the tour for a few weeks— I'll find a way out. There's—"

The music was at death metal concert level, a bone-shattering organ theme filigreed with psychotic tooting.

"You didn't mention Blaustein's death threat because you didn't want him locked up or fired before the book is published," I said.

"George, I'd never [something something something]. I like to think we're friends."

Someone was pounding on the front door.

I held up the phone into the pandemonium. "Are you doing this?" I yelled.

"No, George, when I was creating the world some things like calliopes snuck through on their own. I'd love to hear you whine all day but then I'd have to explain to two million South Sudanese why [something something something] die of draught." She hung up.

I was headed for the front door when a bullet passed through one of the bay windows. Against the calliope uproar it sounded like a balloon popping, leaving no more fuss behind than a small hole radiating cracks. A small puddle of glass dust sparkled on the rug. I scooped up Max; he'd been sitting on the floor with his truck, well clear of the bullet and the drizzling glass, trying to out-vroom! chaos.

I ran to the the study, handed Max to Rebecca, and said, "Get behind the desk. Lie on your stomachs if there's room." Rebecca—a veteran of noisy dorms and battling sisters—was wearing earbuds as she scrolled through her notes for a journal article. She pulled them off. "What?"

"Take Max and get behind the desk!"

The joke she was about to make wilted when she looked in my face.

"What about you?"

"Be there in a minute."

"I don't like this!" Max said.

"Just a game we're playing buddy," I assured him. "Dial 911," I called to Rebecca as she and Max crawled behind the desk.

"What?" she called. "Why?"

"I've got it!" I dialed 911 with a finger in the other ear, leaving the calliope out of my complaint. Police would arrive "shortly." I crawled on my stomach toward the front door till it occurred to me that I'd get there faster by flying. It was the only practical use I'd ever found for flying.

Perhaps it was the dire circumstances or my intense focus, but it was a tic-free flight, very like floating, I'll give you that, Rebecca. The calliope was playing "Rodeo Girl" as I stood up and edged one eye to the door pane. At the foot of our steps Blaustein, ineffectually disguised under a tractor cap, his gun arm at his side, appeared to be assessing the situation.

A circus wagon the size of an eighteen-wheeler was parked a few feet to his left, jutting halfway onto the sidewalk. Old fashioned circus and freak show images covered the side I faced, except for a tiny blacked-out window and the racing lightbulbs along the wagon's edges. The pictures were rendered mostly in garish orange and red, their deep black shadows solid as blunt instruments: a strongman bursting chains, a tiaraed princess waving from a horse, bowler-hatted Siamese twins, a leaping lion, a pyramid of solemn house cats. But scattered among these were images of washed-up celebrities: an ancient former game show host, his face Botoxed to rack-tight serenity; the original Four Tops; a once-mighty Chicago alderman; and some young, glamorous movie stars—washed up already. I gasped at an aged but still recognizable "Schoolbell Sarah," the first person I ever saw on TV. I thought I'd heard that these people were dead.

My baseball bat was still in the corner by the door where Rebecca left it after shaking it at Nelson Baim. I picked it up— prepared to head for the back door, come around, and sneak up on Blaustein while he was thinking—and at that moment the music stopped, its absence more startling than gunfire. Blaustein fired a second bullet through the same bay window; large chunks of it shrugged onto the floor. At that moment the wagon door burst open and four men in roustabout caps and horizontal-striped T-shirts grabbed Blaustein as he was aiming his next shot, pried the gun loose, punched him into a convulsive heap on the sidewalk, kicked and stomped the heap till it stopped moving, picked him up and tossed him through the open door of the wagon. Fuck this! he's still a human being, I decided, and charged down the steps with the bat. By the time I reached the sidewalk they'd piled into the wagon, all except for the one who'd got into the cab, and sped away. As far as I know it was the last anyone saw of Charles Blaustein or the uproarious circus.

. . .

Two police officers took down the details of the shoot-up and the abduction. They'd already been headed to our block to investigate noise complaints. The officers had no other knowledge of the circus—it was gone by the time they arrived— though the younger one said something about rumors. The senior partner cut him off. "We deal in facts, Ronald." Nothing about our account provoked their incredulity except that calling a book "fine" could be construed as a mortal insult.

We needn't have worried that our story would sound implausible. This was still the age of "If George can fly . . ." At the height of my fame America found an infinite number of ways to complete that sentence. "If George can fly, why *couldn't* my dog eat my homework?" "If George can fly, why can't I find a good tomato at the Jewel?" "If George can fly, my dear, why couldn't I have been working late last night?" In short: if George can fly, all is possible. It was a tough time for what some had dubbed "the vanilla truth"; it was the heyday of water shoes (who needs a boat?), alibis, invisible spirit pets, Donald Trump, and The Church of Bad Faith. The courts had been forced to consider whether anything was "beyond a reasonable doubt."

It would be cold to gloss over the abduction and disappearance of my colleague Charles Blaustein. Everyone in the department hated him and no one had better cause than I. But a few months later, when it was clear that his Edward G. Robinson jeer would never again blare through the walls of classrooms, I joined the unanimous vote for a memorial service—really for the sake of his inconsolable wife Karen. The most interesting thing I learned about him at the service was that he was a master of the folk guitar. The chairman had thought that since I knew Blaustein better than anyone else and was therefore the closest thing he had in the department to a friend, I should deliver the eulogy. And so I lied in praise of Blaustein for the last time. "He was a hard man to know," I told the mourners. "But when this private man opened up he revealed a unique and sometimes delightful way of seeing the world. It wasn't till long after we met that I became aware of his playful, razor-sharp sense of humor." The crowd leaned forward, awaiting examples, but he was only brilliant and funny when he was trying to destroy me. Later I said, "I think he was trying to reach out, and I wonder if we failed him. I know I did." I said it without guile. I ended by praising him as "a devoted husband [I had no idea], a complex and interesting friend, a fine hermeneutist, and a fine, fine man."

Afterward I walked up to Karen Blaustein, dreading what she'd made of the eulogy, uncertain what I made of it myself. But I'd glanced at her as I read it and saw her nodding and crying. I'd heard her sobbing when I ended with "a fine, fine man."

With her extreme pallor and her smudges of eyeliner, she looked like an overly thumbed page. Could this broken woman have been his coconspirator? Would she spit in my face? I was startled, relieved, and confused when she closed in for a long hug. At the end of it she drew back and picked up a Nordstrom bag from the refreshments table. "He would have wanted you to have this."

It was, of course, my Twine Award. I suppose I deserved it, in every sense of the word. It remains on my bookshelf.

SIXTEEN

My publisher has been questioning the existence of the circus wagon, accusing me of glibly wrapping up this memoir with a "circus ex machina." They sent over their hulking fact-checker, who just happened to be in Evanston, to try to get me to see things their way (having fact-checked this paragraph he notes, "1) I was visiting my parents; they live in Evanston! 2) I'm tall. Can't a guy be tall in your prose without being 'hulking'?").

I have documentation. While the circus wagon wasn't covered in the mainstream press, its photograph appeared in a story on the front page of *The Daily Northwestern*. I sent my editor that clipping plus the smartphone photo I'd taken through my door pane: the wagon, Blaustein holding the gun, the riotous scene leafy and incongruously still. Granted: the facticity of the event began to evaporate when my colleagues in the English department got hold of it. Their journal pieces treated it as a symbol, a construct. They never actually investigated ("Investigated?" one of them scoffed. "What am I, a cop?") It was never treated as something, always the embodiment of something—the gaudy Age of George, say, or the age of Trumpean gaslighting. Already—it's only been three years—the massive wagon with its teeming images and assaultive noise seems no more substantial than a net-bag of dandelion wisps. Soon it will melt away, along with so much else—this book, for instance.

My publisher wants to suppress the more "incongruous elements." "Does that include the flying?" I asked sarcastically. For a moment he hesitated! "Of course not," he said. "What would the book be about?" But the truth is, the age of "If George can fly . . ." seems long behind us. There's no market for "all is possible." It's like we were all caught believing in Santa Claus. The compromises my publisher demands would be an abdication of the honor of flying, whatever that means, whatever remains of it. He knows this, knows that if he keeps it up (he will) I'll walk away (I will!). I've been an academic more than half my life, and I've known my share of measly men like Ed. He's the perfect embodiment of post-George man. He wants to remove the flying from four-inch flying and keep the paltry inches.

Flying itself is gone. It happened six months after the Blaustein abduction; I went out to the yard before breakfast to practice. For all my practicing my ability had remained unchanged. Occasionally I'd float appealingly, but my default style of flight was so wretched I sometimes wondered if I'd been banished down there for absence of grace. I'd never gone beyond the altitude of four inches, the distance of our hallway, or the speed of the average nursing home resident with a walker. Clearly that's all it would ever amount to, and for a while I'd been on the verge of quitting. I could use that time for prebreakfast sex with Rebecca and for writing this book—though it's apparent I'll soon be writing it only for myself, an exercise as pointless as flying.

"Think of it this way," Harvey Bell had advised when I'd told him I was thinking of quitting. "You're the first amphibian.

You crawl out of the water and gasp and wheeze for a minute, then crawl back in the water and try again later. It's your duty to your race to keep trying." "Once it's clear that this is all I can do, shouldn't I leave the rest to the second amphibian?" "The second amphibian might give up without your heroic example." "And what if there is no second amphibian?" "Then you keep on striving because that's what you do." I could have mentioned that this paste pearl of wisdom was the catchphrase in a series of Geico commercials, but I let Harvey have his smug mystical smile.

The morning I lost flying I went out in the yard in the usual ski pants, two sweatshirts, and thermal underwear, lay down on my stomach on the cold dead lawn (despite the layers, icy lawn stubble bristled against my chest), and willed myself to fly. The result was the same as for every other human being who'd ever willed it. I remained on the lawn, my nose running, my thermal underwear bunching up. I tried again but the ants under my nose remained exactly ant size. I breathed deep, stretched, gave myself three slaps in the face, promised to win one for The Gipper, nodded confidently to my amphibian successors, shouted "Up! Up! And away!" and once again fizzled on the launchpad.

Rebecca came out on the porch with her coffee. "That was quite a shout, dude. Look, here's Max." He always looked moonstruck in the first minutes after waking. He couldn't quite shake off his dreams, and he seemed like an adorable drunk with no idea how he'd got here. He ran out to the yard.

"Daddy can't fly," I announced. "I know, it's something every daddy and mommy has had to face for all time, but—" I stared off at the sky, the clouds parting in sheer mockery.

While Rebecca fetched Max a jacket, he tried to remind me how to fly. He lay down on the lawn on his stomach. I was about to tell him not to get his pj's dirty, but I was entranced by his version of my flying. He pounded his fists on the ground like a toddler having a tantrum, made a moron face, drooled, wrinkled his nose, and bunched his mouth to one side of his face as if it too were trying to escape this earth.

It cheered me to reenact his version of me as a moron pounding the lawn—we pounded the lawn together—but by the time Rebecca returned with Max's jacket and coffee for me, I was staring at the clouds again. "I know," I said taking a sip of coffee, "flying did no good for me or the world. It had no upside." I laughed. What wouldn't I give to get back those tightwad inches!

"Even LeBron James has a bad day," she said. "Have you tried other positions?" The ensuing drill was very much like the one we followed when I lost my keys. On my back, to start with—I dreaded this one might work, and I'd be doomed to flying at four inches upside down. I dreaded crowds of untrimmed noses gathering round, my in-flight view emphasizing the miserable irony that I was flying down here while the earthbound got to be up there. But I remained so definitively on my back that we had to assure Mrs. Housebender next door that I was okay.

We proceeded. On my side, standing up, standing on my head (to entertain Max), and doing a few basic yoga positions Harvey Bell taught me. Rebecca even took me through a few of her stances from ballet class, but their only effect was to make some teenagers in the alley snort.

Rebecca suggested that for the next few days I work on my negative attitude toward flying.

I said, "I get it. Like that story about the guy who can predict the future and who loses his talent when he starts going to the track every day—dishonoring precognition!—just before an unanticipated terrorist bomb goes off at the track and dismembers him?"

"Yeah, George, exactly like that."

"Maybe I'll put in an emergency call to Harvey Bell. On second thought, I'm not ready to break the glass on Harvey yet. I'll see if Dr. Abrams can work me in this afternoon."

"It's way too early for any of this stuff," she said. "See what happens tomorrow."

"When I fell out of bed that morning at the beginning, and rose above the floor, it was only because I knew I could do it. It's the same here. On my first try, I knew flying was over." Do tears rush through the ducts in rapids? Probably not, but that was my image as I held them back. "Anyway, I need someone to officially pass sentence."

. . .

Dr. Abrams was an opera baritone of a man who examined you with a cocked head and a wry set of the mouth. If your malady was susceptible to scoffing, he was the guy. He always found a way to squeeze me in because he was working his way through an inexhaustible list of questions about flying. That day he prefaced each question with "When you could fly—" At first it gave me a wistful ache, but soon I had to look at the blood vessel chart to keep from crying.

"When you could fly could you fly upside down?"

"No."

He jotted my replies in a black notebook.

"When you could fly, did any weight—your son, for instance, on your back—"

I was losing it.

"—did any weight on your back affect your height, speed, and distance?"

"Oddly enough," I said, "no. Or was it all oddly enough?"

"When you could fly, could you . . . back up?" He grinned. "Beep beep beep."

"No."

"When you could fly could you hang a U-turn?"

"Yeah. I guess."

"Hmm. Okay. When you could fly—if you jumped off the observation deck of the Empire State Building would you be able to escape splatting on the ground when you reached your flying inches?"

"Splat!" I replied, summing up the state of things.

He gave me a complete physical and told me I was in great shape for a forty-year-old. He saw no symptoms that I'd lost the ability to fly. What, I asked, are the symptoms of having lost the ability to fly? He admitted he didn't know. And what, I asked, are the symptoms of the ability to fly? He brightened. "Flying!" he declaimed. "Flying is the one known symptom of the ability to fly." We had a good laugh. At some point I stopped laughing and melted into the longest crying jag I'd had since I was eight and slid under a fence that ripped open my thigh.

I know: what's with the sobbing? Until recently I'd cried three times since I was ten—Iris's service, my father's funeral, the birth of our son Max (I'm leaving out occasional book or movie-inspired blubbering). Why so few, you ask now? I don't know. The role model of my father? A career in critical theory? Fortunately we don't have to haul around our lifetime jugs of tears and compare, so back off.

I considered Dr. Abrams a friend. Our sessions, as you can

see, were usually relaxed and informal. At the same time he was a maestro of the examining room, and out-of-the-office Abrams, whoever he was, was never to be seen on the premises. Invade his personal boundaries, and you discovered they were patrolled by Dobermans. He wore thick heavy weapons-grade horn-rims designed, I believed, to keep his patients in some distant clinical elsewhere. Almost forgot: he couldn't bear to run into a patient on the elevator. It happened with me only once. He kept his eyes riveted on the floor numbers as if any acknowledgment of my existence would send us plummeting. I remember asking whether he thought the doors closed sooner when you hit the close door button; he seemed ready to claw them apart! You'd think that a patient crying, even prodigiously, would be a fact of the doctor's profession. Maybe it was the novel problem of how to console a man who couldn't fly. When my tears had abated sufficiently to look around, I discovered that the doctor had deserted me in the office an hour ago, according to the receptionist, and gone home.

. . .

The next morning I phoned Harvey Bell.

"Yeah!"

This snarl in lieu of hello was atypical of Harvey, whom I'd always known as unfailingly polite. "Harvey? Is this a bad time?"

"Ha! It's all puppies, George. Puppies and rides on a fluffy cloud. What can I do for you?"

As I described my flightlessness I heard him sigh. The volume of these sighs rose to a manifest disgust. And yet he'd kept postponing his return to California, living in his sister's guest room near the university to go on being my guru.

"If I'm boring you, Harvey—"

"Let me put your problem in perspective. You've probably heard this one: I was sad when the stumbling oaf scuffed my new cordovans. Then I saw a man with no feet."

"I take it I'm not the stumbling oaf or the man with no feet."

"You know it. You're the man with the cordovans, baby."

"You don't sound like yourself today."

"You'd be amazed what's like myself. I'll be off to prison, oh, by February."

"I think I know you well enough to—what?"

"I'll be off to prison by February."

"God, Harvey, I didn't know anything about this. Is there anything—"

"I'm the man with no feet. Don't feel sorry. Who says I deserve feet? But sure, let's have a final session. I can be there in half an hour."

. . .

Three years after our final meeting it occurs to me: It couldn't be easy being Harvey Bell. You have to balance your ineradicable sense of humor with your famous mystical gaze. You have to extract large sums from your followers for various twinkle-dust projects, and you have to feel ("good" is not enough) blissful about doing it. You have to reconcile yourself to getting beaten up by people who mistake you for a Muslim. And by ex-followers who know exactly what you are (he'd had to fire his bodyguards when the legal bills reached the altitudes of his famous gaze). And you have to wind the damn turban every day—it doesn't go on like a hat. That afternoon he was literally and metaphorically one turn shy of a turban. Sometimes he'd look up at the slack dangling above his eyes, but that problem was way down his list.

"I was indicted today," he said before he'd come in from the front porch. He looked around. "No press mob. I've been expecting an ambush all day." He stood there a few more seconds and took a last hopeful look behind him. "That's the worst of all. When they don't even care."

"I could start a letter-writing campaign," I said as I took his coat. "I've made some influential friends because of the flying. I think if we all just—"

"Thanks, but I'll settle for a double scotch. Rocks, please."

When I returned with it he was seated in the beanbag chair.

"Wouldn't you be more comfortable on the—"

"No, the beanbag chair is all I deserve. If I reincarnate as a beanbag chair I'll consider it just." He took a sip of scotch. "Buddhists believe that every sip must be taken mindfully. Fuck that." He disposed of the rest in one convulsive swallow. "Tomorrow I fly to California for the bail hearing."

Our cat Claude came over and gazed at the short belt of cloth dangling above Harvey's eyes. He longed to take a whack at it but decided, as he did in most matters these days: why bother? None of us was the life of the party.

"What are you charged with?"

"Only the best. Wire fraud and fraud. Plus larceny and a few other things that sound like larceny and fraud. The gist is that I'm a very bad man who bilks trusting people out of money. Guilty."

"In college I thought of you as this kind, sensitive, funny, shy, honest, wistful, thoroughly good and decent guy. Not to mention an insightful, empathetic poet."

"Clearly the road to perdition."

"When you showed up here twenty years later, and I got used

to the turban, the guru mannerisms, the guru gaze, the jargon, the weight loss, and those weird bulging face muscles—"

"It's the bliss. You gotta work your face to sell it."

"—you seemed like the same guy. Apparently not. What happened, Harvey?"

He tried to stuff the cloth into folds of the turban—it jutted out in a loop suitable for miniature basketball. "It was poetry that led me to this. You slap your bloody guts onto the page, and the critics say he's wistful. Pleasantly oddball. Amusingly surreal. Mildly diverting—diverting in the sense of, look, there's his gall bladder on the page. Your Amazon ranking indicates that every person in the United States found time to write a book and it's doing better than yours. But that's okay, Jerkwater College has a position and you and your family won't starve. And meanwhile Billy Collins attends a cocktail party and sets down a few witty observations and everybody in every book club in America goes still. But okay, you're not in it for the sales, and your Amazon ranking sets you free. You can write anything now—you are the audience. And if they stop publishing you—even freer. Navel gazing needn't be avoided, but why stop at gazing? You've always picked at your navel, and now you can poetize the act. Has anyone ever described the smell of navel lint in a poem? You'd think Henry Miller would have eaten out some lover's navel in a novel, but what about poetry? Philip Larkin maybe, but no—it's one more vastness open to your expeditions.

"And then one day you're writing a poem in which a common group of bacteria found in the navel acts as a symbol, and you realize you can't spell it. You're about to look it up, but some imp of the perverse whispers, 'Why look it up? You're the only reader and you know what you mean.'"

He sat up as well as you can in a beanbag chair, waved off my suggestion of a better place to sit, took a bite of an ice cube, and resumed. "Soon after, you're at a party and someone introduces you to a woman in a T-shirt with an iron-on photo of her cat. You're about to excuse yourself when you notice this woman doesn't blink. Terrible for the eyes but it makes her look intense. You find yourself gazing into those eyes, the precise blue, George, of that dizzy wisp of sky where the air runs out. She tells you she's a writer. You ask what she's written. Turns out that in her life as a writer she's written nothing and never will. You profess to find this fascinating. She explains: we don't need more writing—what we need are more people with the sensibility of writers. Maybe she didn't say 'sensibility.' She's trained herself to experience the world as a writer—studied the FBI training manual to learn to make relevant observations, logic and geometry for precision, meditation to rid her brain of clutter, biographies for empathy. Read every book with 'a more powerful vocabulary' in the title. And of course she's read every fiction-writing manual from Aristotle—maybe she didn't say Aristotle—to the three-part-structure guy. All to be sure she's got her mastery of the vocation of writer down pat. Eventually her boyfriend comes over and you finally have the will to go home.

"The next day you're revising a poem, and the whispering imp is back. But the voice belongs to the woman with the iron-on cat. Why revise? You know what you're trying to say; why fancy it up? Why set it down in any form when you know what you mean? Putting down the words just for yourself is the madness of that guy on the subway arguing with himself, maybe even throwing a punch. Does the world need your poem? The libraries are buckling.

"As the consequences of that decision rampage through the years, your wife divorces you, Jerkwater College denies you tenure, and you spend four hours a day traveling among part-time comp classes that barely pay for the gas. And then one day you get a call from Books Ahoy!, a little bookstore in your old neighborhood where you used to give readings. Having heard you're on the skids, no doubt, they offer you a paid reading. You focus on that hundred dollars when you arrive to an audience of four people. A glamorous couple in matching silver unitards steal a copy of your book off the pile and, in the middle of your reading, put it back, and walk out. There's no one left but the cat woman and her boyfriend in the front row—different T-shirt, same cat, different boyfriend.

"She comes up after the reading, and you think of telling her she ruined your life. But you're magnanimous on bookstore wine, so you ask how she's progressing as a writer. She tells you she's found a book that enlarges her writer's spirit, something called *The Golden Throne*. I found my copy the other day. Autographed—by the cat woman! She didn't write the book, she was just being writerly. The author's on the cover with his monk's robe and Michael Jordan haircut. Any professional guru would spot him as a phony. His smile has nothing to do with celestial joy—it's the smile of a man who's looking forward to a Snickers bar after the shoot. And his turban's tilted back like a fedora, which means it's the kind that's attached to a frame—what I've always thought of as the clip-on tie of the trade. Just my personal opinion." Harvey wore that type about half the time.

He went on with his story. "You thumb through the book; seems like a random assortment of D+ surrealism from your old workshops. That's when it hits you. You can make people read your poetry and give you money.

"You spend the weekend assembling passages from your books. You arrange the lines randomly and add transitions. Finally you take out the transitions and you're done."

"Anything from *The Burlap Ventricle*?" I asked. "That was my favorite."

"Of course. That's also the title of our holy book. You mean you haven't read our holy book?"

"Didn't you just say it's all a fraud?'

"But a little support from my friends? Meanwhile I got tons of support from my followers. But they didn't get the poetry. They didn't even get that it was poetry, just something to chant for their lumbago. I tried to assign my original pre-randomized books, but when the time came to discuss them, they hadn't done the reading, they just gossiped about the members who weren't there, as if we weren't a spiritual community at all but a damn book club."

"So you *were* you a spiritual community?"

"The closest I came to thinking that was early in the gig. I asked myself if I actually was the leader of a spiritual community and the answer came back, Yeah, maybe. But these people were using me. Taking what they wanted and never reading my poetry. So I started taking at my end, and here we are."

"Listen. I meant it. I could get the letter-writing campaign going today."

"Thanks, George, but I'm a crook, and you're so scrupulous. What could you say?"

I hadn't thought about that. "A fine man. A fine, fine—"

"You're a good friend but please don't. Let's do your session. What's wrong? You don't trust me now? You're afraid you'll come out of hypnosis as a destitute clucking chicken? Actually I won't be hypnotizing you today. I have something else planned for your last session."

"I hope you'll change your mind about letting us help you," I said and started for the backyard.

"Hold on. Where are Rebecca and Max today?"

"At the pediatrician. And afterward she usually takes him someplace fun. Why?"

"We won't be going to the yard today. We're going up."

.   .   .

I ducked my head under the attic window and slid over the sill. My feet landed on the shingles a few feet below and I straightened out of my crouch. I'd feared the slope of the roof might frog-march me over the edge, but my running shoes had good traction. Nonetheless I started down with my trunk leaning back, as if hoping my feet would go to the edge without me. Harvey was already sitting there, his legs dangling over the gutter.

"Come on, George. This is the easy part. How high is the edge here?"

I sat down next to him. "I know exactly. I had to buy a ladder to clean the gutters. Eighteen feet."

It was an unseasonably cold mid-November, the backyard lawns already straw colored. The yard across the alley still had laundry on the line, those thrashing arms and legs signaling me like frantic runway marshals.

"What happens now?"

"First you jump."

I moved a few yards away from him.

"You're in luck, George. The death window commonly starts at twenty to twenty-five feet, depending on the hardness of the ground."

"Get to the 'but seriously' part." A black girl in Ninja Turtles pajamas waved from a second story window. I had no intention of making her a witness.

"I have a theory about your flying," he said.

"Let me guess. It's my lack of boldness that kept me flying at three or four inches and finally cut me off from even that. But if I laugh in the teeth of death—huh-ha!—and thwack my thigh like Errol Flynn and leap off the roof, then the clouds will part"—it was an overcast day—"and the gods will let me pass."

"Probably not," he said. "It's more likely you'll be seriously injured. Broken bones, maybe internal injuries. Even death is more likely. But is that worse than not trying? If George can fly . . ."

"But George can't fly, Harvey. That's why I called you today."

"So you choose the option of escaping harm. You won't. Think of it this way. Rebecca: you're so beneath her! When you were pursuing her you must have known your chances were at best in the high zeroes. What would your life have been like if you'd played the odds and quit? Traded the likelihood of pain for an endless, muffled, eggshell-white absence of pain. I know, you'd find somebody else, maybe you'd convince yourself you're happy. But your lifelong regret . . . Remember the 'Elvis on Other Planets Weight Chart'? It would be Jupiter. And this will be worse. You want to avoid anything that dishonors flying but you're no longer sure what that means? This is what it means! It'll pancake

277

you! You flew for the first time when you got tangled up in the bedding. And now you want to pull it back over your head."

I was wondering if he was insane. But maybe he was trying to evade his final failure as a guru. If he couldn't help me fly, it was my fault: I wouldn't jump off the roof.

I wondered what he'd do if I actually jumped. Just to scare him I stood up. "Huh-ha!"

He wasn't backing down. "Try to land on the balls of your feet in a crouch, then spring immediately into a forward roll. If you manage that you might not break your feet. Whatever you do, don't land on your head."

"And if I'm flying?"

"Keep going!"

I took off my glasses and handed them to Harvey.

He said, "I know I'm not the holiest guru in the barrel. But I've always been on your side, George. I've never stopped believing in 'If George can fly . . .' "

"Me neither."

He opened his arms. I hesitated a moment then hugged my old friend.

When I returned to the edge I thought of the wind factor. It might slow me down, but it might also wreck Harvey's landing instructions. Or maybe at eighteen feet the wind couldn't do much to change my course. The girl in the Ninja Turtles pajamas was gone from the window.

"Good luck, my friend," Harvey said, "and remember: 'the moment you doubt you can fly—'" He was quoting J. M. Barrie.

We completed it in unison. "'—you cease forever to be able to do it.'"

I tried to read the semaphore of the frenzied laundry. Cleared for takeoff, I decided, and jumped.

. . .

After my near death by drowning at Camp 4-Fun, it took years of therapists and YMCA instructors just to alleviate my fear of the water. Their message was always the same: the water isn't trying to drown you, George, it's trying to bear you up. Gravity, I discovered when I jumped off the roof, was another secret ally, all too happy to release me into the sky. Turns out I was never a small man—I'd been self-crumpled. A larger, freer, grander, taller man had been stooped inside, awaiting his cue to soar. I was flying at an estimated speed of one hundred miles per hour, approximately seven hundred feet above Evanston, Illinois. "Hello!" I shouted to the sun and sky—the clouds were gone and O! that sky! You could fall upward to heights of darker and darker blue, all the way up to your last starved, giddy breath. I greeted a flock of pigeons—"How ya doin'!"—and joined in their spiraling.

Seen from above the ant farm chaos below snapped into grids, squares, diagonals, serendipitously color-coordinated rectangles—everything resolved to geometry but the twitchy dreaming of the lake. Suddenly it was the people down there who looked like ants, and not, as in my old flying, the ants. I unzipped and released my two down jackets, then undid the rest of my clothing—why not!— and set it flapping and miming among the startled birds. And here were the groves and spires and soberly whimsical slabs of Northwestern University. I shouted, "May I have your attention! This is Professor George Entmen! How ya

279

doin'! I have an important announcement! Could you stop moving for a second and listen? Come on, dots! Would it kill you to
stop and hear me out? Attention, this is Quetzalcoatl, winged
Aztec god and lord of the fuckin' sky! Can't hear me this far
up? No, you just don't care, do you? Look what I'm doing for
you and why don't you care?" It occurred to me that this was the
absolute bottom rung of fame.

.   .   .

That recurring dream began a week after the jump. I was going
to start with the jump itself, but you'd say, "That's it?"

You'd have a point. A fall of eighteen feet takes approximately
one second. It doesn't happen in slow-mo as moviegoers have been
led to believe; the ground comes up with the speed of a practiced
fist. There's no time for your life to pass before your eyes, not even
at fast-forward with everyone talking like chipmunks. Same for
any incipient last insight, aphorism, or blinding revelation. You'll
gain no more insight than the drunk who's about to announce
the meaning of life when he's hit on the head by the floor. In my
case I was hit with my frozen lawn. Too dazed to know better,
I stood up. I looked up at Harvey on the roof and exchanged
shrugs. There have been numerous shrugs in this account but
that was the most painful. Literally. I'd broken my right arm.

He drove me to St. Francis Hospital where Harvey was ready
to argue with every nurse, intern, and resident in defense of the
jump: on the eve of his arraignment, he couldn't take one more
count of bad guru-ing. He stressed the poetry of the act. I was
the first amphibian, stepping into his new element. The resident
who set my arm, a skinny guy in his twenties with lightning-
white hair, wasn't a fan. "Wait here," he said. He came back with

a teenager in a black FUCK ALL THIS! T-shirt and a cast on his right arm. The kid kept jerking his head back at the approach of things that weren't there. "George, meet Kev. Jumped off a twenty-foot roof on a dare. Thanks for blazing the trail, *dudes*."

. . .

In the weeks after the cast came off I practiced every night, technically between midnight and two in the morning. Practice consisted of lying down on my stomach on the cold lawn—my old launch position—and continuing to lie there as nothing continued to happen. I could have turned my head but preferred to keep my face pressed into the stabbing grass and frozen ground. I had to stop when neighbors, spotting me from their bedroom windows, would come out to check on me.

"We thought you were dead," they'd say.

"Just practicing!" I'd say, but nobody laughed.

It was peaceful out there, sometimes so quiet I believed I could hear my thermal underwear bunching. But it wasn't the peace of the grave. The silence was broken by cars in the alley, garage doors, footsteps, laughter, scraps of sentences, a barking dog, the Metra train, and, inevitably in this college town, the omnipresent rumble of bass lines. The vibrations came up like Magic Fingers through the dirt, and I listened as if the ground and I were negotiating the terms of my release.

Three weeks of this brought me nothing but a bad cold. I recalled the last thing Harvey Bell had said to me before he flew back to California for his arraignment. He said a true flyboy doesn't lie there, supine, imploring the universe to pick him up like lawn trash. It would take a leap. Of faith? I asked. "No, just jump. It might not happen on the first try or the thousandth.

But whenever you have a spare moment, jump." I pointed out that my last jump hadn't gone well; he advised me not to jump from a height. "But you've got to aim for the stars, George, not the ankles."

And so, late every night I'd sneak out for a walk. When I was sure there was no one around I assumed the superhero's preflight stance: arms extended upward, hands crossed, thumbs interlocked. As I was a confirmed aquaphobe, my resemblance to a high-diver unsettled me. Nonetheless I assumed the stance; I gazed at the stars like a superhero, mindful not to look like a hick craning at the upper stories. I'd tilt my chin up slightly, my gaze respectful but never groveling. And then I'd jump. A pretty good jump for a forty-year-old professor of hermeneutics, but not for an athlete, let alone a superhero.

One night I looked up at a radiant full moon and imagined a portal had opened in the night sky. I launched myself at it from a power-jumper's crouch but landed on my feet a quarter million miles short. My attempted raid on the heavens continued through three more jumps. I was caught on YouTube (I never saw the video-taker), the exposed celebrity, perfectly lit, viral sensation of the year. And so the world discovered I was flightless.

Years later they still come up to me and jump: the mockers with their mincing hops, the fans with their energetic bounds, the true believers awaiting their flight plan.

· · ·

My publisher has at last shit-canned this memoir. He said a flying man *just wasn't plausible.* I pointed out that my flying had been confirmed by dozens of scientists; hadn't everybody conceded it was true? Back when I could fly I'd demonstrated the talent in his office! But flying never *felt* plausible, he insisted, it was plain embarrassing to admit he believed it. I suppose that sums up this new age: reason has been replaced by the Muzak of reasonableness.

This book has been my second exercise in futility. I try to think of it as a way to put flying behind me. That will never happen, but at least it's a way to put flying at the back of a drawer.

Before that happens I'll bring you up to date.

Rebecca's biography of Hugo Freiles, the forgotten genius of German Expressionist filmmaking whose family connection with Wendy Baim led to all our troubles, came out last year to good sales and enthusiastic reviews. Paramount has optioned the film rights! Rebecca cautions me not to get excited and reminds me of her experience in the business. It's a bit like flying. Nearly everything they option dies like the gleam in the eye of the people who say they believe in it. "For a while there's always much talk about 'the property.' But in the business more and more talk nearly always leads to less and less, and then it's dead.

"It never dies officially. They assign a schmoozer to phone every now and then to 'keep the connection going.' Then the schmoozer starts phoning every day, and you wonder if he's fallen in love with you. No, he has big plans for 'the property,' and he says maybe you both should take it to another studio. Then he's calling twice a day, the plans even bigger: he'll—what?—project the presumptive film onto the moon and sell earphone rights. And then the schmoozer's gone and that's as close to officially dead as it gets."

My fame had its own cycle: more and more, then less, then a megaton burst of more (my leap onto YouTube), and finally I was able to stumble off the ride. The looks I get from strangers these days are more forgiving, though I'm never sure what I'm being forgiven *for*. For flying badly or flying at all? Had I aroused their disappointment or their envy? Or had I just creeped everybody out? My fame will never go away, but sometimes they have to blink a moment. "Oh. Right."

There's something familial about this worn fame. It's not that I'm accepted as the man who changed the very idea of reality. It's more that I'm tolerated like the second cousin who once crammed his dirty fingers into the Thanksgiving turkey and made a joke we'd all just as soon forget.

Max is five now and he loves baseball. He wants to be Moose Skowron. Why does a twenty-first century five-year-old want to be a mostly forgotten ballplayer whose career ended in 1967? Because Toby saw Max swinging his little bat at a softball and called him another Moose Skowron. (Later he explained that he'd picked the name "for its euphony and industrial sturdiness.")

Max asks a lot of questions about flying. He wouldn't stop nagging till I committed to appearing at his kindergarten class on parents' job day, and he didn't mean as a hermeneutist. Things turned out as I dreaded. Each thing I said—"three or four inches," "the little crack between me and the ground"; "Now? I can't fly at all now"—knocked the hope out of those kids in an audible whoosh. At the end I watched Max watching me. He looked amused. And not for the first time it seemed there was a forty-two-year-old man sitting in my son, awaiting a plausible moment to start drinking, swearing, fucking, and above all telling the jokes about me he was already saving up.

If that's the case he joins a long, though broken, line of

unreadable men. My father was far from the first. These isolate
Entmens lived decent conventional lives, shared a dinner table
with their happy law-abiding families, and when those wives and
children were called upon at their funerals to sum them up, they
hadn't a clue. My latest theory is that Dad and the rest were secret
flyers.

I wonder about all those conferences he'd go off to. They
just don't *have* that many, but the one thing I think I know is
that he loved my mother. Still, he traveled thousands of miles;
I'd check the odometer. Were the conferences a pretext to drive
across America and stop to fly three or four inches above stubble
fields or disused parking lots or dusty cowboy trails or crum-
bling drive-ins or some forgotten capillary of Route 66? Perhaps
my father, a large booming man, needed a road trip to make
something epic out of all that smallness. I once asked Mom what
clothing she packed for his trips; she said socks, some extra dress
shirts, underwear, another tie, another clean handkerchief, and
his other tweed suit. And so I picture this solemn man in tweed
and elbow patches, flailing and drooling among parking lines
and dumpsters. I try to imagine what he'd feel about the act of
flying itself. Was it shameful, a secret vice? Or was this the great
physicist's rebellion: proclaiming the laws of reality by day, van-
dalizing them by night?

But Max? Nobody who's just pretending to be a five-year-old
boy could manage to look so earnest, happy, and nervous as he
takes his batting stance in our yard. "Skowron always a threat at
the plate," I narrate as I prepare to toss the softball. "The outfield
playing this slugger deep." He narrows his eyes, smiles because he

can't help it, protrudes his tongue in concentration, and watches the air between us.

. . .

As I was typing the paragraph above—what I thought would be the last words of this memoir—Janie Herschorn brought over her glum red-headed son Warren. She said nothing when I greeted her, nothing when I asked whether I'd forgotten about a playdate between our sons—she just gestured toward Warren like the spokesmodel of death. "Look."

He wore an upside-down lightweight plastic fishbowl-thing on his head, fastened with a Velcro collar and generously appointed with air holes; it looked like a space helmet in a micro-budgeted fifties movie. I guess his blue T-shirt with the white infinity symbol was part of the uniform.

"Hi, Warren," I said, "how's it goin' with those intergalactic, uh." I'd forgotten the lingo. Perhaps there was no mythology to go with the fishbowl.

Janie ordered him to turn around, displaying the twin air tanks strapped to his back. They weren't connected to anything. She tapped one of the tanks with a fingernail. "Empty."

"I didn't realize he has a . . . condition. Of course I'll contribute."

"Are you messing with me, George? Because you're the length of your pert nose away from a lawsuit." She wasn't physically intimidating, but even her dried-out frizzy red hair looked poised to kill me.

I didn't know Janie well, but I wasn't surprised. If you're a flying man—even an ex–flying man—your very existence can set off the irritable and the aggrieved. Sometimes an earnest "I hear what you're saying" sets things right.

But it did nothing to distract Janie's focus on . . . whatever this was. "Warren," she said, "do the thing."

Warren looked scared.

"He's scared because I spent half this morning trying to get him to *stop* doing the thing. Warren—"

Warren jumped. Small identical rapid-fire jumps. It reminded me of the morning exercise we'd do in kindergarten— the Jumping Bean—twenty-five joyous five-year-olds jumping to "Jump (For My Love)" by the Pointer Sisters. But his mouth and jaw were set in soldierly determination, his arms unmoving at his sides.

"Janie," I said, "I'm very sorry about . . . all this. But shouldn't you be talking to his pediatrician?"

"His pediatrician doesn't have his face on the package."

"Janie. We're both speaking English but I think we might need a translator."

She pulled a snarl of cellophane from a Target bag and handed it to me. Stapled to the top was a bent cardboard rectangle with the product name: Dharma Jet Pack. Above that was a photograph of my face and my right hand. Cartoony fame-rays shot out of my head. I was giving a thumbs-up—evidently to the product. At the bottom of the cardboard, in smaller type, were the name and internet address and social media icons of Harvey Bell's church.

"I had nothing to do with this," I assured her.

"Then how did your face get on the package? Did it *fly* there?" She seemed inordinately pleased with her joke. "Well *I'm* not to blame. Some kid brought it to his birthday party."

I didn't know her well enough to tell her how Harvey had betrayed me. I'd always thought there was a point in your life when the casual friends, the false friends, the friends who were friends because you saw them every day, the friendships whose basis was a mystery, the friends you could never pry clear of some misunderstanding or feud—by the time you reach forty, I thought, they've fallen away. By then the lifeboats have all gone out, and those who remain sail collegially together toward death. When Harvey came back just after my fortieth birthday I was glad he'd just made it aboard—sorry, I'll can the nautical imagery. My point is, I think of him as the shy, sweet friend in college who wrote long vulnerable love poems that he slid under the doors of baffled women. As the guy who impersonated my dermatologist when I confused their numbers, easing my horrible itching with his kind, calm talk, and he did it not only because it was funny but because he was good. And when he used to erase the eyeballs of people on the cover of TV Guide he did it not only because it was weird and funny but because he believed in other ways of seeing. And I believe that when he persuaded me to jump off my roof he wanted to free my spirit.

Oh, I know he was broke and desperate when he turned up after twenty years, and he still offered his guru-ing for free. And now while I grumbled he was doing hard time in a medium-security federal prison. But I couldn't forgive this. Everything I'd dreaded about fame had come to pass on that strip of cardboard.

"George! Don't fly off on me. Does a five-year-old truly have boundless energy? How long can he go on jumping? Will he have to sleep, or could he just keep jumping until he reaches middle age and has a coronary? Can a five-year-old have a coronary?"

"Can't you just take away his fishbowl?"

She spoke loudly and slowly. *"It's not the fishbowl, George, it's the jumping!* I think maybe the fishbowl gets them started, but they don't want to stop. Ever. You're the flying/jumping man. Talk to him."

I kneeled down. "Hi Warren, are you trying to fly? I used to dream about flying when I was your age, and I thought it would be pretty great." His eyes didn't quite focus, and perhaps his mind was filled, as he jumped, with the image of himself jumping. "It's not as fun as you think. People step on you. You drool. You can't control your arms and legs. They want you to fly their grandma to Albania and when you tell them you can't they swear at you *in Albanian*. You spend most of your flying time looking at dirt and ants and shoes and carpet lint." Nothing I said altered his dead stare or the relentless mechanism of his jumping.

"How does milk and a cookie sound? I know when I've been working out nothing hits the spot like milk and cookies! Notice I said cookies. No reason to stop at one, my friend, you've earned 'em! Janie, I give up, it's like reasoning with a jackhammer." I turned around. "Janie?" I searched the house, including the closets and under the beds. She'd ditched us.

She was listed in my contacts; she'd been on some parents' committees with us. I got her voicemail. "Janie, I have six words for you. Department of Children and Family Services. If you need a break, I'll give you three hours." (She would come back three hours later.)

I found an instruction booklet among the packaging in the bag. "Hey Warren, I found instructions. Let's be sure you're doing everything right. I know! We'll do a checklist. Why don't you stop jumping and you can say check! every time I—whatever." I read aloud: "'Welcome, kids, to the exciting world of Dharma Jet Pack flying.

"'What is Dharma? You know how your parents are always buying phones with a new operating system? Dharma is the operating system of the universe!

"'Soon you'll be up in the sky with the birds and the airplanes, laughing at all the kids down there who thought Dharma flying was a big rip-off. Now let's get flying!

"'1. Put on your Infinity Shirt. It's made of glide-smooth polyester for a happier flying experience.' Check! Though really, Warren, *you* should be the one saying 'check!' Anyway.

"'2. Strap on the Dharma Rocket Pack.' Check! 'The tanks seem empty, but they're filled with Stratospherium. Be sure the tanks are strapped on firmly.' Check! 'Caution: Certain jerks may tell you there's no such thing as Stratospherium. These are the same guys who beat you up. Wave to them when they're dots.

"'3. Put on your Dharma Cosmic-Ray-Fighting Helmet. Tell your mom or dad to be sure the Velcro collar is securely fastened. There's just one more thing you need to do to get in the sky:

"'4. Jump. Now you might think that every time you jump you come right down. *As long as you believe that, you will never fly.* But think of yourself as flying. *See* yourself flying. If you see yourself flying, see it truly and strongly, *you will fly!* Keep trying. I'll be watching the sky for you.'"

Oh, Harvey, you were grifting five-year-olds.

But not exactly. In the Age of George—even the post–Age of George—he wasn't promising the impossible. He was merely promising the overwhelmingly unlikely. It was like a slot machine; with each failed jump you believed you were closer to payoff—to liftoff.

"And so we jump on, aye Warren?" He'd started to jump even faster, the identical dead moons of his eyes brightening.

SEVENTEEN

Iris is alive! Two days ago—three years after I tossed this memoir in a drawer, six years after Iris, locked in a box, spoke her presumed last words: "I'm workin' on it, sweetie"—Toby phoned with the news. He waited quietly through my gale of questions: "Is she okay, where is she, where *was* she, when can we see her, who are this 'they' who found her, had she been hiding from Ricardo, couldn't she have let us know, had Ricardo kept her prisoner, or—or . . ."

"That's it, George, breathe."

"Rebecca, pick up the phone, Iris is alive!"

She picked up the extension; Toby interrupted her delirious free-fire of the same questions.

"I haven't seen her or talked to her," he said, "but I know where she'll be tomorrow. We can't just walk in there. We'll need to make plans. Can you guys be at Wendy and Nelson's this evening?"

"Wendy," Rebecca and I groaned in unison.

. . .

It had taken Toby almost a year to get over his grief and then only by persuading himself that Iris was alive. I'd accompanied him on the first of his investigations. We questioned her friends, relatives, and former neighbors in her hometown of Brecillia, where practically everyone knew Iris and her mom. Nobody looked shifty-eyed when they said they hadn't seen her. I remember it was a ferociously sunny, windy day, everybody smiling and squinting. At the center of town teenagers congregated near a stoplight swinging on a wire; a colossal American flag whumped on a pole next to the dry cleaner's. Toby managed not be condescending, except once when we were walking around town and he said through the side of his mouth, "Let's stock up on these clothes. You never never know when it will be 1952." And when we stopped at a Woolworths we did find things we'd assumed had gone out of existence: Hubba Bubba cola, Halo shampoo, Bab-o cleanser, Wildroot Cream Oil hair tonic, Woolworths.

We decided not to call ahead to Iris's mom in case Iris was hiding there. Maureen sported a dirty blonde version of Iris's Mary Tyler Moore hairdo; she looked like a sleepy water-logged version of Iris, with a sand-blasted version of her daughter's voice, the southern accent more distinct. When we claimed to be "passing through" she cocked her head. She asked whether we were visiting Brecillia for the cuisine or the waters; she must have dealt with hundreds of amateur investigators that year. But she was happy to speak to Iris's Chicago friends. She showed us Iris's old room, the walls decorated with posters of . . . I can only remember Gloria Steinem, Flannery O'Connor, and TV megahunk Ashton Kutcher. (Toby found excuses to look under the bed—"I always used to hide stuff under my bed"—and in the closet—"Let's see what she used to wear." When he went to use the bathroom he snuck into the other rooms.) She showed us the little shrine in the living room: Iris's prize-winning high school essay on *The Sorrows of Young Werther,* her diving medal, an issue of *The Paris Review* with her first published story (she was seventeen), framed replies to her fan letters from Vanna White and Pat Sajack, a framed certificate for second place in a Velveeta cheese recipe contest. It raised the eternal question about our friend: "Was Iris kidding?" We'd always wondered how sincere she could be about her tastes, this tenured professor who professed to unironically love all manner of kitsch (though she'd never call it kitsch). Maybe she'd outgrown that stuff and *was* making fun of it, but we'd both seen her cry at "*Wheel of Fortune.*" Cautiously I asked Maureen about her daughter's "wide-ranging tastes." Could she truly love both Goethe and Velveeta? The solution to the riddle occurred to me as I asked the question: Toby and I were elitist assholes.

We all teared up when Maureen answered, "Sweetie, that girl had a big heart."

We thumbed through Iris's yearbooks; I would have thought that this gloomy odd duck with her idiosyncratic jokes and Edgar Allen Poe pallor would be a no-show in those pages. I was surprised to find them bristling with bookmarks. Here was Iris looking sad among the debate team, pensive among the yearbook staff, anxious among the high school newspaper staff, troubled among the lit club, uncertain among the biology club. You could tell by looking at the classmates with their arms around her shoulders: they saw her not as an oddity but a rarity. Their black swan. And here was Iris looking into the abyss from the center of a pyramid of cheerleaders.

As we stood at the door Maureen said, "My adviser and I saw on the news that you lost your flying. He says you should try it in your pajamas. He says all our powers come from dreams, and pajamas are the uniform of dreams."

I asked whether she thought Iris was alive.

She smiled. "The police say it's not possible, but like my adviser says, 'Nobody really knows anything.' If George can fly, right? She was a lifeguard at the public pool, you know. A real strong swimmer. Rescued this dumb high school football player who got badly injured belly-flopping off the high-dive board. He was screaming and flapping around in the water like a fish out of water and my daughter had the privilege of knocking him cold."

On the drive back all Toby could think about was the diving medal. "A strong swimmer, George. A strong *diver*! She swan-dived into the Chicago River, and somewhere she's entertaining people with the story—fortified with great jokes." I questioned her ability to survive a twelve-story plunge into the river, not to mention the ability to climb out of the Chicago River downtown in gold-spangled tights and remain unseen. He described various flotsam in the police photos from that night and listed the items that could be used as flotation devices, allowing her to escape downriver.

. . .

Once a month over the years Toby would take me to lunch and fill me in on the progress of the investigation. A few months ago he told me he was looking into Ricardo Dean. Ricardo had been telling friends he was bored doing his magic act.

"He wanted to create a magic circus, something like the old-fashioned circuses of our nightmares—seedy, mysterious, wondrous, vile-smelling and terrifying. He often spoke about circuses in his interviews, their 'alluring crumminess,' his regret that they'd lost their filth and their balls. When he was a kid Ricardo saw a movie called *Circus of Horrors* and knew he wanted one of those. And after he read *Something Wicked This Way Comes*, young Ricardo wished he could build a circus that could come for a guy late at night, silently rolling down Main Street, and the guy 'was never seen again.'"

It was Toby's contention that that was the circus that came for me.

I conceded that they took away Blaustein and he'd never been seen again. I asked what happens to all those guys who are never seen again.

He said he was looking into it. He said he'd been speaking to magicians, acquaintances of Ricardo, who cautioned that this circus was the most dangerous and closely guarded secret in magic.

And how, I wondered, could you keep a *circus* secret?

He said, "There are parts of America that have no connection to *this* America." We were sitting in Tiffany's, a restaurant on Sherman Avenue in Evanston, where the tables were lit by ugly imitation Tiffany lamps and you squinted to read your menu through the garish murk. Nobody thought it was good idea; it was a quiet place to talk. He squinted at his burger, as if seeing it better might make a difference. "Towns where you'd have to drive five hundred miles raising dust all the way just to reach actual flyover country. If the circus comes to Badger's Tooth, Nebraska, does it make a sound here?

"Well it turns out it does," he said triumphantly and set his phone on the table. "This is from YouTube. Press play."

It was a short clip of Iris reading a few paragraphs from her novel *Attack of the Honeybees.*

"It doesn't look like a circus tent," I said.

"I think she's reading against a backdrop," he said. "The videographer is sitting near the back and she looks blurry when he zooms in. Don't be distracted by all the tractor hat guys coming and going in the foreground. Wait till she pauses and you'll hear something. Here it comes."

I had to play it twice to hear anything.

"It's very faint," I said. "A whistling noise. Probably the wind."

"Here." He took his earbuds out of his briefcase.

I could make it out now. "A calliope. Odd, but it doesn't prove anything. Hold on. She never toured for *Attack of the Honeybees.* It came out after she disappeared. Goddamn! She's alive!"

"Just hold your horses. First of all, she did give one reading from the novel before it came out."

"Oh."

"But it was at the Museum of Contemporary Art. Not a tractor hat in the joint."

"Then she must be—"

"Don't say 'must,' George. This is the internet. People are always faking videos to prove one conspiracy theory or another. The person onstage is blurry enough that we can't be sure she isn't a stand-in—with Iris's Chicago reading on the soundtrack. I'm hopeful, but for now hold your horses, put 'em back in the barn and stock up on hay."

The video was still running. "Keep watching," Toby said. "The videographer must have been uploading this while he was shooting." A blurry figure in a tractor cap put his hand over the lens. The image turned sideways and shook violently, somebody yelled 'hey!' and the screen went black.

. . .

"You think you've experienced the absolute bottom rung of fame?" Toby dismissed the idea with the tiniest flick of the hand. "You weren't looking down, my friend—not all the way."

The Baims' enormous dining room was lit with a few dim skittish candles. Perhaps they thought this dying-campfire effect would promote conversation. But when I saw Toby puffing up to hold forth, I protested that raconteurship was the last thing we needed. We, or at least Rebecca and I, needed to know where Iris was and what we were going to do about it.

Wendy leaned across the table and put her hand on mine. Her perfume had always seemed unsubtle, but in that darkness, in my febrile state of mind, it walked right up and sat on my face. "George, Rebecca, relax. We have a plan. It's all but taken care of—tomorrow we'll bring her home."

"The hard part," Nelson said, "will be comprehending . . . all of it. If you start right in asking questions you'll have ten new questions for every answer. Give Toby a chance. In a few minutes you'll know everything we know." Nelson had lost twenty pounds and his gut. His beard was professionally trimmed and book jacket ready. He'd dispensed with the powder-blue prom tux—he was wearing a corduroy sport jacket—and had stopped trying to string his side hair across his bald immensities.

After Charles Blaustein disappeared, the English department had honored Nelson's contract with Monitor Press. When he was abducted by circus roustabouts we voted to publish the book anyway because the department had a contractual obligation to—all right, because we were afraid of Wendy. There was one thing we'd failed to foresee. It was a good book. *Against Joy* was published to great acclaim among philosophers and the reading public. The philosophy department of Columbia University had overruled Nelson's old dissertation panel and he was finally awarded his Ph.D. His courses at Lake Forest College are the most popular in the college's history. The author of Nelson's *New Yorker* profile called him "perhaps the most cheerful nihilist in America," and why wouldn't he be?

I don't even think his ascent in late middle age had required Wendy's decades-long reign of terror—or, if you're a romantic, her selfless love. Let's compromise: her implacable love. Twenty years ago she'd seen a scraggly, spiteful but determined man reading his rejected dissertation aloud at the Broadway gates of Columbia University. To eighteen-year-old Wendy he seemed brilliant, commanding. I can imagine the few moments that determined the rest of their lives and eventually set my own life careening. He was talking back to his hecklers, which only drew more heckling. A half-cup of coffee bounced off his shirt, a man on a unicycle circled him laughing, but he remained defiant. It was one of those transparent October days when each thing proclaims itself in sharp outlines, and the tendrils of a greasy ginger beard can look radiant. The grind of shivering leaves spoke to something in Wendy. She decided, and never wavered, *that* was the guy! Over the decades, whenever reality begged to differ, she took an axe to it and chopped away everything that was not the reality she chose. But apparently Wendy's reality—Nelson is a genius, his ideas are groundbreaking—had been plain *reality* all along. We're still straightening out reality in the post–Age of George.

"Toby?" Wendy prodded. "Please?"

Toby had been petulantly studying an imaginary manicure. He continued. "Everybody knows about the trajectory of fame. But the people who chart it usually fail to see that at *every* point, your fans already hate you. Even back when they loved you they already hated you—or if not hate, raging envy. They want to see out of your eyes. They want to walk around in your appropriated skin."

Rebecca and I traded exasperated looks but knew we'd have to let him finish.

"Only the vastly rich get to enjoy the ritual of a celebrity at the absolute bottom rung of fame. You came so close, George. Remember that magician you spoke to? Clarence Fonderbein, the rabbit guy? He works for them. His job is very simple. Clarence comes to your door on some pretext—he wanted to talk about agents, is that it? And while you're talking a circus wagon pulls up in front of your house. Clarence is excited! Is that a circus wagon? Oh my goodness, he's always wanted to go inside one of those! What do you think, Professor Entmen? 'Oh, I don't know, I'm a distinguished hermeneutist, mustn't muss up the reputation by associating with circus folk.'" Toby's imitation of me was never more unnervingly good than when he said things I'd never say.

"The kid walks up to the circus wagon's door, and suddenly he can't do it. Shy. No social skills. Bottle-fed. Ate lead paint off the walls as a toddler. You'll show him how it's done. You roll back your sleeve, summon all your scholarly hauteur, knock. The door opens, Clarence shoves you inside, slams the door—it locks from the outside— and the circus has its latest attraction (kind of a simpleminded tactic, yes—these are carnies not jewel thieves).

"But you screwed them up by storming out of the house before the wagon got there. Clarence tried to stall you, but you got away. Their final attempt was playing loud calliope music in front of your house, hoping you'd come out and knock on their door, but Blaustein showed up—strictly by coincidence—and started shooting at your house."

I'd opened my mouth to call him on this exercise in fabulism, but then I remembered Blaustein's abduction and filled the mouth with beef bourguignon.

"But let's imagine they'd managed to collect you. At first being their prisoner isn't as bad as you'd expect. Sure, living in a cage and sleeping on a bed of straw at night isn't the three-star life. But it makes the rubes happy to feel superior to a Jew professor who performs—performed—miracles. The small town police? Bought off."

"Where do the rich come in?" I asked. "Where does *Iris* come in?"

Ignoring me, he imperiously forged on. "Anyway the food's good. Nothing but the best for the most famous person in the world. Sure, you're chained to the wall at times, but that's just to please the rubes. And they give you a key to the locks to set your mind at rest—though two strongmen guard your cage. I suppose your act would be a one-man show along the lines of An Evening With George: My Adventures in Flying. After work you get to hang out with the other celebrities and the freak show and circus stars. You're given the perk of sleeping with any of the other performers: I'd go for Rubberosa, 'the most flexible woman in the world,' but I know you'd stay faithful. But while you plot your escape, life isn't quite as horrible as it could possibly be.

"And then late one day they hitch a truck cab to your cage and drive off to a more isolated venue, a burned-out cornfield, say. The audience in the folding chairs is well-dressed; you've never seen a circus crowd in Armani and Donna Karan before. They're an appreciative audience. They laugh and applaud at the right times and get most of your jokes except the hermeneutics ones. When it's over they hand you their autograph books through the bars, and you manage to sign them handcuffed by setting the books on the podium. But you can't shake the thought that you were being *assessed*. For what? You've never fathomed the purpose of kidnapping celebrities just to perform in a circus— haven't these people heard of booking celebrities through their agents? And you're awake all night with mad conjectures: Why is the food so good? What are they fattening you up for?

"At the bleeding edge of dawn you see a man approaching, it's practically always a man approaching in the distance. Eventually you see he's wearing evening clothes. He has a jaunty, perhaps even debonair stride one doesn't expect to see in a bare field in Kankakee or Cedar Rapids. For all his high spirits it's an autumnal scene: the empty field, the elongated shadow with its scarecrow limbs, the dim golden light transforming the scene into a tintype—something a child might come across in an old book, and for reasons she can't explain it makes her sad."

"Good one, Tobe," Rebecca said.

"The well-dressed man stops outside your cage to take a parcel from the guard. He unfolds it; it's a full-body apron. He puts it on, accepts the key from the guard, steps in. You're at least slightly relieved that he doesn't seem to have a knife or a gun. What happens next depends on the particular well-dressed man. Some like preliminary conversation. They'd ask about flying, maybe ask how you've dealt with fame. All these men have gone to the best universities, so if you're lucky, maybe yours brings up hermeneutics, and you spend a few reassuring minutes discussing Gadamer or Habermas. But it's all just a respite from the inevitable, and about the time you're analyzing Wellmer's conception of absolute truth, the well-dressed man delivers a punch to your kidneys. Regrettably they've kept your chains on since last night ("a temporary security measure," they'd assured you). He beats the crap out of you; I won't go into grisly detail. You're an adorable man, of course, so he'll go for the face. Same for all the well-dressed men to come."

I opened my mouth.

"Why?" he preempted. "It was the rich, you know, who staged the infamous hobo fights of the eighties and nineties. I guess the old brand of Calvinism never entirely died in that class. Beating up people beneath their station affirms everybody's place in the grand design. But mainly this is about raging envy: 'Why does George get to fly four inches above the ground? Those are *my* inches!'"

"I know how much you care for Iris," I said, "and if she was being beaten up in a circus cage somewhere you wouldn't be regaling us like some drunken toastmaster."

"*Half*-drunken," he said. "We all have to be at our sharpest tomorrow. Iris *is* with the circus, but we're nearly positive she's uninjured. We've had an observer in the audience for weeks. And forgive me for my speechifying; I find the sound of my own voice soothing. It relaxes me in a crisis. You, on the other hand, fret. I hope that gets you to sleep tonight.

"Ten years ago—I'm going as fast as I can, Rebecca—Iris gave a reading at 57th Street Books in Hyde Park. It was a long reading, and she hoped the audience would be too tired to make

her take questions. But there's always that one. This time it was
Vanessa Gobwin. A billionairess. Her grandfather invented the
ding! You know, the sound your car makes when you leave the
lights on or the door open. You seem to have accepted everything
else I said, George, and *this* is what makes you incredulous?"

I was googling her. It was all there: Gobwin, billions, ding!

He was saying, "She puts the question crisply, authoritatively,
and loudly: 'Do you write from life?'

"You know how polite Iris is, but she was falling asleep on her
feet and—"

"Toby, *please*," Rebecca said, "get where you're going!"

"Iris said, 'I write from the *after*life: life plus distance. Or wait,
is that an airline fee? Anyway goodnight.' Iris wasn't even sure
what that meant, but Vanessa Gobwin looked stricken. Normally
Iris would have apologized but she needed to get out of there. As
she was turning her back, that crisp, loud, authoritative voice—
the radio voice of doom, Iris called it the next day— shouted, 'Do
you write from life!' Vanessa shrieked it on Fifty-Seventh Street
as Iris was running for her car.

"For years afterward Vanessa showed up for every reading
Iris gave in metropolitan Chicago. Iris tried to do away with
questions altogether, but Vanessa knew how to act pathetic—
'Oh, please Ms. Ransler, just one question?' —and the audience
would make those sympathetic awww noises. And so Iris would
halt her progress to the door, unbutton her coat, and nod stoically
to the firing squad. Vanessa would begin in sycophantic mode.
'Oh, Iris, I'm such a fan! You can't know how much this means
to me! I was just hoping you could answer a question that comes
to mind every time I read a work of fiction.' She'd draw a massive
breath then, and Iris swore she doubled in size. Sometimes Van-

essa extended the pause, savoring the fear of her prey. Iris had grown up in the rural South, so she'd heard her share of guns and fireworks. As a child she snuck up too close when they dynamited the old Savannah Hotel and she was deaf for three days. But no sound was as terrifying as the one she knew was coming, and the removal of the element of surprise only increased her hopelessness.

"Finally the event itself. 'Do! You! Write! . . . From life!' Afterward the audience would gape, dig fingers in their ears, giggle anxiously, or shake their heads as if listening for the broken pieces. A few of the bravest and angriest might approach Vanessa threateningly but they always backed off. (If you're wondering why you know nothing about this, it's because Iris stopped notifying her friends about her readings.) Once she asked Vanessa how she learned to yell so expertly: she attributes her skill to opera classes, assertiveness training, wrath, and yogic breathing.

"Iris had her banned from readings; the bookstores faced higher rents and a plague of city inspectors. Iris stopped reading in the vicinity of Chicago; Vanessa turned up at her readings in New York, Los Angeles, Paris, London, and Hong Kong, where she was detained for disturbing the peace and released within minutes."

I turned to Rebecca. "I just remembered. About eight years ago we were at one of Iris's readings and that woman gave us both splitting headaches. Toby makes everything ten percent more vivid, but there's no denying the woman was loud."

"Oh, yeah. Very loud."

"But it's not till Iris lost all the battles and won the war," Toby resumed, "that our story truly begins."

"Great," Rebecca muttered.

"She'd been on the verge of giving up readings, but instead she adapted. As she put it, 'I gave up hearing for literature.' I'm sure you noticed that in the later years you often had to repeat yourself for her. This wasn't all a negative for a resourceful writer. As Ted Berrigan said, 'all mishearing is poetry.'"

"Once she gave me this horror-stricken look," Rebecca said. "It turned out she thought I'd said, 'Why aren't those kids on the hoods of cars where they belong?'"

"She put that line in a children's story, 'The Mean Neighbor,' remember? But Vanessa Gobwin had hoped that her program of focused yelling would have reduced Iris to a pile of ash by now. She wasn't willing to settle for stoic resignation. She tried standing on Iris's porch and yelling for hours, but not even billionaires can get away with that in Evanston.

"So she tried Ricardo. He and Iris had performed for her charity benefit once and they'd had a knockdown argument in the middle of a trick. Vanessa had heard the rumors among her set of Ricardo's circus and its enticements for the truly rabid fan. He refused to consider letting Iris be beaten up—he was trying to be a better boyfriend. But he came up with an alternate idea. What if Iris actually disappeared during his disappearing act and he spirited her away to his circus? She *would* be kept in a cage, though. And she'd give as many private readings as Vanessa wished. Vanessa could ask her question as often and as loudly as she pleased. Ricardo offered to split the take if she extended the invitation to all her resentful book club friends. They'd finally get in-depth answers to the questions authors dismissed or answered sarcastically—where do you get your characters?; if I have a character in one place, and then someplace else, do I have to show the character traveling to the second place, or can she just be there?;

how does the reader know something is a symbol?; does the *New Yorker* want stories to be double-spaced, and do I have to put the title at the top of *every* page? And if Iris smart-mouthed them, then for an additional fee (one million dollars) they'd be granted the right of eternal repetition.

"Vanessa thought it would be a nice fairy tale twist to tell Iris she could have her freedom whenever she gave the right answer to 'do you write from life?'

"The version of the plan Ricardo presented to Iris was considerably different. He promised her that most of the time she'd be alone in her sound-proof cell—perfect for writing. 'Think of it as the McDowell Colony with its own supply of ready-made gothic characters.' It would just be for a year, after which she'd reappear in Ricardo's magic cabinet at Club Blasé—think of the sensation! And with her part of the split she'd collect around five million dollars. I doubt Iris was in it for the money: I have it from my sources that what she's writing is an exposé of Ricardo and all his crimes. If he knows I doubt he's worried: I don't think he was ever planning to let her go. It's been six years. Questions?"

"How do you know all this in such detail?" Rebecca asked with a tinge of skepticism.

"I had two main sources. Remember my Russian ex-girlfriend Ludmilla? The performance artist who could pile furniture on her head and keep it there while doing deep knee-bends and touching her elbows to the floor?" He smiled dreamily. "Anyway . . . remember how offended she got if you called her a circus performer? I'll just observe that for a performance artist she knows a surprising number of circus performers. Nobody who's actually in Ricardo's troupe, but a few who know people who are. And at the other end, nobody is better connected to the billionaire grapevine than our hostess." He raised his glass. "To Wendy!" We toasted Wendy.

"How did Ricardo make her disappear?" I asked.

"The secret of a magic trick is always boring and an air horn to our dreams. You remember that when we were searching for her that night we checked the hidden corridor and the secret stairway? Would you be shocked, George, to learn that the concealed corridor has its own concealed corridor, and the secret stairway has a hidden secret—"

"No, just disappointed. In the trick. Delighted she's alive." I raised my glass to Wendy.

"What's the plan?" Rebecca asked.

"The circus is ready to hit the road on ten minutes' notice," Wendy said. "They do drills. There's no printed schedule. Nobody knows where they'll be tomorrow. Each day's lucky billionaire sadist only learns the location on the day itself.

"But a friend of mine got herself on the list. We'll learn the location in the morning and head out. So George? You'll be wandering around knocking on trailer doors. Security has photos of all her friends, I'll bet, but the guards won't rough you up. They'll let you wander wherever you want until they're ready to push you into one of those trailers. They know how valuable you are, they'll treat you like Venetian Renaissance glassware. But we don't have to worry about a bunch of carny security guards. *We* have The Boys! We've added women to the corps but they voted unanimously to remain The Boys."

She took a small remote from beside her plate, pressed a button, and the sound system began blaring relentless pounding aerobics class disco. "I love my boys!" Wendy gushed. The lights came up and three dozen men and women in dark glasses and navy blazers and pants bounded into the room, flexing, mouthing grimly into walky-talkies, quick-drawing firearms. Wendy ran up to join them, mussing hair, rubbing her ass against a guy's crotch while he frisked her.

I glanced at Nelson; nothing could disarrange his serene smile. "A few months ago Wendy decided our security force needed a pick-me-up," he said. "We had a great time going to stripper bars and recruiting. They're about a third of the force now. Don't worry; we leave the dangerous stuff to the ex–FBI and Secret Service." The thought of Nelson turning into a swinger literally made me dizzy; Rebecca put a hand on my shoulder.

"You really can't tell them apart from the law enforcement people," he said. "The dancers have been trained to shoot, the agents have been trained to grind."

I decided I preferred the glum, surly, sponging Nelson to this guy.

"I hope you don't think this is all a lark," Rebecca said. "Because if anything happens to Iris while you're having fun, George and Toby and I will find a way to kill you. That said, we're grateful to you and Wendy for all your help. Please don't be hungover tomorrow." She, then Toby and I, stood up.

"It's not a lark," Nelson said. "She's worried about me. She thinks she sees signs I'm falling back into depression. So I guess I'll have to endure being saved all over again. You can't say 'helping'—not around here anyway—without 'hell.'" He waved to Wendy, still twerking. "She thinks this sort of thing will be liberating for us. She's not having any more fun than I am, but I don't know what else to do except play along. For all her flirting, we're actually the two least swinging people on earth. You don't have to worry about us having a lark."

I exchanged glances with Rebecca and Toby, trying to decide whether we were at all reassured.

Wendy was holding her arms out toward Nelson while she continued rubbing against the agent or dancer.

"Gotta go," Nelson said. "Be here at six in the morning."

He ran into the dancing paramilitary mob and tore open his shirt. He flashed Wendy a by-the-book smile, pumped his fist, and grimly turned his hips.

. . .

I hoped the man speaking into his cotton candy was one of ours. He and his girlfriend were following me among labyrinthine rows of trailers and cages at the periphery of the circus. They both wore NASCAR IS FOR LOVERS! T-shirts.

The acts in the trailers were mostly accessible by private appointment only. It was Wendy's theory that I'd have more freedom to wander and snoop if I were unaccompanied. About twice a minute I wondered how much I should trust Wendy and tried to control my panic when I realized I had no idea. I'd picked up a conga line of followers muttering into popcorn or teddy bears or goggle-eyed fuzzy owls.

"Hey bud," said a man in a cage. He sported a well-tended gray pompadour, huge orange-tinted glasses, and a dusty pink suit and was chained to the metal frame of the bed he sat on. He held up two fingers in a V, brought it to his mouth, inhaled, and exhaled so persuasively I could smell cigarette smoke among the shit and sawdust.

I shrugged regretfully. "Say, aren't you Wink Martindale?" The line behind me had ground to a halt and tried to look plausibly engaged by the surrounding trailers and cages.

"No, but I'm honored. Wink's my role model. Compared to him all other game show hosts are babies playing with cue cards. That man reached out of the TV and shot a lightning bolt of entertainment into every viewer. I'm Tommy Mink. Maybe you saw my show, *Sex in a Box?*"

"No. Is it what it sounds like?"

"Absolute truth in packaging. Some people said we were a rip-off of *Sex Box*. But on that show, *Sex Box*, you don't see or hear anything that goes on in the box. You just have the couple going into the box, and the audience and a panel of *therapists*"—he pronounced the word mincingly—"sits around the box waiting for them to finish. Then they discuss the sex with the therapists and the audience and everybody *evaluates* how the sex went and whether they're *reaching their full potential as a couple*. So first of all, we did away with ten minutes of people staring at a box. We mic-ed the box. We were hoping for a first in broadcast television: an in-box sex cam or a transparent box, but they said we'd have to move to an adult network."

"I'm not much of a porn fan, but what does the box add? I mean, why not just show the people having sex?" I didn't care about the answer; I was trying to look peripherally at my followers and decide what they were. It occurred to me that they might not be on either side. I hadn't been followed around by fans for a while, but maybe this was my comeback.

Tommy Mink said, "You don't see the difference between *Sex in a Box* and porn? Fuck you."

I started to walk away and he said, "I'm sorry, please don't go." He got off the bed and came up to the bars, dragging his ankle chain. "Pretend we're talking aesthetics," he whispered as he passed me a folded sheet of paper. "These carnies think they're tough but they've never been up against the William Morris Agency. Ask for Donna. The box," he said at conversational volume, "is what makes it art. That's the form, man, and form is limitation. Like the fourteen lines of a sonnet. I suppose the cage is what makes *this* art, but fuck this."

"I promise to call Donna at the William Morris Agency," I whispered. "Have you seen a writer here—Iris Ransler? Blonde, a bit of a southern accent?"

"Oh, sure. Middle of the next row. The trailer says literary fiction."

The line following me had expanded, the new faces muttering into balloons, a Deadeye Shooter trophy, and a box of peanut brittle. I phoned Wendy. "George? Do—"

"I'm close. Send in everyone. There. I'm looking at it. The trailer says Literary Fiction in psychedelic circus colors. There's this trompe l'oeil effect with a painted book standing open at a picture of an empty highway, and it seems like you could start walking down that road and never stop. It's sort of a Wile E. Coyote terrain, cloudless blue sky, little buzzards—"

"Get a grip, George. Breathe. We're tracking your cell. Be right there."

The line of object whisperers was ten yards back and closing. I tried the knob. It turned.

"George?" Iris stood up from a card table, walked over, and gave me a hug—all in the manner you'd greet a friend you hadn't seen for two weeks. We'd been told to expect PTSD or Stockholm syndrome. "Thanks for driving all the way up. You play canasta? I'm on a roll." She wore jeans and a sweatshirt and had her hair in a ponytail.

I closed the door and turned the lock under the doorknob.

The bald muscular man who'd been sitting across from her had a long spike sticking out the top of his head. His T-shirt read ASK ME ABOUT THE SPIKE IN MY HEAD.

"Have a seat, sweetie."

"I shave to guard the door. We're going to get you out of here. Toby and Rebecca and the Baims and about thirty armed private security are on the way."

"You gotta love this guy," she said to the man with the spike. "Always thinkin' positive. Mr. Blockhead, this is my friend George Entmen. George, do you know what a blockhead is?"

Someone was jiggling the doorknob. I pressed my back against the door.

"Uh, George? I've tried to block that door, and—remember when Ricardo punched me in the eye and I pretended I got hit by a door? Turns out getting hit by a door is worse." I kept my back against it.

"Anyway, a blockhead is a guy who pounds a long nail or spike up his nose. It looks like it's going right up into the brain but a good blockhead knows how to angle it toward the nasal cavity. Now I know you're thinking, Yes, Iris, but that doesn't explain the spike *sticking out the top of his head*. True. When he was eighteen, Yevgeny was a blockhead in a Russian circus. He loved a girl named Berta and when she wouldn't marry him he pounded that spike we're looking at now, more than forty years later, into the top of his head. Now surviving a spike in the head wasn't unprecedented. In the nineteenth century a man named Phineas Gage had his skull penetrated by a four-foot rod."

I could hear a helicopter.

"The rod went straight through the top of Gauge's jaw and the other end came out of his skull. And he lived. Every block-

313

head has heard of Phineas Gage. Yevgeny wanted to make a grand romantic gesture that he at least had a chance of surviving. But unlike Phineas Gage he decided he'd never get it removed— not as long as Berta refused to marry him."

Why did everyone keep *narrating* at me? I could hear more than one helicopter now. "Iris, don't you want to hear what's happening out there?"

"Oh sweetie, I know what's gonna happen and none of it's good . . . The doctors warned him about the nearly certain risk of infection. But Yevgeny has a heart as big as all outdoors and an intellect you could fit in a thimble." She looked at an imaginary thimble in her palm—it was adorable. "And to give him his due, he's already outlived many of us without spikes in our heads. He's already outlived me." It was the saddest thing I'd ever heard her say.

Yevgeny laughed triumphantly. "Mister, if we go to hospital now and do tests, and other doctors read tests, they think *you* have spike in head!"

The door banged open, flinging me down on the linoleum. It was Ricardo—looking slightly risible in a black silk cape—and two armed tuxedoed goons. The goons hauled me to my feet and by the time the scuffling ended, Ricardo held Iris and me with his arms around our shoulders, the goons crouched behind us with guns at our heads; Yevgeny was frantically trying to replace the hunk of latex and gunk and the fake spike sticking out of it (some of the prosthetic scalp was caked to the floor; the remainder sat on his head like a beanie); Toby, Rebecca, Wendy, Nelson, and The Boys were crowded in front of the doorway, the press behind them; police with bullhorns were trying to disperse the mob; and farther back the SWAT team stood on top of their trucks taking aim.

"Watch very closely," Ricardo said to the audience. "My lovely assistant Iris and I are about to disappear—forever. Now you might well ask where we could disappear *to*, surrounded as we are by tightly packed humanity, the gunsights of the SWAT team, and the unrelenting gaze of the press. No mere puff of smoke can get me out of *this* jam. Or can it?

"I've known you were here for hours, George," he whispered, "and I had plenty of time to make preparations. When the smoke comes up and the trapdoors open and Iris and I disappear, you'll disappear to your own special place. You think you've seen the absolute bottom rung of fame? Wait till you're wasting away alone in perfect darkness for the rest of your life. I think you'll appreciate all the thought I put into it. Just as it looked like there was nothing left to do I said, 'Make it damper.'"

The crowd was getting noisier but he was in no rush. "I won't have to hear any more crap about how *my* miracles are fake and your small-dick miracle's the real thing. Let's face it, George, the world wants you forgotten in some hole. No wonder your father kept his distance—you're a freak. Not some mutation on the way to the next stage of evolution—flying's in our *past*, millions of years ago when we were birds. You don't even rate a spot on the blooper real."

He turned to Iris and whispered, "Remember, baby, you've got to turn the flange. The whole gag depends of the flange." He raised his arm, brought it down, smoke came up, and when it cleared everyone was coughing and Ricardo was still there. "Speaking candidly," he said to the audience, "something has gone awry. Let me explain. There are tricks so close to impossible, so close to flaunting the laws of God, that the universe itself intervenes and declares, 'It can never be so!' Most magicians would walk away now. But if he has the nerve, the great magician will stare down God and say, 'Your puny laws of physics no longer apply!'"

I thought his crew were getting their revenge. Ricardo was conceded to be the hairiest asshole in magic, and today would be their last chance to fuck him up.

Mine too. "Your mascara's running," I said. "Let me get that." I smooshed it down his cheek. Pointless as it was it's the bravest thing I've done.

"Hey, enough of that," said the gunman behind me, throttling a laugh. "If you do that again I'll shoot you." For a moment Ricardo looked frantic. He looked like he'd call off his war with God for a mirror and a paper towel.

He took a deep breath and said, "Here are my demands to God. Accept our molecular and atomic and subatomic dematerialization—even though it defies your most basic laws—or strike us down now!"

"Not really a joint declaration," Iris muttered.

He whispered, "You forgot to turn the flange."

"What? I'm a little deaf in this ear."

"Iris, baby, you have to turn the flange!"

She laughed and said, "Sweetie, you've found your famous last words. Better than 'either that wallpaper goes or I do.' Take your bow and off you go with the nice people in uniforms."

"On the count of five," he whispered, "turn the flange. Five four three two one." He raised his arm, made a throwing down motion, smoke came up; he raised the other arm concealing himself and Iris behind the cape, people coughed, and at the end all of us were still there.

Toby squeezed through the people pressed against him and walked in. Iris ran up and threw her arms around him, and they kissed to trailer-shaking applause. "I was wondering," Toby said to the goons. "If I were to punch Ricardo in the face would you guys shoot me?"

"Nah." "Godspeed, dude."

State troopers were coming through the door.

Ricardo whispered, "Will you *please* turn the flange!"

But he and the goons were already being cuffed. He whispered, "The little key, Iris. For the cuffs. Kiss me and pass on the key."

She pointed to her ear, shrugged, waved goodbye.

An imposing woman who sounded like she belonged in a horned helmet thrust her head in the doorway and shouted, "Do! You! Write! From life!" She too was cuffed and led away.

. . .

People sometimes ask, "You're a Herman's Hermitist or whatever. You study what things mean. So? What did it all mean?" I explain that I study the meaning of *texts*. They say pretend it was all a text. I say, Actually, my field is the *theory* of the meaning of texts. Sure, they say, but come on, nobody here but us chickens, what's it all mean? I'm ashamed to admit I do what I always do when I'm cornered that way: I bore them into submission. The truth is, I don't know. Let's let Iris take a crack at the meaning of it all. Here she is at her press conference the day after her liberation. She was a bit more sharp-tongued than usual that afternoon, but who could blame her?

The final question came from a nervous young man who seemed to have just graduated journalism school and been released blinking into the world. "There's a sense in this country that we've lost our grounding in reality after the Age of George. As someone who lived through one of the more extreme—" and so forth.

Iris seemed moved by the question. Stupid people always touched her heart, and she smiled at the questioner like Florence Nightingale serving in the idiot ward. "You're asking *Ricardo Dean's former abused girlfriend* about her sense of *reality*? Oh sweetie, you're speaking to someone who *voluntarily dated* Mr. Blockhead—a circus freak show employee who pounds spikes up his nostrils for a living."

Mr. Blockhead was seated in the front row, turned out in his best duds: gold lamé cape, gold-spangled tights, and his best formal spike jutting, supposedly, from his brain. "You are right, dearest," he said graciously. "You deserve moon and stars."

She winced. "Sorry, Yevgeny . . . But reality? I know nothing about it except what I see on *Nova* or read in the Sunday *New York Times*, but anything that can happen *must happen* in at least one of an infinite number of universes, according to the latest theories. Don't ask me why it has to be everything. How do we know this multiverse doesn't repeat itself like a bad writer? Recycling old work, falling back on its greatest hits? But the theorists have Ph.D.s in this stuff, and I can't even balance a checkbook except on my head. So it's not just that everything is possible, *everything is actual*. But when we ask 'em where's the really unlikely stuff, the talking dogs or whatever, they say 'off in some other universe,' that old junk drawer of existence. I'm beginning to think that we are that universe."

. . .

They're still out there jumping; I see them on my late-night walks. Usually they're each alone, out of the light, their jumping wistful or oafish or hopeful or manic or joyful or coy or energetic or fatalistic or interpretive (inhales) or angry or ironic or ditsy or longing or frenzied or button-down or performed merely so they can feel they've left nothing undone. I don't want to turn this into "I See America Jumping" but I've seen every race, creed (on their T-shirts), nationality, and gender bouncing in that sequestered darkness. I've seen them in wedding dresses and pajamas and escaped-patient gowns with the back open. In tube tops and undershirts and the inevitable jumpsuit. In Wall Street pinstripes that brook no obstacles on the march to thinnest air.

In the darkest places you can still find people struggling to launch in my classic mode—lying on their stomachs drooling and flailing. On warm spring nights I've found them mumbling to the earth or attempting snow angels on the bare sidewalk. You never see these groundlings in crowds, but the jumpers sometimes gather: black-hatted congregants jumping in unison, frat kids out for a quick-roiling barf, hipsters in long johns with the iron-on faces of their lamest heroes—Droopy, Mr. Magoo, and yes, my own. Mostly they're glad to see me. "George, baby, give us some inches!"

So I jump for them. Nothing athletic these days, my jumping is reserved, a series of modest thuds, as accepting of the coming down as of the going up.

ACKNOWLEDGMENTS

Thanks to everyone who read the manuscript or excerpts, offered criticism, helped with research, published the book, or just behaved kindly when I felt like I was down there with George among the shoes, cats and dustballs: Jim Stockwell, Doris Stockwell, Richard Friedman, Darlene Pearlstein, Peter Kostakis, Richard Schechter, Lore Segal, Jacob Segal, Athena Bryan, Dennis Johnson and Melville House.

Thanks to Chuck Klosterman and his "The 23 Questions I Ask Everybody I Meet In Order To Decide If I Can Really Love Them." In question 1 he posits a magician who can perform some of the oldest, corniest tricks "with real magic." Klosterman asks, "Would this person be more impressive than Albert Einstein?" The character of Clarence Fonderbine is my attempt to answer that question.

About the Author TK